Thunder in the Blood

By the same author

RULES OF ENGAGEMENT
REAPER
THE DEVIL'S BREATH

GRAHAM HURLEY

Thunder in the Blood

**MACMILLAN
LONDON**

First published 1994 by Macmillan London Limited

a division of Pan Macmillan Publishers Limited
Cavaye Place London SW10 9PG
and Basingstoke

Associated companies throughout the world

ISBN 0–333–60217–X
    0–333–62775–X (Airside Edition)

9 8 7 6 5 4 3 2 1

A CIP catalogue record for this book is available from the British Library

Phototypeset by Intype, London
Printed by Mackays of Chatham PLC, Chatham, Kent.

To Bill Flynn with love

Dimmi se mai fu fatto qualche cosa?

Leonardo da Vinci

Prelude

Yesterday, according to my father, was the first day of spring. He hauled out the old push-mower and tramped up and down the lawn beneath my window, and when the grass was cut he took the mower to pieces, wiping off the winter grease, freshly oiling the moving parts.

I took a break from the book, watching him through the open window. When he'd finished, he looked up at me, wiping his hands on a length of rag. I leaned out of the window, amazed, as ever, by his logic.

'Why do that first?' I said. 'Why make life so hard for yourself?'

He didn't answer for a moment, just stood there smiling, gently amused. 'Good question,' he said, 'coming from you.'

He's got a point. I've been here now for nearly four months, back in the bedroom I grew up in, six hours a day at the tiny fold-down table by the bed. On the floor, all around me, are the sources I've drawn on for what follows in this book, the raw material which has made the account possible. There are diaries, cuttings, books, magazine articles, letters, transcripts of various interviews and three boxes of video and audio cassettes. The material is carefully organized and I've lived with the stuff for so long that I can access anything in a matter of seconds, but to anyone else I know it looks a mess: an ocean of paper, spilling across the carpet. It's a scene which has greeted my parents every time they've come up with a cup of tea, or a sandwich, or a message from a caller, and I know they're as puzzled now as when I began, three cold days into the New Year.

Last time I occupied this room for any length of time, I was seventeen years old and on the verge of university: cheerful, trusting, headstrong, exuberant and quite fearless. Now, more than a decade later, I'm none of those things. The Sarah of my father's dreams has become a solitary obsessive: sober, thoughtful, not given over-much to conversation, unprepared for now to share the secrets of the growing pile of typescript at my elbow. This new me, the lodger upstairs in Sarah's bedroom, isn't someone they recognize or perhaps even like, but that, I suspect, is the way it has to be. Telling a story like this exacts a certain price.

These are the facts, the way I first heard them. In September 1991, a journalist on a specialist UK defence magazine was attending a three-day conference in Geneva. On the first evening, late, he found himself talking to an American. The American was a senior design engineer with a major defence contractor. He was very drunk.

The journalist bought more drinks. They talked about the Gulf War. They moved on to a night club. Past three in the morning, in the cab back to the hotel, the American told him that his own company had done exceptionally well out of the war. Their equipment had showcased on the Basra Road and he had the videos to prove it. Better still, post-war, they'd won a multi-million dollar re-equipment order from the Kuwaitis. For this, the American had been duly grateful. In the post-Cold War sales vacuum, Saddam Hussein was effectively keeping his company afloat.

Back at the hotel, the journalist sensed there was more to come. Over brandies, in the privacy of his hotel room, the American got into the small print of the re-equipment deal. His company, he said, had been contacted at the highest level by the US State Department and given specific instructions on when to pitch to the Kuwaitis and what bid would be acceptable. The instructions were very precise: a specific day and a specific price. His company was left in no doubt that the business was there for the taking. All they had to do was follow the chalk marks on the trees. And so it had proved.

The journalist said that sounded very interesting. He'd heard similar stories from other sources. The American nodded and fell silent for a while. Then, according to the journalist, he looked up. The point about the State Department, he said, was the date of their covert approach. They'd been in touch on 7 January 1991 . . . nine days *before* Desert Storm had even begun.

The journalist thought about the conversation overnight. To him, the Gulf War had never made any kind of military sense. The Allied casualties had been impossibly low, lower even than the budgeted deaths for a peacetime exercise of equivalent scale. Not because of luck or some special genius in the Americans' conduct of the war but because Saddam had consistently pulled his punches, making a long tally of elementary mistakes.

Why no overseas terrorist strikes? Why only one serious attack on Allied shipping? Why withdraw the best Iraqi warplanes, Saddam's precious MiG–29s, so quickly? Why such poor targeting of the Scud missiles? Error margins so gross that they began to look deliberate? Why deploy the best Iraqi army units to totally ineffective positions? How come the Allies got through the mine-fields so quickly? With such little loss of life? Why no use of chemical weapons?

In review, the cumulative scale of military blunders had occasionally made the journalist wonder whether Saddam had *ever* been serious about 'the mother of battles'.

Now, the conversation with the American businessman fresh in his mind, the journalist began to think the thing through all over again. The Gulf War had, after all, conferred blessings on both leaders. Internationally, George Bush had emerged with enormous political and military prestige, architect and master of a 'new world order'. Domestically, likewise, he'd become the hero-president: guardian of American lives, saviour of the American arms industry, moral leader of the Free World. God knows, thanks to lavish dollar contributions from non-participating nations (like the Japanese), he'd even managed to run the war at a *profit*. For the expense of little blood, he'd acquired huge amounts of treasure.

And Saddam? Remarkably, despite the attentions of the best-equipped coalition army in the history of warfare, he and his regime had survived intact. Bridges were down, sewage flooded the streets, food was scarce and the chemical and nuclear pro-grammes had been set back a decade, but Saddam's grip on Iraq was, if anything, even tighter. The Republican Guards were as loyal as ever and huge portions of the troublesome conscript army had been incinerated on the Basra Road. In the immediate aftermath of the war – thanks to the passive connivance of the

Americans – Saddam had even managed to deploy his gunships and armour and smash a dissident Shiite rebellion in the south.

So why the symmetry? How come so much violence had finally resolved so little?

The journalist brooded. On the face of it, a behind-the-scenes, covert understanding between Washington and Baghdad on precisely how the war should be fought seemed inconceivable. Yet the more he thought about it the more this explanation seemed to fit all the facts. What if the two leaderships had conferred through third parties after the invasion of Kuwait? What if an agreement had been hammered out? A shooting script for the conduct of the war? A painstaking, highly publicized build-up of arms in the Gulf followed by the swift expulsion of Iraq from Kuwait? Baghdad spared? Saddam spared? American lives spared? George Bush (and the American arms industry) walking tall?

Next morning, the journalist went looking for the American. He had more questions to ask. He needed detail: names, dates, phone numbers. He knocked on the American's hotel door. There was no reply. Downstairs, he enquired at the desk. The clerk checked his bookings and then looked up. Unaccountably, at six in the morning, the American had checked out and returned to the States. The remaining two days of the conference were, it seemed, no longer of any interest.

That was the way I first heard it. Later, I got to know the journalist. His name was Wesley Keogh. I knew the American, too, a man called Grant Wallace. I visited his grave last month, a corner plot in a small, shadowed half-acre within sight of the Shenandoah River. I went there for two reasons: partly to pay my respects and partly to make sure the man was really dead. Three months with Wesley had that kind of effect on me. Believe nothing until you've seen it for yourself.

Wesley's dead, too. I was very close to him in the months before he died, and everything that follows is based on what he told me, what I found out for myself and on the tapes, notes and diaries that he left behind, the material that surrounds me now.

Towards the end, when it was obvious that he wasn't going to make it, Wesley brooded on whether or not to ask me to take over, to risk unleashing me on the foothills of the mountain he'd tried so hard to climb. He was far too proud to put the thought into words and when I did it for him he pretended that the idea had come as a great surprise. He thought about it for a day or two. Then he said yes, on two conditions. It had to do justice to the story. And it had to be worth my while, something I truly believed in.

He need never have worried. Wesley Keogh was an exceptional man, the bravest person I ever met, and I loved him for it. Hence, if he's still listening, this book.

Book One

I

The story begins, bear with me, in Africa.

I arrived in Kinshasa on 28 July 1984, three days short of my twenty-second birthday. I had a second-class university degree in English and a large canvas holdall stuffed with the clothes I thought I'd need for the next nine months. The holdall had been a going-away present from my father, a relic from his more active years in the Royal Marines, and I hauled it around like a talisman. It had seen him through some tricky postings in Northern Ireland and I saw no reason why the eleven-hour flight from Gatwick should have affected its karma.

At Kinshasa, I joined a river boat called the *Colonel Ebeya*. There are quicker and more comfortable ways of making the thousand-mile journey to Kisangani, but three years at Cambridge had given me a hearty appetite for real life. The *Colonel Ebeya* was an old boat. It plied up and down the Zaire River pushing six double-decker barges before it. The barges were jammed solid with people. I never counted, but there were evidently more than five thousand. They packed the gangways and rooftops. They spread sleeping mats where there was space. They napped, played cards, plucked chickens, butchered monkeys, chewed manioc, pounded plantains, washed clothes and doused their kids in river water from powdered milk cans lowered carefully over the side.

The first evening, I abandoned my shared first-class cabin aboard the *Colonel Ebeya* and clambered on to one of the barges. The companionways were virtually impassable. *Commerçants* at makeshift tables sold soap, salt, sugar, fishhooks, medicines and bread. The decks underfoot were slippery with enormous catfish, giant eels and glistening piles of grotesque bottom-fish netted from the river. When I finally located a seat, I found the space below the table occupied by a ten-foot crocodile, still alive, trussed to a pole. The crocodile had green eyes and smelled, unaccountably, of diesel oil. Its jaws were bound shut with lianas and every minute or so it farted. If equatorial Africa was a culture shock, the *Colonel Ebeya* was instant trauma.

It took twenty-nine days to get to Kisangani. In some ways the journey changed my life and I arrived with none of my comfortable European assumptions intact. Every morning I awoke, sweating, to the same smells: smoked fish, roasting palm grubs and the overwhelming stench of the latrine. The noise of the *commerçants* and the kids and the tribes of orphaned young monkeys on the deck overhead was deafening, and when I rolled over in the narrow bunk and peered through a crack in the welded metal shutters, the view always seemed the same: the unending tropical rain forest, huge and clammy and green, a soupy broth of life-forms crowding down to the sluggish brown water at the river's edge. I'd never been anywhere so fertile and so forbidding. By the time the *Colonel Ebeya* docked at the journey's end and I managed to find an old Peugeot taxi to take me to the Mission Hospital, I felt comprehensively outnumbered. The Europeans had got it all wrong. In terms of the life-force, what the planet could *really* do, we were doomed.

I'd come to Zaire to spread the good word about AIDS. I'd applied for the job through a Christian newsletter my mother takes but seldom reads. I travelled up from Devon for the interview and spent a pleasant enough afternoon with two elderly presbyters and a retired district nurse. My qualifications, aside from a working knowledge of French, were non-existent. I never went to church. I knew nothing about epidemiology. I knew precious little about AIDS. But I had a good degree and a nice smile and I was candid to the point of bluntness about the speed with which I could pick things up. By teatime, after a lengthy discussion of a transatlantic crossing I'd done aboard a forty-foot yacht, I knew I'd got the job. The younger of the two men leafed again through my hastily typed CV.

'You've certainly been around,' he said. 'Was there ever a favourite place?'

'America,' I said without hesitation, 'last year.'

'Whereabouts?'

'New York, Chicago, West Coast . . .' I shrugged. 'I loved them all.'

'And you were there *alone*?'

'Yes.'

'No companion? No boyfriend?'

'No.'

'Was that wise?'

'Probably not.' I smiled again. 'But it never got dull.'

I spent six months in Kisangani, working from a tiny office in a near-empty wing of the old Mission Hospital. A lot of the time I was out in the bush, accompanying a young French nurse called Monique who was as close to a saint as anyone I've ever met. We travelled together from village to village by jeep and motor-driven wooden canoe. We had a blackboard and a box of chalks and an ancient generator-driven projector for after-dark slide shows, and we offered a cartoon account of the interplay between the body's immune system and the tiny packet of protein and nucleic acid they call the HIV virus. Interestingly, in our presentation the T-cells and the B-cells, the body's trusty warriors, were always black, while the HIV virus, the unwanted interloper, was always white. In the end we made a joke of this, we white girls from Kisangani, and it never failed to raise a quiet laugh.

The Africans called the disease 'Slim' and many of the people we met, either in the bush or the Mission Hospital, were already victims. After a month or so I could spot the symptoms at first glance: weight loss, lassitude, fatigue, yeast growths in the mouth, visible swellings in the neck and groin. The disease had been rife for years, part of the landscape, and for the most part the sick were remarkably sanguine about what awaited them. Monique, a practising Christian, put this down to faith but I wasn't so sure. These people lived here. They knew the jungle. They knew the biological odds. They knew where the food chain began and ended, and if it wasn't a leopard or a crocodile or a snake that got them then it might as well be a virus. This sense of resignation, of mute acceptance, was pervasive. In Lingala, the local language, there were no separate words for yesterday or tomorrow. Time-wise, there was now, and not now. Somehow, the HIV virus fitted nicely into this stoic view of human life. The virus was the untamed beast, the hand that reached out from the rain forest, immune to white man's medicines, eager for fresh kills.

Towards the end of my six months, on our blackboard, we gave the virus a name. The taker of lives and layer-waste of whole communities we called George. In the light of later events, it was a curiously prophetic choice of name, though it was to be another five years before I realized why.

At about this time, in New York City, Wesley contracted HIV. I've got a photo of him from that trip, part of my precious archive, and it shows a tall, gangly twenty-eight-year-old standing on a street corner on one side of Times Square, the eager young reporter recently taken on by a big national tabloid, the provincial boy made good. Whoever took the picture knew nothing about photography because the background, sunlit, is in perfect focus, while Wesley is in shadow, dramatically blurred. The smile's still there, though, his head cocked slightly to one side, the hair savagely barbered, the eyes slightly bulbous, the ears too big. He looks immensely pleased with himself, that very special combination of mischief and genius, and the forefinger of one hand is looped into the belt of his jeans, his own awkward parody of high camp.

Wesley had flown to New York on assignment. I found what passed for the brief amongst a pile of other souvenirs he'd kept from the trip. According to the features editor Wesley was to unearth background on a drugs feature but, ever curious, he'd decided to broaden the brief with a visit to a selection of the city's bathhouses. Gay himself, with a limitless appetite for what he called 'really horrible sex', he'd become rather less than objective and at some point between the second and the fifth of April, he'd taken one risk too many. Later, it became a source of some regret that he could never put a name or a face to the person who'd effectively ended his life. It could, he said with a frown, have been any of three dozen men.

Either way, back in England, he fell ill almost immediately with a flu-like fever – muscle aches and sweating – which lasted rather longer than usual but nevertheless cleared up. Impatient to return to work, he ignored a friend's advice to get himself tested. Only seven months later, as part of the research on another story, did he allow a doctor to draw 10 mls of his blood and send it away for analysis. The results came back five days later and Wesley kept the letter they sent him through the post. 'Dear Mr Keogh,' it goes, 'Further to your recent test, we would ask you to return for additional discussions with Dr Webber. You may wish to bring a relative or a friend...' Wesley, typically, did neither. Bad news, he always said, was like life. Better confronted alone.

I returned from Zaire in the late spring of 1985, staying with my parents in their house in Budleigh Salterton. Budleigh is a small, genteel seaside town in east Devon. The locals call it 'God's waiting room', and it's much favoured by retired folk of the moneyed kind. There are avenues on the southern edge of the town, up towards the golf course, where it's difficult to find anyone below the rank of Rear-Admiral, but my father had long since settled for something a little more modest, a neat thirties house near the town's centre, with a decently kept garden and a couple of fruit trees and distant glimpses of the sea from the upstairs bedrooms. I'd grown up there, an only child, and I'd loved it.

The summer came and went. I'd managed to save a little money from Africa, and when that had gone I began to commute daily to Exmouth, a bigger town along the coast. A young couple my mother knew had opened a nursing home and they were always short-handed. They'd bought a property called Beacon Hill House, a handsome Georgian mansion with wonderful views down the coast. Inside, the place was shabby and chaotic, but the couple who ran it – Eileen and Pete – became good friends, and I spent three months emptying bedpans and spoonfeeding elderly women until the novelty began to fade. By September, both my parents and I agreed that my life, post-university, was going nowhere.

Part of the problem was my spell abroad. People say you don't leave Africa by getting on a plane. On the contrary, you take the place with you, its smells, its madness, its frequent and at times brutal reminders that life isn't all fast food and bus stops.

One particular episode had made a deep impression. A couple of weeks before I was due to leave, there'd been an incident down by the docks, a brief flurry of violence between a group of fishermen from upriver and a couple of local merchants. The cause of the quarrel was obscure, but the fishermen returned upriver with one of their number savagely beaten. Later that night, they came back. Unable to find the merchants, they kidnapped a relative of one of them. They woke him up, bound his wrists behind his back and walked him on to the street. There they beat him unconscious with lengths of rubber hosepipe and cut his throat with a gutting knife. Then they hacked off his genitals and stuffed them in his mouth. Next day, he was still lying dead in the street, his body in full view. I saw him on the way to the Mission Hospital. I recognized what was left of his face because he'd recently helped us fix a puncture on the jeep. His name was Malu and he was barely eleven years old.

There was an investigation of sorts, but no arrests. Everyone knew who'd done it, but no one seemed to care. Monique and I attended his funeral and laid flowers on his grave. His family hardly dared look at us. The message was plain: we were white; we didn't understand; Malu had been taken; there was no point making a fuss. For months, back in England, I brooded on this incident. Economically, Zaire had long been a basket case even in Africa, and I'd seen plenty of suffering. The place was a real mess and I'd gone way beyond the point of being surprised or angered by it, but the sight of Malu's broken body, already swelling in the heat, had tripped a switch deep in my head.

I'd never been remotely political, but that single image forced me to think for the first time about the glue that sticks society together. Old-fashioned things. Like justice. And law. And order. Sometimes, on the occasional evenings I spent at home, I tried to discuss it with my father. We'd never been especially close – he'd spent most of my childhood away on various postings – but my descriptions of daily life in Kisangani struck a chord with him, too.

The British, it seemed, were also locked in conflict. The miners' strike had dragged on through the winter I'd been away, no quarter offered or given, and the prime minister seemed to have turned confrontation into a way of life. Everything, quite suddenly, had become black and white. There was good and there was evil. There was right and there was wrong. The middle ground had gone. Either you were a believer or you weren't, and if you weren't then you were simply ignored. The moderates, according to my father, had been neutered, and the only language that now mattered was the language of violence. Anarchists on the rampage. Riot police on horseback. Thirty pounds of Semtex in a Brighton hotel, the prime minister escaping death by the width of an en suite bathroom.

Recently attached to some kind of forward planning unit in the Ministry of Defence, my father was now close enough to the heart of it all to understand what a delicate structure our society really was. Concepts like law and order, he said, rested on an elaborate conjuring trick, an illusion. There were more, lots more, of them than us. Exactly who 'they' were and what my father meant by 'us' I never quite fathomed, but the moment 'they' realized the true odds, the sleight of hand at the heart of democracy, then the trick was revealed and the game was over. What remained was chaos and violence and the slow surrender to corruption and anarchy. Poor Malu.

In retrospect, I shouldn't make too much of these conversations. They happened twice, perhaps three times, and what mattered most about them to me was the interest my father took in what had happened in Zaire. I warmed to his questions. They seemed to me to be the beginnings of a real relationship and accordingly I told him everything. But my father, I suspect, took a great deal more from our heart to hearts. Behind the slow smile and the occasional asides, he was thinking, as ever, on practical lines. I was twenty-three years old. I was highly educated. I could handle myself in most situations. I was wasted at the Beacon Hill House Nursing Home. I, and perhaps my country, deserved rather better than that.

The phone call came in October. Autumn had descended on Budleigh Salterton, and I was cutting back the roses behind the conservatory when my mother signalled through the sitting-room window. She gave me the phone. I recognized the voice at once.

'Rory!'

'Sarah. Long time . . .'

We chatted for a while. Rory had been a young instructing officer at the Commando Training Centre at Lympstone. We'd met a number of times before I went to Africa. He was tall and wild and very funny, with a ruddy, raw-boned face and a passion for windsurfing. He was nearly ten years older than me, but we'd always got on extremely well, mainly, I suspect, because he regarded me as 'a good bloke'. I wasn't dainty, like the other girls. I didn't lie around mooning about rock stars or fashion spreads in *Vogue*. On the contrary, like Rory himself, I was game for virtually anything, providing it offered physical excitement and a few laughs. Now, after a brief exchange of news, he suggested I come up to London. He, too, was working at the MOD. I caught myself frowning. Something in his voice made me hesitate.

'Why?'

'People I want you to meet. People who want to meet you.'

'What kind of people?'

'Good guys. You'll like them.'

'Why do they want to meet me?'

'No idea. I've told them you're an old slag. Made no difference.'

'Will you be there?'

'Sure. They're civilized. Speak the Queen's English. You'll need an interpreter.'

I laughed. We agreed a time and a place. He hung up. Lovely man.

It was about the same time that Wesley found himself in trouble. At first, he'd greeted the news of his infection with disbelief, keeping it at arm's length and treating it with a mix of derision and contempt. HIV was someone else's nightmare, something that wouldn't – couldn't – happen to him. The diagnosis, Dr Webber's glum letter, had been a mistake, some wild medical fantasy, a rumble of stage thunder in the on-going play that passed for his life. Accordingly, he decided to ignore it.

This period, he later told me, lasted about a week. Then, like any good reporter, he began to ask questions. He went to several voluntary bodies. He tried to work out who made sense and who talked bullshit. He did his best to separate the medical facts from the political hysteria. The latter, a bush fire whipped up by various gay factions, he found particularly hard to take. They were, he said drily, a pain in the arse.

But the facts, none the less, alarmed him. By 1985, doctors were putting a two-year tag on the period between infection with HIV and the development of full-blown AIDS. To some degree this was a guess, but the evidence from the States, acquired in bulk by Wesley, made grim reading. Guys in San Francisco were dying in their hundreds. The word on the lips of the spokesperson from the Center for Disease Control was 'exponential'. No matter how bad things looked today, tomorrow would be a whole lot worse.

Sobered by his research, Wesley conducted what he later described as 'a brief audit' of his life. Two years meant twenty-four months meant 104 weeks. Ever impatient, he did the sums again and again, wondering how much of the two years would be surrendered to the doctors and nurses and how much he could rely on as his own. Without doubt, by now, he was in shock. An express train of his own making, he'd sighted the buffers rather earlier than he'd anticipated. No longer immortal, he was obliged to make a few decisions.

One of them had to do with his work. Wesley had never been remotely casual about journalism. From early adolescence, it had been his only choice of career, the one thing in his life that he wanted to do properly and do well. By nineteen, he was starring on a small Essex weekly. Two years later he moved west, to Bristol, accepting a job on a big provincial daily. He started on the general reporters desk. Within a year, he was business editor, filing copy by the yard, building a reputation for dogged foot-work, exhaustive research and a bloody-minded defence of his right to ask the truly awkward questions.

Colleagues I've contacted from that period talk of him with affection and some awe: a driven man in his mid-twenties with an uncertain grip on the world that most of the rest of us inhabit. He had no dress sense, no social life, little time for small talk or gossip. He had few close friends and never forgave anyone who lied to him or let him down. On the other hand, he was utterly loyal and immensely generous. Money, I can vouch, meant nothing to him. If someone else's need was greater than his, he simply emptied his pockets and gave it all away.

On 16 October 1985, after nearly a year on Fleet Street, Wesley made an appointment with his editor. The appointment and its aftermath occupy several pages in the loose-leaf ring binder that served at this period in his life as a kind of diary. Sitting down in front of the editor's desk ('totally fucking empty – just like his head'), Wesley explained that he was HIV positive. The editor, wrongly thinking Wesley already had AIDS, was shocked. In the interests of the paper, for the sake of his colleagues, he said, he'd have to review the situation. Wesley, appalled, explained the difference between HIV and AIDS. He had the virus, no question. The virus was at large in his body, knocking off the warrior cells. He was infectious, certainly, but he had no plans to screw anybody and it would be a while before the virus got the upper hand. Once it did and his body's defences were shot to pieces he'd doubtless succumb to something horrible, but until then he was still good for the odd story or two.

At this, the editor had evidently looked a bit dubious, and although he'd done his best to temper his disgust with a little sympathy, Wesley knew in his heart that his days in the sun were over. The newspaper world thrives on gossip and in his own small way, Wesley himself had become the current news story. 'So how's this for a sign-off?' he confides to his diary. '*Gay Plague Sweeps Fleet Street. Hack Banned From Newsroom. Bleach Sales Hit New High.*'

I went to London in mid-October. I met Rory in the coffee shop at Paddington Station and we took a cab to a small Malaysian restaurant in Soho. Upstairs, at a discreet table by the window, he introduced me to two colleagues. One of them was in his late fifties, a sombre, jowly man in a dark suit, not Rory's kind at all. The other was much younger, crop-haired, neat, watchful. Neither, as it turned out, was much interested in small talk.

2

I joined MI5 in time to attend the Curzon House Christmas party, an awkward, joyless affair that descended from perfunctory conversation and the exchange of witty presents to deep eddies of gossip, vicious and, past midnight, wildly drunken.

The recruitment process had seemed, to me at least, utterly haphazard. The lunch with Rory and his friends had lasted no more than an hour, me doing most of the talking. Rory filling the occasional silences with a series of badly told stories that he'd dredged up from our social get-togethers in Devon. Several of the stories were pure fiction, designed somehow to convince our hosts that I was on the level, a good sport, heart in the right place, a safe pair of hands, and afterwards, when our hosts had paid the bill and left, I asked him what he'd been up to.

The atmosphere throughout the meal had been chilly. Neither of the two men had bothered to explain themselves and I'd no idea why I'd been invited, or who or what they represented. If their intention had been to offer me a job, I wasn't at all sure that I wanted to accept. Who were they? What did they want? And why did they find it so bloody hard to smile?

Rory dismissed my questions with a wide grin and a wave of the hand. The restaurant was nearly empty now. A waiter hovered patiently in the background with our bill.

'Spooks,' he said.

'What do you mean?'

'Intelligence. Security wallahs.' He tapped the side of his nose. 'Brothers in arms.'

'You mean spies?'

'No. Spycatchers. MI5. The home team.'

'What do they want with me? What have I done?'

Rory hooted with laughter. Laughter suited him. The pale, freckled planes of his face were seamed with deep lines, and when they filled with laughter he created the sensation, at once dangerous and playful, that something was about to happen: a prank, a joke, some wild physical adventure. For a man in his early thirties, with a mortgage and two kids, he could sometimes be deliciously adolescent.

'They want you,' he whispered. 'They want you to work for them.'

'Why?'

He leaned forward. The melodrama, the big eyes, the clowning had quite gone. Instead, there was another expression, utterly serious. 'Because you'd be bloody good at it.'

'Who says?'

'Me.'

'What do you know about it?'

'Quite a lot,' he said, reaching for the bottle, 'as it happens.'

Ten days later, back in Devon, I got another phone call, from a woman this time. I was to return to London for a formal interview. The interview took place two days later in an over-heated office on the second floor of an anonymous building in Gower Street. The office was shabby. The paint had bubbled on the big iron radiators and the nylon covers on the chairs were printed with swirly patterns in orange and olive green. The place reminded me of my one and only visit to the DHSS outpost in Exeter: good intentions, zero budget and absolutely no taste.

The interview was conducted by two men and a woman. One of the men was the younger of Rory's colleagues I'd met at the restaurant. Ten days had done nothing for his conversation and he spent most of the morning making notes on a large yellow pad. The other man was older, with a small, white face and a habit of gazing out of the window. Of the three of them, the woman did most of the talking and it was she who led me patiently through my life, pausing from time to time to ask a question, note a date or ask me to expand a little on this or that. She was evidently senior to the other two – there was a very definite sense of deference when they occasionally conferred together – and when she'd mapped out my twenty-three years to her satisfaction, she became suddenly brisker, closing her file and returning her fountain pen to her bag.

'You'll be sitting a couple of tests: English language and mental agility,' she said. 'The latter is a bit of a game.' She smiled. 'You ever play dominoes?'

I took the tests in a room down the corridor. The dominoes were arranged in certain sequences. The test was to guess the next sequence. I spent half an hour toying with various pieces. As a preparation for defending the state, it seemed a curious exercise.

The woman reappeared before lunch. She carried her bag in one hand and a sheaf of papers in the other. On top of the papers, clearly visible, was a copy of the Official Secrets Act. She put it carefully on the desk. Beside it, she laid another official-looking document.

'This is the Maxwell-Fyfe Declaration,' she said. 'You're welcome to read it but I'm afraid you can't take it away. The photo-copier's broken.' She smiled thinly, nodding at the document. 'It's the only one we've got.'

I picked up the declaration and read it quickly. It turned out to be a statement of the aims of the security services. I looked across at the woman. Thus far, no one had spelled out what I was doing or why I was here.

'Are you offering me a job?' I said.

'Yes. Subject to the usual checks.' She paused. 'We'll need four names. Four referees. Just to make sure.'

'But what for? What's the job about?'

She paused again, frowning.

'It's a government post,' she said at length. 'Security service. F branch. I understood you'd been briefed.'

'No.'

'Oh.' She nodded, sighing, 'I see.' She looked at me a moment, speculative, then glanced down at the papers on the desk. 'Do you have a pen?'

'Yes.'

'Then perhaps you'd like to sign this.' She picked up the copy of the Official Secrets Act and indicated the relevant page.

I didn't move. I was still looking at her. 'But what if I don't want the job?' I hesitated. 'Whatever it is?'

'It makes no difference. You still sign.'

'Why?'

'Because you're here. Because you've met us. Because—' she

broke off, glancing at her watch. 'It'll save time later.'

'Later?'

'Yes.' She glanced up, that same thin smile. 'After you've had a little think and accepted.'

I joined MI5 on 15 December 1985. Each of my four referees had been interviewed by a suave young man from the Ministry of Defence Police and he completed his trawl through my life with yet another personal interview. Quite what he made of my ramblings about Zaire I can't say, but a thick bundle of forms arrived through the post five days after he left, and I began my induction at the MI5 Registry and Documentation Centre at Curzon House in Mayfair.

The important thing to say here is that at no time did I express any real enthusiasm to join the intelligence services. I certainly welcomed the prospect of a regular wage and I had no objection to a year or two in London, but I was totally honest about my impatience with paperwork and my loathing of desk jobs. Something they called 'fieldcraft' sounded more enticing and when they pushed the conversation in the right direction I readily admitted a liking for unusual encounters and physical risk. But in every other respect I was never less than sceptical, an attitude which I now believe exactly matched what they wanted. Thus, perhaps, the offer of the job. And thus, amongst the pink balloons and the cheap champagne, my first taste of MI5 at play.

Christmas 1985 also found Wesley on the move. The outcome of his exchanges with the editor was an invitation to resign and he finally left on New Year's Eve with a boxful of office stationery and a generous cheque. The latter was big enough to keep him eating for the best part of the following year, and he retreated to Stoke Newington and set himself up as a freelance, generating a stream of stories from the battered Olympia portable he kept on the desk beside his bed.

Because he was such a good journalist – tireless, nosy, bold – he achieved a remarkable strike rate, cashing in on the goodwill and respect he'd already earned in Fleet Street, and pushing his copy to any editor who'd pay. Each published story he scissored carefully from the appropriate paper and glued it into the scrapbook which now lies on my bedroom floor. Beside each item, usually in his favourite green Biro, he added his own judgement on the worth of the story and what he'd managed to do with it. Many of these judgements are harsh, a kind of relentless self-mutilation, but what's very evident is the direction his journalistic interest quickly began to take.

For a while, that winter, he stuck to the style he'd made his own: tabloid, punchy, the vivid conga of breathless three-line paragraphs he was later to dismiss as his 'Doc Marten period'. This idiom had won him his first real job in Fleet Street, but by early spring he was plainly tiring of it. Working at his own pace, freed from the tyranny of the news desk, he at last had time to sink his teeth into real stories, hunting a succession of quarries, dragging one or two of them to earth. Many of these stories had a business background, totally unsuitable for the tabloid cosh, and he began to develop a new style, still direct, still a treat to read, but making room for analysis and irony and the complex arithmetic of the real world.

The papers changed, too. By mid-summer, he'd given up on the tabloids altogether. Instead, he was writing for some of the weightier broadsheets, not too often and none too regularly, but winning for himself a reputation for solid, authoritative analysis, wedded to a growing contempt for some of society's better-disguised secrets.

This contempt occasionally boiled up into something close to fury, and once I got to know him, putting a face and a voice to this scalding prose, I was able to recognize at once where it came from. Wesley wrote this way because, when it mattered, he really cared. Drunk or tired, he'd talk for hours about how much need there was for honesty and tolerance and simple courage, and the fact that the real world wasn't about any of these things was a frustration he took to the grave. If that sounds like a speech it probably is, but I can hear him saying it now, shaking his head, the voice thickened with red wine and roll-ups, the big eyes wide with wonderment and rage.

But all of that came later. For now, Wesley was working and well. His career, to his own surprise, was flourishing and he'd begun to believe that he might yet have time to make it as a journalist. What happened next was Derek Aldridge.

Aldridge I've met on a number of occasions, a tall, good-

known him on the paper in Bristol, where the pair of them had briefly shared a flat. Aldridge's emotional life was as complicated as Wesley's, though for different reasons. He had a passion for women, evidenced by a string of office conquests, and an early marriage to a girl from the valleys had already ended in the divorce courts.

Wesley and Aldridge spent a great deal of time together in their Bristol days. They were both loners, contemptuous of the pack, and although there were obvious differences between them, the chemistry seemed to work. Aldridge, according to Wesley, had an awesome sense of direction, knowing exactly where he was headed. Evidently he kept a private schedule, a blueprint for his career, a carefully tabulated list of dates by which he should have achieved certain targets. He showed it to Wesley once, the pair of them drunk, and Wesley memorized most of it and wrote it down when he'd sobered up, amazed at the man's single-mindedness.

To Wesley, who believed emphatically in fate, having any kind of life plan was purest folly – where was the mystery? where were the surprises? – but the real point about Aldridge's schedule was that it all came true. By twenty-seven, he was in Fleet Street. Two years later, he'd made defence correspondent on a big national daily. And by his thirty-fourth birthday, on the dot, he was occupying a desk in a large office on the fourth floor, the newly appointed deputy editor charged with infusing the feature pages with fresh blood.

One of his first calls went to Wesley. He said he wanted to offer him a job. Wesley, after some thought, asked two questions. One had to do with his health. He hadn't seen Aldridge for several years. Aldridge might have picked up the rumour or he might not. Either way, it made no odds. Wesley now came as a package deal. Me and my virus. All or nothing. The second question also had to do with the virus. HIV had concentrated his mind wonderfully. He, too, now had a schedule, a series of deadlines he kept in the back of his mind, doubtless shorter than Aldridge's, but no less important for that. So far, on the freelance market, he'd done well. He'd enjoyed the freedoms, the latitude, the time. He didn't want any of that to change and the onward march of the virus gave him the right to insist it wouldn't.

The two men met for lunch at an expensive restaurant off Covent Garden. Aldridge, according to Wesley, had put on a little weight. He showed Wesley the label on his new Armani suit and told him how much the local garage was charging him for routine services on his Mercedes. He talked at length about his marriage, and suggested Wesley might like to pop down for supper. His wife's name was Caroline. Until recently, she'd been working as a television presenter and media personality. Now, heavily pregnant with their first child, she was trading it all in for motherhood and a big mock-Tudor house on the outskirts of Godalming. It was the kind of relationship that Aldridge had always dreamed about and now it had come true. Wesley remembered the phrase from their days together in Bristol, and over liqueurs, bored, he enquired about the job. Aldridge had nodded at once.

'Sure,' he'd said, 'no problem. Start whenever. Trust you to death.'

Wesley had smiled telling me the story and I'd smiled too, not at Aldridge's talent for tactful dialogue, but at how similar it was to my own arrival in London, the door to MI5 opening with barely a touch.

I spent most of 1986 at Curzon House, commuting daily from a tiny flat on the Fulham Road. Attached to a succession of departments, I learned a great deal about intelligence: what it is, where it comes from, how you lay hands on it, and why analysis (the dominoes?) is so important. Destined for F branch, the bit of the empire responsible for countering domestic subversion, I learned about telephone taps, mail intercepts, on- and off-street surveillance, covert penetration, various cosy arrangements with other government agencies and the many techniques for shuffling quietly into other people's computer systems.

Our own computer system lay at the heart of the whole operation and a great deal of those early months was spent making myself comfortable with the way it worked. 'Comfortable' was a favourite MI5 word. It was a word we wrapped around ourselves. It insulated us. It kept us snug and warm. We were 'comfortable' with the prospects for a certain operation. We were 'comfortable' that Special Branch, or MI6, or the RUC or countless other agencies didn't know what we were up to. We were 'comfortable' that the intelligence yield (something we often referred to as 'the

that the intelligence yield (something we often referred to as 'the harvest') would be put to good and proper account. And we were 'comfortable', above all, that the growing calls for accountability would be faced down. We were, after all, simply defending the state. That, in particular, was a great source of 'comfort'.

Looking back, I'm astonished at how easily I slipped into it all. Most of what I had to learn was totally new to me, but its sheer novelty – the daily challenge of trying to make sense of this technique or that computer program – kept me from thinking about the wider questions. The days sped past in a blur and at the end of the day I had neither the time nor the energy to ask myself what might happen to the fruit of our painstaking labours. The anxiety I'd felt in Zaire, all the stuff about how fragile society was, had quite disappeared. In its place was a determination to master my brief, tinged with a faint awe at the sheer reach of the machine of which I was now a part.

People at Curzon House often referred to the place as 'the Factory' and to some degree they were right. The commodity we produced was intelligence and mere mortals like me were simply workers on the assembly line, putting together little parcels of data, seeing whether they looked like other little parcels, testing this fact against that, comparing dates and locations and the small print of some businessman's travel records, wondering all the time about circumstance and coincidence, quality-checking the product at every stage until it slipped out of the door and away to what the older hands referred to darkly as 'the end-user'.

The end-user was, of course, the government, but if I thought about them at all, those faces around the cabinet table, it was only in a distant, uncurious, faintly benign way. Governments were like rain or gravity, always there, a fact of life. They needed intelligence in exactly the same way they needed taxation. In that sense, we were simply another of the oils that made the machine work, and as long as the machine worked then everyone would benefit. Wasn't that how it went? Wasn't that Rory's favourite line?

Rory I was now seeing on a fairly regular basis: drinks, meals, the odd visit to the cinema or (a passion of his) the opera. I enjoyed his company enormously, partly because he was such good fun and partly because he freed me from the chore of picking up with somebody else. I'd already had offers from work, serious young men with heavy glasses and appalling skin, but I was perfectly happy living by myself and I had absolutely no appetite for getting involved with anyone else. By twenty-three, I'd had quite enough relationships to know the difference between love and a good fuck and just now I'd no need of either. In this sense, Rory was perfect, a big uncomplicated friendship warmed by the odd bottle of wine and a great deal of laughter.

Exactly what Rory was doing in London he never made clear but as we saw more of each other it became something of a challenge for me to find out. I was, after all, supposed to be in the intelligence game and after six months at Curzon House I began to use a little of my time on the computer to wander into certain Registry files, looking for the odd clue. This was harder than it sounds. Many of the files were technically closed to people at my level, but I'd acquired some supplementary access codes and one of them, coupled with the odd slip by Rory himself, led me to form some very definite ideas.

'DIS,' I said, 'for sure.'

It was mid-June. An early heatwave had taken us to a Putney pub. We were sitting by the river in the half-darkness, watching a lone sculler pulling hard against the falling tide. Rory was in jeans and shirt-sleeves. The remains of his third pint stood on the table beside his motorcycle helmet. Lately, I'd noticed he was drinking quite heavily. I'd no idea why.

'Defence Intelligence Staff?' he murmured. '*Moi?*'

'Yes.'

'Evidence?' He glanced across. 'Care to tell me why?'

I shrugged. 'You got me into this. You must be connected. You're not on the MI5 register. You don't work for Six. You're still a serving soldier—' I looked at him. '. . . Aren't you?'

'Yes.'

'Then it must be DIS.' I paused. 'Unless there's another lot they haven't told me about.'

'Ah . . .' he nodded, non-committal, 'the Wild Bunch.'

He fell silent, refusing once again to elaborate, and I thought about the proposition some more. The Defence Intelligence Staff was an outpost of the Ministry of Defence. They worked closely with MI6, keeping an eye on foreign armed forces. Rory, with his Aberdeen University degree and his near-perfect Arabic, would have been a likely recruit. The way the system worked, he'd be on some kind of attachment. Then, after a couple of years, he'd return to the stockade.

I reached for my drink. The lone sculler had disappeared under Putney Bridge. Rory was yawning.

'I'm bloody tired,' he said, 'and you should be in bed.'

'Thanks.' I lifted my drink. 'Am I keeping you up?'

'No,' he said. '*Au contraire.*'

He looked at me for a moment, a strange expression on his face, an uncertainty I'd never seen before. Then he shook his head, leaning back on the wooden bench, closing his eyes. For a second or two I assumed he really was tired – a busy day, an early start – and I reached across, patting his arm, his sympathetic chum from the West Country. He caught my hand in his and squeezed it, opening one eye as he did so. Rory was never less than honest. He had a candour that was occasionally close to brutal. It was one of the reasons I thought the world of him.

'I've fallen in love with you,' he said quietly. 'You're supposed to have guessed. Your line of work . . .'

I blinked. 'What?'

'Love. I've fallen in love with you.' He paused. 'I've thought about some of the other words, but love comes closest.'

'Why?' I said. 'When?'

I winced at the questions. They sounded, at best, infantile, but I was trying to catch my breath, wondering why on earth I hadn't picked up the signals, seen the smoke in the wind, headed off this appalling scene. Intelligence, for God's sake. Analysis. What a joke. I withdrew my hand, reaching for my drink.

'You're pissed,' I said gently.

'No.'

'It's the heat.'

'No.'

'Summer flu.'

Rory gazed at me for a moment. 'Fuck off,' he said softly. 'At least allow me to do it properly.'

'What?'

'Make a fool of myself.'

'You're not.' I reached across the table again and took his

hand. 'You're a lovely man. You've got a lovely wife and great kids and you shouldn't be living up here. Miles away from them.'

Rory nodded, thinking about it. His hand was warm in mine. 'And you?' he said.

'I've got a terrible memory. Famous for it.'

'Meaning?'

'You never said it.'

He looked at me for a long time, unconvinced. I'd never seen him so deflated, so utterly forlorn. He looked about twelve. Or seventy.

'Yeah,' he muttered at last. 'I never said it. You're right.'

We went back to Fulham on his motor bike. Outside the flat, he pulled into the kerb and waited for me to get off. I stood on the pavement, shaking out my hair, offering him the spare helmet.

'Thanks,' I said.

Rory took the helmet and attached it to the back pannier. He hadn't killed the engine and he was trying his best not to look at me. I stepped towards him, calm at last, back in control. This was a friendship I didn't want to lose. There'd been a misunderstanding. He'd simply got things out of perspective. A little time and it would all sort itself out. I put my hand on his arm.

'Do you want to come up?' I said. 'Coffee? Something to eat?' I shrugged. 'Whatever?'

He stood upright, straddling the machine, adjusting the buckle on his own helmet. He looked, if anything, angry. 'Christ no,' he said, his voice muffled. 'God forbid!'

3

I didn't see Rory again for nearly four years and by that time events had taken both Wesley and me by the scruff of the neck. In my case, it meant what my bosses termed 'a career adjustment'. In Wesley's case, it was rather more serious.

The fifteenth of June 1987 was the day it first occurred to Wesley that an early death might be less than physically pleasant. Dying before his time was something he'd almost come to terms with, but somehow he'd never got round to translating the graph lines and the paragraphs of cold prose into a physical reality. The last thing he seems to have expected was pain.

By now, he was keeping a diary in earnest. Lots of HIV positives do it. It's meant to be a help and I suspect it probably is, a private cupboard for storing the darker and less acceptable nightmares. Wesley kept his on a series of lined pads, which he later filed in the same ring binders I've raided for some of the earlier material. There are four of them in all. I had a chance to read them before he died and we discussed some of the key bits. What follows is the closest I can get to the way it must have felt for him. Reproducing the entries themselves, for June and July 1987, would be pointless. He was so ill, and so frightened, he could scarcely manage to complete a sentence.

It began with a headache and a general feeling of nausea. Wesley had been away, in southern Ireland, spending some of Aldridge's features budget on a big, ambitious story about drug smuggling. He'd driven round the coves of West Cork and Kerry, armed with leads from contacts he'd made in a number of North London pubs. He was trying to source a recent flood of high-quality cannabis, and by the time he returned from Ireland he was near certain that he had the makings of a sensational exposé.

The guts of the story concerned the involvement of an MI5 agent who had the smuggling operation under surveillance and was actively helping to move the stuff into the UK. In its own right, this was startling enough, but what gave it (in Wesley's phrase) 'legs' was the fact that profits from the drug runs were going, via a series of laundering operations through Kilburn betting shops, to the IRA High Command in Dublin. This, of course, was why MI5 had got involved in the first place, but this kind of logic wouldn't, Wesley felt, be immediately obvious to the Great British Public. Instead, they'd doubtless see it as yet another example of the spooks and the criminals working hand in hand.

When he got back from Ireland, the headache got worse. Crouched over the electric fire in his bedroom, the typewriter on a tray on his knees, he began to shiver. He wrapped himself in a dressing gown. Over the dressing gown he put on an anorak. For the best part of a day, sensing the shadow at his door, he typed and typed, checking and re-checking his notes, getting down what he could and sending it by courier to Aldridge with a brief note and a list of expenses.

That night, for the first time ever, he began to sweat. He'd read about the sweats that often accompany HIV. They didn't come as a surprise, but as the fever took a real grip and the pile of sodden T-shirts grew on the floor at his bedside, Wesley began to panic.

By this time, he'd taken a lover, a quiet, gentle twenty-three-year-old called Mark. Mark was an aspiring actor, and, like Wesley, HIV positive. He features again in this story and I've talked to him at length about what happened next. His recall is perfect, largely because he was sure that one day the same thing would happen to him.

Mark came looking for Wesley three days after the fever began. He found him exhausted, curled under a pile of blankets, his knees to his chin, shuddering with cold. The mattress beneath his body was soaking wet. The path to the lavatory was strewn with paper cups. There was a terrible smell. Mark did what he could, helping Wesley out of bed, propping him up on a chair, changing the sheets, turning the mattress, opening the windows, filling the place with air freshener. When the doctor came, he retreated to the kitchen, making another pot of Wesley's favourite herbal tea, watching through the half-open door while the doctor ran a stethoscope over Wesley's chest. In three days, he seemed to have shrunk. Weight, in Mark's phrase, had just fallen off him. Chalk-white, wild-eyed, still shivering with cold, he crouched in the chair, his hands pushed into his crutch, staring at the carpet while the doctor went tap-tap across his chest, up over his shoulder and down his back.

The doctor sent him to hospital. Within an hour he was occupying a bed at St Mary's, Paddington. By now, he'd lost all track of time. Dimly aware of the activity around him – nurses taking blood samples, Mark's face at the foot of the bed, two visits to the X-ray department – Wesley surrendered to the fever. With his temperature nudging 103°, he was quite certain he was fighting for his life. His head was bursting. His stomach felt hot and raw. There wasn't an inch of his body that hadn't been scorched by this monstrous, implacable fever.

He stayed at St Mary's for nearly a month. After a week or so, the antibiotics began to get the upper hand. His temperature fell, he was able to keep liquids down and as the fever gradually receded he was left with a feeling of total exhaustion. He slept a great deal, sweating again when his temperature rose at night, then sinking into a kind of half-life, detached from his surroundings, monosyllabic, acknowledging visitors with a weak handshake and a glassy smile.

One of the visitors was his mother, a small, timid woman of whom he saw very little. She lived out on the coast in Essex, and Wesley had never told her a word about his HIV. Mark, alarmed enough to phone her, had been less than specific and when she arrived, the consultant obliged Wesley with a vague reference to viral pneumonia. She stayed for half an hour, her woollen gloves folded on her lap, telling Wesley how terrible the trains were.

Another visitor was Aldridge. He sat by the bed for the best part of an afternoon, reviewing the prospects for Wesley's Irish drugs story, trying to mask how shocked he felt, what a difference a week could make to someone he thought he knew well. At the end of the visit, the nurses wheeling the screens into place around the bed, he bent quickly to Wesley's ear and promised to return as soon as he could, but Wesley reached up, caught a fold of his jacket and shook his head. He didn't want Aldridge to see him this way. He'd get better, quicker, on his own. Time, he muttered as Aldridge turned away. Just give me a bit of time.

The tests, at first, revealed nothing. The consultant, aware of Wesley's HIV, told him that it could be any of a dozen infections. His immune system wasn't working too well. Some bug, resident or otherwise, had got the upper hand for a while. Wesley thought about it, the hot dark spaces of his body crawling with infection. He felt, he said, a sense of betrayal. Not by fate. Not by the guy in New York. But by the feeble chemistry of his own system. Sitting in a bath in the tiny tiled room at the end of the ward, he looked down at his pale flesh, astonished at how thin he'd become. As he tried to shave, his eyes followed the razor in the mirror, exploring unfamiliar territory, the skin tauter, thinner. Even the bone beneath, he told me later, felt raw to the touch.

After the first bout of fever came the depression. Wesley lay in the bed, quite still, a needle in his arm dripping yet more anti-biotics. When the trolleys from the kitchen appeared, clattering down the ward, he shut his eyes and turned his head into the pillow. The smell of food, any food, made him want to vomit and he tried to visualize other things, scenes from his recent trip to Ireland, the shape of a fold of land, the twists and turns of a particular conversation, peat smoke shredding in the wind, fat little parcels of cloud bellying in from the Atlantic. Once or twice he tried to read, picking up a paper, letting his eyes wander down the page, unable, for the first time in his life, to make sense of any of it. This failure of concentration compounded the physical hurt, and by the tenth day he was wondering whether there was any point in carrying on. Part of him, an old man already, had had enough. But there was another part, too, that was still angry, still hurt, still determined to get better.

A week later, the doctors no wiser, the fever returned and with it came yet more tests. Semi-delirious, Wesley tried to concentrate on counting the tiles in the ceiling while the nurse coated his upper body in KY jelly and a technician arrived with an ultra-sound scanner. The pictures of his spleen and liver, though, revealed nothing, so the consultant decided to do a liver biopsy, half a syringe of local anaesthetic and two fine wires inserted through the body wall while Wesley lay immobile, on his side, forbidden to move for hour after hour. The following day, still in the dark, they wheeled him away for a CT scan, inching his body through a big white plastic arch, building up a 3D picture of his stomach. Back in bed, surrounded by bottles of Badoit, Wesley felt worse than ever. Every bit of him hurt. The bits that touched the pillow hurt. The bits beneath the sheet hurt. The bits in contact with the mattress hurt. Even the soles of his feet hurt. Unable to sleep, he simply lay there, thinking about the next hour, and the hour after that, and all he felt was dread.

Next morning, the consultant arrived. It was 8 July. He was smiling broadly. The CT scan had caught the offending bug. Wesley had TB of the stomach. Now they could set to work and make him better.

And they did. Within ten days, still very weak, Wesley left the hospital with Mark and took a taxi back to Stoke Newington. Waiting for him there, a nice touch, was a letter Aldridge had sent by courier that same afternoon. In it he promised Wesley that his job was safe for as long as he wanted it and that he should take his time getting better. Only at the end of the letter did he mention the Irish story. The piece, he wrote, was sensational. Wesley had done a fine job. But certain aspects had proved especially sensitive and after a great deal of thought Aldridge had decided not to run it. Nothing personal. Just an old-fashioned editorial decision he hoped he'd understand. Wesley didn't understand, but what was more important was the realization that, just now, he didn't much care. Mark, coming in from the kitchen with yet more soup, had watched the letter flutter to the floor. Years later, he still remembers the expression on Wesley's face: pure indifference, a residue of the fever that had very nearly killed him.

My own career, meanwhile, had ground to a halt. By now, I'd been at Curzon House for well over a year. The novelty had gone, the challenge had worn off and I'd had more than enough time to ask myself some of the harder questions. One or two of them had to do with a growing sense of claustrophobia. The offices themselves were dull and airless. No one ever seemed to laugh. There was no spark, or sense of real involvement. My colleagues, most of them, were obsessed by status and petty slights. My superiors were largely invisible. And away from the building, out in the real world where the product was gathered and spent, there was only a mysterious void. I'd said yes, all those months ago, because I thought I could contribute. Now, I spent my working life in front of a computer screen, a million miles from what I fondly thought of as the action.

MI5 has a form for moods like these. It's called an HR7. You fill it in and send it upstairs. After a while, if you're lucky, they ask to see you. In my case, it was autumn before the summons came, a peremptory phone call telling me to report to an office on the fourth floor. I recognized the voice at once. It was a voice you didn't forget: flat South London vowels half-buried under a thin, nasal whine. It belonged to the younger of the two men I'd met with Rory at the Soho restaurant, the one who'd subsequently reappeared at my formal interview. Since then, I'd seen him perhaps half a dozen times, awkward meetings in lifts or the central lobby, a nod and a grunt and a passing reference to the weather, nothing I could dignify with the word 'conversation'. The only thing I really knew about him was his name, Eric Stollmann, and that fact that he'd come to us a couple of years back from Customs and Excise.

The latter was occasionally a subject of canteen gossip. Customs and Excise were well known as zealots, keen-eyed shock-troop types with terrible complexions and inner-city educations and absolutely no sense of humour. As far as I could judge, Stollmann was the perfect example of all three. Quite why he'd transferred his affections to our little brotherhood no one seemed to know, but he was universally mistrusted, not least because no one had a clue what he did.

I knocked twice on his office door and stepped in. He was sitting behind a desk with his back to the window. The sun, low, cast a long shadow over the blotter. He was toying with a paper clip, thin bony fingers, bitten nails. For the first time ever, he smiled.

'Long time,' he mumbled, 'no see.'

We talked for nearly an hour. I remember everything about the conversation because – to be frank – it was the first time I'd got any real sense out of any of my superiors. He began by saying he was sorry. My induction had taken rather longer than had been planned, more the firm's fault than mine. Unexpected resignations in Registry had left the department undermanned. In consequence, I'd been obliged to backfill. Under the circumstances, the view was that I'd done rather well. A series of source reports I'd analysed on certain developments in Northern Ireland had attracted a great deal of attention. I obviously had a knack for the work. I could recognize what was important and what was rubbish. I had the intellectual courage not to qualify my conclusions. I was bright and forthright and I obviously wasn't frightened of hard work. One of the things he wanted to say, he muttered, was thank you.

By this time, as you might imagine, I'd rather warmed to the man. With the blinds down on the window behind him, shielding me from the sun, I had the opportunity to take a real look. He was certainly young – I guessed maybe early thirties – but the tightly cropped hair was beginning to grey at the temples, and his face was hollow with fatigue. Physically, he was medium height, thin, with a white, indoor face and coal-black eyes. He was carefully dressed – blue shirt, subtly striped, nicely cut suit, quietly original tie – and there were no rings on his fingers. The desk, likewise, was virtually bare – blotter, wire basket, telephone, internal directory, two cheap Biros in a plain white mug – and it somehow matched the impression I was beginning to form about the man himself. It looked spartan. It spoke of efficiency, hard work and long hours. Empty of photographs or ornament, it made no concessions to a life outside.

After a while, he enquired whether I'd like tea. I asked for coffee instead and he grunted, smiling at my usual obduracy, lifting the phone. When he put it down, he opened a drawer and took out a file. It was a red file. Red files, at Curzon House, are subject to internal restrictions. He slid it across to me.

'Read it,' he said. 'I've got some biscuits somewhere.'

I opened the file. Inside was a thin sheaf of source reports. The numbers on the tops of the pages weren't consecutive. I was only getting part of the story. I read the first report. It quoted at length from a letter which had been received a week and a half earlier. It was on House of Commons notepaper and signed by an MP called Lawrence Priddy whose name I recognized from the papers. I glanced up.

'Tory? Somewhere in the West Midlands?'

'Yeah.'

I nodded, returning to the file. Priddy had received a visit from a constituent, a woman called Beth Alloway. She'd come, in strictest confidence, because she was worried about her husband. Clive Alloway was a businessman. He ran a small consultancy in the engineering field. Priddy had evidently met him on a number of occasions and described him in the letter as 'a minor player'.

There was a tap on the door and the coffees arrived. I began to close the file but Stollmann signalled for me to read on. I did so, dunking the first of his stale digestives in the thin black liquid, committing the information to memory, brick by brick, the way I'd been taught. Clive Alloway sold high-tech tooling, much of it for export. In consequence, he spent a great deal of time abroad, winning orders, doing deals, troubleshooting hiccups. For the last year or so he'd been in Iraq a lot, often for weeks at a time. In ways that only a wife can recognize, these trips appeared to have changed him. He'd become secretive, evasive. He wasn't sleeping well at nights. Strange calls on the house phone had begun to disturb him.

Beth Alloway had answered one or two of these calls herself when her husband wasn't at home and it had always been a foreign voice at the other end, polite enough but never offering a name or a number for a return call. This had made her wonder a bit but then, very recently, she'd been readying one of his jackets for the dry cleaners and she'd found a plain brown envelope, unsealed, in one of the pockets. Inside the envelope was a thick wad of fifty-pound notes. She'd counted them. They came to £2450. Astonished that he should be carrying so large a sum when she'd been told repeatedly that times were hard, she'd confronted her husband with the money, wanting to know more, wanting to know where it had come from, wanting to find out what it was that had changed him so much. Brusque and defensive, he'd dismissed her questions, demanding the money back, accusing her of 'meddling'. There were some things, he told her, he simply couldn't discuss. Not with her. And not with anyone else.

After some thought, Beth Alloway had decided to search the house. Under the desk in her husband's tiny office she'd noticed a loose floorboard. Under the floorboard she'd found a revolver.

With the gun was a box of bullets. She'd put them both back and not told her husband, but she'd known then that she needed help. Going to colleagues would have been disloyal. A psychiatrist, though tempting, would simply enrage him. So in the end, half convinced she already knew the answer, she'd put the question to her local MP, a man whom her husband seemed to count as a personal friend. What was happening to Clive? Why was he going off his head? Who was getting at him?

I looked up. Stollmann was sipping his coffee, watching me over the cup.

'Well?' I said. 'Who *is* getting at him?'

'We are. And the Iraqis.'

'Why?'

'Because he's selling them the goodies they're after.'

'What goodies?'

'Arms-making equipment. Lathes. Computers. State of the art stuff. The kind of gear they need just now.'

I nodded, fingering the next report in the file. Iraq was still at war with Iran. They'd been at it for years and they were getting through a lot of everything: shells, mines, military hardware of every description. Much of the equipment had once come from the Soviets, but now the Iraqis wanted to make it for themselves. For that, they needed the right tooling, and you didn't have to have a business degree to see the openings for men like Clive Alloway. I frowned.

'I thought it was illegal,' I said, 'exporting lethal equipment to Iraq? I thought we'd given up all that? I thought there was an embargo?'

'There is.'

'Then who gave this guy the go-ahead?'

'The DTI.'

'But aren't they supposed to police it? Issue the licences? Make sure everyone stays in line?'

'Yes.' Stollmann nodded. 'Of course they are.'

I gazed at him. Around Whitehall, the Department of Trade and Industry had a reputation for a certain maverick independence, though I wasn't aware it extended to sanctions-busting.

'They really let him get on with it?' I said. 'Help the Iraqis on their way? Despite all the other guff?'

Stollmann didn't answer for a moment. Then he shrugged. 'That's not the point,' he said. 'Licences are only as good as what you put on them. It's a question of how you phrase it. You can stretch and bend these things. Call the stuff dual-use. Say you're building tractor parts. Happens all the time.'

'Then what *is* the point?'

Stollmann looked at me for a long time. Then he leaned forward, putting the cup carefully to one side, and I sensed at once that our conversation was about to change gear. My days at the computer keyboard were numbered. Thank God I'd sent the bloody form.

'Alloway's working for Six,' Stollmann said quietly. 'They debrief him regularly. Every time he comes back.'

I nodded. 'And us? Are we interested?'

'Yes.'

'Why?'

'Because the Iraqis are making moves here, too. They've targeted certain firms. Alloway's is one of them. Small though he is.'

'Targeted?'

'They want to buy him. Plus others. Build a network...' He shrugged. 'The DTI call it foreign investment. It's music to their ears.'

'And us?' I said again.

'We keep tabs on the Iraqis. See what they're up to, who they're talking to, what they're spending money on.' He paused. 'Helps keep things neat and tidy, knowing what they're about.'

'And Alloway?'

'He knows what they're about. He's advising them.'

'And does he tell us?'

'So far, yes.'

'Why?'

'Patriotism.' Stollmann shrugged. 'His word, not mine.'

'I see.' I nodded, glancing down at the file again. Mrs Alloway had a point. Sandwiched between MI5, MI6 and Baghdad, her husband was doubtless finding life extremely uncomfortable. I looked up again. 'So what next?' I said. 'What do you want me to do?'

There was another silence. Stollmann reached across for the

file and extracted a photograph from a pocket at the back.

'Mrs Alloway,' he said.

I looked at the photo. Beth Alloway had a nice smile, a small shy grin, revealing slightly crooked front teeth. I glanced up. Stollmann was flicking through the digest of the MP's letter, his finger racing down each page.

'So far she's only gone to Priddy,' he said carefully. 'It would be a shame if she went anywhere else.'

'What's he told her?'

'Nothing.'

'How much does he know?'

'Quite a lot.'

'But he doesn't want to be compromised?'

'Exactly.'

I nodded, turning over the photo, reading the scribbled message on the back. The message had been for Clive Alloway. The photo was evidently a relic from happier times. I glanced up. 'You want me to go and talk to her?'

'Yes.'

'On the quiet? Tell her not to rock the boat? Talk about...' I paused, 'the national interest?'

'Yes,' Stollmann said, 'and take a look at Priddy, too.'

4

Stollmann let me photocopy three of the documents in the file. I read them on the train to Wolverhampton the following afternoon. I felt very odd, clattering through the trading estates north of London, trying to work out how Whitehall would ever square the circle: making lots of money out of the Iraqis while denouncing them to all and sundry. There was doubtless a logic in it somewhere, but from where I sat it looked like simple hypocrisy. What was I going to say to Mrs Alloway? How was I going to put it?

The MP, Lawrence Priddy, met the train at Wolverhampton. I'd phoned him from London on Stollmann's advice. He was younger than I'd expected, tall, slightly stooped, with a careful parting and a mirthless smile. He stood on the platform, looking me up and down, a physical appraisal no less disgusting for being so frank. I'd dressed carefully for this occasion – sensible skirt, high-necked sweater, minimum make-up – but there are bits of me it's hard to disguise.

'Sarah,' he said at once, offering a cursory handshake. 'Welcome.'

We drove to a nearby hotel, a gloomy, red-brick Victorian establishment. Priddy ordered tea at reception and led me through to a small parlour. The staff were immensely respectful. Evidently, he came here often.

In the parlour, we settled into a couple of uncomfortable mock-leather armchairs, Priddy immediately in command, the kind of facile, effortless charm that comes with a five-figure majority and a promising career. Overnight, I'd done a little research. The man was bone dry, right of centre and had recently become parliamentary private secretary to one of the junior ministers at the DTI. His constituency was out in Shropshire, a comfortable forty minutes from the ghettos of the black country. Clive and Beth Alloway lived there too, though I fancied in rather less style.

A waitress brought cakes and a tray of tea, and I played mother while Priddy told me a little more about Clive Alloway, not bothering to hide the fact that he had little regard for the man. He was, he said, one of the smaller cogs in the West Midlands machine tools sector, running his consultancy partly from home, partly from his car phone and partly from a seedy two-room office somewhere in the depths of Walsall. He'd been acting as an agent for a handful of local firms and although he appeared to have done well enough, there'd been recent rumours that he'd overstretched himself. In his line of business, Priddy suggested drily, that wasn't difficult. The man would have big overheads: airline tickets, city-centre hotels, hospitality and the incessant need to keep up appearances. If the orders dried up, he could quickly find himself in real financial trouble. And that, it seemed, was what had happened.

I nodded, watching him reach for his third cake. 'How do you know?' I said.

Priddy looked up, surprised. Like many men, he excelled at being patronizing, scarcely bothering to conceal his amusement. My mother always said it came from insecurity or a deep hatred of women. Watching Priddy, I wasn't sure about either. 'My dear,' he licked a curl of cream from one finger, 'how do you think I know? The man's a mess. His marriage is on the skids. His business is up the chute. His poor bloody wife's a basket case. And his bank manager's threatening to foreclose. We call that a disaster in my trade.' He smiled. 'What's your word for it?'

I said nothing, favouring him with a smile of my own.

After a moment or two, he bit deeply into a chocolate éclair, savouring it, then wiped his mouth with a corner of his napkin. 'I suspect you owe me a proper briefing,' he said at last, brushing the crumbs from his lap. 'And I suspect now isn't the time.'

'No?'

'No.' He shook his head, leaning forward, his elbows on his knees. 'I'm in London after the weekend. I have a little place round the back of Dolphin Square.' He paused. 'Lunch or dinner? Your choice.'

By the time we got to the Alloways' place, it was nearly dark. The cottage was beside a river. The lights were on upstairs and the empty bottles were already on the step for the milkman. I stood in the road for a moment, listening to the sound of water over rocks.

Priddy's window purred down. 'Alloway's abroad,' he said briefly, 'as I expect you know.'

I nodded, glancing down at him. 'Are you coming in?'

'Briefly. To pay my respects. Then you're on your own.'

Beth Alloway opened the door at the second knock. I'd left it to Priddy to make the arrangements for my visit and I could tell at once that she didn't like the man. She offered him a brief nod and invited us in, a small, busy woman, strands of greying hair escaping from a badly secured bun at the back of her neck. She was wearing a thick jumper and a pair of paint-stained tracksuit bottoms. One knee had a hole in it. I stood by the door while Priddy did the introductions. I liked her on sight.

Priddy, his camel coat carefully buttoned against the cold, turned to go. He was already treating me like an old friend, as if we'd known each other for years.

'Sure about the taxi back?'

'Yes, thanks.'

He looked at me a moment, one eyebrow arched, then kissed me lightly on the cheek and walked out into the night. We were still standing beneath the tiny porch, watching the lights of his Rover disappear round the bend, when I decided there was little point not voicing the obvious.

'What a terrible man,' I murmured and glanced at Beth.

'Yes,' she said, turning back into the house.

I stayed at the cottage most of the evening. Downstairs, the place was a mess, piles of ironing on a chair beside the fireplace, bundles of rhubarb in a bucket of water under the table, dog biscuits scattered around a bowl behind the door. A fire was laid but unlit and the room felt cold enough for me to regret taking off my coat. While Beth hurried from room to room, apologizing for not being ready, I looked around for family photos, clues to the way the marriage had started, snaps of the kids I knew she'd had, but the only photo on display was a small black and white shot of the wedding itself, carefully mounted in a cheap wooden frame. The couple were standing, arm in arm, outside a registry office. Clive Alloway, much younger, looked pleased with himself. Beth, under the short skirt, had nice legs.

I was still looking at the photo when Beth finally joined me, shutting the door at the foot of the stairs and stooping to the fire. She lit it with an old candle end, then broke open a bottle of sherry and poured two large glasses. 'Mr Priddy says you're from London.'

'Yes.'

'Something to do with . . .' She frowned, a totally artless pause, genuinely perplexed.

'Intelligence,' I said quietly. 'I work for intelligence.'

'Oh?'

Beth looked alarmed, as if her worst nightmare had come true, and I wondered for a moment what on earth Priddy had told her. He'd made it quite plain in the hotel that his own involvement was to be minimal. 'Arm's length' was the phrase he'd used.

'I work for MI5,' I said. 'You should know that.'

'Isn't that . . . secret?'

'Yes.' I smiled. 'You and me.'

'And Clive?'

'No.' I shook my head. 'Not Clive.'

'Ah.'

She looked away, reaching for her sherry, and I could tell at once that she was relieved. One less secret to share. One less scene to risk. I reached for my own glass and invited her to tell me how things were. She did so, deciding to trust me, an instinctive thing, woman to woman, her other options quite obviously exhausted. She talked in a low, slightly hesitant voice, rueful, saddened by what ambition and the lure of big business had done to the man she'd married.

She'd never wanted him to be rich. She'd no real interest in money. In fact she and Clive had both been happier, much happier, when he was still in the world of education, teaching day-release courses in engineering. They'd lived in Walsall, then. They'd had two kids in quick succession, both grown-up now with homes of their own. Laura, who was in bed with flu upstairs, had been an afterthought, a brief burst of sunshine between the squalls. After a while, she got to the point of the story. Her husband had changed beyond recognition. The bills and the business were driving him mad. But there was more to it than that. She knew it.

I nodded. The bottle at her elbow was two-thirds empty. 'Is there anyone else?' I said.

'No.'

'Are you sure?'

'Yes. I asked him. It was one of the first things I thought of but—' She shook her head, emphatic. 'No.'

She gazed at me for a moment. The light from the fire danced on her face. She looked utterly miserable. 'I think he's frightened,' she said at last. 'He must be. But I don't know why.' She paused again, looking at me. 'He's never had a gun in his life. He wouldn't know what to do with it. He hates violence. We both do. I just hope to God—' She broke off again, shook her head and began to cry.

There was a box of tissues on the table. I took a handful and gave her one. She shut her eyes and blew her nose. When the question came, I barely heard it.

'Is it to do with you?' she whispered. 'Your lot? Is that why you're here?'

I gazed at her for a moment. 'Yes,' I said.

'Is he in danger? Will they . . .?'

'No.'

'None of them? Not you? Not . . .' she opened one eye, 'whoever else it is?'

'No.'

'Are you sure?'

I hesitated, balling the Kleenex in my hand, pressing very hard. The woman needed help, real help, not platitudes. She was looking at me again, the eyes wide, an old face, ravaged by grief.

'It's not that I'd be alone,' she said. 'It's not that. I can cope with that. I've thought about it and I'd hate it, but it's not that. No. It's . . .' She began to cry again, reaching out for another tissue, shaking her head, trying to dislodge some awful thought. 'He's a good man, a truly good man. He doesn't deserve all this, whatever it is, whatever's going on. It shouldn't have happened, not to him.' She paused, watching me, wanting answers, her life out of control. 'How *can* it happen?' she said at last. 'How come we've ended up this way? What's he *done*?'

I stayed another hour, before phoning for a taxi that took an age to appear. I asked her about Priddy, the kind of relationship he'd had with her husband, trying to determine what she hadn't told me, but the deeper I probed, the more I realized that she knew very little about Priddy and probably cared even less. Her real concern was Clive. Her husband's safety. Her husband's sanity. When I tried to assure her that he was in no danger, she shook her head.

'He's spying,' she said flatly.

'He's giving us information. Keeping his eyes open. Keeping us in touch. If I tell you he's a brave man, you'll get the wrong idea. He isn't at risk. He's simply doing . . .' I hesitated.

'He's spying,' she said again. 'He's a spy.'

'OK.' I nodded. 'He's a spy.'

Beth was silent for a moment, staring at the wall. 'And me?' she said at last, then, gesturing upstairs: 'Us?'

'You're his wife. You come before everything.'

She nodded, gazing round the room, thinking about it, her eyes moist again. 'I know,' she said. 'I think that's his problem. If I didn't love him, it wouldn't matter.'

The taxi arrived soon afterwards. I stood in the pool of light beneath the porch, thanking Beth for her time, looking back at the chilly chaos that was all she had left of the marriage. The rapport we'd established earlier had somehow gone. I was, by the evening's end, just another messenger from that other world that had taken her husband away.

Turning up my collar against the driving rain, I fumbled in my pocket and scribbled the number of my Fulham flat. It wasn't much, but it was the closest I could get to telling her that I really wanted to help. In truth, I hadn't a clue about the small print, about what her husband was really up to, but in the parlance of my new trade, that was strictly irrelevant. What mattered, in professional terms, was trying to insulate her against further contacts. I hoped that I'd done that. I hoped she wouldn't talk to the media, or discuss it with friends. More important, I hoped she trusted me and would feel confident enough to pick up the phone if things got really bleak.

'My home number,' I said, giving her the already sodden piece of paper.

She looked at it for a moment, quite blank, then mumbled her thanks. I kissed her on the cheek, wished her luck and ran to the waiting taxi. Looking back, starting to wave, I was surprised to find the front door already shut. As the taxi began to move away, I looked back again, watching her shadow move across the curtains, reaching for the light switch, returning the cottage to darkness and the rain.

I was back in Stollmann's office three days later. Getting an appointment had been far from easy.

'She's frightened witless,' I said. 'She thinks he's going mad.'

Stollmann looked at me woodenly. His eyes were blacker than ever. 'We knew that,' he said.

'But she's half mad herself. Truly. She's out of her mind with it. Worrying about him.'

Stollmann nodded and reaching for one of his Biros added a line to a list of notes on a pad. I wondered for a moment whether the note had anything to do with Beth. Somehow I doubted it.

'She going to talk to anyone else?' he said at last.

'No.'

'You sure?'

'As I can be.' I nodded. 'Yes.'

'How do you know?'

'I told her she'd be putting him in danger,' I lied. 'I told her it wouldn't be a clever thing to do.'

Stollmann said nothing for a moment. Then he looked up. 'You're right,' he said. 'It wouldn't.'

There was a long silence. Stollmann's eyes were back on the pad. Our conversation was evidently over. I got up. Then sat down again.

'About Priddy,' I began. 'Remember you asked me to take a look at him?'

Stollmann glanced up. 'Yes?'

I shrugged. 'What did you have in mind? Exactly?'

Stollmann ducked his head a moment. 'I just wondered how you got on, that's all, you know . . .' He was uneasy, even embarrassed. 'Chemistry? Would that cover it?'

'Did I like him? Is that what you're asking?'

'Yes.' He nodded. 'More or less.'

I stared at him a moment, remembering the touch of Priddy's

hand on my arm, the way he modulated his voice for certain questions, an interest all the more insulting for being so obvious.

'No,' I said quietly. 'Sorry to disappoint you, but I thought he was ghastly.'

Stollmann looked briefly pained, then reached for the phone. His eyes went to the door, indicating that our little chat was over.

I got up again, watching his finger stabbing at the grid of buttons. 'Do you want a formal report?' I said. 'About Beth Alloway?'

Stollmann shook his head, not bothering to look at me. 'No,' he said. 'Nothing on paper, thank you.'

I spent the rest of the month back at my desk. I couldn't get Beth Alloway out of my mind, the photo on the mantelpiece, the pair of them outside the registry office, her face years later, the look of total bewilderment. Twice I tried to talk to Stollmann again. I wanted more detail. More background. The first time, he refused to see me. The second time he told me we weren't a branch of the social services. I took the latter comment as an insult and told him so. Then I returned to my computer. If Stollmann wouldn't tell me any more, I'd have to find out for myself.

By now, I knew a great deal about Registry files. I knew the way they were organized, what the experts call 'the architecture' of the system. I knew the strength of the internal walls they'd thrown up, insulating one file from another, the ditches they'd dug, impossible to cross without the right access codes. I knew, as well, about the other precautions they'd taken, the tricksy little electronic tags they'd attached to this section or that, the priority classifications they'd given to particular entries, the lengths they went to protecting special sources. It was a maze, impenetrable to outsiders, and even to people like me, only accessible on a need-to-know basis.

But it didn't end there, because the Curzon House system formed part of a larger network, serving every department in Whitehall, a wholly logical arrangement which put a great deal of information at our fingertips and saved a fortune in time and money. But access to these 'daughter-systems', likewise, needed codes, and they were issued only on a case-by-case basis. To acquire a particular code you needed proper authority, and once you'd laid hands on the code your problems weren't over because they changed them every week. In this sense, the codes were a bit like railway tickets. What I really needed was a rover ticket, taking me everywhere. But the best I could hope for, given the proper authority, was a series of day returns.

I thought about it a great deal: where I'd look, what I was trying to find.

If Alloway was selling to the Iraqis, he'd need DTI export certificates. Without these, the stuff wouldn't get past the docks. But DTI certificates were only issued in compliance with certain guidelines. In the case of Iraq (and Iran), the government had banned the sale of something they termed 'lethal equipment'. According to Stollmann, this was precisely Alloway's line of country. How, then, had he got round the government's embargo?

Part of the answer would lie in the DTI files. They'd have copies of the export certificates. Alloway might also have been using the Export Credit Guarantee Scheme, a form of government insurance in case businessmen had trouble getting paid. They, too, might have documentation.

I began the search by tapping into Central Registry, poking around our own files, checking whether we might have anything on the shelf. Even this exercise could be risky, and when my supervisor paused behind me and enquired what I was doing, I told him I was 'housecleaning'. 'Housecleaning' was what you did when you got in a muddle on your computer. It happened a great deal in MI5.

Alloway, as it turned out, did have a file of his own. Some of the intelligence was a straight donation from MI6, crumbs from their table, and there were additional source reports from one of our own guys who'd since resigned after a row about his pension rights. Scrolling quickly through the entries, I got a picture of a small, overworked entrepreneur, building what bridges he could between the Iraqis and a group of firms in the West Midlands. The stuff he was selling included machine tools and various peripherals like software programs for the computer-controlled jigs, and there was a brief analysis of the dozen or so contracts he'd so far secured. Detailed information about what the Iraqis were doing with all this equipment was listed in a separate annexe. Beth Alloway's visit to Priddy was carefully noted (the same

Wolverhampton hotel!) and there was an accompanying recommendation that she be handled with extreme care.

At this point my supervisor returned, and I greeted him with a triumphant smile, backing out of the Registry files, wiping the screen clean and switching the machine off with a flourish.

'Done it,' I said cheerfully. 'Nice and tidy again.'

The supervisor looked at me for a moment, amused. 'Until the next time,' he said at last, 'eh?'

By now it was obvious I'd have to look elsewhere and I began to think about the problems of tunnelling into some of the precious daughter-files. At Curzon House this is known as 'B & E' (breaking and entering), and one way of doing it is simple, old-fashioned corruption: finding someone with a key and bending their arm until they lend it to you. The question was therefore simple: who might have the codes I'd need? And how would I persuade them to share?

I gave this problem a great deal of thought, but I soon realized that the only real option was Lawrence Priddy. I still hadn't made much sense of Stollmann's line about 'chemistry', but the MP had phoned twice and both times he'd left messages asking me to get in touch. It wasn't a call I looked forward to making, but the man plainly had good connections at the DTI and it was possible that these might extend to the kind of access I was after. I found him, at the first time of calling, in the office he shared at the House of Commons. He sounded surprised to hear me and slightly wary. I suggested we might meet.

'Sorpressa,' he said, naming an Italian restaurant in Belgravia, 'half past one.'

I arrived at the restaurant at ten to two. The place was a swirl of pink tablecloths and loud conversation: sleek, well-heeled MPs bent over dainty forkfuls of designer pasta. Priddy was at a table near the back, reading a copy of the *Spectator*. He barely bothered to look up.

'Is it fashionable to be late?' he enquired. 'Only I was about to go.'

We sparred for nearly an hour. By now, I'd been a civil servant long enough to know that every conversation in Whitehall has a sub-text. What you say isn't necessarily what you mean. It's the gaps and the silences and the occasional ironic asides that often light the real path home. MI5, as it happens, are expert at this kind of dialogue and while I'm not especially comfortable playing games like these, it certainly helps to know the rules. Priddy, of course, had mastered them years ago, a fact I ought to have taken into account much, much earlier.

We were in a cab, heading for Dolphin Square, before he hinted that he might – *might* – be able to accommodate me.

'Tell me again,' he said. 'Make me believe it.'

I nodded, the wide-eyed young ingenue from Curzon House. 'Clive Alloway lives in your constituency,' I said, 'and he's selling into Iraq. That's two reasons why you should be interested.'

Priddy was sitting back in the corner of the cab, gazing out of the window, his long, pale face quite blank.

'Agreed,' he said.

'He's working for Six, and for us as well. You probably know that already.' I paused, half-expecting a response, but Priddy didn't say a word. 'He's frightened.' I said, 'His business is collapsing and his marriage as well. In the office, they'd say that made him dangerous.'

Priddy frowned. 'Dangerous?' he murmured.

'Yes.'

'You mean that?'

'Yes.'

'Dangerous to whom?' He looked at me for the first time, the beginnings of a half-smile playing on his face. 'Well?' he said finally.

'I don't know,' I said. 'That's why I need a little help.'

We went to his flat, a big, sunny apartment with tall, handsome rooms and some exquisite furniture. I stood at the window in the sitting room, looking out, while Priddy made coffee in the kitchen. When he returned, he was carrying a cafetière and two cups on a tray.

I nodded at the big overmantel, the detail beautifully picked out, daring shades of green, wholly successful. 'Who's the interior decorator?' I said. 'Your wife?'

Priddy nodded. 'Yes,' he said, 'as it happens.'

'Is she up here a lot?'

'Often enough.'

He sat down on the sofa and began to pour the coffee, and I

wondered how long it would be before he got to the point. He'd spent most of the meal examining me through half-closed eyes, letting me prattle on while he explored the possibilities. I hadn't the slightest intention of going to bed with him, but I was uncertain how I'd handle saying no. He glanced up, holding out my coffee. Thin, bone-china cups. Not cheap.

'Customs and Excise,' he said abruptly. 'Tell me about Customs and Excise.'

I gazed at him. It wasn't at all what I'd expected. 'I don't know about Customs,' I said. 'Should I?'

He looked at me a moment, speculative. 'Yes,' he said at last, 'I think you should.' He paused. 'Working for that busy Mr Stollmann.'

I blinked. 'You know Stollmann?'

'Of him. Not personally.'

'I see.' I paused, looking up. 'So what do you want to know? Specifically?'

'About Alloway. What the Customs people make of him. Where he fits in that little world of theirs.' He paused again. 'Can do?'

I nodded, automatic assent. 'Yes,' I said, 'of course.'

'Good.'

He finished his coffee and glanced at his watch, and for the first time I realized quite how cleverly he'd played the last hour and a half. I'd agreed to meet him in order to bend his arm. Instead, without any great effort, he'd bent mine. I swallowed the last of the coffee and put the cup on the tray.

'A steer on the DTI codes would be a help,' I said.

Priddy glanced up at me, and nodded. 'I'm sure,' he said. 'Give me a ring.'

He got up and straightened his tie. Half-way to the door, he paused in front of the mirror in the overmantel, checking his appearance and running a hand over the back of his head.

'You like the place?' he said. 'Approve?'

'Yes, it's very nice.'

'Good.' His eyes met mine in the mirror. 'Then you'll know where to come next time.'

5

In one of the cardboard boxes on my bedroom floor is an audio cassette. In Wesley's scrawl, it's labelled 'Bollocking, Derek, 17 September 1987'. On the cassette is a complete record of an exchange between Wesley and Derek Aldridge at the point when Wesley was out of hospital and on the mend, and well enough to realize what had happened to his precious dope-smuggling exposé. I'm including bits of it here, not because the story itself is especially significant (it isn't), but because the conversation launched Wesley on the path that led to Geneva and to the revelations that begin this book. It's also, more importantly, the authentic sound of the man in action. At full throttle, as I later realized, Wesley Keogh could be a terrifying spectacle.

The tape begins with Wesley switching on the machine. He and Aldridge have obviously just met because Aldridge is telling him to park his coat on a hanger behind the door. My guess is that Wesley had one of those little hand-held recorders in his coat pocket and switched it on as he put it on the table. There's certainly a clunk on the tape, the machine hitting something solid, and a silence during which I imagine Aldridge staring at the table and Wesley hanging up his coat.

Either way, Wesley now sits down. The next bit of the conversation goes as follows. The first voice belongs to Aldridge.

'Is that what I think it is? That Sony?'

'Yeah.'

'Is it on?'

'Yeah.'

'Why?'

There's a pause here. By the sound of it, Wesley's lighting a cigarette. Whatever's happening, Aldridge still wants an answer.

His tone of voice has changed a little. If anything, he's sounding wounded.

'Wes, I asked you why. Are we on the record or something? You want to sue me?'

'No. Shit, no.'

'What then? Why tape it all? Don't you trust me?'

'Not exactly, no.'

'Why not?'

Wesley draws breath. He's clearly in no hurry. This absolutely fits the man I later met. Scenes like these, confrontational, potentially embarrassing, he enjoyed enormously.

'Because I think I know what you did with the Irish piece.'

'I spiked it. You know that. I told you. I sent you a letter.'

'Yeah. But now I think I know why, why you spiked it. I think you got the phone calls. In fact I'm pretty certain you got the phone calls.'

'What phone calls, for fuck's sake?'

'Our friends in Curzon House.'

'MI5?'

'Yeah. I think they nobbled you.'

There's another silence here. Four years later, Aldridge's name came up in my background research on Wesley. I looked him up in Registry's surname index, what we spooks call 'the in-tray', A for Aldridge, and it turned out that Wesley was right. Aldridge got a number of calls from us, four in all, which probably explains the abrupt change in his style on the tape. He is, at first, very bluff, very male, very aggressive.

'Am I hearing this?' he says. 'You think MI5 were on? You think that's why I didn't run with it?'

'Yes.' There's a pause here. Then Wesley comes back, his voice a little softer. 'I'm not saying it's as crude as that. It never is. I'm sure it was all very grown up, arms round the shoulder, see it our way, sensitive material, agents' lives, national interest, all that shit. I expect—'

Aldridge explodes. No more hurt. Just anger. 'Give me fucking credit, Wes. In God's name . . .'

Another pause. Wesley unrepentant.

'How did they put it? Straight threats? D-notice? Phone call to the chairman? What?'

'Listen, mate—'

'No, honestly, I'm interested. You know the story. You know what they were into. Don't get me wrong. I can see their point of view. I just don't think it should have been ours. Or yours, at least . . .'

Aldridge mutters something here I never quite caught. Then there's the scrape of a chair. I fancy he may have got up at this point. At any rate, when he speaks again, he's much closer to the microphone.

'Is that why you came here, Wes? Is that what you've been up to? Getting the dirt on me?'

There's another pause. Then Wesley again, almost sympathetic. 'They did phone you?'

'You know they did.'

'And what did you say?'

'I told them to fuck off.'

'No, you didn't.'

'No, you're right, I didn't, not in those words. But I told them it wasn't any of their business.'

Wesley laughs here. He had a very distinctive laugh, high-pitched, a percussive sound, slightly manic, almost a cackle. Aldridge responds. He's sounding hurt again.

'What's the matter?'

'What you just said. What you told them. None of their business. That's the whole point, mate. That's why they were on to you in the first place. It *was* their business. Most of the fucking piece was about their business. That's why they were were shitting themselves. Jesus, there we were with this monster story, about to go public, MI5 caught with their knickers down, smuggling all those tons of dope. No wonder they gave you a bell, shit . . .'

Wesley cackles again. There's nothing from Aldridge for a bit. Then you get the scrape of a chair, and Aldridge's voice, more distant. 'Listen, mate, this job—'

'Isn't as easy as it looks? Yeah, I know.'

'Don't be so fucking smart.'

'I'm not. I'm trying to do a fucking job. The one you pay me for. Remember?'

'OK, OK, OK, you're disappointed, I can understand that. OK, so yes, they did. They were on . . . and yes, there was pressure, lots of it, round the clock: them, the board, the bank, our city friends, you name it, so . . . You're right. I bottled.'

'You bottled.'

'Yeah. *Mea* fucking *culpa*. And now you're upset about it.'

'Yeah. And you know why? Because next Sunday it'll be in print anyway.'

'Where? Who?'

'The *People*.'

'You *know* that?'

'Yeah.'

'All of it?'

There's another pause here. It's Wesley's turn to be slightly hesitant. 'No . . . not the whole thing.'

'The MI5 bits?'

'No, not them. But the rest, the Micks, the dope, all the stuff about the betting shop and the laundering scams . . . it's all there. Believe me, I've talked to the bloke who's doing it. He's pissing himself. They all are. Can't understand why we, you, never—'

'But they're not running the MI5 bits?'

'No.'

'Then what's the story?'

At this point, Wesley goes barmy. The tirade lasts for several minutes. At the end of it, unusually, he apologizes. Aldridge accepts the apology and mutters something about not playing a blinder himself. Then the conversation changes course completely. Aldridge is taking Wesley into his confidence. Two old mates. The tape still running.

'Listen, Wes, things have been happening. Stuff you don't know about . . .'

'You're sacking me.'

'No, on the contrary—'

'You want me to do your job.'

'God forbid. You'd never forgive me. Who'd fucking want it?'

'What, then?'

Here, there's the sound of blinds rattling down. Then Aldridge again. 'Just you and me? Off the record?'

'Sure.'

'I've had an offer.'

'Surprise me.'

'Seriously. An amazing offer.'

'Doing what?'

'Heading up a defence magazine. Specialist weekly. Leader in its field . . . C'mon, Wes, you know what I'm talking about . . .'

'*Defence Week?*'

'In one.'

Another pause. Wesley sounding slightly shocked. 'They want you to edit *Defence Week?*'

'Yes.'

'And you want to do it?'

'Yes.'

'Why?'

Aldridge takes his time answering. His voice has the tone of someone contemplating a good meal: excited, pleased with himself, anticipatory.

'It's authoritative. It's the best in the field. It's read in the right places. It's . . . shit, a real opportunity.'

'To do what?'

'To move out a little. Spread my wings. Get some profile.' He pauses here. 'You know the way it goes, Wes. The embassy drinks circuit. The odd *Newsnight* invite. The odd consultancy. Seat at the top table. The high and the fucking mighty.'

'And you.'

'Yeah. And me.'

'What are they paying?'

'A lot.'

'More than you get now?'

'Yeah.'

'How much more?'

'I told you. A lot.'

There's another silence. I can imagine Wesley brooding, that pose of his, head down, eyes half closed, a cigarette hanging from his long fingers. He doesn't say a word. Aldridge picks up the conversation again. The size of his new salary remains a secret but it's still party time, and he's plainly sending out at least one invitation.

'I want you on it, Wes,' he says, 'which is why I'm glad you're here. I've told them I need to expand on the staff side. I've got it in writing. Five extra jobs.'

'So what do I write about? MI5?'

'Fuck off, Wes. You know what I'm saying.'

'I do?'

'Yeah. Listen, mate. I'm looking at an open cheque book. They want it sharper, more focused, more investigative. They want more aggression. They think there's an appetite for it. They've identified new markets. It's the big push, their word, not mine.'

Another pause. Wesley grunts. The old game. Hard to please.

'So what do I write about?' he says again.

'Up to you, mate. It's a straight offer. Yes or no.'

'You haven't answered my question.'

'And I'm not going to because you know the bloody answer already. If I didn't think you were the best fucking weasel in the business, we wouldn't be having this conversation. So do me a favour. Yes or no.'

'When do you go? Start? Whatever?'

'In the New Year.'

'Do they know upstairs?'

'It's irrelevant. Just tell me. Yes or no. No, and you're on your own. New boss. New policy. New everything. Yes, and we'll do something amazing.'

'We just did. And you binned it.'

'You really think that?'

'Yeah.'

'Then bollocks to you.'

There's a long pause here. I see them glaring at each other. Then Aldridge again. 'OK, get your coat on and let's go and have a bevvie.' Final pause. 'And turn that fucking thing off.'

Wesley resigned from the paper the day after Aldridge himself announced his latest career move. A month later, early in 1988, he accepted a staff job on *Defence Week*. The magazine, then and now, is headquartered in Guildford, occupying two floors of a big new block between the High Street and the railway station. For nearly a year, Wesley commuted three or four times a week from his flat in Stoke Newington, waiting for the virus to make another move. When nothing happened, he moved south to Guildford, pleasantly surprised to be alive, putting down a deposit on the top half of a thirties semi on the Dorking Road. It was there, nearly four years later, that I first met him. By then, though, a great deal else had happened.

First, I began to get somewhere with my private enquiries about the background to the Alloway story. I say that, not because I made any obviously spectacular advance (I didn't), but because my superiors became extremely tetchy about my out-of-hours activities. In Whitehall, as any insider will tell you, you gauge your real progress by changes in the way that other people relate to you. With your immediate colleagues, it might be jealousy or (if your ship is sinking) a week or two of sympathetic amusement. With your superiors, it's simple attention. The moment they take any notice of you, it's time to ask yourself why.

It was January 1988. I'd now been with MI5 for two whole years. The call, once again, was from Stollmann and this time he didn't bother with the compliments.

'You've been seeing Lawrence Priddy.'

I remember looking at him, startled. I'd been at work barely five minutes. Stollmann had obviously been fretting a lot longer than that, his head down, his eyes on the pad on the desk.

'Yes,' I said.

'Why?'

'Because . . .' I shrugged. 'Is it any business of yours?'

'Quite probably.' He nodded. 'Yes.'

I looked at him for a moment or two. On these occasions, I find myself concentrating on the silliest detail. In this case, it was a particularly angry boil, half an inch above the collar of Stollmann's shirt. Poor diet, I thought. Or stress.

'He invited me out a couple of times,' I said at last, 'and I accepted.'

'Why?'

'Because that's what you do if you're in my position.' I shrugged again. 'Single girl, time to spare, glad of the odd change of scenery.'

'You fancy him?'

'*Fancy* him?'

'Yes.'

'No. Not remotely. Not at all.' I stared at Stollmann. 'Why?'

Stollmann said nothing, just carried on playing with his pen.

Irritated at sounding so defensive, I refused to pick up the conversation, preferring silence to any more of his questions. The silence went on and on. Finally, he looked up and sat back in his chair. The next bit was unbelievable.

'You slept with him,' he said simply, 'so either you fancied him, or you wanted something in exchange. I can't imagine it was money, so . . .' he shrugged, 'what was it?'

I stared at him. Gusts of anger came and went. Stollmann, as it happened, was right about Priddy. I had slept with him, though the experience wasn't something I ever planned to repeat. In my defence, I was extremely drunk, though not drunk enough to forget the ghastlier parts.

'How do you know?' I said. 'As a matter of interest?'

Stollmann's eyes were back on the pad. The pad, for once, was bare.

'Maybe he told us.'

'I doubt it.'

'Maybe he told somebody else.'

'Possibly.'

'Does it matter?'

'Yes, of course it does.'

I thought for a moment about the other explanation, unvoiced by either of us. MI5 were routinely wiring targets all over the country. Anyone could ask for a phone tap, or something we referred to as a 'device emplacement', and there was a whole section of the service that was devoted to nothing else. They had bugs that could activate telephones, turning domestic receivers into listening microphones. Priddy had a phone by the bed. I'd seen it there next morning. I shuddered to think what kind of cassette Stollmann might have been sent, had they looped Priddy's phone and listened in. The man had been extremely vocal, and the sound effects would have left little to Stollmann's imagination. No wonder he was looking pensive.

'Tell me,' he said, 'what did he want to know?'

'You mean out of bed? When we weren't being taped?' Stollmann didn't answer, just nodded. 'Nothing. I told you. It was purely social.'

'So what did *you* want to know?'

'I . . .' I hesitated, only too aware that the interview wasn't about Priddy's sex life at all, or mine, but something far closer to home. Lately, before Christmas, the top floor had been running checks on computer usage. I knew that because a colleague in the office had told me so. He'd been interested in county court judgements against his landlord, and they'd caught him poking around in DHSS files. Doubtless the checks extended to my computer terminal, too. Which explained a great deal about Stollmann's interest in Priddy.

'He gave me access codes,' I said simply, 'DTI codes.'

'Why?'

'Because I asked for them.'

'Why?'

'Because . . .' I shrugged, 'I needed a little information.'

'For Alloway?'

'About Alloway. I'm a curious girl. I want to know things, find out things. I thought it was part of my job.'

Stollmann nodded, his eyes still on the pad. Then he looked up. 'And Priddy? What did he want in return?'

'Me.'

'What else?'

'Some stuff about Customs.'

'What stuff?'

'Whether or not they're investigating certain firms. About export orders. To Iraq.'

'And did you get it for him?'

'No.'

'Why not?'

'Because I couldn't get into their system.'

'Did you try?'

'Of course I did.' I looked at him. 'As you probably know.'

Stollmann nodded and permitted himself a small, private smile, and I wondered again about the circumstances surrounding his transfer to MI5. He'd worked for Customs. He'd come to us. Had he preserved the old friendships? Were the channels in good working order? Could he still lift the phone and plug straight in? Or had he folded his tent and stolen away, leaving nothing behind but enemies?

Stollmann got up and went to the window. In all our exchanges, something had been bothering me, something I'd never quite managed to define, but suddenly I knew what it was. Despite the frustrations of talking to the man – his brusqueness, the way he rationed out information in tiny little parcels, his sheer lack of response – I sensed he liked me. The evidence for this was, I admit, pretty sparse but it was definitely there. He was gauche, and wary, and anti-social to the point of near silence, but he did care. I knew it.

'About Priddy,' I began. 'The least you owe me is a clue or two.'

'About what?'

'About how you found out.'

I waited for an answer. He was still at the window, his hands in his pockets, staring out. The seat of his trousers was very shiny. At last he shrugged, part of some private dialogue, and turned back into the room. His face, like his desk, was quite empty.

'Sorry,' he mumbled, 'but it wouldn't be helpful.'

The conversation, in any important sense, ended there. It left me more frustrated than ever, my usual ignorance compounded by the unanswered questions about my private life. MI5 was entitled to a great deal of my time and loyalty, but I drew the line at the bedroom door. Whatever I chose to do with Lawrence Priddy, or anyone else for that matter, was no concern of theirs.

I thought about the conversation for a couple of days. Then I decided – at last – that playing the system was a waste of time. Stollmann, unchallenged, wouldn't tell me anything. What the situation needed was a dollop or two of direct action. Time, in my father's favourite phrase, to seize the initiative.

Stollmann, I knew, left the office two or three times a week, always at half past twelve, always on foot, always carrying a plastic shopping bag. Quite where he went I hadn't a clue, but my marks on the surveillance course had been way above average, and I saw every point in putting a little of that talent to practical use.

The first lunchtime I staked out the Curzon Street entrance, he failed to appear. Next day, prompt at twelve-thirty, he pushed through the big plate-glass doors and walked briskly south, towards Green Park. I followed on the other side of the street, fifty yards behind, nicely buffered by half a dozen lunchtime strollers. The park itself was trickier, Stollmann picking up speed, a stiff black figure in the big green spaces, his head down, the beige Sainsbury's carrier bag swinging at his side. I let the gap between us widen, knowing I couldn't possibly lose him here, only quickening my step when he got to the Mall, pausing for a second or two before darting into a gap in the traffic. I followed, cheating death at the hands of passing cabbies, and spotted Stollmann heading for the bridge across the lake in St James's Park. By now I was beginning to wonder exactly where he was headed. Beyond St James was Westminster and Whitehall. Both were plausible destinations for middle-ranking MI5 officers using their spare time for personal advantage, though in Stollmann's case I somehow doubted it. Everything about the man told me that he was a genuine outsider: no chums, no alliances, no time for the barbed pleasantries that pass, in Curzon House, for conversation.

We were in Victoria Street now, London at its busiest, an endless queue of buses and delivery vans, the air blue with exhaust fumes. Stollmann crossed the road. I was close behind him, invisible in a scrum of shoppers, watching him plunge into the maze of tiny streets behind Westminster Abbey where the wealthier politicians pitch their tents. For the first time, it occurred to me that I could have been wrong about Stollmann's isolation. Maybe, after all, he had friends in high places, a top politician, someone hungry for the kind of information we're paid to file away. Maybe he'd been brokering some deal on the side. Maybe that's why he was so obsessed by Lawrence Priddy. I paused for a moment, wondering which address he'd knock at and whether or not I'd recognize the face at the door. Instead, at the end of Great Smith Street, Stollmann hurried across the road and disappeared into a large, civic-looking building. I hesitated a moment, fifty yards behind, one foot off the pavement. Over the entrance, it said 'Public Baths'.

I gave him a minute or two to buy his ticket, then went into the reception area. Most public baths have a supply of spare bathing costumes, left by accident, and the Westminster Baths were no exception. For £1.30, I got a swimming ticket and a low-cut little number in electric blue.

The changing rooms were busy, mostly secretaries. I wriggled into the one-piece and examined myself at the full-length mirror by the showers. The costume was at least a size too small and left absolutely nothing to the imagination, and I knew already that Stollmann, despite his efforts to play the monk, wasn't blind. Once or twice I'd caught him looking at me in a way that had absolutely nothing to do with my professional skills. Within the security of his office, on home turf, that had meant very little, but meeting semi-naked in a public swimming pool was a very different proposition, and I sensed that if I wanted something even half-candid from him, then now was the time to try. That, at least, was the theory.

The pool, like the changing rooms, was busy. I spotted Stollmann at once in the poolside lane, his head bobbing up and down as he fought to keep up with the rest of the action. He had an awkward breaststroke, more effort than grace, the long thin arms hauling the water past his body, his legs not quite co-ordinated with the rest of him. His hair was flattened against his skull and he had an odd expression on his face, a grimace, almost a snarl, pure determination. I watched him for a minute or two, wondering how long he kept it up, how many lengths he set himself, not quite sure how to play it. People who swim like Stollmann have a daily target and hate interruptions. Maybe, after all, this wasn't such a good idea.

In the end, still undecided, I plunged in, joining the swimmers in the lane next to Stollmann. I had a seaside childhood – Devon again – and I've been at home in the water for most of my life, and I caught up with him on my second length, slowing as I surged past. His body was a foot or two from mine, strangely vertical in the water, his arms chopping back, his breath coming in hard gasps, the big veins in his neck standing out with the effort he was making. We swam side by side for perhaps ten yards. Then he glanced sideways, frowning, and his eyes met mine. Unlike most of the other swimmers, neither of us were wearing goggles or bathing caps and I knew at once that he'd recognized me. For a second or two, his rhythm broke. Then we were at the end of the lane, the shallow end, my feet finding the bottom, my arms draping over the rope that divided us. Stollmann stopped. He had no option.

'Surprise, surprise,' he muttered.

'Yes.' I grinned, standing up now, brushing the hair out of my eyes, the water barely waist-deep.

Stollmann said nothing. He was squatting on his haunches, trying to make room for the queue of swimmers coming up for the turn. I levered myself on to the edge of the pool, out of the way, and gestured for him to do the same. He looked up at me, plainly reluctant, and when I extended a hand, helping him out, I understood why. His back and shoulders were purpled with the burned-out remains of a savage attack of acne. Adolescence, for Eric Stollmann, must have been a misery.

He sat beside me, his feet in the water, hopelessly vulnerable. His body was thin, what my mother would call 'skinny'.

'Nice style,' he said.

'Who?'

'You.' He glanced sideways at me. 'You go swimming a lot?'

I looked at him a moment, knowing that I'd been right, knowing that for a few precious seconds I'd stolen the advantage.

'I'm surprised you have to ask,' I said lightly, 'I'm surprised you don't know already. All those sources of yours.'

Stollmann stared at the water, then permitted himself a small, shamefaced smile.

'Don't get the wrong idea,' he said at last. 'It's not as bad as it looks.'

'What's that supposed to mean?' I moved a little closer, aware of other swimmers looking our way. 'You mind telling me?'

Stollmann shook his head. 'Nothing to tell,' he said.

'I don't believe you.'

'I'm sure you don't.'

'Then why don't you trust me? Explain a bit more about Priddy? Why the interest? Why the tape? God knows, I might even be able to help instead of sitting on my backside all day. Or is that being naïve?'

Stollmann studied me briefly and then looked away again, down the pool, towards the deep end. I have perfect recall of the next ten seconds because they've shaped my life ever since and changed it in ways too numerous to list. My dealings with Wesley, some way down the line, are one consequence. This book, oddly enough, is another. Stollmann was sitting on his hands now, the way kids do when they get cold.

'We're sending you to Northern Ireland,' he said. 'It's got nothing to do with Priddy, but it's the closest you'll get to active duty.'

6

I spent two years in and out of Northern Ireland. It's not a part of my life that I can write about in any real detail, nor do I want to, but it was certainly a world away from the numbing routines of PO Box 500.

Most of the time I was based in Belfast. In its own way, the place was as dense a puzzle as Curzon House, riddled with ambiguities and contradictions, but the people I worked with, mostly men, often army, couldn't have been more different. The way you got on with it mattered there. With each other, you had to be straight. You had to be honest. And quite often you had to be very brave. The older hands, battle-tested, had a phrase for it. 'Three parts tradecraft,' they'd say, 'to one part Jamieson's.' I never bothered with the whiskey, but the other bit they'd got about right. Unless you did your homework, unless you took a great deal of care about the small print, you'd quite possibly end up dead. In this respect, it's wise not to rely too heavily on the media. Ireland was a dangerous place. A number of my ex-colleagues are buried there, way out of sight, not a single column inch to tell the tale.

Before I flew to Belfast, I attended a two-week course at an MOD facility in Hereford. For the first three days I commuted from a small boarding house near by and sat through a series of lectures on self-defence. The lectures included the use of small arms and afterwards we practised with various weapons, sometimes on a range with targets, sometimes in a specially built complex ringed with razor wire. The building included a number of rooms we were required to 'sanitize'. The latter meant kicking open the door and responding to whatever you found on the other side. The guys who ran the place would have made a fortune in Disneyland. They had a real talent for mixing high explosive with a certain black humour. The ear defenders we had to wear were wired to a Walkman. The Walkman had been programmed to play rock music at critical moments in the exercise. The theory had something to do with disorientation, but to this day I can't listen to the Pogues without seeing the room plunged into darkness and smelling the hot sweet chemical smell of freshly expended cordite.

After the ranges and the killing rooms, we took to the hills. So far, life outdoors had never offered me anything but immense pleasure. I'd always been physically fit and in London I'd been running three or four times a week, sometimes more, but here the routines were brutal – deliberately so – and until you worked out exactly what they were trying to do, it was extremely hard to take.

As a climax to the course, they sent you out on your own for two long days, completing a huge fifty-mile circuit of the Brecon Beacons, and you carried everything you needed to survive except water. That was hidden in special caches every ten miles or so and if you didn't find it you went thirsty. That put a premium on keeping your wits, which was doubtless the point of the exercise, but the instructors spiced our days with a series of sick jokes designed to make you lose faith – first in them and latterly in yourself.

A favourite happened at the end of the course. A Land Rover would be sent to pick you up. It would be waiting for you at the last R/V (rendezvous), normally the end of a long, straight track. Exhausted, but aware of the watching NCOs, you'd put everything into that last quarter of a mile, only to watch the Land Rover drive slowly away, leaving you totally spent, close to tears, sick at heart. That, of course, was the intention, and once you'd recognized them for the bastards they really were, then it became infinitely simpler and more personal. One of you would prevail. And, you told yourself, it wouldn't be them.

After Hereford, I had a week's leave. I went home, to Devon. I was fitter than I'd ever been in my life, an astonishing combination of appetite, self-confidence and sheer physical zest that my father must have recognized at first glance. He sat me down in front of the fire and fussed around me in a way that he'd never done before. At first, I put all this down to senility, or the cloudy, farm-bottled cider that he used to drink. Only later did it occur to me that it was simple pride. His girl. Young Sarah. Out in the mountains with a Bergen on her back for a taste of the real thing.

We went to the pub one night, just the two of us. I demolished a huge plate of pasty and chips while my father sat in the snug beside me, one leg crossed over the other, plugging and replugging his pipe. We talked about life in London and about his recent return to a Brigade HQ desk in Plymouth. He told me how glad he'd been, and how lucky, to have made it to the Falklands in 1982. Wars, real wars, were getting hard to come by, especially if you were as strapped for cash as the Brits appeared to be. I humoured him and called him an old war horse, Budleigh's answer to Genghis Khan, and he smiled and patted me on the knee, and quietly recommended the rhubarb crumble, a shyer, nicer, gentler man than I'd ever, somehow, been led to expect.

Towards the end of the evening, in passing, he mentioned Rory. 'Seen anything of him?'

'A bit. A while ago. To begin with.' I paused. 'Why?'

'Just wondered. He was asking after you. Last week, as a matter of fact.'

'Oh?'

I glanced up. It must have been something in my voice that made him look at me rather harder than usual. He nodded.

'He was back for the weekend. Collecting some bits and pieces.'

'Back?'

'Yes. He and Ruth have rented a flat in London. I thought you knew.'

I shook my head, remembering the riverside pub at Putney and the lone sculler in the half-darkness and the lurch inside me when Rory told me he thought he was in love. I'd done the right thing. I knew I had. I'd told him to think about his wife, his family. Since then, though, I hadn't heard a word. Until now. I was still gazing at my father.

'What about the kids?' I said carefully. 'What's happened to them?'

'Emma's started at Norton Grange. Giles went to Fernside. Been there two years now.'

'Both away then?'

'Yes.' My father nodded. 'That's why Ruth's up in town.' He smiled. 'Keeping the boy on the straight and narrow.'

'Good for her,' I said automatically, wondering where they lived, what the place looked like inside and whether or not – after all – it was what Rory really wanted. Ruth, to be honest, I'd never been really sure about. I knew her socially, a thin, slightly gaunt woman with a long, fine-boned face and an interest in bereavement counselling. They'd been married for more than eight years, but for someone with Rory's appetites, she'd always struck me as a bit of a surprise: too serious, too intense, too introvert. My father was still looking at me. Behind the bar, the landlord's wife was hosing my crumble with whipped cream.

'He told me you'd saved him from the funny farm,' my father said, 'those first few months in town. He said he was going barmy until you turned up.'

'Really?'

'Yes. Apparently you cheered him up no end. Turned the lights back on was the phrase he used.' He smiled again. 'That sound like the Rory you know?'

I nodded, watching the steaming plate of crumble, glad of the interruption. 'Yes,' I said, reaching for my spoon, 'it does.'

In Belfast, after a brief spell in barracks, I moved into a rented flat off the Ormeau Road. No one ever bothered me with anything as formal as a job description and after a couple of months I realized why. At some exalted level, my bosses had decided to push for something called 'primacy' in UK mainland dealings with the Provisional IRA. Primacy meant MI5 taking a lead in the war against the terrorists. If the plan worked, then the police would be the losers, and my bosses – never ones to underestimate a challenge – had accordingly dug themselves in for a long struggle.

To make a credible case in Whitehall, they had to argue from a position of strength. They had to know a great deal about the Provos. They had to fatten their intelligence files, improve their strike rate and demonstrate to the Home Office that their knowledge of the enemy was second to none. That meant extra assets on the ground, agents who would bed down in Belfast, touching base occasionally with the RUC, with Army Intelligence and with MI6. Most of all, it meant building a stable of informants, men and women from deep within the Republican command structures, people whom, for one reason or another, you'd turn and nourish and put to good account. The latter job, amongst one or two others, was mine.

The logic wasn't difficult to follow. I had youth on my side. I had the right academic background. And some judicious arm-twisting gave me credible cover as a research student at Queen's University. The fact that I was single entitled me to a half-decent social life, and from my bosses' point of view I thus acquired the most precious asset of all: I could plausibly mix in most company.

It was a strange life, me and my other self, and if I felt anything at all it was a kind of lingering guilt at enjoying it so much. Raw intelligence is a commodity unlike any other. It doesn't respond to fixed hours and a five-day week. You can't manufacture it on an assembly line, behind a set of factory gates. On the contrary, the best bits are often wholly unpredictable, big juicy windfalls that drop off the tree without the faintest stir of breeze, a phone call or a meeting or a note through the door that seems, at the time, pure chance. In reality, of course, that's not the case at all. Nothing happens without months of careful preparation, of friendships carefully nurtured, of pressures oh-so-subtly applied, of dance steps so intricate and so deft that it's hard, often, to even be aware of the music. But the music is there, and as time goes by it becomes slowly but unmistakably addictive.

'Off-duty' isn't a meaningful word in this context because it never happens, but there were times when the sheer beauty of the place very nearly got the better of me. I used to go to the Republic a lot, trips south over the border. Most of these excursions took me no further than Dundalk or Donegal, places of considerable interest to people like us, but occasionally I could justify going way down, past Dublin, across the Midlands, to the wild, empty coasts of Kerry and Galway. These were landscapes I'd never seen in my life, the mountains shouldering down to the sea, the weather ever-changing, the fine soft drizzle drifting in from the Atlantic, the abrupt squalls of wind, the heaving ocean puddled a sudden, brilliant blue. I loved it, the taste of it, the smell of the peat fires, the curls of smoke around the tiny cottages, the dogs chained to the milk urns, the way the hill farmers worked their stony fields, their jackets buttoned tight against the wind, one finger raised, a passing salute. Sometimes alone, sometimes not, I marvelled at it all, brief interludes, simple pleasures, buried in an otherwise complicated life.

Throughout my time in Belfast, I kept one eye on the newspapers, thinking more often than not about Beth Alloway. The Iran–Iraq War had finally come to an end and there was a flurry of press speculation about arms and related sales in its aftermath. As far as I knew, the embargo still applied, but the reports about sanctions-busting UK firms never made the front page, and if I thought anything at all, it was strictly in connection with Beth.

Once, and once only, I tried to talk to her on the phone. She answered almost at once, a flat, worn voice, a child crying in the background, and after a brief series of awkward pleasantries, I knew that the conversation was going nowhere. She wasn't pleased to hear from me. Her husband was 'away'. Life, to no one's surprise, was going on much as before. After a minute or so, I apologized for interrupting her from whatever she'd been doing, knowing that the gap between our separate worlds was probably unbridgeable. Sympathy, alas, wasn't enough. All Beth Alloway wanted was her privacy. That, and some vestige of the life that we, and the Iraqis, had taken away from her.

My life in Northern Ireland came to an abrupt halt one December night in 1989. A complicated set of events had taken me west, across the province, to a modern hotel on the banks of the River Foyle a couple of miles downstream from Londonderry. There I was to meet a young Catholic businessman called Padraig MacElwaine. He ran a local chain of builder's merchants. Like everyone else in the construction business, he paid a sizeable monthly sum to the local IRA godfathers, but his eldest son had recently been beaten up in a carefully laid ambush in the city centre, and gruff Provo regrets about mistaken identity had done nothing to temper his rage. Evidently, the man was incandescent. He had debts to settle. He had names to impart, information to pass on and – most important of all – he said he was in a position to make an informed guess or two about what we in Five always referred to as 'forthcoming attractions'.

This kind of intelligence was exactly the collateral that my bosses needed to make their case in Whitehall. I was therefore ordered to Londonderry post-haste for a rendezvous at the riverside hotel. I was to pose as a visiting businesswoman from the UK, order a drink in the bar and await developments. The hotel was way off the local Provo circuit – too classy, too expensive – and I was assured that the usual cover arrangements, unspecified, would be in place.

I drove to Londonderry. By the time I found the hotel, it had been dark for nearly three hours. I parked outside reception in a well-lit bay and left a spare key on top of the front wheel. The meet in the bar went according to plan. Padraig turned out to be a beefy, thick-set man with tight curly black hair and a shirt collar one size too small for his neck. He was attentive and courteous and made a beautiful job of picking me up.

After the meal, we were to adjourn to Padraig's room. There he'd give me chapter and verse: names, addresses, dates, forthcoming attractions, the kind of priceless operational data that I'd haul back to Belfast for onward transmission to London. That's what the plan said. That's what I expected. Instead, Padraig leaned forward over the table, slightly comical, the corner of his mouth blobbed with cream from the second helping of cheesecake.

'I haven't got a room,' he said.

'Why not?'

'They're full.'

I laughed, offering him a napkin. He wiped his mouth with it, reddening with embarrassment. I was still laughing.

'Good job you're not for real,' I said. 'What kind of pick-up would this be?'

He shrugged, scarlet now. We'd already established he had a wife and four kids. He clearly adored them all. I looked at my watch. It was nine-fifteen.

'Would you have a car?' he said. 'Only the wife dropped me off.'

'A car?' I gazed at him in mock alarm. 'What did you have in mind?'

'I . . . we. . . .' He shrugged again, tapping his wallet, the closest reference he'd yet made to the evening's real business. 'I can give it you all. I've written it out.'

'Why not give it to me now?'

He hesitated a moment, frowning. Then he tossed the napkin

to one side and began to get up. 'There are things we ought to talk about. It's not a lot of your time I'm after. You'll be away in ten minutes. Unless . . .'

'What?'

'You've got a room of your own.'

I shook my head. 'No,' I said, 'I've booked somewhere else.'

I paid the bill and we left the restaurant. Outside, in the car park, it was still raining. I stepped out of the shelter of the hotel porch, Padraig at my elbow, his coat already on. He'd get a taxi afterwards, he was saying. I paused by the hired Escort, bending quickly to the front wheel, looking for the spare key. The key, for some reason, wasn't there. I glanced up, feeling foolish, the rain dripping off the end of my nose. The last thing I expected to see was the gun in Padraig's left hand. It wasn't small, a Browning Parabellum, eight-shot magazine, accurate to thirty yards. I'd used one at Hereford. At point-blank range, like now, they could leave an exit hole the size of a ten-pence piece. Padraig was already walking me round the car.

'Get in,' he said.

'What?'

'Get in.'

The passenger door swung open. There was someone else in the back. I could see the shape of a head, silhouetted against the lights of the hotel. I hesitated, knowing that now was the moment to run, to make a move, knowing that in a second or two it would be infinitely more complicated, but Padraig was already pushing me into the car, forcing the door shut behind me. A gloved hand had appeared from the back, clamping hard across my face.

'You feel this?'

I nodded.

'You know what it is?'

I nodded again, recognizing the pressure at the base of my skull, something cold and metallic, another gun. The hand unclamped its grip, but the pressure of the gun never wavered. Watching Padraig circling the front of the car, I could feel the man's warm breath on my ear. I could smell him, too, a sour mix of spearmint and wet clothing. Padraig got in, not looking at me, adjusting the mirror, closing the door.

We drove out of the car park and on to the main road. We

turned north, skirting Lough Foyle, headlights coming at us out of the rain.

'You'll have a short,' Padraig said to me after a while.

I didn't answer. 'Short' is Provo slang for a handgun. We were going faster now, the car rocking from time to time in the buffeting sidewind from the lough, and I wondered whether it was sensible to risk a bullet in the head by waiting for a corner, grabbing the wheel and trying to force the car off the road. Unlike Padraig, though, I wasn't wearing a seat belt. If anyone was going through the windscreen, it would probably be me.

'You'll have a gun?' Padraig asked again.

I looked at him.

'Nice meal,' I said drily.

I saw his eyes flick up to the mirror, the merest tilt of the head, then the hand was back, plunging inside my coat, searching left and right, finding the little Beretta at once, clipped neatly inside the shoulder holster they'd given me at Hereford. Best on the market, the instructor had told me. Unlike its new owner.

We drove on in silence. I heard the scrape of a match behind me and the car was suddenly filled with the bitter tang of cheap tobacco. For the first time it occurred to me that there might be more than one person in the back. I looked at Padraig again. He was concentrating hard, peering ahead through the rain, then up at the mirror.

'Nice odds, too,' I said, 'three against one.'

Padraig appeared not to hear me. The car was slowing now, his eyes fixed on the mirror. Something was wrong. I knew it. It was there in his face. I began to turn round, wanting to look behind, but the moment I moved the gun at my head cracked sharply against my temple and I reacted against the blow, pulling away, the other side of my head hitting the door pillar, my hands coming up, involuntarily, the blood warm to the touch.

We were going faster now, Padraig dropping through the gearbox, oblivious to the rain, and I felt the rear wheels beginning to slide as he lurched sharply into the next bend, fighting for control. We stayed upright, just, the road straight again, the Cat's-eyes receding into the darkness, the speedo nudging eighty. I didn't need to turn around any more. Whoever Padraig had seen, whatever had made him so nervous, was close now, only yards behind, the headlights on full beam, the interior of the car bathed in a hard, white glare.

I reached up for the seat belt and pulled it across my body, braced for another blow, but nothing happened. I glanced across at Padraig. He was driving in a strange hunched position, trying to avoid the blinding dazzle from the mirror, peering ahead. My right hand felt for the anchor point, and I heard the buckle engage as I pushed it home. The car lurched again and I heard a woman's voice behind us, a muttered oath. I looked round. There were two figures behind, both crouched against the back seat, their bodies half turned. The bigger of the two, the man, was trying to steady the gun against the parcel shelf. The car behind was only yards away. Beyond the headlights, there was nothing but darkness.

I looked at Padraig again. His lips were moving, but there was no sound, nothing recognizable, just the high-pitched whine of the engine. Another bend was coming up. I could see it in the distance, a tight left-hander, a low bank and a frieze of trees beyond. The bend raced towards us, an image from a film, someone else's life, someone else's nightmare, and I knew with absolute certainty that we'd never get round. So, I think, did Padraig because the last coherent thing I remember is his hand reaching down, hunting for a lower gear, and the woman screaming, a wild animal yell, and the gun going off in the back, a huge hollow sound that seemed to last for ever.

Briefly semi-conscious, I registered a face above mine. It was a face I thought I knew. I tried to smile but nothing happened. Then I heard a siren and the sound of people shouting and the face wasn't there any more, curtained by the darkness and the rain.

7

Quite a lot of the next three months or so is indistinct, a blancmange of hospitals, nurses, pain, tests, operations, more operations, more pain and brief bedside interludes with a series of gloomy consultants.

My parents flew over to see me that first week, at the Gransha Hospital in Londonderry, but I remember very little of the detail except the expression on my father's face, bending over the bed, trying to feed me chicken soup. It must have been Christmas, because there was holly on the wall and balloons on the ceiling, but what drew my eye was the tears running down his face. I remember watching them, quite dispassionate, almost used to the pain by now, thinking that there must be something wrong with him, something that the ward sister could put right with a couple of tablets or a glass or two of Lucozade. The fact that he might have been crying about me, the sight of me, the state of his precious daughter, never crossed my mind. At this point, I should add, the nurses had been wise enough to spare me the benefit of a mirror. Which, under the circumstances, was probably just as well.

From Londonderry, after Christmas, I was helicopted to Aldergrove Airport and transferred on to an RAF plane to London. I was stretchered all the way and ended up in a private ward at the Churchill Hospital, near Marble Arch. Curzon House, ever sympathetic, sent a modest bunch of flowers to welcome me home. Unfortunately, a mix-up over the delivery date meant that they didn't turn up until Stollmann had appeared for the debrief. That way, the flowers seemed to me to be a sardonic reward for what little I was able to tell him. Padraig, the builder, had seemed on the level. The meal we'd shared at the hotel had been delicious.

Events in the car park had been a big surprise. The rest, beyond doubt, he already knew.

Stollmann had noted it all down without comment, sparing me the tonic of small talk. When the nurses arrived to wash the bits of me that still showed, he retrieved his coat from the back of the door and beat an embarrassed retreat. I watched him as he left. He stood outside in the corridor for a minute or two, a stooping, cadaverous figure, studying his notes, shaking his head. Hopes for Padraig had evidently been high, but the yield, as we agents say, was minimal. Three more headstones in the Republican plot at St Joseph's Cemetery. And a largish hospital bill for little me.

By now, I was word perfect on my tally of injuries. The Escort, according to the report Stollmann had received from our friends in the car behind, had left the road at about seventy miles an hour. It had gone sideways up the bank and turned completely over before hitting the trees. Padraig's side got the worst of the impact. Both he and the girl in the back were killed outright. The man behind me, not belted in, had been thrown clear. He never recovered consciousness and died three days later.

My own injuries, by comparison, were minor. Both my legs were broken, one of them in three places. My right arm was fractured between my elbow and my shoulder and a number of ribs were also cracked. I'd sustained a collapsed lung, and there was concern for a while about the likelihood of serious disfigurement. Apparently, the casualty staff at Gransha Hospital had spent most of the night picking glass out of my face, and a deep laceration around my right ear had given the plastic surgeon plenty to work on. The wound had effectively meant re-attaching my ear to the side of my head. The join had taken a total of forty-nine tiny stitches, a long crescent-shaped track around the back of my ear, but the tail of the wound curved down beneath the earlobe and out on to the cheek itself, and there was nothing that plastic surgery could do to disguise the scar. At first, numbed by analgesics and quite unable to distinguish between one source of pain and another, it didn't concern me. But as my body began to mend and I re-entered the world of mirrors, I became more and more aware of the way that my face had changed.

I've never been especially conscious of my face. It's wide and friendly, with tawny skin and big dimples. I've always smiled a lot and enough men have told me I have a nice mouth for me to believe it might be true. Either way, it had always been a face I'd been happy with, in that carefree, mostly unconscious way you simply take things for granted and get on with it. It was a trouble-free face, a face you didn't have to worry about. Until that night in Londonderry.

After Londonderry, after the crash and the operations and the moves from ward to ward, it became a different face. It became a face that I fretted about, the focus for all that delayed shock, all those nightmares that the pain and the trauma had postponed. To begin with, it was a mechanical thing. The fact was, they'd sewn my ear back on. Consequently, whenever I lifted my head from the pillow, glanced around, nodded or made any other sudden movement I worried that the ear might fall off again. What if the flesh hadn't healed properly? What if the skin was too thin to take a proper stitch (it seemed very thin on the other side)? What if the stitches themselves had been botched?

These questions dogged me for weeks, making me nervous of the slightest head movement. After a while, one of the nurses got quite concerned, ignoring all my excuses about a stiff neck, rightly diagnosing a near obsession with my still swollen ear. A day or so later, she had a quiet word with the resident plastic consultant, who arrived one afternoon with a couple of textbooks and a pad. Sympathetic, if slightly formal, he drew lots of helpful diagrams, showing me exactly what the guy at Gransha had done and told me that he'd personally give the repair a score of nine and a half on a scale of ten. His tone of voice suggested that I was lucky to have ended up in such skilled hands on a wet night in London-derry, and when he'd gone I did my best to accept what he'd said. The ear wouldn't come off. The mend was a fine piece of work. In fact I was bloody lucky to have two ears at all.

To some degree this worked, but as time went on I became convinced that my face was lopsided. In the mirror, OK, it didn't look too bad. I was pale, certainly, but face-on the scar was barely visible, and even with my head half-turned, the reality wasn't quite as awful as I'd imagined. Once my hair had grown back and I'd got a bit of colour in my face, it would just be an oddity, a piece of bad luck that I'd simply have to live with. Yet the evidence of my eyes wasn't enough. Inside my head, where it mattered most, the wound had become grotesque, a hard, livid ridge of raised tissue, a wholly new feature in that familiar stretch of landscape I called my face. It made me not me. It made me different. Above all, it made me uncertain. I'd never been uncertain in my life. I'd never had a problem with men. I could pick and choose as I liked. But now I wasn't so sure. Who'd want to have anything to do with me now? And what would happen when they'd got over the shock of seeing the scar on my cheek and we'd become friends and they were running their fingers through my hair and they found the rest of it? All forty-nine stitches?

In the hospital, they gave me some liniment called Aqueous Cream. It came in a big white tub and it was cool and rich. I was supposed to work it into the scar twice daily, softening the tissue, but I quickly became obsessed with it, applying it hourly, the fingers of my right hand rubbing and rubbing, as if, somehow, I might erase the bloody thing entirely. The end result of all this was a litter of repeat prescriptions and another session with the consultant. He asked to see my right hand and examined the index and middle fingers. The tips were soft and wrinkly. He looked up at me.

'It won't work,' he said. 'Not the way you want it to.'

'How do you know?'

'It just won't. Believe me.'

I withdrew my hand, embarrassed and angry, knowing he was right, not wanting to accept it.

'OK,' I mumbled, 'so what else do you suggest?'

Convalescing, back in Devon in early March, I told my mother about the exchange and about my obsession with my wrecked face, the first time I'd discussed it with anyone. She understood exactly what I meant at once, brushing back the newly grown hair from my temples, running her fingers over the scar, reassurance, benediction.

'Do you really?' I said. 'Do you really understand?'

'Yes. Of course.'

'How? Why?'

She smiled. 'It happened to me once,' she said.

'Did it?'

I blinked. My mother's face was flawless. Fifty-three years had left barely a wrinkle. She nodded, still smiling.

'I got stung by a bee. On the upper lip. Here.' She touched the corner of her mouth. 'Your father was abroad, thank God.'

'Why?'

'It blew up like a football. I felt like Quasimodo, you know, all *wrong*.'

'Yes . . . all wrong.' I frowned, my right hand straying involuntarily upwards, probing for the ridge of scar tissue. 'That's it exactly, all wrong.' I looked at her. 'So what happened?'

'It went down again.'

'And?'

'I still felt all wrong. For months. Then . . .' she shrugged, 'your father came back, and it was suddenly all right again.'

'And did you tell him?'

'Good Lord, no, of course not.'

I nodded, smiling, trying to apply the lessons of this parable to my own life. My mother, as ever, got there first.

'You need a little entertainment,' she said. 'Someone to take you out of yourself. I'll see what I can do.'

Rory called the following weekend, phoning first, ever the gentleman. He was down for a bash at CTC, the Commando Centre at Lympstone. Ruth was with her mother in Cheltenham. The kids were at school. How did I feel about a couple of miles along the beach at Exmouth and a pint or two afterwards? I smiled down the phone. It sounded fine to me. With my ear on his blind side, it might even be mildly therapeutic.

Rory appeared an hour later. By now, I hadn't seen him for nearly four years, an interval that had done nothing to sort out exactly how I really felt about him. Were we still friends? Could we pick up where we left off? Or had that single indiscretion, that one brief flirtation with the truth, moved the relationship on to a different track? Standing in the front room, watching him push through the gate and saunter up the garden path, I hoped not. He was wearing his usual civvies – cotton shirt, jeans, thin leather jacket, impossibly Spartan gear for such a chill March day – but his head was up, his hair was blowing in the wind and he was whistling some tune or other, way off-key, the same old Rory. I went to the door. I was off the crutches now and out of plaster, but I still had to walk with the help of sticks. Rory stood in the sunshine, looking at them, grinning.

'I've left the Kawasaki at home,' he said. 'Probably just as well.'

We took the bus to Exmouth, five miles to the west, where I'd worked in the nursing home. The town has a lovely beach, and a slightly fifties feel. Out of season, it's quiet and restful, and we walked along the promenade, beside the rows of wooden beach huts. The tide was on the ebb, the water pouring out of the estuary, the tidal stream dotted with windsurfers, stitching back and forth to the sandbank offshore. Rory watched them as we walked, his arm through mine, a steady pressure, what my mother calls 'the Marine two-step', sympathy with menaces.

Beyond the big green buoy that marks the edge of the shipping lane, Rory jumped down on to the sand and I followed, waving away his proffered hand. The beach slopes away towards the water and I tottered down without a thought, no pain, no anxiety, listening to his running commentary on this performance or that. Rory himself was an excellent windsurfer and in this – as in most other things – he took no prisoners. One particular guy got the full treatment. The man was out of his depth. If he was very lucky, he might survive. If he was even luckier, his girlfriend might take his board away and give him something more appropriate. Like a wheelchair. He stopped in mid-sentence, aghast, and looked at me.

'Shit,' he said. 'I'm sorry.'

'No need.'

'No, really. It can't have been much fun.'

'It wasn't.' I glanced up at him. Just being with the man made me want to smile. 'It's OK now though.'

Rory frowned, his hands deep in the pockets of his jeans. He looked genuinely astonished.

'You've got over it?' he said. '*Already?*'

I shook my head. 'No,' I said, 'that's not what I meant.'

'It's not?'

'No.'

'Oh . . .'

He hesitated a moment, half wanting me to go on, but I knew I was trespassing again, the stretch of wild country that lay the other side of the last evening we'd spent together, and I shook my head.

'About that pint,' I said brightly. 'I'm freezing.'

By nightfall, I was back home in Budleigh Salterton. Rory stayed for supper, and afterwards he and my father pulled up their chairs around the fire and compared notes about various Corps issues. This was another Rory, one I'd never really met before, infinitely more serious and grown-up, a man who weighed his words with great care, treating my father with exactly the right blend of informality and respect. Listening to them both, watching Rory's face in the firelight, his body bent forward, his elbows on his knees, the way he used his hands, I sensed what it was that made him such a good leader, why men followed him, what it was in his voice and manner that gave them the confidence to risk their lives. It was nearly ten before he left, running up the road in case he'd missed the last bus. I shut the door behind him. My mother was at the foot of the stairs.

'Well?' she said.

'Well what?' I looked at her, quite lost, still wondering about the bus.

'Did it make any difference?'

'Difference to what?'

'Your ...'

She touched the side of her head, behind her ear, and I gazed at her a moment longer, still none the wiser. Then it dawned on me. My scar. My wound. My poor lopsided face.

'Didn't give it a thought,' I said truthfully. 'Not once.'

I returned to London at the end of March. I felt, after Devon, immeasurably better. My legs still ached from time to time but I could walk without sticks and I began to put back some of the weight I'd lost. My other bones were well and truly mended and I'd finally found the courage to throw away the tablets that I'd more or less relied on for a decent night's sleep.

Drug-free, I also began to ask myself some of the more obvious questions about the cause of my injuries. If the cover arrangements at Londonderry had extended to the hotel car park, why on earth had I been allowed to walk into a trap? If they'd seen Padraig's friends get into my car, why hadn't they intervened? The answer, of course, was all too obvious. The hotel car park was only the start of the trail. The smart money was on holding off, on keeping a low profile, on seeing where the trail led. But if that was the case, why turn a simple piece of surveillance into a car chase? Why declare your hand? Why frighten them? Why drive them, quite literally, off the road? To this latter question I had no answer, and the more I thought about it, the stranger it became.

Back in my flat, I settled in. Jenny, a colleague from work, had been popping round since Christmas and the place was spotless. The shelves in my tiny larder were stocked with food and there was fresh milk in the fridge. There were flowers in a vase in the living room, and three months' worth of calls on my answering machine were neatly transcribed on a list by the phone. Most of them I'd already dealt with, friends who'd tried to get through to wish me well and had later phoned the hospital. But down towards the end of the list was a name I didn't know. It was someone called Karen. There was no second name. Just Karen. She'd phoned twice, first a couple of weeks back, 17 March, then again three days later. Each time the message had been the same. I peered at Jenny's careful script. 'Please get in touch as soon as you can,' it read, 'it's really urgent.' There was a phone number beside the message, a prefix I didn't immediately recognize. I lifted the phone and dialled the number. After a bit a woman answered, a flat Midlands accent, slightly nasal.

'Karen?'

'Yes.'

'It's Sarah. Sarah Moreton.'

'Who?'

'Sarah Moreton. You left a couple of messages. On my answerphone.'

'Oh . . .' the woman's voice went faint, then came back again: 'it's you.'

'Well?'

'It's about Mrs Alloway.'

'Who?'

'Beth. Beth Alloway. She's had a breakdown. She's in hospital. She . . . I can't talk on the phone like this. I've got her daughter here. Laura.' She paused. 'Are you still there?'

I took the train to Wolverhampton the following day. Karen

met me at the station. She was a large, brisk, impatient woman, middle aged, with a Japanese station wagon and two large dogs.

We drove west on the motorway towards Telford, while Karen told me what had happened. She lived in the same village as Beth. She helped in the local nursery school that Laura, Beth's daughter, attended and the two women saw quite a lot of each other. Lately, since Christmas, Beth had become very withdrawn, almost reclusive. She'd started behaving oddly, neglecting the house, not bothering to cook. Twice, to Karen's certain knowledge, she'd forgotten to give her daughter any breakfast, sending her off to nursery school on an empty stomach. Both times, Karen had saved the day. She'd tried to talk to her. She'd known something was wrong and she'd tried to find out what. But Beth had told her to mind her own business.

Then, two weeks ago, Laura hadn't appeared at nursery school at all. After a couple of hours, anxious, Karen had gone to the cottage. She'd found Laura in her mother's bedroom, huddled in an armchair, knees to her chin. Beth was still in bed, deeply asleep, a bottle of pills on the floor beside her. The bottle wasn't empty and to this day Karen doesn't know what had happened, but she'd phoned for the doctor and agreed to look after Laura while Beth was encouraged to spend a little time in hospital, under observation. We were driving to the hospital now. There I could draw my own conclusions. As far as Karen was concerned, the diagnosis was obvious. The woman was off her head. Simple as that.

I nodded, watching the damp, flat fields speed by.

'How did you find me?' I said. 'How did you get my name?'

'Beth told me.'

'What did she say?'

'She said you'd once told her to ring. If anything went wrong.'

'Did she say anything else?'

'No.'

Karen looked across at me, totally uninterested in who I was, or how, exactly, I was connected to Beth. Since we'd met at the railway station, I'd been wondering how much she knew about Beth's husband, Clive Alloway, what he did, where he travelled, who he mixed with, and now I realized that none of it mattered to her. Her only concerns were Beth herself and the child. The rest, very sensibly, was irrelevant.

The hospital was smaller than I'd expected, a psychiatric facility with limited accommodation for longer-stay patients. Beth occupied a corner bed in a flat-roofed annexe in the grounds. Squirrels were playing in the trees outside her window and she was watching them when we arrived. She recognized me at once and it was obvious I wasn't welcome. Karen stood over the bed, hands on her hips, while I made small talk for a minute or two. Finally, I looked up.

'It might be better if we talked alone,' I said, 'if you don't mind.'

Karen pursed her lips and for a moment I thought she was going to be difficult. Then she shrugged and made for the door. I turned back to Beth. She was staring up at me. The initial hostility had gone.

'What happened?' she said. 'To your face?'

My hand went up to my ear, a reflex action, and I felt myself reddening.

'I . . . had an accident,' I stammered.

'When? How?'

'Before Christmas. In a car.'

'Was it bad?'

'Yes,' I said truthfully, 'it was terrible.'

She looked at me a moment longer, then she patted the bed, abruptly maternal, and told me to sit down.

'What happened?' she said. 'Tell me.'

I shook my head, totally wrongfooted, more distracted than I should have been by the hospital smells, the clatter of the trolleys and the sight of the screens going up around a bed by the door. I'd left all that behind me. I was better. I was whole again. Beth was still looking at me, still waiting.

'Well?' she said.

I told her about the accident. I made it as simple as I could. She followed my every word, her eyes never leaving the curl of scar tissue tracking out across my cheek.

'You poor love,' she said at the end. 'You poor, poor love.'

'I'm better,' I protested. 'I'm OK now.'

'Really?' she frowned. 'You don't look better.'

'Don't I?'

'No. You look thin. You look ill. I can tell. Believe me.' She paused. 'It must have been terrible.'

I shrugged and said nothing. What little I'd told her had taken more out of me than I cared to admit. I was here to try and help and all I could manage was one long bleat.

Beth bent forward, her hand on my arm. 'Are you married, dear?'

'No.'

'Boyfriend?'

I hesitated. 'No,' I said at last, 'not just now.'

'Worried about it?'

'No. Not at all.'

I frowned, the questions intrusive, the boot for once on the other foot.

'I've come about you,' I began. 'I've come to find out how you are.'

Beth looked at me for a moment, saying nothing. Then she squeezed my arm, very gently, genuine warmth, the last thing I'd expected.

'You and me,' she began, 'we're on the same side, really. Aren't we?'

I gazed at her, not beginning to understand, watching her eyes moisten, the tears beginning to fall.

'What's the matter?' I said. 'What's wrong?'

'Nothing.'

'What's happened? Tell me? Why . . . ?' I gestured round. 'Why all this? Why are you here?'

Beth reached for a corner of the sheet and tried to dry her eyes. I could see a nurse coming now, walking down the ward towards us. I bent towards her, my face very close to hers.

'Tell me,' I said, 'tell me what's wrong.'

Beth looked up, the smile quite gone. We were back in the cottage, months ago, years ago, that same conversation, that same ravaged face.

'They've hung a man in Iraq,' she said simply, 'and my husband thinks he's next.'

8

'He's not.' Stollmann was emphatic to the point of near contempt. 'It won't happen.'

'How do you know?'

'Because Bazoft was a journalist. The Iraqis hate journalists.'

'And Alloway?'

'Alloway's a businessman. They need businessmen.'

'Is he in prison there?'

'Christ, no.'

'Where is he?'

'In the UK, as far as I know.'

'Is he still going to Iraq?'

'You tell me.'

'She says he is.'

'Then maybe he is.'

'Shouldn't we know?'

'Of course we know.'

'Then don't *you* know?'

'Yes.'

'Then why not tell me?'

Stollmann leaned back. He was losing patience fast. I could see it in his eyes, the way he kept looking at the ceiling, shaking his head, not believing my persistence, my naïvety. Though technically still on sick leave, I'd shamed him into giving me half an hour of his precious time.

'Do you ever read the papers at all?' he said at last. 'Superguns? Nuclear triggers? All bound for Iraq? Does any of that sound familiar?'

I nodded. The last few days, the papers had been full of stories about UK firms exporting illegally to Iraq. Customs officials had seized parts of what they called a 'Super Gun' on the dockside at Teesport. Firms in the West Midlands and Sheffield were under fire. Some of the names quoted I recognized from our own files, heavily starred for maximum security classification, and I'd been surprised to see any of them in print.

Stollmann was still staring at me. For once, I appeared to have stirred a real response. 'Doesn't it bother you at all?' he said. 'A maniac like Saddam? Prepared to gas his own people? Getting his hands on all that technology?'

'That's not the point.'

'No?' Stollmann leaned forward again. 'It's not?'

'No.' I shook my head. 'It's not.'

There was a long silence. Stollmann was back in control again, reined in, the voice low, barely a mumble, and I suddenly remembered him sitting by the swimming pool, two years back, how vulnerable he'd seemed and how frail.

'This Alloway woman,' he was saying, 'you shouldn't have gone up there. Professionally, it was crass.'

'I care,' I said quietly. 'I care what happens to people. To Mrs Alloway. To her husband. The dangers we expose them to. The risks we make them run.' I paused. 'She reads the papers. She sees the Iraqis hang people. She's got a name. Farzad Bazoft. He's a journalist. I know that. Iraqis hate journalists. I know that, too. But that isn't the point. The point is that he carries an English passport, just like her husband, and he had a perfectly good reason for being there, just like her husband, and now he's dead.' I paused again. 'Can't you see that?'

'Of course.'

'And can't you see what it might do to her? A woman in that state? Half mad already?' I leaned forward, angry now. 'She thinks we're close to killing her husband. That's what she thinks. I know she does. She doesn't actually say it. But that's what she means.' I leaned back. 'And she might have a point. No?'

Stollmann slumped in the chair a moment, his head back, his eyes closed. He looked, if anything, exhausted.

'Sooner or later,' he muttered at last, 'you should expect arrests.'

'In Baghdad?'

'No.' He opened one eye. 'Here. In the UK.'

'You mean Iraqis?' I frowned. 'Buying arms?'

'No.' He offered me a thin, mirthless smile. 'Brits. Selling them.'

I gazed at him a moment, the penny beginning to drop.

'You mean people like Clive Alloway?'

'Of course.'

'Why?'

'Because they're breaking the law.'

'By doing what?'

'By selling to the Iraqis.'

'But we encourage them. Or the DTI does.'

'I know.'

'And he's been helping us, too. It's in the file. I've seen it.' I leaned forward again. 'Doesn't that count?'

Stollmann said nothing. Just looked at me. Finally, he bent across the desk, his face close to mine. 'The law's the law,' he said. 'Or that's the way the Customs people see it.'

'And you? You agree with all that?'

'Yes.' He nodded. 'As it happens, I do.' He shrugged. 'Parliament makes laws. We enforce them. Seems pretty straightforward to me.'

'And the rest of it?' I stared at him. 'Our involvement? The DTI? Whoever else? Doesn't that matter? When people like Alloway get hurt? Total innocents? People just making their living? Doing their bit? Doing their best?'

Stollmann opened his mouth and began to say something, then thought better of it. Instead, he got up and went to the window. When he turned round, his voice was almost inaudible. 'I'm sorry about what happened,' he said. 'I've seen better operations in my time.'

I felt myself going scarlet. I kept my hand away from my face, but only just. 'They did their best,' I muttered. 'It could have been worse.'

'That's not what I meant.'

'It's not?'

'No.' He stood up. 'The reports from Londonderry are conclusive. Someone fucked up.'

I shrugged, affecting indifference, still keen to get the conversation back to Alloway.

'Happens,' I said. 'No one's fault.'

Stollmann looked at me for a moment or two. There was a strange expression on his face, an expression I'd never seen before. Partly speculation. Partly something close to regret.

'Nice try,' he said quietly, 'but wrong.'

I returned to work on 30 April 1990. I arrived to find myself allotted a desk in the big open-plan office on the second floor. The desk had a keyboard, a computer screen and the personnel department had already phoned through the combination that opened the drawers. In the top drawer there was a long white envelope. The envelope contained a copy of a letter from my Belfast controller and a brief covering note from Stollmann.

The Belfast letter detailed my operational record in Northern Ireland. It was extremely flattering and had drawn a small round of applause from Stollmann. He said it was 'meritorious' and 'evidently no more than you deserve'. He had lodged it on my record and he was happy that the Treasury had seen fit to approve his application for a compensatory payment. I read his note twice before looking at the accompanying cheque. The prose was as wooden as ever, but he appeared to be saying that he was proud of me.

The cheque was made out in my name to the sum of £76,000. A curt line of officialese on the attached remittance advised me that the monies were 'in full and final settlement of any later claim', and included 'an apportionment for pain, suffering and inconvenience'. I shook my head, remembering the months of hospital ceilings and bed baths, and the long nights spent wondering quite what I'd look like when they'd finished with me. There were several words which I might have used to describe it all, but 'inconvenience' wasn't one of them.

I stayed at my desk throughout the early summer. After the first afternoon of smiles and handshakes, most of my colleagues were slow in picking up old friendships. They hadn't a clue what I'd been doing in Northern Ireland and they knew it was pointless asking, but the apostrophe of scar tissue curling on to my cheek appeared to tell its own story. If they felt anything, it seemed to me to be a kind of embarrassed acknowledgement that my career had come full circle. I'd done my training. I'd been out in the trenches. And now I was back, tap-tapping my way into those same Registry files, an early casualty returned to the rear area. It was a journey that reeked of failure and no one drew that conclusion quicker than me. Slowly, week by week, I began to fall apart.

Looking back with the benefit of a great deal of good advice I can now see what was happening. My body, fitter than most, had largely survived the trauma of the crash. My gold medal hopes for the hundred metres were over, and I'd be wise to think twice about sky-diving or anything ambitious in the sub-aqua line, but I was back on a modest training schedule and I felt, physically, in reasonable shape.

But that, in a sense, was irrelevant, because my brain, or my soul or whichever bit of me is really me, hadn't in truth begun to cope. At the Gransha Hospital, in Londonderry, a wise old priest had once spent half an hour at my bedside. He knew I wasn't a believer and we had a nice secular chat about Africa (which he knew well), but when he was on the point of leaving, he'd bent low over the pillow and given me a blessing. I'd thanked him through my swollen lips and he'd paused for a moment or two by the door. 'In God's good time,' he'd said. 'Believe me.' My limbs encased in plaster, my head bandaged, my brain numb with drugs, I'd half registered the phrase, thinking it was nice of him to come, sweet old thing. Only years later, in very different circumstances, did I realize what he was on about.

Three things happened next, all interlinked. On 21 June 1990, more than two months after my conversation with Stollmann about Clive Alloway, a Customs and Excise team descended on an engineering factory in Coventry. They spent most of the day asking questions about sales of machine tools to Iraq and they carted away a great deal of documentation. I was one of the first to know because I was cross-indexing some source reports that day, which meant open access to the inter-agency loop on the computer, and I noticed specially flagged 'alert' messages dropping into a number of departmental 'baskets'. These alert messages normally generated traffic of their own, electronic ripples in the Whitehall pond, and in this case the volume of stuff coming out of the DTI was astonishing.

Sitting back from the computer, my own task well in hand, I watched the internal phones begin to wink. At our level, no one quite knew what all the fuss was about, but later that afternoon there were a number of heavy meetings on the top floor and by close of play the office gossips were talking in terms of 'headless chickens'. The chiefs were evidently scurrying around, leaving the building in droves, commandeering our small band of chauffeurs to run them to this ministry or that. Only Stollmann, curiously enough, stayed put and I remember thinking at the time that he, above all, should be wise to the ways of the Customs and Excise people. I met him in the lift in the early evening, descending to street level, but when I asked him about the Coventry developments and whether or not the arrests he'd mentioned might follow, he just shrugged. Anything, he muttered, might happen, and probably would.

The following week, on the Saturday morning I got up late. By now, I was having the paper delivered every morning, a small domestic gesture that somehow smacked of permanence and routine, important glues in a life that I knew was close to disintegration. By now I was a wreck. I couldn't sleep properly. I couldn't think straight. I couldn't make the simplest decisions. Whatever I did, wherever I went, I ended up shaking. Big deep tremors. Impossible to anticipate or control. So far, thank God, I'd managed to hang on to my job, mainly by keeping the lowest of profiles, but I knew it was only a question of time before someone noticed and filed the inevitable report. Not even my chums at MI5 could be that blind.

I picked up the paper and went back to bed. There was a big piece on the front page about Bush suspending talks with the PLO. I read it twice, making little sense of it on either pass. Irritated at my inability to concentrate, I opened the paper and began to leaf through. On page three, half-way down, there was a single-column report from Birmingham. A businessman had been found dead in a car, in woodland, near Bridgnorth. The man had run a small business consultancy in the engineering field. He'd left a widow, two sons and a daughter. His name was Clive Alloway.

I remember staring at the name. I remember the shakes coming back and hearing the thunder of my own blood, swirling around my head. I remember groaning, turning over, putting my head under the pillow and crying and crying until the sheet was wet. Then I got out of bed and tried to find my address book, and couldn't. Finally a little calmer, I phoned my mother.

'Rory and Ruth's place,' I said when she answered. 'What's the number?'

Rory came to the flat. I remember thinking what grown-up clothes he was wearing, corduroy trousers, heavy brown brogues, shirt and tie. I let him in and offered coffee, but he shook his head and sat on his own in the living room while I got dressed. More than anything else I wanted to talk, but he had Ruth in the car downstairs and he was keen to get me back to their place. Back home, we'd all have brunch together. Then we could have a proper sort-out. I nodded, quite numb. It sounded very sensible. Not Rory's style at all.

We drove across London, down to Greenwich, where Rory was renting a top-floor flat in a big Victorian terrace. The flat was small and cosy and I spent most of the weekend sitting in a puddle of sunshine in the living room, the windows wide open, gazing across the rooftops towards Blackheath, trying to make some sense of what was going on inside my head. Ruth was with me a lot of the time. Her concern was scrupulous. She sat for hours in a straight-backed wicker chair beside me, holding my hand in hers, encouraging me to talk, scream, rage, weep, whatever it took to empty out the poisons and make me better again.

Part of me, utterly detached, listened to her voice, a low monotone, unrelenting. She'd learned her psychology from books. She was word-perfect on the latest theories. She was caring and articulate, but it was like being part of a seminar back at Cambridge, the careful application of logic and reason and a great deal of reading. There were ways to get me better, ways I could help myself. I nodded and grunted and said how grateful I was, and once or twice I looked beyond her, seeing Rory in the shadows, sprawled on the floor, half listening, his nose in the paper. Once, just once, he looked up and winked, the therapeutic high point of that long, exhausting weekend.

I returned to Fulham on Sunday evening in a taxi. Rory and Ruth had an invite for a dinner party in Docklands. They offered to cancel, but I said I wouldn't hear of it. Rory walked me down to the waiting cab. Saying goodbye, I could see Ruth up at the window, looking down, her arms crossed, watching Rory.

'Take care,' he said. 'Stay in touch.'

I nodded, standing on tiptoe, kissing him on the cheek.

'I will,' I said, as I got in the cab.

The following week came and went. A doctor's note spared me from Curzon House and I had a number of conversations with Beth Alloway. At first, she sounded remarkably sane. She'd left hospital and returned to the cottage. Her husband's suicide had come as no surprise and Laura seemed to be coping. The word suicide was hers. During the third conversation, I asked her how she was so certain.

'He'd talked about it,' she said, 'often.'

'He came to see you? In the hospital?'

'Yes.'

'And what did he say?'

'He said that life was impossible. He said he was the meat in the sandwich.'

'Whose sandwich?'

There was a silence at this point. Then I asked the question again.

'Yours,' she said at last. 'Your sandwich. And those Iraqis. Actually, he never told me that much but I'm not stupid. I can tell. Your lot wouldn't give up. And neither would they. Something was bound to go wrong. He knew it was.'

'Like what?'

'I don't know.'

'But something *did* go wrong?'

'Yes.' She hesitated. 'The week before he died, before they found him. Something upset him, something bad.'

'What was it?'

'He wouldn't say.'

I nodded, remembering the DTI messages dancing across my computer screen, the Customs and Excise heavies in action in the Midlands. So far, to my knowledge, they'd made only one visit. Maybe Clive Alloway was next on their list. I went back to Beth at this point, trying to pick up the conversation again, trying to nail down the connections, but she told me she didn't want to know.

'He's dead,' she kept saying, 'and gone.'

I tried to apologize again, to find some form of words, but Beth had already put the phone down and so I sat there, staring at the floor, wondering whether I'd got it all out of perspective. Northern Ireland had certainly taught me a great deal about casualties, about the umpteen victims of political violence, but it had all seemed somehow different across the water. There, like it or not, we were fighting a war. In war, you expected bloodshed, grief, loss. Back in the UK, there was no such war. All Clive Alloway had tried to do was make a living. And now, thanks no doubt to the national interest, he was dead.

Mid-summer is a blur. My doctor was kind enough to extend my sick note. I phoned work and told them I wouldn't be in for a bit. Then I drew £2000 from my compensation and flew to Paris. I booked into a modest hotel on the sunnier side of Montmartre and spent the days walking the streets. I knew the city well from my student days, and each morning I set off with no plan whatsoever, content to surrender to the kind of existential half-life I'd only ever read about in books. When I was hungry, I stopped to eat. When I was tired, I ducked into a bar, or sprawled on the grass in the Bois de Boulogne, or found myself an empty bench on one of the *quais* down by the Seine. In the evenings, I went to the cinema, sitting anonymously in the back, the storylines a mystery, the dialogue pure gibberish.

I returned to London at the end of July, no better, no worse, just as confused as ever. Deep down I think I now knew what I wanted, but three weeks in Paris pretending to be Albert Camus had taught me that getting it was another matter entirely. The priest, bless him, had only been half-right. Maybe in God's good time. Maybe never.

Rory turned up the day before the Iraqis invaded Kuwait. He arrived, unannounced, at seven in the evening. He was wearing a suit and tie and carrying a briefcase. I was immensely pleased to see him and I told him so. He kissed me at the open door and ruffled my hair. He smelled, I remember, slightly desiccated: that distinctive Whitehall smell that goes with shiny linoleum, mushroom walls and the dusty, bomb-proof net curtains I knew they favoured at the MOD.

I took his briefcase, sat him down and poured him a large Scotch. I'd had the bottle in the kitchen for weeks. I hadn't touched it. Rory looked up at me, his glass raised. Like me, he was grinning.

'Cheers,' he said, 'your very good health.'

I offered to cook for him but he said he wouldn't hear of it. He knew of a place in Bayswater. He'd been there a couple of times. It served southern Indian food, wholly vegetarian, and he thought I'd like it. I felt, at a stroke, newborn. I didn't know why he'd come and I wasn't about to ask. All that mattered was that he was there. That lovely priest again. Thank God.

The restaurant was empty. We sat at a table at the back, the dishes of Chana Dhall and Mushroom Dupiaza garlanded with onion and fresh coriander. For a while, we talked about Ruth. She had, it turned out, gone away on a conference. Rory thought it might have been to do with something called Gestalt therapy.

'She was very helpful to me,' I said, 'last month.'

'I know. I was there.'

'It was kind of her. All that time she spent. I must have bored her witless.'

'Not at all. She showed me the notes.'

'*Notes?*'

I stared at him and he grinned back. Ruth had written me up. In two short days, I'd become a case history.

'What of?' I said 'What was the matter with me?'

'Affective depression.'

'What's that?'

'God knows.'

'Do you think she's right?'

'I don't know.' He reached across and touched me lightly on the face. 'I just want you to get better.'

Afterwards, we walked back to Fulham. It was a beautiful summer's evening, the grass in Kensington Gardens newly mown, couples strolling in the warm darkness. At home, in the flat, I made a pot of coffee and laced it with more Scotch. Rory had taken off his jacket and was flat on his belly on the carpet next door, sorting through my collection of CDs. His taste in music, like his whistle, was dreadful.

'No Neil Diamond?' he said vaguely. 'Nothing half-decent?'

I knelt beside him with the coffees. He had a long, narrow body, very wiry, thin hips. I'd seen him once in the shower, after a windsurfing expedition to a club in north Cornwall. Like me, he had red hair, though in his case it was slightly sandier. I touched his arm, indicating the mug of coffee. He rolled over and looked up at me.

'Seriously,' he said, 'how are you?'

I thought about the question, rocking back on my heels. I hadn't felt so peaceful for weeks. Months. It might have been an illusion, a happy conjunction of good food, Kingfisher beer and the company of this glorious man, but it didn't feel that way. It felt like something entirely different. Something I'd never felt before.

'I love you,' I said simply.

Rory said nothing for a moment. His expression, thoughtful, mellow, gave nothing away. Then he reached up for me, pulling me gently down, until I was lying on top of him, nose to nose. Then he kissed my eyelids, one after the other.

'I know,' he said.

About three in the morning, I woke up in the tiny bed curled against the wall, my back in Rory's lap, his arms around me, the warmth of his breath against my cheek. We'd made love past midnight, Carmen on the CD player next door, the curtains drawn back, the wall stencilled with the lights of passing cars. It had been slow and tender and richly physical, the promised land I'd dreamed about in Paris, and afterwards I'd bent over him, blowing lightly, my lips an inch from his flesh, cooling him, caressing him, rousing him again, lapping and nibbling, taking him in, pleasing him. Then, he'd said very little, watching me, his eyes half closed. Now, up on one elbow, he traced a line across my face with his fingertips. When he got to the scar, he paused, feeling me flinch beneath him.

'You were lucky,' he said, 'believe it or not.'

'You think so?'

'I know so.'

'Why?' I frowned. 'How come?'

He smiled down at me, his fingers behind my ear now, tracing the knobbly stitchwork. Then he bent low and kissed my ear, his voice the barest whisper.

'I was there,' he said, 'in the car behind.'

9

If I needed a coda for Rory's extraordinary admission, more evidence that the world was going mad, I didn't have to wait very long. Early next morning, Saddam Hussein invaded Kuwait and within hours Curzon House was gripped by war fever.

While Iraqi tanks rolled south, our bosses on the top floor cannoned around Whitehall, desperate to secure a piece of the action. The issues were clear cut. The Iraqis were guilty of naked aggression. They'd violated treaties, spilled blood, seized an entire country under the thinnest of pretexts. They had one of the biggest armies in the world and they were plainly prepared to use it. Unless they were stopped now, then God knows where it might end. Saudi Arabia? Dubai? Weybridge? Our bosses eyed the subversives files, the ones we kept on suspect foreign nationals, muttering darkly about the dangers of a fifth column, of betrayal from within, and someone deep in the government machine thought we must have a point, and lifted a phone and told us to get on with it.

Down on the second floor, I and some of my colleagues watched this tiny sub-plot unfold. We all knew the files had been neglected and were way out of date. One or two of us had even written memos on the subject, months before. But headlines about international rape and pictures of marauding tanks do funny things to people and the premium was suddenly on action. Arresting dozens of luckless Palestinians was hardly going to stop Saddam in his tracks, but under the circumstances it seemed the best we could do. Later, in a series of discreet court hearings, the vast majority of the guys we picked up were shown to be completely innocent. Some, it turned out, were even members of the Iraqi underground, exiles *opposed* to Saddam. But at the time, none of that mattered. War is a narcotic. We lost our heads, our judgement. And even then, some of us knew it.

Not that I cared. The first I heard of events in the Gulf was Rory standing naked by the bed, a cup of tea in one hand, my ancient transistor radio in the other. He was listening to the breaking wave of news reports with obvious relish. For the first time since the Falklands, there appeared to be a real opportunity for him to get shot.

While he looked for his underwear, I tried to pin him down. 'Tonight?'

'Ruth's back.'

'Early? Before she expects you home?'

'Maybe.'

'Tomorrow? Lunchtime?' I smiled. 'Here?'

'Maybe.'

'Only maybe?'

'Aye.' He nodded at the radio. 'Hostilities permitting.'

He phoned me at Curzon House later in the day. The news, he said, was bad. There were no plans for mobilization, no immediate prospect of the dispatch of British troops. Worse still, if and when the UN got its act together and the prime minister agreed to contribute to some kind of Task Force, there seemed little likelihood of Royal Marine involvement. You didn't waste your precious commandos on the Iraqis' tanks. Instead, you sent heavy units of your own.

'Seventh Armoured,' Rory said in disgust, 'and the bloody Crabs.' The Crabs were the RAF, another of Rory's pet hates.

We met that evening outside Green Park tube station. He kissed me on the lips, chuckling.

'Home?' I said.

'Home,' he agreed.

We went home to Fulham. I'd picked up some groceries at lunchtime – cooked Tandoori chicken, potato salad, a bottle of red wine, stuff I knew he liked – but we left most of it in the kitchen, taking the Rioja and two glasses to bed. After we'd made love, a little drunk, I rolled over and asked him about Londonderry again. We'd talked the night before, but I needed to be certain.

'You'd been out there for a while?'

'Eight months. I was in barracks. They gave me a room of my own. At Bessbrook.'

I nodded. Bessbrook was a big army base outside Newry. It lay in a hollow behind coils of barbed wire and big thick walls, an old converted linen mill. I'd been in and out dozens of times, sometimes by car, sometimes by helicopter. Looking back, it seemed odd that Rory had been there too.

'I wish you'd told me,' I said. 'I wish I'd known.'

Rory shook his head. 'Couldn't,' he said, 'and wouldn't.'

'Why not?'

'Unfair on you. Unfair on me. Plus I was Mr Invisible. Meant to be.'

'DIS?'

He smiled at me, not answering, tipping the bottle to his lips and swallowing the last of the Rioja. When I kissed him, he tasted ripe, his tongue in my mouth, his hands pulling me on to him again. I resisted, pushing him away.

'But you knew? You knew about the Londonderry operation? Padraig MacElwaine?'

'Yes.'

'Coincidence?'

'Not really. We had an interest in the man. He'd been on to us before. It came to nothing and we'd had our doubts ever since. That's why . . .' He shrugged.

'Why what?'

'Why we suggested cover. Four-five Commando were still finishing their tour in Londonderry. I knew some very good guys in the unit. We needed men on the ground, proper stake-outs. We thought we knew where MacElwaine would be taking you. So I was put in charge.'

I nodded, listening, running a finger across his chest. Last night he'd told me he'd seen everything at the hotel. He'd watched Padraig pull the gun, he'd followed the Escort out of the car park and he hadn't interfered because he knew exactly what was going to happen next. An informer of his own, a man he said he trusted, had sworn blind that I'd be taken back to the city. The man had two addresses in the Bogside, one a flat, one a terraced house. Both had been carefully picketed by marksmen hidden in a variety of vehicles. I'd be taken to one address or the other, and before anything terminal happened to me, the trap would be sprung.

In the on-going war, it would be a small but satisfying skirmish. Padraig off the plot. Three or four others off the plot. Another reason for the Provo High Command to start asking each other some of the harder questions. But it hadn't turned out that way at all. Instead, the Escort had turned left, heading north, and Rory had found himself in enemy territory, no assets, no fall-back plan, just three terrorists, a couple of handguns and a woman he knew he loved. I looked at him.

'Tricky,' I said.

'Very.'

'You should have let it develop. That's what the book says.'

'I know.'

'But you didn't.'

'No.' He nodded. 'You're right. I didn't.'

I put my head on his chest, feeling his hand on my head, his fingers in my hair. I could hear the whine of the Escort's engine again, Padraig crouched behind the wheel, the smell of roll-ups, scraps of conversation from the back, the harsh Belfast accents.

'I didn't want you to get hurt,' Rory said quietly.

I looked up at him. 'Great,' I said.

'It could have been worse.'

'I know. I could have died.'

'Worse than that.'

'Really?'

'Yes.' Rory nodded. 'MacElwaine had a nickname. In the Bogside they call him Tupper.' He paused. 'You wouldn't have known that, the way the operation was set up.'

I frowned. This was new. This, he'd never told me.

'Tupper?' I said blankly.

'The man had a reputation. With the women. Liked to help himself. Famous for it.'

I nodded, absorbing this new piece of intelligence, thinking again about the meal at the hotel, the big meaty hands picking at the Dover sole, how plausible he'd sounded, and how naïve I'd been to trust him.

'My lot knew all this?'

'Yes.'

'And still sent me?'

'Of course.' He shrugged. 'Given the arrangements our end, it should have been routine.'

'It wasn't.'

'I know.'

'I nearly got killed.'

'I know,' he said again, soothing me. 'And now we're here.'

'At no expense to anyone. Except me.'

'Wrong. I was pulled off operations. Returned to mainland duties.'

'Why?'

'Because I didn't let them run with you.' He paused. 'The phrase they used on paper was poor operational judgement. Face to face, they said I'd panicked.'

I looked at him, thinking of Padraig again, the hands, the darkness, three guns and a locked room.

'Christ,' I said softly. 'Thank God you did.'

We met as often as we could for the rest of the summer, sometimes at lunchtime, mostly in the evenings. We built walls around ourselves, pet names on the telephone, letters left under pillows, presents of books, poems or photos snipped from magazines, picnics in bed, a bottle of Rioja or white Burgundy, big fat rolls stuffed with cheese and watercress and ripe tomatoes. We ate and drank and laughed a great deal, the same sense of humour, the same sense of awe and dread at what we were doing, at the risks we were taking, at the whole lunatic folly of the thing.

We drew up rules, agreeing nightly that it couldn't go on, that we wouldn't let it, that we wouldn't want to damage anyone else, that when the real world intervened and the spell wore off, we'd slip quietly back to our respective lives, wiser and fonder, friends for ever. We discussed Ruth exhaustively, how much respect Rory had for her, what a good mother she was, how bright she must be, how important it was to protect her from our terrible secret. And then, with what little honesty we had left, we'd look each other in the eye and giggle and pull up the sheet, shutting out the world, making love all over again. It was an astonishing relationship, a kind of on-going nuclear reaction, the secret no one else had ever discovered, just the pair of us, eternal warmth. I think I knew very quickly that it was the most important thing that had ever happened to me. And I think I knew as well that –

for better or for worse – it would soon change us both.

Events in the Gulf gave Rory the best of excuses for saying he had to work late, and most evenings he'd stay at the flat until ten or eleven, showering before he left. An infinitely more careful man than I'd ever suspected, he went to enormous lengths to avoid detection. He brought his own soap to my flat, refusing to use mine. When I asked him why, he said it was obvious. Ruth knew what he smelled like. Smelling of someone else's soap would be a total giveaway. At the time, I nodded. It seemed sensible enough. The last thing I wanted was Ruth finding out. Yet that pebble of green Palmolive, sitting in my shower tray, slowly began to get on my nerves. It symbolized her. It was the shackle of his other life. It was the reason we couldn't meet out in the open, like everyone else.

One evening in early October, Rory arrived late. It happened to be his birthday. I'd taken the afternoon off and prepared a meal I knew he loved, a North African dish, a fiery couscous with chicken and lamb and little peppered sausages called *merguez*. Rory had said he'd be along about seven, the normal time, but it was gone eight before I heard his key in the lock. When he walked in, he looked drained and slightly nervous. I'd sent him a birthday card at work, typed envelope, Moscow rules. On the front of the card was a pen and ink drawing of the Cobb at Lyme Regis, the scene of our one and only excursion out of London, and inside I'd transcribed a line or two from a Laurie Lee book we'd both been reading. The quotation had to do with walking through Spain, another of our fantasies.

Taking off his coat, sitting down, accepting a hug and a kiss and a glass of champagne, Rory didn't mention it. The day had been a bitch. Planning for the Gulf was grinding to a halt. The MOD was on a drip-feed of funds. The politicians, as ever, wanted glory on the cheap. For the sake of an extra couple of million quid, we were bloody close to putting men's lives at risk. Listening to it all through the open kitchen door, I began to recognize the diatribe for what it really was, a breakwater, a dam that Rory was throwing up against his own guilt. It was his birthday. He should have been at home, with Ruth. Not here with me.

Over the pudding, slightly drunk, I tried to put it into words.

I wanted it to be tender, concerned. Instead, it sounded blunt and slightly aggressive.

'D'you miss her?'

'Who?'

'Ruth?'

'What?'

'Ruth, your wife.' I paused. 'I just get the impression ...' I shrugged. 'It doesn't matter.'

'No, tell me.'

'I just feel ... I dunno, I just feel you're not here ... not with me, not really ...' I offered him a weak smile. 'You're not any-where really, are you?'

Rory blinked and said nothing. We finished the syllabub in silence. Then I stood up, knocking over my glass of wine, pure clumsiness.

'Come here,' I said. 'Make love to me.'

Rory was staring at the carpet. I'll remember the expression on his face until I die. For the first time ever, to me at least, he looked ordinary, just another man, hemmed in by life, threatened by circumstance.

'You've spilled your wine,' he said.

'Make love to me?'

'There. Look.'

'Now?'

He got up and went to the kitchen. I heard him emptying the bowl, filling it again, brisk angry movements. Then he came back with the bowl in his hands and a scourer from the sink, and I sat on the sofa, quite numb, watching him on his hands and knees, trying to mop up all that spilled Rioja. After a bit, he looked up. I think he knew by now quite how much he'd revealed of himself and there was a tight little smile on his face.

'Come with me,' he said, extending a hand.

We walked through to the bedroom and he took off my clothes, as tender and attentive as ever, down on his knees, kissing me and nuzzling me, while I lifted a hand to my face, glad that he couldn't see me crying. Afterwards, in bed, we made love, over-athletic, all-too-conscious of the question mark we'd left in the living room, the big wet stain beside the sofa.

'I love you,' he whispered in the darkness.

'Happy birthday,' I replied.

A little later, I jerked awake. The bed was empty. Next door, I could just hear a voice, tinny, somehow amplified. It was saying something about a train. I recognized a list of stations. I slipped out of bed and went to the door. The door was open, no more than an inch, and when I peered through the crack I saw Rory sitting on the sofa, the phone to his ear, the voice coming from a tiny cassette player beside him. He was fully dressed. He was talking to someone. He was explaining about a delayed train, pretending to be on the concourse at Waterloo. He'd been down to Salisbury. The train had been late arriving. He'd be back as soon as he could. The conversation came to an end. He put the phone down, reached for the cassette player, turning off the sound effects he must have recorded earlier. Then he looked round, over his shoulder, and saw me in the doorway. He managed a smile, but only just.

'Ruth?' I enquired.

He nodded, pocketing the cassette player.

'Needs must,' he muttered, getting up.

I looked at him for a moment. I wanted to tell him what I really thought, what a fool he was, staying with a woman he didn't love, sustaining a marriage for the sake of appearances, but in that one small moment of time I knew, too, that I didn't want to lose him. Not now. Not ever. The man meant more to me than anyone else I'd ever met, or was ever likely to meet. He'd saved me from insanity and glued me back together again. Without him, I was nothing. I opened the door properly and went to him. I gave him his coat, buttoned it for him and walked him to the door. He smelled, as ever, of Palmolive. I reached up for him and kissed him. I knew, above all, that he wanted to look at his watch.

'Half eleven,' I said. 'Still plenty of cabs.'

He smiled down at me. 'I love you,' he said.

'Honestly?'

'Yes.'

'Thank Christ for that.'

I kissed him again and opened the door, not wanting to prolong the scene. A minute or so later, putting on the kettle, I heard a cab slow and stop. I listened for a moment, wanting to hear the sound of his voice, then I reached for the bar of Vanish and a saucepan of water, and returned to the living room. The carpet was still wet, and there were blobs of red wine everywhere.

Rory's birthday was a turning point. Afterwards, we still met nearly every day and in many ways he was keener than ever, but somehow I became more aware of the rest of his life, of what he wasn't telling me, and this other Rory began to obsess me. This was, I admit at once, wholly irrational. The man was married. He had responsibilities, two children, a mortgage. These were serious foundations for any life, not lightly discarded, and though I believed him when he told me how good we were together, I knew I'd be an idiot to assume that several months of illicit passion were any substitute for real life. Deception, as I'd begun to recognize, can be the ultimate aphrodisiac and I'd started to wonder, against my better judgement, how on earth we could ever put the thing on a proper footing.

One decision I took was to make myself less easily available. Since the summer, I'd been totally steadfast, a traffic cone in the swirl of Rory's life. Whatever was happening to him during the day, he knew where to find me at work. I'd be at my desk, from nine until six. He had the number, and when he felt like it, he'd ring. Likewise, in the evening, I was always at home. He knew where to come. He had his own key. A meal, and a glass or two of wine, and me, were only ever a cab fare away. Don't get me wrong. Rory never treated me as a convenience. I never once felt he was taking me for granted. But as the nights drew in, I became more and more aware that I'd surrendered control of my own life. Ruth was turning me into a recluse. I needed to get out. I needed a life of my own.

I looked round for things to do. Another relationship was out of the question. I didn't want it and wouldn't have known what to do with it had such a thing turned up. No, it had to be something else. Something that would take me out on the odd evening. Something I could put my heart into, be proud of. Something of some relevance. Something, for God's sake, *worthwhile*.

After a week or two, to my surprise, I found the answer. I saw Rory the following evening. He arrived at the flat as I was getting ready to go out. For once, unusually, he hadn't phoned.

My blouse half ironed, I met him in the hall. Rory was carrying a large cardboard box, Scotch-taped over the top. There were crude holes stabbed in the box, and noises from inside. I stared at it.

'What's that?'

'Pressie.'

'What is it?'

'It's for you.'

Rory leaned forward and kissed me. I was wearing knickers and a loose singlet, no bra, a combination, as it happens, guaranteed to turn Rory on. He put the box on the floor and picked me up.

'What's going on?' I said. 'What's in the box?'

Rory carried me into the bedroom. 'First things first,' he said, lifting my singlet and burying his nose between my breasts. I pushed him away. He looked surprised.

'What's the matter?'

'I'm going out.'

'*Out?*'

I laughed, not unkindly, just at the expression on his face. Treat time, it said. I pulled my singlet down and returned to the living room. I picked up the iron and ran it down the hem of my blouse. Whatever was in the box was definitely on the move. Rory reappeared, adjusting his trousers. If anything, he looked hurt.

'I was going to phone,' he said. 'Honest.'

'You should have.'

'Why?'

'I'd have spared you the journey.'

He looked at me a moment, then sat down. 'What have I done?' he said. 'Give me a clue.'

'Nothing. You've done nothing. It's just . . .' I shrugged. 'I'm going out, that's all.' I smiled at him, a genuine smile. 'You're welcome to stay. I'll be back later.'

'When?'

'I'm not sure. Depends.'

I looked at Rory, waiting for the next question. Nothing happened. I stirred the cardboard box with my foot. There was another scuffling noise inside.

'It's a kitten,' Rory said woodenly. 'I've bought you a kitten.'

'Ah.' I nodded. 'Company.'

'What?'

'Company. For little me. These long winter nights.'

I finished with the blouse and peeled off my singlet. I stood there for a moment but Rory didn't look up. My bra was on the armchair. I put it on. Then the blouse. Rory reached for his shoelaces and began to undo them.

'Don't you want to get it out?' he said. 'Have a look?'

'Of course I do.'

I finished buttoning the blouse and bent to the box. I tore off the Scotch tape and opened the flaps on top. Inside, amongst the remains of yesterday's *Daily Telegraph*, was a tiny black and white kitten. It looked up at me. It was adorable. I sensed Rory behind me.

'Well?' he said.

'It's lovely. Beautiful.'

I picked the kitten up. Purring, it sounded like a small, noisy boiler. I held it close to me. The kitten grabbed at me, suddenly frightened, huge green eyes, claws like needles. Rory reached out, tickling it, and for a moment I toyed with making a phone call to cancel my plans and staying in. Then I shook my head, gave Rory the kitten, kissed him lightly on the nose and went into the bedroom. By the time I'd found the right combination of sweater and jeans, he was standing in the open doorway. His shoes were back on. He looked less than happy.

'So where are you off to?' he said. 'Or is it a secret?'

I hesitated a moment in front of the dressing table, examining the contents of my make-up drawer. I could still see him in the mirror. He had the kitten in his arms. He was stroking it, nice tableau, orphans both.

'You remember all that stuff about Africa I told you?' I said. 'With Monique? The French girl? All those jungle lectures? All those poor bloody Africans?'

'Yes.'

'Well . . .' I shut the drawer, deciding after all against lipstick, 'I'm going to an outfit called Charlie's. It's a support-group. They need people who know about AIDS.'

I glanced up at the mirror. Rory was staring at me. Like most military men, he had limited time for life's casualties and none at all for homosexuals.

'AIDS?' he said.

'Yep.' I stood up. 'They're looking for people to train as counsellors. People who can help. People who can listen.' I smiled. 'In this case, me.'

10

Charlie's turned out to be just what I was after, a new support group formed by a Jesuit priest and some disaffected gays who'd peeled off from the mainstream AIDS agencies. They operated from two rooms over a Jewish tailor shop in Finsbury Park. The tailor's son was a haemophiliac, and had contracted HIV from an infected batch of Factor 8, and the tailor – appalled at the lack of facilities for people with HIV – had donated the rooms free of charge. He was a small, round, powerful man whom I'd met through a colleague at work. His first name was Charlie, and in the absence of anything better, the priest had called the project after its sympathetic landlord.

I took the tube up to Finsbury Park twice a week. For a while, I sat in on other people's groups and updated myself on the literature; then I was given my own slot in the counselling rota and my own quota of clients. There were five in my group, four of them men, the other a girl of eighteen, a junkie who'd been on the game. The men were all gay, all newly diagnosed and we sat together for hours, one-on-one to begin with, as a group a little later on. We talked a lot about the small-print things, insurance policies, various welfare benefits, travel restrictions, problems with vaccinations and so on, and once we'd got to know each other and there was trust between us, we ventured even further. Being HIV positive meant anticipating AIDS, and that, in turn, meant evenings discussing issues like living wills, hospice care, and – trickiest of all – how to cope with any one of the dozens of infections that would, in the end, kill you. None of this sounds terribly cheerful, but oddly enough we all drew a sort of comfort from stripping the disease down to its essentials and asking ourselves what we could actually *do* about it.

One advantage I had, oddly enough, was my scar. Unless you were blind, it was perfectly obvious that I, too, had been obliged to weather one of life's rougher passages. At first, in the counselling sessions, this didn't occur to me. Five months with Rory had done miracles for my physical self-confidence, and I was largely oblivious to the odd stare from passing strangers. People with HIV, though, are extraordinarily aware of the problems of others. They approach life from an entirely different point on the compass, and the girl, especially, was eager to know what had happened to me. When I told her I'd been in a car crash she was immediately sympathetic, and I suspect that of everything I said to her during our time together, this was by far the most therapeutic. I'd been there. I knew something of what it was like. I carried the scar to prove it, the stigmata. I was a fellow sufferer, one of the afflicted. To my shame, I have to say that I made the most of this, not exploiting it exactly, but certainly doing nothing to hide the evidence that I'd been to the edge, and looked over, and crept back again. In a deeply private way, it gave me immense satisfaction to try and turn the whole ghastly experience to good account.

By now, it was mid-December. For a while, I'd been dreading the end of the year. Christmas would mean Rory returning to his family. There'd be presents to buy for the kids, decorations to hang, a tree to dress, mince pies to warm, carols to sing. They'd all pile in the Volvo and drive back down to the family home in Devon, and the chances are that I'd probably be there too, the ghost at the feast, haunting my parents' house at Budleigh, thinking of nothing but Rory.

My work at Charlie's cushioned the approach of this nightmare to some degree, but the three evenings in the working week that I wasn't there I still spent with Rory at the flat in Fulham, and deep inside I knew that I relied on him no less. My little bit of independence had made him, if anything, even more attentive, while I, without question, was obsessed by the man. He had, in a very exact sense, become the most important part of me, the part without which I simply couldn't function. With him, with the knowledge of him, with the certainty that we'd see each other, at the very least, within two days, I could do anything. Work was no problem. Even the bloody computer had its charms. But without him, without Rory, I knew with the same absolute certainty that there'd be nothing but darkness. Rory meant everything to me. We were inseparable. We were beyond division. One way or another, the thing would resolve itself. Had to.

A week before Christmas, for once in our relationship, we ventured out of the cave. It was Rory's idea. His treat. He'd found a pub by the river, in the Thames Valley. We arrived after dark and the car park was already packed, but Rory had booked a table and there was already a bottle of champagne chilling in an ice bucket between our chairs. The food, as promised, was delicious and afterwards Rory relaxed with a cigar and a second glass of port. We'd been talking about the situation in the Gulf. Events were moving towards a climax. At Curzon House, we were now running a sweepstake on when, exactly, the war would begin. I'd drawn 10 January. Rory pulled a face.

'No chance,' he said.

'Why not?'

'They won't be ready in time.'

'Who? The Americans?'

'Aye. Powell was up at one of the House Committees yesterday. He's saying mid-February at the earliest.'

I looked at him a moment, surprised. General Powell was Chairman of the Joint Chiefs of Staff in Washington. When it came to the fighting, he'd be calling the shots. He thus had every incentive to keep the Iraqis guessing.

'You *believe* him?' I said. 'You don't think he's playing games? Flying kites? Stringing us all along?'

'No, I don't. Logistically, he's boxed in. Mid-February. At the earliest. A week or two of bombing. Then the big push. *Months of fighting.*'

'Phooooey.'

I laughed, tidying the remains of my brandy butter into a neat pile at the side of my plate. In almost exactly a year's time, I was to remember this conversation, but now I didn't give it a moment's thought. When I glanced up again, Rory was still looking at me.

'You're a cynic, Miss Moreton,' he said, 'one hundred and ten per cent.'

'You're right.' I smiled at him. 'Goes with the job.'

'Off-duty too?'

'Of course.' I smiled again, reaching for his hand, and reassurance.

We drove back to Fulham. Ruth, it turned out, was away again, in Paris of all places. Rory stayed at the flat and we spent the night together in my narrow little bed, tucked into each other, like children.

Next morning, by common consent, we opened each other's presents. Afterwards we celebrated Christmas yet again, on the floor, by the sofa. Rory looked up at me. Moist and warm, I was still straddling him.

'Your favourite position,' I said. 'Happy Christmas.'

He smiled and revolved his eyes again, and reached up for me, cupping my breasts.

'We're having a party,' he said, 'Boxing Day.'

'We?'

'Ruth and I.' He paused. 'Your parents are coming. I know. Ruth told me.'

'Ah.' I nodded. 'And me?'

'Yes, please.'

'Bit near the knuckle, isn't it?'

'Not at all. Season of goodwill. Old friends . . .' He grinned. 'What could be nicer?'

I spent most of Christmas Day getting nervous. My parents and I shared a quiet meal around the table in Budleigh, and later we watched television. My father, for some reason, was quiet to the point of near silence, but after mince pies and clotted cream, my mother broke out the Martell I'd brought down from London, and he began to cheer up a little. We'd been talking about Ruth's party, what it might be like.

'You won't have seen Rory for a bit,' he said. 'Been busy, I expect.'

'Yes.' I nodded. 'Is he still at the MOD?'

My father glanced up, a turn of the head that was just a fraction too brisk, and he looked me full in the eyes for a moment. Then he settled back in his chair.

'Yes,' he said quietly, 'I gather he's waiting for the balloon to go up.'

The party at Rory's was an all-day affair. My mother had been warned to get there about noon, before the vultures descended on the buffet, and we duly turned up in my father's old Rover. Rory and Ruth had a house on the edge of a village called Topsham, upriver from the Commando Centre. It was a neat Victorian villa, red brick, with a double bay at the front and distant glimpses of the Exe estuary. Inside, the two rooms at the back of the house had been knocked into one and it was here that the party took place.

There was a trestle table along one wall, covered with plates of food. There were boxes of wine everywhere and crackers galore and heaps of toys for the kids. Ruth met us at the door. She was dressed in black – tight jeans and designer T-shirt – and she was wearing a huge pair of Elton John glasses one of the kids had given her for Christmas. She had a drink in one hand and a small cheroot in the other, and her dark purple lipstick was already smudged. Used by now to the earnest, slightly dour Ruth of Rory's description, I was astonished. Here, in front of my eyes, was a very different Ruth. She was laughing. She was natural. She looked really attractive. And when Rory appeared, funny hat, clown's make-up, empty glass, she grabbed him by the hand and gave him a big hug.

'Meet Coco,' she said to my mother. 'I've hired him,' she winked, 'strictly on approval.'

I drank steadily through the afternoon. Most of the people at the party I knew already, old friends from my youth, instructors at the Commando Centre, the kind of conversations you pick up as if they'd never stopped. Twice, people asked me if I was all right and both times I nodded vigorously, favouring them with a big empty smile, steering the conversation away from the rocks, asking them about their children, or their new posting, knowing all the time that I was giving myself away, my eyes glassy with alcohol, following Rory around the room as he dipped into this conversation or that, a bottle in each hand, filling glasses, sharing jokes, chasing children, playing the fool, the perfect host.

Once or twice he looked my way, risking a smile or even a wink, and much later, dark outside, we met in the kitchen, amongst the litter of empty bottles and paper plates. His daughter was on her hands and knees under the table teasing the family spaniel with a rubber spider from one of the crackers. Otherwise, for a moment or two, the room was empty.

'Lovely party,' I said flatly.

'Enjoying it?'

'Great.'

'Truly?'

'Truly. You've got a real flair for it. I'd never have guessed.'

'Flair for what?'

He beamed down at me, the deep green eyes behind the mask of circus make-up. On his cheek, very clearly, I could see the imprint of a pair of lips. The imprint was purple. Purple lipstick. Ruth's lipstick. Her kisses. My man. I turned away, sickened with it all, with Rory, with his family, with myself. I'd got it all wrong. All these months, I'd got it wrong. Not one Rory. Not my Rory. But two. By the door, I felt his hand on my arm. He pulled me back, urgent, almost rough. Outside, in the hall, there were couples playing football with a balloon. Rory looked down at me. I realized, for the first time, that he was probably as drunk as I was.

'What's the matter?' he said.

I gasped at the question, at how crass it was, not caring any more. All I wanted to do now was to get out of the house, get back to Budleigh Salterton, put all this merriment and laughter behind me, take the train to London, to the warm claustrophobia of the life we'd called our own. Rory asked me the question a second time, his hand still on my arm, and I shook my head, trying to hide the tears, aware of his daughter looking up at us both.

'I don't know why you asked me,' I muttered, 'that's all.'

Back in London, the start of the New Year, I didn't see Rory for nearly a week. We talked on the phone, endless conversations, me going through the argument time and again, him saying I'd got it all wrong. A party's a party. His job was to be host. He was there to keep it all together, to get people pissed, to make sure the kids had a great time, to jolly things along. What had I wanted him to do? Cruise around looking shitty? Tell everyone the truth? Announce our engagement? The latter suggestion, in particular, stung me.

'That's cheap,' I snapped. 'I've never asked you for anything. Anything. Except to be straight with me.'

'And I've lied?'

'No. Not in so many words.'

'What then?'

'It's—' I shook my head, angry and confused. 'It's just that nothing makes sense. It doesn't, you know ... *tally*.'

'That's intelligence talk. Curzon House bullshit.'

'Wrong. It's me telling you you're better off where you are. You're a great father. You're probably a great husband, too, for all I know. And she's probably a great wife, as well.'

'You believe that?'

'I believe what I see.'

'Me and Ruth? After everything we've talked about?'

I paused a moment, deep breath, starting again. I didn't want all my bridges burned, not quite yet. I loved the man. I didn't want to see him hurt. That's partly why we were having the conversation.

'No, my love,' I said gently. 'Not what we talked about. What you talked about. It's you, sweet, you. You do the talking. You do the phoning. You're the one who decides where, and when, and how often. You're—'

'We've been through all this.'

'I know. I know. But I'm saying it again. Because I have to say it again. Because it's true. None of it mattered very much until last week. Until last week.'

'Fuck last week. Last week was Christmas. Christmas is a sham, a joke. Everyone knows that.'

'No, my love, Christmas isn't a sham. It's not a joke. Neither are families. And that means wives. Rory, I have eyes in my head. I can see. Give me some credit. The woman *loves* you. She needs you, for Chrissakes. You must know that. *Must* do.'

'Aye ...'

'Well, then. Spare me the rest, eh?'

'What?'

'You heard.'

I looked at the phone for a while, arm's length, hearing his voice, a new note, uncertainty, contrition, then, very gently, I cut him off. I've never done it before, not to him, not to anybody, but I knew it was the only way to bring the thing to an end, and if I'd meant what I'd said, then it was my only remaining option.

Rory appeared the following evening. I'd been meaning to go out, but I felt so ill I decided against it. He stayed for half an hour. He sat beside me on the sofa and told me that he'd been up all night thinking about what I'd said and he'd decided that I was right. He'd been selfish with me, a pig to his wife and irresponsible about the kids, and now was the time to try and put it all back together again. He wouldn't be phoning any more and he wouldn't be coming round again. The last six months had been the high point of his life, and he never expected anything like it to happen again. He'd loved me for years, he loved me now and he couldn't see it ever stopping. But stop it must and now was the time.

It was a curiously stilted performance, old-fashioned, awkward, not like Rory at all. At the end, he kissed me and held me for a while, and then he got up and left. I heard the front door closing, and I sat on the sofa for probably an hour, maybe longer, thinking about absolutely nothing. I wasn't surprised. I wasn't hysterical. I was just numb. Then the phone rang, my mother asking about tickets for a concert she wanted to go to, and we talked for a bit and then she said goodnight. I put the phone down and went out into the hall to bolt the door. On the mat, with its little curl of string, was Rory's key. I looked at it for a moment or two. And then I wept.

Of the next few months I remember very little. I did what I could at Charlie's, forcing myself to turn up three or four evenings a week, but I was only going through the motions, listening to myself drone on about positive thinking and self-empowerment, wondering why none of it worked. The Gulf War came and went, video games on the television every morning, and by the end of February we appeared to have won. There was a major celebration in the office, loose talk about a new world order, speculation about closer ties to Washington and I shared a brief drink with Stollmann who told me we were bloody lucky Saddam had been so clueless. A lot of the gear he had was ours. Questions about British deaths from British-supplied equipment might, in some quarters, have been tricky to answer.

Quite what to make of these muttered asides I never really

knew, but I'd recognized a face in the paper that morning, a mutual friend of ours who'd just been appointed Parliamentary Under-Secretary for Trade and Industry. The promotion, according to the *Guardian*, had been carefully timed. The arsenals of the Gulf were virtually empty, and the pickings for the arms salesmen were very rich indeed.

'Lawrence Priddy,' I'd said to Stollmann, 'who'd have thought?'

Stollmann, at the mercy of a small glass of sweet sherry, had pulled a face and then looked quickly away, changing the subject when I tried to pursue it. I was doing a fine job in Registry, he'd said, and he held out great hopes for an imminent pay rise. He knew it wasn't my first choice of posting, but I wouldn't be shackled to the computer for ever and he'd try and sort something out. I'd looked duly grateful at this piece of news, but in truth I'd ceased to care. Neither the future, nor the present, had any meaning. I just lived from day to day, hour to hour, praying for the phone to ring, slowly realizing that it probably never would.

I was wrong. Late September, summer gone, I was sitting in the flat, spooning Whiskas into a saucer for the cat. The cat was a good size, now. She had the sense to eat for both of us. I lifted the phone. It was Rory.

'Hi,' I said woodenly.

'I'm at the end of the road. In a call box.'

'You want to come up?'

'Please.'

I let him in a minute or so later. It was raining outside and his mac was soaking. He stood in the hall for a second or two, dripping on to the carpet. He looked much thinner. I gazed at him for a long time, then I shrugged and went to him and put my arms round him. I could feel him shaking. After a while, he produced a handkerchief and we shared it, drying our eyes. I led him through to the living room, and we sat down, our arms round each other. After a bit, my head on his shoulder, I sniffed.

'Hopeless.' I said.

'You're right.'

'But better now.'

He said nothing, his arms tightening around me. Then the cat jumped up, fat old thing, and we both laughed.

Two days later, at Rory's insistence, we took the night sleeper to Inverness. At Inverness, we changed on to another train, and clattered west, across the Highlands towards the Kyle of Lochalsh. End of season, we had the carriage to ourselves, and we huddled together by the window, gazing at the view, the stands of pine, the soaring kestrels, the ice-blue water of the lochs, the mountains mirrored beyond, their summits already capped with snow. We said very little, because there was no longer any need, and when we got to the Kyle, we stepped off the train and walked to the end of the platform, shivering in the wind. Across the water was the Isle of Skye and to the north, plainly visible now, were the Cuillin Hills.

Since I'd met him, years back, Rory had talked about the Cuillins. They were, he said, the finest range of mountains in the world, the one occasion when God and geology had got it exactly right. As a youth, holidaying on Skye, he'd climbed them all. In various conversations since we'd come together, he'd climbed them again, choosing the hardest tracks, leading me by the hand, describing every step of the way. Most of these conversations had happened in bed, nose to nose, and the Cuillins had become our talisman, our private estate. One day, he'd always promised me, he'd take me there. And then we'd climb them for real.

That first night, we stayed at a hotel in Portree, an hour on the bus from the ferry. The hotel, fittingly enough, was called Cuillin View, and we had a room at the front of the building, big picture windows, the last of the daylight expiring on the sea loch, the wind beginning to stir the pine trees, the mountains themselves already invisible behind a wall of cloud.

The weather got worse. For the three days we'd managed to escape, it never stopped raining. Once or twice, on our hands and knees on the bedroom floor, we pored over the map Rory had brought with him, convinced that the weather would improve, but it never did and we left Skye with the Cuillins unclimbed. We hadn't once seen the sun and most of the cloud never left ground level, but we'd had some delicious meals, most of them in bed, and I'd been happier than I can ever remember. Walking down the little road from the hotel to the town centre for the bus back to the ferry, we wiped the rain from our eyes and joked about our paper assault on Rory's precious mountains. One day, I told him, we'd be back. And then, in God's good time, the buggers would fall. I squeezed Rory's hand, watching the bus turn into the town square.

'What's a couple of years,' I said, 'between mates?'

Back in London, three days later, I fixed for us to go to the movies. There was an Indian film on, *Salaam Bombay*. I'd read the reviews and I'd once spent a couple of unforgettable weeks in Bombay and after all the chatter about the Cuillins I wanted to treat Rory to some memories of my own.

It turned up outside the cinema a minute or two early. I waited and waited but Rory didn't appear. After an hour, worried, I phoned the MOD. The desk officer tried his extension. It didn't answer. I frowned, replacing the receiver, wondering what I could possibly do next. I had his London phone number, the flat in Greenwich, but I was loath to use it. Since Skye, Rory had been planning to tell Ruth that the marriage was over. It wasn't a conversation he relished having, and the last thing I wanted to do was interrupt it.

I waited on the pavement another fifteen minutes, half expecting him to turn up. When nothing happened, I went back to the phone box. I dialled my own number, thinking Rory might have had the dreaded conversation and gone to my place forgetting about the cinema. When there was no answer, I waited a couple of minutes more. Then I phoned the number in Greenwich. It answered on the second ring.

'Is Rory there?' I said carefully.

There was a moment's silence. Then a woman answered. Her voice, familiar, was chilly. I recognized it at once. It was Ruth.

'Who is this?'

'It's Sarah. Sarah Moreton. I was just—'

'What can I do for you, Sarah?'

'Is Rory there?'

There was another silence, longer this time, then she was back again. There was no mistaking the new edge to her voice. As I'd suspected, phoning was a real mistake.

'Rory?' she said. 'I thought you'd be the first to know.'

'Know what?'

'He's gone to Iraq. To look after the Kurds.'

'What?'

'Iraq, Sarah. The Kurds.'

I blinked. The last time I'd seen Rory, we'd been sitting in a pub in Soho looking for the cinema listings in the *Evening Standard*. That had been yesterday. Now he'd gone to Iraq.

'When?' I said.

'This morning.'

'But when did he know?'

'Weeks ago.' She paused. 'Ten days ago.'

I shook my head, not wanting to believe her. 'How long?' I said. 'How long has he gone for?'

'God knows.'

'But when's he back?'

'Christmas, I hope. We've taken a chalet in Val d'Isère. He swears he'll be back in time to join us.'

'*Join* you?'

'Yes.' She laughed. 'It's the last promise he made me before he left.'

Next day, I was called to Stollmann's office. He was brisk and surprisingly cheerful. A journalist on a defence magazine was chasing a story in which we had a considerable interest. We needed to find out where he was heading and, if necessary, go with him. The journalist had a reputation for being difficult. He was also HIV positive. At this point, Stollmann glanced up at me.

'You know about AIDS,' he said. 'You work with these people.'

'Yes.'

'Still?'

'Yes.'

He nodded, opening a drawer. He gave me a large white envelope. I was to read the contents, make an operational plan and report back. I looked at the envelope. It had a Guildford postmark. On the way out of the office, I paused.

'This journalist,' I said, 'what's his name?'

Stollmann glanced up again. He was already working on another file.

'Keogh,' he said, 'Wesley Keogh.'

Book Two

11

What happened with Rory came as a complete sur-
prise, naïve as it may sound. It was the last thing I'd expected
and for days I don't think I really believed he'd gone. But the
phone never rang and nothing came in the post – no letter, no
explanation – and slowly my feelings about him hardened into a
cold, implacable anger. I'd loved the man. I'd trusted him. And
now, for the second time, he'd taken what he wanted and stolen
away. Betrayed would be too mild a word for the way I felt.
Rage, loathing and contempt are much closer, though none of
these emotions is much fun to live with. Thank God, I remember
thinking at the time, for Stollmann and his little files.
    My dealings with Wesley Keogh began with Derek Aldridge,
his editor at *Defence Week* and his long-term chum who'd been
the one to raise the alarm with Eric Stollmann. We met at a
French restaurant in Guildford. The meal had been his idea and
he was already studying the menu by the time I arrived, rising to
greet me the moment I walked in. He was a heavy man, carefully
barbered, with a sallow, indoor face and a warm smile. He was
drinking Campari from a tall glass and there was a folded copy
of the *Daily Telegraph* lying beside his plate. Stollmann's brief
had described him as 'vulnerable' and 'eager to please', music to
our ears, and I could see at once why.
    Aldridge settled into his chair. He hadn't once taken his eyes
off me.
    'Mind a recommendation?'
    'Not at all.'
    'You like onion soup?'
    'Yes.'
    'Good.' He smiled again. 'And pheasant?'

'Yes.'

'Excellent.'

He glanced up at the waiter and ordered both dishes in passable French. In the light from the window, his face was mapped with tiny broken blood vessels. He looked at me again.

'Burgundy OK for you?'

I smiled. 'Anything you say.'

'Sure?'

'*Bien sûr.*'

The waiter scribbled the order and headed for the door. Aldridge reached for his napkin. He had beautiful hands, long fingers, buffed nails, a single signet ring.

'I got the impression you were older,' he said, 'somehow.'

'Oh?'

'Yes. Your voice on the phone.' He shrugged. 'I always get it wrong. Daft old sod.'

Rory had cured me of many things. One of them was believing garbage like this. I smiled politely at Aldridge, making no comment, thinking about the man's relationship with this Wesley Keogh. Stollmann had called it 'intermittent' and 'close', two words that seemed to me to be a contradiction in terms. Were they buddies? Working colleagues? Or what? On the phone, Aldridge had refused to comment. Now he was telling me about a place he and his wife were planning to buy in France. It was eighteenth century. It came with forty acres and included a small lake. At a million and a half francs, it was dirt cheap.

'About Keogh,' I said.

Aldridge stopped in mid-sentence. One of the things he obviously wasn't used to in life was being interrupted. He looked at me for a moment, then reached for the remains of his Campari.

'On the record,' he said finally, dabbing his mouth with the corner of his napkin, 'or off?'

'Whatever you like,' I said, 'makes no difference.'

'To whom?'

'To me.' I studied him for a moment. 'As I understand it, you made the approach to us. Your idea. Your call. You were having problems with Keogh. You were worried about him. Wasn't that it?'

'Yes. Poor bastard.'

'And you thought you ought to get in touch?'

'Yes.' He hesitated. 'I've talked to your people before. As you probably know.'

'Yes.' A trawl through the files had revealed his previous dealings with us, caving in when we applied pressure over Wesley's precious drug-smuggling story. Aldridge was shaking the creases out of his napkin, spreading it on his lap. He glanced up, all innocence.

'So . . .' He shrugged. 'I called again. Thought it might be helpful.'

'Why?'

Aldridge studied me for a long time. Then he glanced out of the window and sighed. The courtship was over. In its place was a new game.

'This is hard for me,' he said at last, 'harder than you might think. I've known the guy most of my working life. He's like a brother.' He frowned. 'He's brilliant, too. Did you know that?'

'Only from you. From what you told us.'

'It's true,' he nodded. 'Hacks like me, been around a while, you get a nose for that kind of talent. Blokes like Wesley . . . Jesus . . . make you feel this big.' He gestured with his right hand, thumb and forefinger, an inch apart.

'But you say he's a problem. That's the impression I get. Reading between the lines.'

'It's true.'

'Why?'

'Because . . .' he sighed, watching the waiter approach with a bottle of Burgundy. He poured two glasses and Aldridge lifted his, the smile back on his face. After a moment's hesitation, I leaned forward. The train I'd ringed to get me back to London left at three. At this rate, we'd be barely past the soup.

'The recession's awful,' I said, 'circulation's down. Sales are hopeless. And Keogh has just upset one of your major advertisers. Isn't that it?'

Aldridge blinked, the glass at his lips. 'Yes,' he said.

'American firm called Extec? From Dallas?'

'The Extec Corporation.' He nodded. 'That's one of them.'

'There are others?'

'Of course. They hunt in packs.' He paused.

'And the others are upset as well? Because of Keogh?'

'Yes, more or less.'

'Why?'

Aldridge looked at me again, the smile quite gone, and I sensed for the first time exactly what it was that had taken him so far, so fast. Behind the petty vanities and the drink, he was certainly no fool.

'There are different kinds of defence journalism,' he said slowly. 'You may know that.'

'No,' I said truthfully, 'I don't.'

Aldridge nodded. 'There's real journalism. Real questions. Real issues. Broadsheet stuff . . .' He paused. 'And then there's our sort.'

'What's your sort?'

'Our sort?' He frowned. 'Our sort's different. The broadsheet guys, they're out in the corridor, hands and knees, peering in through the keyhole, making themselves a nuisance.'

'And you?'

'We're tucked up inside, nice and cosy, no hard questions, nothing embarrassing.' Another pause. 'We kid ourselves we're in the same business. We call it the data game. We like to pretend it's grown-up journalism, journalism without the hype. In fact, it's nothing of the sort.'

'What is it?'

'It's mostly copy that the industry sends through. We read it and we change it around a little and we put a modest spin on it from time to time, but that's all. In essence, we're just another branch of the industry, a mouthpiece if you like. We rely on their advertising, their support. We feed at the same trough. What hurts them, hurts us. In a recession like this, you're just happy to keep eating.'

'You sound bitter.'

Aldridge looked up, shaking his head. 'Not really,' he said. 'You get into bed with these guys, you expect to get screwed. It's not so bad after a while. It has its compensations. Providing you forget about journalism.'

'And Keogh?'

Aldridge shook his head again, genuine regret. 'Never forgot. Not once. Never understood why he should, either. Guy in his position . . .'

'That's past tense.'

'You're right.' He nodded. 'I sacked him this morning.'

The soup arrived but Aldridge didn't touch it. My bluntness seemed to have opened a door he didn't want to close. Wesley Keogh had been a good friend. As a fellow human being, he had unlimited time for the man, but as a member of *Defence Week* he'd always been a major risk. He was brilliant, but he lacked perspective. He had no time for compromise, he refused to temper his journalistic instincts for the good of the magazine. Fit and well, pursuing genuine stories, he'd always been a handful. Now, his health and his judgement gone, he'd become a real liability.

'How bad is he?'

'He's terrible. He's sick.' He shook his head. 'You'll see for yourself if you meet him.'

'But is he still working?'

'Until this morning,' he nodded, 'yes.'

'What happened this morning?'

Aldridge looked away. Then he smiled, a small, quiet adjustment of the bottom half of his face, almost rueful.

'There's a guy sits across from Wesley. He runs the North American desk. He's very good, very dependable, gets the stuff out, no waves, no drama.'

'Your sort of journalist?'

'Yes. Lovely man.'

'And?'

'Wesley needed one of his files. The guy keeps files on everything. You should see them. Hard copy from the disks, everything cross-indexed, absolutely immaculate.'

'And?'

'Wesley wanted the file on Extec. He's been after it for weeks. The other guy wouldn't let him get near it. Not after what Wesley's done to his contacts.'

'What's this guy's name?'

'Doesn't matter.' He paused, looking at me. 'Ellison.'

I made a note on the pad beside my plate. Then I looked up.

'Ellison wouldn't part with the file,' I said. 'So what happened?'

Aldridge said nothing for a moment. Then he smiled again, shaking his head, the story evidently still fresh in his mind.

'Ellison wanted to take a leak. Wesley followed him to the loo. I happened to be on the editorial floor at the time. The loos are down one end. I saw him come out. The man was raving.'

'Why?'

'Wesley had pinned him to the wall and threatened to bite him.'

'*Bite* him?'

'Yes,' he paused. 'You can imagine the guy's reaction.'

I put my pen down, thinking it through. According to the tabloids, one bite from someone with AIDS is tantamount to a death sentence. It's not true but Ellison had obviously believed it. I glanced up, trying to hide a grin.

'People know? About Keogh's condition? What's wrong with him?'

'Oh, yes.' Aldridge nodded. 'That's the whole point. Wesley doesn't believe in secrets. Least of all, his own.'

Over the pheasant, at last, we began to talk about Wesley's story. The version Aldridge had sent to Stollmann was the one that starts this book: that the Americans had staged the Gulf War for their own – and Saddam Hussein's – benefit. Umpteen Iraqis may have died, but Saddam was still in power, George Bush was a mega-hero and the American arms industry was going from strength to strength. As an exercise in cynicism, the story made me catch my breath, but what I'd seen of the rationale was more than plausible. In six weeks of hostilities, the Americans had lost just seventy-nine men, many of them to accidents and friendly fire. As Stollmann himself had pointed out, that was fewer than a fortnight's homicides in New York City. On the basis of figures like these, participation in the biggest conflict since Vietnam was – if you were wearing the right uniform – four times safer than staying at home.

By this time Aldridge was half-way into the third bottle of Burgundy. When he offered to fill my glass, I shook my head. I'd drunk far too much already.

'So tell me,' I began, 'do you believe it?'

'What?'

'Keogh's little thesis. About the Gulf.'

Aldridge gazed at his glass for a moment. Then he reached for it, one finger circling the rim.

'No,' he said at last, 'I don't.'

'Why not?'

He smiled, rueful again, an honesty I was beginning to like.

'One, because I can't afford to,' he said, 'and two, because it simply couldn't have happened.'

'Couldn't?'

'No.'

'Why not?'

'Because . . .' He shrugged, 'these things take organization. It's too big a secret to keep. You'd have to involve too many people.' He glanced up. 'Conspiracy's a fuel. It keeps most journalists going. It's what makes them get up in the morning. It's a beautiful word. It explains everything.'

'But not this?'

'No.' He shook his head, emphatic. 'Life's more complex. More difficult. Conspiracy sells newspapers. But that's about it.'

I nodded, saying nothing, tidying the remains of my pheasant into a neat pile at the side of my plate. When I glanced up again, Aldridge was studying me over the rim of his glass.

'What about you?' he said. 'What's your interest?'

I pondered the question for a moment or two. It had preoccupied me for most of the previous week, though three successive attempts to get Stollmann to part with the background had achieved nothing more helpful than a reminder about my overtime. Anything over five hours a week, I had to get authorized in writing. Unless, that is, I chose not to book it. I looked at Aldridge again. He radiated neither power nor glamour, but in certain lights he had a kind of shabby charm.

'Tell me about arms sales,' I said carefully, 'into the Middle East.'

'Before the war? Or after?'

'After.'

'Easy.' He smiled. 'Most of them are going to Washington.'

'Most?'

'Twenty-one billion dollars' worth so far and counting.'

'And us? How are we doing?'

Aldridge took another sip of wine, enjoying himself now, back on home territory.

'Us?' He shrugged. 'Crumbs from the table. Bits and pieces. Back in the spring there was a Kuwaiti re-equipment agreement. You probably read about it. The Americans sort out the air side. The French look after the navy. We replace the rest.'

'Rest?'

'Army stuff. Tanks. Artillery. Mines. Various ordnance.'

'And?'

'The Americans said yes, sure, great idea. Then they started calling the debts in. Their guys are everywhere. They're selling everything. They're all over the ragheads and the ragheads love it, which I suppose makes sense. They're going to buy where the power is. They're going to stick with the big guys. That means dollars, not pounds.'

'What are they after?'

'Anything. We're trying to sell the Challenger into Kuwait at the moment. The Challenger is our battle tank. The Americans say theirs is better. Heavier. Faster.' He paused. 'A smarter buy.'

'And the deal? That agreement you mentioned?'

'Worthless. Either they never meant it in the first place or it's all out of control.' He leaned forward. 'And one other thing you have to remember. America's a democracy. Next year's election year. The last thing Bush wants is empty factories out west.' He smiled. 'The Americans understand two things. Winning and losing. The big guys won. That gives them *carte blanche*. At least, that's the way they see it.' His hand strayed back towards the half-empty glass, the voice quieter, more reflective: 'So maybe that's it, maybe we think they've been cheating. Maybe we're looking for the big stick.'

I smiled, looking across at him. 'God, no,' I said. 'That's Keogh's line.'

Afterwards, in the street outside, I stood beside the waiting cab, saying goodbye. Aldridge buttoned his coat and leaned forward to kiss me. His eyes were moist and his breath was heavy with brandy. He kissed me on the cheek, holding me lightly by the shoulders.

'Nice to meet you,' he said, 'truly.'

'Me, too.' I nodded. 'And thanks for the meal.'

He looked at me for a moment, uncertain, then he reached in his pocket.

'You'll need this,' he said.

'What is it?'

'The keys to Wesley's place.'

'Why should I want them?'

'Because he won't be there this afternoon.' He glanced at his watch. 'He's seeing me at half past three. We have to discuss terms.' He pulled a face. 'Money.'

'Ah . . .' I nodded, still looking at the keys.

Aldridge pressed them into my hand, closing it with a tiny squeeze. Then he reached for the door of the cab, ever the gentleman. 'Number 216, Dorking Road,' he said, 'upstairs. Post the keys back when you've finished.' He smiled. 'And call me some time.'

It had begun to rain by the time the cab got to Wesley's place. I told the driver 250 and we cruised slowly past, peering at the numbers, giving me the chance to take a look before we stopped. The house was semi-detached, solid thirties pebble-dash, with double bays and a rectangle of front garden behind a low brick wall. There was a 'For Sale' sign by the gate and another sticker in one of the downstairs windows. Upstairs, where Wesley lived, the curtains were still drawn.

When the car finally stopped, I paid the fare and walked back down the road. Five doors from Wesley's was a phone box. I ducked inside and dialled Aldridge's number. When his secretary answered, I asked for Wesley Keogh. There was a brief pause, then she said he was in with Aldridge. I thanked her, left no message and hung up.

Wesley's front door was at the side of 216. I tried one of Aldridge's two keys and it turned first time. Inside a flight of stairs led to a long, boxed-in landing. At the end of the landing was another door. I opened it with the second key, standing in the corridor for a good half-minute, listening for noises inside. The place smelled of bleach and stale joss. Somewhere a tap was dripping.

At length, a small black cat emerged from the gloom and wound itself around my legs. I bent to stroke it, feeling the metal disc attached to the underside of the collar. The cat began to meow and I picked it up, fondling it, turning the disc to the light from the window. Beside Wesley's phone number was the cat's name. The cat's name was Scourge. I tickled the cat behind the ears, calling it by its name and it began to purr, pressing itself into me, the tiny paws outspread on my chest.

Still carrying the cat, I went into the flat. The place was in semi-darkness, every curtain drawn. The main living room lay off the entrance hall. I switched on the light and looked round. The place was over-furnished, an upright piano in one corner, cushions everywhere, a table in the window, three old armchairs drawn up around an ancient gas fire. One of the armchairs was surrounded by a litter of books and magazines. Some of the books were open, face down on the carpet. I crossed the room, looking down at them. A biography of Oliver North. Two fat paperbacks on the Gulf War. An atlas open at the state of Texas.

The cat began to wriggle and I tried to calm it, whispering the name again, Scourge. It looked up at me, big green eyes, the black face striped a grubby white down the middle. I grinned at it, tasting the brandy in my mouth, and put it down carefully on the threadbare hearthrug. It looked up at me, then tottered away towards the open door, a strange crab-like walk, not at all well. I watched it disappear into the hall, thinking again of the notes Stollmann had arranged to be lifted from Wesley's GP. According to the photocopies I'd seen, his T-cell count was down in the low three hundreds. Barring miracles, that meant the imminence of full-blown AIDS. Scourge, I thought again, hearing the cat scratching at the kitchen door.

I turned back into the living room. Over the gas fire was a mantelpiece. On the mantelpiece, secured beneath an empty bottle of Guinness, was a pile of receipts. I glanced through them. Most of them were tear-offs from Access slips. Some of the slips were from bookshops. Others were from a local off-licence. One, for £499, was made out to a company called TravelSave. I peered at the date, feeling for a pen in my bag, writing it down. The slip was barely a week old, and a pencilled note beside it read 'DFW'. I gazed at it a moment longer, then crossed to the window. In the bay was a small table, covered in pages of manuscript. The manuscript was closely typed, single spacing, the pages spread in no apparent pattern.

I bent to the table, curious now, regretting the brandy, picking up the pages at random, trying to get the drift. The stuff was highly technical, long paragraphs about error probabilities and optimum fire rates, and it took me longer than it should have done to realize that it wasn't Wesley's work at all, but had come from somewhere else, probably America. Spellings like 'defense' and 'center'. References to various individuals in the Pentagon. I hesitated a moment, then glanced at my watch and left the pages where I'd found them. It was barely four o'clock, but the questions I had left were brutally direct and I knew more or less where to look to find the answers.

Wesley's bedroom was the next door along the hall. The curtains here were also drawn, the room nearly dark. I switched on the light. The room wasn't big. A single bed lay along one wall. Beside it, on an upturned tea chest, was a pile of neatly folded towels. At the foot of the bed was a chest of drawers. On top of the chest of drawers were more towels and a pile of T-shirts. I opened one of the drawers. It was full of underwear, including a number of pairs of woollen tights, elasticated at the top. The tights were obviously well used because some of the heels had holes in. I glanced around at the bed again, recognizing the scene for what it was, evidence of the twin HIV preoccupations: with hygiene and with warmth.

I returned to the chest of drawers, rummaging deeper, finding what I'd been looking for almost immediately: a small white box with a dispensing note taped neatly round three sides. I glanced at the note. Wesley was to take four capsules daily, as prescribed. He was to avoid over- or under-doses. I opened the box. Inside were a number of white capsules with a thin blue band around the middle. In all, the course numbered thirty-six capsules. Only twelve had gone. I looked at the label again. It was dated 5 July 1991. I replaced the capsules and shut the drawer. The capsules were AZT, a drug that binds itself on to bits of the immune system and slows the advance of the HIV virus. It has some horrible side effects, but if you take it while you're still HIV positive, but not actually ill, then in theory it can give you a couple of extra years. Once you begin to develop full-blown AIDS and the virus gets the upper hand you normally stop.

I gazed at the bed. Wesley had stopped taking the capsules, probably because of the side effects. If I'd got it right, if the stolen T-cell counts were accurate, then he was indeed on the edge of full-blown AIDS. In fact he might already be sick, tussling with whatever infection would finally kill him. I thought about it a little longer, trying to match him with some of the people I'd been counselling at Charlie's. Without a detailed conversation, any real prognosis would be largely guesswork, but the evidence to date wasn't wonderful.

I stepped towards the bed, impressed by how clean everything was, newly washed, newly ironed. Then I saw the rows of pencil marks on the wall beside the pillow. For a moment they made no sense, a series of neat vertical lines, each set crossed out with a long diagonal stroke. I stared at them for a moment, wondering where I'd seen something similar before, then I had it. These were the marks you found on cell walls in prison, part of the dialogue prisoners had with themselves, banged up in solitary confinement, the days crawling past, an eternity of nothingness. I smiled trying to imagine this strange, possessed man in bed, adding another precious day to the life that was trickling away from him. Wesley Keogh, I thought, with his poorly cat and his careful pencilwork, turning mortality into the blackest of jokes.

'What else?'

Stollmann emptied another sachet of sugar into his coffee and reached for the plastic stirrer.

I shrugged. 'Not much. Spare bedroom. Next to Keogh. Unused.'

'You went through the stuff on the table? In the living room.'

'Some of it.'

'You find anything else?'

'No.'

'You look for anything else?'

I glanced up at him, recognizing the impatience in his voice. I'd phoned him from a call box on Guildford station. For some reason, he'd insisted on meeting me off the train at Waterloo. By now, my headache was turning into a full-blown migraine. Half an hour with Stollmann I emphatically didn't need.

'I had no time,' I said. 'I just wanted a look. A nose around. That's all.'

'You've still got Aldridge's keys?'

'Yes.'

'Why does he have the keys in the first place?'

'I don't know.'

'Didn't you ask him?'

'No.'

'But you'd have an idea?'

I looked at him for a moment, remembering Aldridge in the restaurant, the long fingers, the practised innuendos, the way he'd kissed me when he said goodbye.

'Yes,' I said, 'I'd have an idea.'

Stollmann nodded, pushing a cup towards me, turning away, his elbows on the counter of the kiosk, half of London swirling past us in the nightly race for the trains. I shivered and cupped my hands around the thin plastic. For mid-October it was already surprisingly cold. Stollmann picked up his coffee, wetting his lips, not swallowing. When he was tired, he had a habit of talking without moving his lips, as if he was trying to conserve energy.

'You seeing him tonight, then?'

'Who?'

'Keogh.'

'No.'

'Why not?'

I put my cup down. I was beginning to fantasize about *Coronation Street* and an early bed.

'I'm tired,' I said, 'and I'm going home.'

'You understand the urgency?'

'Yes. You mentioned it.'

'I meant it. We need to know about him. What he's doing. Who he's seeing. What he knows. Not next week. Not tomorrow. Now.'

'I told you. I'm going home.'

Stollmann looked at me a moment, then shrugged. 'I've got a car on the forecourt,' he said. 'We'll give you a lift.'

Fulham is twenty minutes from Waterloo, on the north side of the river. Instead, we turned left at Putney, slotting into the traffic streaming south out of London. It was raining again, a foul night, but the Curzon House driver anchored himself in the fast lane, dismissing cars in front with bursts of mainbeam, pushing the big Rover past ninety miles an hour. By the time the roadside boards were indicating Guildford, I was calm enough to risk a conversation.

'Is this wise?' I said. 'Me arriving unannounced?'

Stollmann barely registered the question, staring ahead at the road, totally impassive. 'We fixed it this afternoon,' he said, 'through Aldridge. You're expected at seven.'

'I am?'

'Yes. Aldridge has been worried. He knows you through a friend. You're an AIDS counsellor. You're happy to help. Aldridge has asked you to call in.'

'And what did Keogh say?'

Stollmann hesitated a moment, the faintest smile on his lips. 'He told Aldridge to forget it. He told him there were better ways to square his conscience.'

'Like what?'

'Aldridge didn't say.' Stollmann tapped the driver on the shoulder and muttered something I didn't catch. A mobile phone appeared between the front seats, the driver handing it back. Stollmann took it and punched in a set of numbers from memory. Then he passed me the phone.

'Wesley Keogh,' he said. 'Best to confirm you're still coming.'

12

For the second time in three hours, I paused outside Wesley's front door, wondering what the man would be like. On the phone, from the car, he'd been blunt to the point of rudeness, a flat, slightly hoarse London voice telling me it was a waste of time even making the call. He was busy. He was tired. He had better things to do than sit around listening to do-gooders all night. Do-gooders drove him up the wall. If I had any sense, I'd turn round and go home. In the background, loud, I could hear music. I recognized the piece because it had been one of Rory's favourites.

'Puccini,' I'd said, when he paused to take a breath, '*Turandot*.'

'You know it?'

'Well.'

'You like it?'

'Yes. Very much.'

'Really?'

'Yes.'

He'd laughed at this point, a high-pitched cackle of mirth, far from benign.

'Fuck me,' he'd said, before putting the phone down, 'you'd better come over then.'

Now I heard footsteps on the stairs. The door opened. He had a huge face. The rest of him was very thin. He was wearing a collarless shirt beneath a loose pullover and a pair of tracksuit bottoms several sizes too big. His ears were enormous, his eyes bulged slightly, and when he opened his mouth, I saw he'd lost one of his front teeth. He looked at me, a figure from a strip-cartoon, *Viz*, maybe, or the *Beano*.

'You never told me your name.'

'Sarah.'

He nodded, peering out into the dark. 'You gotta car?'

'Came by train.' I paused. 'And cab.'

'Oh?' He frowned a moment, then shrugged. Upstairs, *Turandot* was coming to an end. I stepped inside, shaking the rain from my coat, following him up the stairs. Stollmann and the driver were half a mile away, in some pub or other. Already, I knew I'd got the right end of the deal.

Upstairs, we went into the living room. Light from a small table lamp spilled on to Wesley's armchair. Beside it was a four-pack of Guinness and a copy of the *Daily Mirror*. The cat sat in a nest of cushions on the chair. Wesley tipped him off, sinking into the scuffed leather, carefully arranging the cushions behind him. The room was very hot, the gas fire turned up high. Wesley looked up at me, grinning in a slightly manic way. He reached for one of the cans, tearing the ring-pull, tipping it to his lips. He had long, bony fingers, big red knuckles and the watch on his wrist slid up and down every time he moved his arm.

'What happened?' he said.

'I'm sorry?'

'To your face.' He touched his cheek. 'There.'

I looked at him. The man came at you in gusts. It was like having a conversation with the beginnings of a typhoon, sudden flurries of questions, totally unpredictable.

'I had an accident.'

'Where?'

'Abroad.'

'When?'

'A while ago.'

He nodded, taking another mouthful of Guinness, stooping to fondle the cat.

'Scourge,' he said briefly, 'my buddy.'

I smiled, recognizing the dig for what it was. In the AIDS world, buddies team up with the sick and the dying, staying with them until the end. Wesley, as ever, had found an alternative.

'He's very thin,' I said.

'Yeah.' He paused. 'He's expressing solidarity.'

'Is he ill, too?'

'Feline leukaemia. Same kind of virus as HIV. That's why I

took him in. He's read the books. Knows the script backwards.'
He bent to the cat again, one huge eye upturned, waiting for me
to react. His hair, long, was very thin. I could see his scalp
beneath. 'So why are you here?' he said at last. 'Friend of Dirty
Derek's? Piece on the side?'

'Hardly.'

'No?' He laughed again, that same percussive cackle. 'Guy's got
a real problem, you know that? Can't keep his dick to himself.' He
paused, still looking up at me. 'I'm amazed.'

'At what?'

'That he hasn't tried it on. With you.'

'Oh,' I shrugged. 'Maybe he doesn't fancy me.'

'He fancies everyone. Anyone. Anything in a skirt. Judgement
never comes into it. Just as well, really, because he hasn't got any.
That's why they made him editor. You know all about that, too?'

'No, not really. He's a family friend. I don't get mixed up in
the rest.'

'Ah,' Wesley nodded. 'That would make it incest. Probably not
his game.'

He looked disappointed, sinking back into the cushions, closing
his knees to make a platform for the cat. I sat down in the
chair opposite.

'I really can help,' I began. 'I'm not here to kid you along.'

Wesley glanced up at me, a new expression, attentive, wary,
one eyebrow raised. 'You're not?'

'No.'

'You're sure?'

'Absolutely.' I paused. 'What have you had so far? In the way
of outreach?'

'Oh,' he shrugged, 'the usual. Kindness. Help. Support. You
have to put up with a lot of all that.' He frowned, tickling the
cat. 'People are clueless really but I don't think they mean any
real harm. It's just . . .' He shrugged again, reaching for the can
of Guinness. 'You drink this stuff?'

'Yes.'

He held a can out for me. 'Take it. There's a glass in the
kitchen. Clean as a whistle.'

'I'm sure.'

I went into the kitchen for the glass. I found one in a dresser beside the sink. Everything was spotless, just like the bedroom. Leaving the kitchen, I noticed a photo on the pin-board by the door. It had been carefully scissored from a newspaper but carried no caption. I paused by the door, peering at it. There were tiny dots on a grey/white background. Each dot trailed a line behind it, like a spoor. I began to count the dots. There were a dozen or so.

'Guess.'

I turned round. Wesley was standing in the hall. He had a can of Guinness in one hand. I nodded at the pin-board. 'These things?'

'Yes.'

'Haven't got a clue.'

He nodded, saying nothing, reaching for my glass. The Guinness foamed and bubbled as he poured.

'You're supposed to ask questions,' he said, 'in your line of work. Why don't you start with the obvious? Like when I first got sick?'

'But you hate do-gooders.'

'Do I?'

'Yes. You told me you did. On the phone.'

'Sure.' He nodded. 'It's true. I do.'

'And?'

He glanced up, crumpling the empty can, aiming for the bin and missing. He stooped to pick it up, carefully wiping the line of drips with a rag from a bucket under the sink. Then he opened a cupboard and took out another four cans of Guinness.

'Let's start at the beginning,' he said. 'I've got lots more of these.'

We talked for the rest of the evening, back in the living room, the empty cans of Guinness forming a neat line beside Wesley's chair. He told me everything I'd reasonably need to know about his medical condition, plus a great deal more. He went into the smallest print of half a dozen sexual encounters, some here, some in the States, partly to test me, to probe my shock threshold, and partly because I think he genuinely enjoyed talking about it. He described each episode the way a man on a desert island might remember a particular meal, what it looked like, the way it presented itself, the sense of anticipation, of excitement, that subtle contract between curiosity and sheer lust that had, in the end, taken him to a selection of the glitzier New York bathhouses.

One particular place, his favourite, he described with enormous relish: the clever lighting, the different kinds of pine, the bodies ghosting about amongst the steam. The cubicles where you got changed had smelled of amyl nitrate and expensive leather and everywhere you looked, he said, there were guys fucking each other. They were doing it at the side of the swirl pool. They were doing it under water. They were even doing it through specially cut holes in the cubicle partitions, crutch height, a real gas, no face, no name, no conversation, just the goods. The whole thing had been wonderland, pure anarchy, buckets and buckets of raw sex laced with drugs and laughter.

Sprawled in the armchair, Wesley closed his eyes, grinning at the memories. He'd loved it, he said, in New York. He loved the energy of the place, America on speed, the pace of life on the street, the way that no one dared look at you, the risks you could run, the rules you could break, the relationships you could nurture and trash in the same crazy twenty-four hours.

'Brilliant,' he said, 'daft and brilliant.'

'No regrets?'

'None.'

'And now?'

He shrugged. 'Now's different. When you're at it, you don't think about now. Do you? All this?' he gestured limply with one hand, the roll-up in his fingers still unlit.

'All what?'

'This. All this. Me, Scourge . . .' He paused. 'Nice ladies like you, popping round to help.'

'No?'

'No.' He shook his head, reaching for a match, lighting the roll-up. 'A lot of it's in your head, you know that?'

'A lot of what?'

'This. All this. AIDS. You. Me. All that stuff.'

'You mean getting it?'

'No. Fuck, no. I've just told you. That was a rage, getting it.' He shook his head again, expelling a long plume of blue smoke. 'No, having it, having it.'

'I don't understand.'

'Yes, you do. You must do. You meet guys, guys like me, my

kind of state, OK, so maybe quieter . . .' He paused, frowning, looking for another word. 'Deader? That make sense?'

I looked at him, storing the phrase away, surprised at how exact it was.

'Deader,' I agreed, 'less vital.'

'Sure. So you'll meet these guys. And most of them, most of us, are in the same fucking room in our heads. We're all frightened. We're all completely lost. Anyone tells you different's lying. But it just matters how you deal with it, that's all.' He glanced across at me. 'We agree?'

'Yes,' I nodded, 'I think we do.'

'You're serious?'

'Yes. Perfectly.'

'Good . . . you know something about AIDS?'

I shook my head, not wanting to break the flow, already mesmerized by this extraordinary man. 'No,' I said. 'Tell me.'

'It's amazingly dull. That's the real problem. Dull.' He stopped, inhaling another deep lungful of roll-up, seeming to expect some reaction or other. I obliged with a smile.

'Dull?' I queried. 'Dull as in boring? Or dull stupid?'

'Both.' He grinned. 'Actually, there's a period early on that's truly weird. Worse than weird. Surreal. That's when they've told you what's wrong and you've drawn the obvious conclusions, and you still need a new car because the old one's completely clapped out, and you're listening to the guy at the local garage trying to sell you a three-year warranty on some fucking banger and you're thinking three *years*? Or the vehicle licence thing comes through the door, the renewal thing, and you start wondering seriously about six months or a year, whether to risk the money or not, whether to waste the hundred quid or whatever it is for the whole year when you might be in the box.' He smiled, watching me. 'Then there's that whole world of old, of being old, people like my mum. She's old, seriously old. She's sixty fucking six, for God's sake, and there she is, banging on about the pension and the Darby and Joan club, and you're standing there shaking your head thinking sixty-*six* . . . Jesus . . . she should be so lucky.' He shook his head, looking away. 'Yeah, surreal . . .'

There was a long silence. Scourge had departed. I could hear him in the hall, scratching away at the front door. I thought for a moment about letting him out, but didn't.

'D'you talk like this to everyone?' I asked. 'Chapter and verse?'

'No.' He shook his head. 'Why?'

'Just wondered.' I paused. 'Only with most people it's the other way round. They sit and fidget and don't say very much. Blood out of a stone.'

'Yeah?'

'Yeah.' I nodded, tipping the can to my lips. 'Cheers.'

Wesley lifted a limp hand in response and sank a little deeper into the cushions. Behind the wild gusts of dialogue and the extravagant gestures, he was watching me very carefully indeed.

'Dull,' I prompted, 'tell me more about dull.'

'Dunno.' He shrugged. 'Maybe it's because the thing's so unpredictable. You never know. Not from week to week, day to day, hour to fucking hour. You know the bastard's knocking off the T-cells and you know you're not in great shape, but you can never be quite sure which bit's gonna pack up next, and that becomes very knackering because you're always on patrol, up and down, trying to work out what's going on.' He paused, shifting in the chair. 'They tell you all this stuff about visualization, giving the bastard a name, the virus, trying to work out what it looks like, what it eats, whether it likes tomato sauce or not, and you do that for a while, but no one tells you how fucking exhausting it is, permanently out there, up and down, all weathers.' He glanced across at me. 'Bastard never sleeps, you know. Never. Not once in its bastard life. Just keeps hammering away, day and night, turning a buck, keeping busy, real eighties stuff.' He shook his head, disgusted. 'I know how the bastard votes, anyway.'

'But dull?' I said for the third time.

'Yeah.' He nodded, emphatic. 'Dull, because once you get sick, it's basically all the same. Bits packing up. One after the other.'

'You're sick now?'

'Off and on.' He frowned. 'Sometimes I'm really sick, laid out. Other times, like now, it's not too bad. But even now, I'm not right. Not well. Not the way I remember being well. It's like living with a permanent hangover.' He gazed down at the row of empty cans. 'That's one of the reasons I use these. Bastard never drinks. Hates it. No imagination. No sense of fun. I do it to spite him. When I've got the energy.'

He looked at me for a long time, then shook his head, unfolding slowly from the armchair, one limb at a time, an old man in his mid-thirties, upright now and catching his breath. Watching him, I thought briefly of Stollmann and his chauffeur chum from Curzon House, sitting in some pub down the road, killing time. Wesley was looking down at me, swaying slightly, and for the first time I realized that he was drunk.

'Don't think dull means I've given up,' he said, 'because I haven't. Giving up means missing out.'

'On what?'

'Dunno.' He shrugged. 'Whatever. No,' he shook his head, emphatic again, 'I'm into rationing, that's all. The important things. Time and energy. What's left. In between the bits when the bastard goes ape. That's as close as we get to a plan round here. Listen—'

'What?'

'Come with me. Real treat.'

He was already heading for the door. I followed him. At the end of the hall was a red velvet curtain. So far, I'd assumed it covered a window of some sort, but when Wesley pulled it back there was a map of the world underneath. He looked at it for a moment, speculative. There were holes in the map, all over, the kind you make with a drawing pin. He glanced over his shoulder at me, a sudden grin on his face, one hand reaching into an alcove beside the kitchen door.

'Treat,' he said again. 'Guest of honour.'

'He produced three darts and gave them to me. 'Home rules?'

I nodded, none the wiser. 'OK,' I said.

'You stand there.' He pointed to a small rush mat at the other end of the hall. I did what he asked. 'Now shut your eyes.'

'OK.'

'Throw the first dart.'

'Where?'

'At the map.'

'I might miss.'

'Doesn't matter.'

I threw the dart. I heard it hit the wall and clatter to the floor.

'Terrible. Try the next one.'

I did so. The same thing happened again. My eyes were still closed. I felt Wesley beside me.

'OK. One more. Last one. This time, be gentle. Otherwise, I'm buggered.'

I threw the dart. I heard it hitting the map. It stuck there. I opened my eyes. Wesley was already at the other end of the hall, peering at the dart. When he turned round, he was grinning.

'Nice one,' he said. 'Definite improvement.'

'Why? Where's the dart?'

'Here.'

'Where's here?'

'Morocco.' He paused, checking again. 'Just south of Tangiers. Very promising.'

'What does that mean?'

'It means I'll die there. It's a game. I play it when I'm happy. It takes the wondering out of waiting.' He turned back to the map. 'Last week it was here.' He indicated a hole off the bottom of South America, an inch or so from the Falklands. 'Can you imagine anything worse? All those fucking penguins?'

Back in the living room, we started on the remains of a bottle of Bells. It was way past eleven. Stollmann would be out in the cold by now, sitting in the car, waiting for me. I looked across at Wesley. The cat was back on his lap, a deep throaty purr, staring down at the fire.

'Are you frightened?' I said.

'Of what?'

'Death.'

'No. Not at all. I'm pissed off about one or two other things. But not death.'

'What, then?'

He glanced up at me. 'Is that a serious question?'

'Yes.'

He nodded, saying nothing for a moment, the madness and the laughter quite gone. 'Pain,' he said. 'I'm not crazy about pain. And blindness I can do without. That's in the script, too, towards the end. A lot of guys go blind.'

'I know.' I paused. 'Anything else?'

'Yes.'

'What?' I glanced up.

'Toxo,' he said quietly. 'No bullshit. I'm terrified of toxo.'

Toxo is AIDS shorthand for toxoplasmosis. It's an infection

which affects the brain and nervous system. Two of the consequences are seizures and partial paralysis. Another is dementia,
medical code for early senility. Your memory goes. You forget
how to speak. You lose all physical control. You dribble your
way to the grave.

'Horrible,' I agreed. 'Ghastly.'

'You're right,' he muttered, 'but it might happen.'

I looked round for the bottle of whisky, sensing the cue for
another shot of Bells. Wesley was on his feet again, bending over
a small table beside his hi-fi stack.

'Scotch?' I asked, holding out the bottle.

Wesley didn't say anything. He appeared not to have heard me.
He turned round, an audio cassette in his hand.

'How old are you?' he said.

I blinked. 'Twenty-nine.'

'That's young, isn't it?'

'What for?'

'Your line of work.'

I began to answer him, some nonsense about voluntary agencies
recruiting lots of young graduates, but he ignored what I was
saying, slotting the cassette into the hi-fi stack and turning up the
sound. He set the counter and pressed the fast forward button,
watching the numbers spool by. After a while, he stopped the
tape.

'Another game,' he said, 'different rules.'

He pressed the play button and wound up the volume still
more. I heard a key turning in a lock. Then the creak of a door
opening. After a while, there were footsteps on bare lino. Then,
very distinct, the sound of a woman's voice. My voice.

'Scourge,' it said, 'Scourge.'

I felt the blood rising to my scalp. I lay back in the chair. I
closed my eyes. Wesley stopped the tape. There was absolute
silence. After a long time, I heard him stirring. He obviously put
the tape machine on record when he went out. Or maybe it was
wired to the front-door catch. Either way, I should have checked.

'Who gave you the key?'

'Aldridge.'

'When did you meet him?'

'Today. Lunchtime.'

'Have you met him before?'

'Never.'

There was another silence.

'How did you get here tonight?'

'By car.'

'Where is it?'

'Up the road.'

'Who else is with you?'

I opened my eyes. Wesley was standing beside the hi-fi. The cat was winding itself around his ankles. He repeated the question. I ignored it.

'You knew,' I said. 'You knew it all. From the moment I walked in. Tonight.'

'Of course.'

'Is that why . . .' I looked at him, gesturing round at the empty cans of Guinness, the overflowing ashtray. 'All this? Everything we've talked about?'

He said nothing for a moment. Then he reached for my glass. There was an inch of Scotch left in the bottle. He gave me all of it.

'Who do you work for?' he said.

'I can't tell you.'

'Special Branch?'

'No comment.'

'MI5?'

'I said no comment.'

'I heard you.'

'Then you'll understand.'

Wesley nodded, the empty bottle still upturned over my glass. 'How much freedom do they give you?'

'Who?'

'Whoever it is. Those bosses of yours. The big guys upstairs?'

Despite everything, I began to laugh. The situation had gone beyond embarrassment to something close to farce.

'Listen,' I said. 'You've been very clever and very amusing, and if it matters at all I've liked all this a lot, but you can't expect me—'

'All what?' he said.

'All this. Tonight. Talking to you. Being here.'

'That matter? Any of that?'

'Of course. But—'

'You *do* know about AIDS?'

'Yes.'

'And you're telling me there's some kind of other problem? Some kind of career thing? Loyalty thing? Moves you don't want to make? Something you don't want to put on the line?' He paused. 'You think any of that shit *matters*? You think I care about any of that? You think you should?'

I put the glass down, uncertain now, hazy with drink, unsure whether this was more playacting or the real thing. Wesley had baited the trap, skewered me beautifully and spent most of the evening watching me make a fool of myself. Now, it seemed, the games were over.

'Listen,' I said quietly, 'I'm sorry.'

'*Sorry?* What does that fucking mean?'

'I didn't want to . . .' I shrugged. 'You weren't supposed to . . .'

'Yeah. But I did. So what happens now? Have you searched the place? Taken stuff away?'

'No . . .' I hesitated.

'Why not?'

'I didn't have time.'

'Pathetic.'

'Thanks.'

'Pleasure. Here,' he picked up the glass of whisky, 'drink it, shit.'

He turned away, shaking his head, bending to the cat, lifting it up. When he turned round again, his eyes were moist.

'You know what's really hard?' he said.

I shook my head. 'No.'

'Tonight. I really enjoyed it. Liked your company. Doesn't happen too often. You know that? God's truth.'

I looked at him for a long time. Then I lifted my glass. 'Cheers,' I said softly. 'Your health.'

13

Next morning, Stollmann rang at half past seven. I answered the phone, still wet from the shower. Six hours earlier, driving back from Guildford, I'd told him very little. Keogh, I'd said, was probably close to full-blown AIDS. The man was difficult and wild and probably brilliant, just the way the brief had phrased it, but he had no special affection for people like me, and – as yet – the disease hadn't left him helpless. He'd indicated no great urge to meet me again and as far as I could see our brief relationship was over. Of the evening's final conversation – the tape, the anger, the hint of tears – I'd made no mention.

In the Rover, coming back, Stollmann had said virtually nothing. Now, he asked me whether I was dressed.

'No,' I said. 'Why?'

'I'm sitting in a car outside your flat. I thought I might come up.' He paused. 'I've bought a couple of rolls. Cheese...' he paused again, 'and pickle.'

I went to the window and peered round the curtain. Stollmann was gazing up at me through the windscreen of a blue Metro. A brief flutter of his right hand was the closest he got to a wave.

'Give me five minutes,' I said. 'I'll put the kettle on.'

By the time Stollmann appeared, I had the coffee brewed and ready. He stood in the hall holding a small white paper bag. He looked tired and a little hesitant. When I offered to hang up his coat, he shook his head. Out of his element, away from the office, he was incredibly shy.

'This needn't take long,' he mumbled, offering me the bag. 'Want one?'

I shook my head and put the rolls on a plate for him, soft white baps with curling sheets of orange cheddar and a smear of

Branston, very Stollmann. He sat on the sofa, munching the rolls in total silence, trying to keep the crumbs off the carpet. I spared him the chore of conversation, half listening to the weather forecast on the radio from the kitchen. High winds and more rain. Welcome to winter.

'We're pulling you out of Registry,' Stollmann said at last, 'as of now.'

'We?'

'Me.'

'Why?'

'I want you to work from here. There'll be no need to go near the office. You'll be reporting to me personally. If you need access to Records, give me a ring. I've got a couple of numbers for you.' He reached inside his coat and produced a slip of paper. The way he held it suggested I'd won a prize in some raffle or other.

I reached for the coffee pot. 'Doing what?' I said carefully.

'Keogh. I want you alongside him. I want to know exactly what he's up to, how far he's got, what might happen next.'

'That's what you wanted yesterday.'

'I know.'

'But I told you. The man's difficult. He's no fool, either. So what am I supposed to do? Beat it out of him?'

'You'll have to find a way . . .' Stollmann paused, the slip of paper still in his hand, 'make a friend of the man, make him need you.'

'But he doesn't need me,' I lied, watching him carefully now, determined to find out exactly what lay behind this visit. Apart from my brief liaison with Priddy, Stollmann had never before expressed a moment's interest in my private life. Indeed, until this morning I wasn't aware he even knew where I lived. Something must have happened, though God knows what.

'You think he's some kind of ferret?' I said lightly. 'You want me to bag him up and cart him around with me? Only it would help if you told me a bit more. Like which holes to pop him down. And why. Nothing difficult. Nothing ultra-classified. Just the odd clue.'

Stollmann stared at me. The way I put things always made him uncomfortable. He hated directness, the straight question, though he himself was never less than blunt. Now he pushed his precious piece of paper towards me and picked up the other roll.

'There's a problem with time,' he said, through a mouthful of cheese and pickle. 'He's going to America on Wednesday.'

'How do you know?'

'I've been checking the passenger lists. He's booked on American Airlines. To Dallas.'

I remembered the Access chit on the mantelpiece with its pencilled note. DFW was airline code for Dallas/Fort Worth.

'That's tomorrow,' I said. 'What do you expect me to come up with by then?'

'I told you. A relationship.'

'I'm not with you.'

'He's got to need you,' he said again. 'Medically. Socially. Any bloody way you like.'

'Why?'

'Because you're going with him.'

'To America?'

'Yes.'

I stared at him for a moment, wondering whether he'd gone mad. As far as I knew, Stollmann was still swimming three times a week. Maybe the chlorine had got to him. Maybe he'd fallen in love with one of the lifeguards.

'Listen,' I said slowly, 'there's something I haven't explained.'

'Oh?'

I told him about my afternoon visit to Wesley's flat, the tape-machine running, our brief late-night confrontation about its contents. The man knew already. There was no way I could fool him. Agent Moreton. Counsellor turned spook. Stollmann was still demolishing the last of his roll. He wiped his mouth, reaching for the coffee.

'Doesn't matter,' he said. 'You still go.'

'As me?'

'As whoever you like.'

'And do what?'

'Keep an eye on him. Stay alongside him. Meet whoever he meets . . .' he paused, 'and keep me briefed.'

'What happens if he says no?'

'He won't.'

'How do you know?'

Stollmann glanced up at me and for a moment his eyes strayed down my body. It's tempting to think I misinterpreted this little piece of fantasy, but at the time I couldn't believe the inference.

'The man has AIDS,' I said quietly. He's gay. And infectious.'

'Of course,' he said, 'I understand that.'

'So explain to me how I get him onside. Hypnosis? Heavy drugs?'

Stollmann shook his head. 'It doesn't matter. Play it any way you like. You have *carte blanche*. As long as you make it to Dallas. And as long as you stay in touch.' He nodded at the phone numbers, still on the table. 'OK?'

I shrugged, picking up the piece of paper, checking the scribbled digits, noticing that they weren't the phones on Stollmann's desk. I glanced up. Stollmann was studying his hands, not saying anything. He looked exhausted, even a little lost, an orphan from some storm he refused even to acknowledge. I'd never seen him so deflated, so careworn. He looked as if he needed a good cuddle.

'These numbers,' I began, 'they're new. They're not even Curzon House.'

Stollmann nodded, still not looking at me, stifling a yawn, glancing at his watch. 'You're right,' he said at last. 'They're not.'

Stollmann left ten minutes later. We'd agreed that I'd report to him on a daily basis and to no one else. My work in Registry had already been reassigned and word was being circulated that I'd been released on indefinite leave. He'd send round a ticket for the Dallas trip, plus a substantial float in dollar traveller's cheques. The way he put the latter detail left me in no doubt that the operational budget was, for once, no problem. I was to empty Wesley Keogh of everything he knew. If money was the price, then so be it. Watching Stollmann from the window as he stooped to get into his Metro, I wondered yet again why Wesley's thesis should have rung quite so many bells. Maybe Aldridge had been right after all. Maybe there was some conflict of interest over arms sales. Too many American snouts in the trough. Precious little left for the likes of us.

A few minutes later, I phoned Wesley. He took an age to answer, and for a second or two I wondered whether I was talking to the same man. He seemed to be having trouble getting the words in the right order. He sounded about seventy.

'It's your friend from last night,' I said carefully. 'The one who left in disgrace.'

He tried to laugh, but ran out of puff.

'Who do you work for today?' he said finally. 'Or haven't you decided yet?'

I smiled. A conversation I'd been dreading seemed more natural than I could ever have hoped.

'You sound terrible,' I said. 'What happened?'

'I found a bottle of schnapps. After you left.'

'And?'

'Most of it's gone.'

I tut-tutted on the phone.

'You should be careful,' I said, 'drinking neat spirits like that.'

'Bad for me?'

'Terrible. Shorten your life.'

He laughed then, a mini-cackle, and when I asked whether he'd be in if I drove down, he said to come anyway, regardless.

'But you need to be in,' I said patiently, 'to answer the door.'

'Why,' he said, 'when you've already got the key?'

I got to Guildford around noon. When I pulled up outside the house, two men in the front garden were taking down the 'For Sale' board. One of them looked like an estate agent. The other was doing the work. I let myself in at the side door and climbed the stairs to Wesley's flat. I had two tins of designer cat food for Scourge and a huge bunch of freesias I'd bought at a lay-by on the A3. I was still bewildered by Stollmann's brief, but I thought I might as well start with a peace offering. When I opened the door at the top of the stairs, I found Wesley on his hands and knees with a pair of rubber gloves and a bucket of bleach.

'Heavy night,' he confirmed, scrubbing hard at the lino, working his way slowly towards the kitchen.

I made coffee for both of us. Afterwards, we sat in the living room. The curtains were still drawn and the gas fire was still on. Apart from the change of clothes, it was almost as though I'd never left. Wesley sat in the armchair, his knees to his chin, surrounded by pillows. He looked terrible.

'Self-abuse,' I said after a while, 'or something nastier?'

'Self-abuse.' He nursed the hot mug between his hands and nodded at the video remote-control unit on the table between us.

'Press the button marked play,' he said thickly. 'I don't know how much they've told you, but there's something I want you to see.'

I did what he asked. A shape appeared on the screen, a big blue 'E' that whirled into focus from nowhere, accompanied by a series of self-important chords on a synthesizer. The 'E' fattened and elongated. More letters appeared, the chords building and building until finally the company's logo settled centre-stage. 'THE EXTEC CORPORATION', it read, 'EXCELLENCE IN TECHNOLOGY'.

The screen went abruptly black, the music fading. Then we were airborne over a stretch of desert, the urgent American commentary voice underscored by the steady 'whump-whump' of helicopter rotor blades. It was 26 February 1991. One of the biggest armoured battles in history had just come to an end. Allied tanks had smashed through Saddam's defences, rolled north and thrown a noose around tens of thousands of retreating Iraqi troops. Allied deception plans had been a complete success. Saddam's army had blundered into the killing zone and American technology had done the rest. The Iraqi rout was, the voice-over assured us, a triumph for leading-edge companies like Extec.

I glanced at Wesley. His eyes were half closed.

'Watch this,' he said softly. 'If you can.'

I went back to the screen. We were still airborne, the music back again, a driving bass note, the kind of stuff you normally associate with certain kinds of car commercial. Objects began to appear in the desert, unrecognizable bits of machinery, blasted apart, the sand scorched and blackened around each one. The chopper flew on, more and more wreckage appearing. From several hundred feet up, it was slightly abstract, shapes and colours, totally devoid of human content, but as the music slipped into the minor chord we came down to earth, the camera moving slowly amongst the charred bodies and the shattered tank hulls, the roadside littered with unimaginable horrors.

'There's a button beneath play,' Wesley said. 'I'll tell you when to hit it.'

I looked down, finding the button. It said freeze frame. I looked up. On screen, there was an upside-down truck. The wheels had gone and there was a hole where the driver's door had once been. The American voice on the soundtrack returned, telling us about Extec's laser-designation skills. The shot changed. We were looking at the truck from a different angle. Two Iraqi soldiers were lying in the sand. One of them had no head.

'Now.'

I fingered the button. The image glued itself to the screen, shuddering slightly. Wesley was sitting forward now, one thin arm pointing at the television set. I wondered how many times he'd viewed the sequence, how many times he'd stopped the tape.

'Guess,' he said.

'Guess what?'

'Guess how many there were. Guys like that.'

I shook my head, sickened already. 'I can't,' I said. 'I don't know.'

'Thousands. No one knows for sure. Tens of thousands . . .' He paused, looking across at me. '. . . movie fucking extras.'

I nodded, pressing the play button again, and the video wound on, mile after mile of wrecked Iraqi hardware, intercut with lengthy technical asides on the miracles of something called 'multi-targeting'. After the fourth close-up of a shattered Iraqi face, Wesley told me to turn it off.

I did so, glancing across at him. 'That's it?' I said.

'No. It gets worse.'

'You want me to see the rest?'

'No.'

'You want to see the rest?'

'No.'

He shook his head, his knees up to his chin again, the mug of coffee empty. After a moment or two, it occurred to me that he was shaking. I got up and took his arm. It felt freezing. I left the room. There was a spare blanket on his bed and a big duvet. When I got back to the living room, he hadn't moved. I tucked the duvet around him, aware of the huge eyes following my every movement.

At length, he stirred. 'Was the AIDS stuff bullshit, or did you mean it?'

'What AIDS stuff?'

'Last night. You telling me you knew all about it. Counselling. The medicals. All that.'

'Oh,' I nodded. 'All that.' I looked down at him for a moment or two, taking my time.

'Well?' he said, suddenly tetchy.

'No.' I shook my head. 'No bullshit. I'm certainly no doctor but . . . yes, I know enough.'

Wesley gazed up at me for a moment, then looked down at the video. 'Thank Christ for that,' he muttered.

I took him to lunch in a pub in a village near Dorking. He ordered scampi and chips in a basket, but left the scampi and picked at the chips, dipping them into a pond of Brown Sauce he'd poured on to the middle of his plate. In the weak autumn sunlight, the first for nearly ten days, he looked gaunt and pre-occupied and as I listened to him I tried to imagine what he must have been like before the virus. Aldridge had said he'd been big – physically commanding, thirteen stone, well over six feet – but the only evidence left of this earlier Wesley were the bony bits. His feet were still large and his hands, too, and that enormous head, perpetually lowered, the eyes looking at you through a thin curtain of hair. His face was slightly lopsided and it was only now that I realized why. His nose, prominent and rather fleshy, was crooked. He was telling me about the American he'd met, the design engineer from Extec, Grant Wallace.

I leaned forward, touching him lightly on the arm. 'Your nose,' I said. 'What happened?'

He looked at me in astonishment. There was a small comma of brown sauce at one corner of his mouth. 'What?' he said blankly.

'Your nose.' I touched my own. 'It's a funny shape.'

'Oh, that . . .' He frowned, fingering it. 'It got broken.'

'When?'

'Years ago.'

'Rugby?'

He looked at me. Then laughed, derisive. 'No,' he said. 'Guy bottled me in a pub. Said I'd propositioned him.'

'And had you?'

'Yes. Of course I had.'

'Was that wise?'

'*Wise?* What's that supposed to fucking mean?'

I shrugged. 'Some stranger in a bar. It's just . . .' I reached for a chip. 'Some people can't take a joke.'

'It wasn't funny. Not at the time. He wasn't a stranger, either. I'd been sleeping with him for a month. I even knew his name.'

'And he hit you? Broke your nose?'

'Yeah.' He paused. 'I don't blame him. He was making a point, that's all. It just got out of hand.'

He looked at me a moment longer, then dismissed the episode with a shrug, returning to the subject of Grant Wallace. He too had been gay. That's why they'd got on so well. That's why, even now, they were still talking.

'You met him in Geneva?'

'Yeah. Last month.' He frowned. 'Aldridge sent me to cover the conference. I think he wanted me out of the office. Me and Grant got smashed on the first night. Some club. Down by the lake.' He was smiling, mischievous. 'You ever try Tequila Slammers?'

'Never.'

'Don't. We had six each. Grant's idea. Some Texan trick you play on strangers.'

'Potent?'

'Lethal. And incredibly expensive. Twenty Swiss francs a throw. That's ten quid each in real money. Aldridge went bananas when he saw the exes. He added them up on his calculator, right there in the office, demanded to know what I'd got to show for it—'

'And?'

'I told him.' He shrugged. 'Seemed quite reasonable to me. Hundred and twenty quid for the best story he'll ever get his hands on—' He broke off, suddenly angry, shaking his head, and I smiled, sympathetic.

'But he doesn't want stories any more.'

'Who said?'

'He did.'

Wesley looked up, startled. 'When? When did he say that?'

'Yesterday. Over lunch. He said it's all changed. He told me it's the advertising that matters now, the revenue, not the rest of it, your bits and pieces.'

'He *told* you that? Admitted it?'

'Yes.'

'Shit.' Wesley turned away, disgusted, shaking his head again, and I leaned forward across the table, helping myself to one of his chips.

'This conference,' I said, 'last month.'

'Yeah?'

'How were you? Physically?'

'Brilliant. No problems. You know the way it goes. Up and down . . .' He paused. 'I was up, way up. That's partly why I got so . . .' he shrugged, 'so hectic. My state of health, you don't waste stories like that. Guy tells you the war never really happened, you go for it, give it everything you've got. You've talked to Aldridge, you've listened to him banging on, you know the way he operates, all that stuff about moderation and responsibility and seeing it from every angle. That's great when you're sitting in fucking Guildford with a family and a pension and some prospect of being around to spend it. But people like me, that's all fantasy. *Pensions?* Jesus . . .' He laughed. 'I should be so fucking lucky.'

'So who did you upset?'

Wesley peered at me, not understanding the question. 'You want a list?'

'I meant about Wallace. This story of his. Of yours. About Extec.' I paused. 'I want to know who you upset. Why,' I shrugged, 'they sent me down.'

'You don't know?'

'No.'

'They haven't told you? Whoever they are?'

'No.'

'They tell you *anything*? These people of yours?'

'No,' I said truthfully, 'not much.'

Wesley looked at me for a long time, an expression I recognized from last night, and I knew he was trying to decide whether or not to believe me. Finally, he reached forward, pushing the basket of chips across the table towards me.

'This might just work,' he said, 'if you don't fuck around.'

We were back in his flat by mid-afternoon. In the car, he'd told me to level with him. 'Level' sounded a little dramatic, and I'd asked him to put it some other way. He'd thought about it for a mile or two, not saying anything, then he'd told me to stop the car. I'd done so, finding a muddy lay-by beside a sodden field. Then I'd turned to him. In any of my other lives, I'd have expected something physical – a hand on my thigh, some clumsy proposition – but Wesley lit a cigarette and made himself comfortable, his back against the passenger door, his eyes never once leaving my face. To this day, I'm word perfect on the next piece of dialogue. Nothing else came as close to spelling out the shape of the next few months.

'You work for who you work for,' he'd begun, 'probably MI5.' He'd paused here. 'Yes?'

I'd looked at him for a moment or two, still haunted by the way he'd put it last night. '*You think any of that shit matters?*' he'd said. '*You think I care about any of that? You think you should?*' Now, in the car, I nodded. In the great scheme of things, it suddenly seemed a pretty minor admission.

'Five,' I agreed.

'OK. So the way these things go, you'll be reporting back. They'll want that. They'll expect it. Am I right?'

'Yes.'

'So who do you work for? Report to? What's his name?'

'I can't say.'

'Won't say.'

I'd nodded. 'Won't say.'

'OK.' Wesley had conceded the point with a shrug. 'So let's talk about the story. So far, I'm nowhere. I've got enough to tell me it's huge, but that's about all. I've got names, phone numbers, contacts. I know where to look next, where to go, who to talk to. It all takes time and money. Money's not a big problem. Not yet. But time is. You with me?'

'Yes.'

'So . . .' he'd smiled, 'you have a decision to make. We can go into this thing together, or we can carry on playing games.' He'd paused here. 'Your call.'

'What do you want?'

'Where I am now, I don't have a lot of choice.'

'What does that mean?'

'I need you.'

'What for?'

'Everything. Physical help. Another pair of hands. Company. A few laughs.'

'Don't you have other friends? Someone else who could help you?'

'No one who works for MI5.'

'Is that important?'

'Of course it is.' He'd smiled again. 'You're the offer I can't refuse. That's why they've sent you. Don't you understand that?'

There was a long pause here. I remember the rain beginning to fall again, the sound of the droplets drumming on the roof.

'So what do you want from me?' I'd said at last.

'I'm asking you to join me. Be part of it.'

I'd looked away at this point, another silence, gazing out at the dripping hedgerow, thinking of Stollmann on my sofa, giving me back-up I'd never dreamed existed, telling me to get beside Wesley, to help him along the way, to get him to journey's end before the virus and mortality intervened. He and Wesley, it now turned out, were asking exactly the same question. Wherever I belonged, whatever I decided, the answer was the same.

'Yes,' I'd said. 'I'm saying yes.'

'You're with me?'

'Yes.'

'And the rest of them? The office? That boss of yours?' He'd paused. 'How much does he get to know?'

I'd looked around at him at this point, beginning a little speech about loyalty and obligation and how incredibly difficult the whole thing was, but he'd waved it all aside, so many empty words, totally irrelevant, so in the end I'd reached for the key, started the engine and wiped the condensation from the rear-view mirror.

'Just trust me,' I remember muttering. 'Please.'

Back at the flat, Wesley was suddenly all business. We'd reached some kind of bend in the road and we'd got round in one piece, and whatever he'd made of our conversation in the car, he'd put it behind us. As he'd said himself, he didn't have a lot of choice. Whatever happened, he needed help. Mine, with or without strings, was the best he could expect. I had limitless time and, thanks to Stollmann, a great deal else. We could meet anyone, ask anything. Our reach was infinite, our curiosity boundless, and if our interests were still separate, then so be it.

Now, Wesley was stooped over the table in the upstairs bay window. The curtains, for once, were open, spilling daylight on to the pages of manuscript that lapped around his battered old Olympia portable. He sorted through one pile, then another. Finally, he found what he wanted. He stapled five pages together, and gave them to me.

'How are you off for visas?' he said.

I glanced at the top sheet. At the top, it said *'Grant Wallace'*.

'Where for?'

'The States.'

'Fine. I've got a B1/B2. It's up to date.' I looked across at him. 'Why?'

'We're going tomorrow. Dallas. Noon.' He grinned. 'But I expect you knew that already.'

14

Dallas/Fort Worth Airport, the following afternoon, was hot, humid and incredibly busy. The flight over was half an hour early, but the immigration hall was already packed with arrivals. There were five queues for the glassed-in kiosks and it was Wesley's idea that we should have what he termed 'a relationship' for the purposes of getting our passports stamped. Entry to the USA is barred to carriers of HIV. They don't insist on tests, or a certificate of immunity, but if they sense the need, they do ask you whether you're infected or not. If you say no, they let you in. If the answer's yes, you're shipped out on the next flight.

The kiosk at the head of our queue was occupied by a small, tough-looking woman and she'd already given a couple of German youths a grilling by the time our turn came to step up. Wesley went first. From behind the yellow line, I could see her looking hard at his passport photo. I'd examined it on the plane. It showed a younger, bigger Wesley. If you knew what you were looking for, it was a dead giveaway. The latter phrase I'd used on the plane, reducing Wesley to helpless laughter, another brick in the wall we seemed to be building around ourselves. Now, I could see him shaking his head, gesturing towards me, full of righteous anger. The woman didn't look impressed, but once she'd done the usual computer checks and made a lengthy phone call, she reached for her stamp and waved him through. When I caught up with him in the arrivals hall, minutes later, I asked him what she'd said. He ignored the question, grinning down at me and kissing me gently on the forehead.

'What's that for?'

'You.'

'Why?'

'That's what fiancées are for, isn't it?'

Grant Wallace was waiting for us by the Hertz desk. Wesley hadn't said much about him on the way over, but I'd read the notes he'd given me and the impression I'd formed of the man was somewhat at odds with the real thing. I'd somehow imagined Wallace to be a thin, nervy American executive, imprisoned in a world of performance targets and management-speak. Instead, I met a smallish, rotund little man with a chubby face and a warm handshake. His hair, cut short, was receding over a high forehead and his big wire-rimmed glasses made him look slightly owlish. Wesley enveloped him in a hug and introduced me.

'Sarah,' he said. 'Friend of mine.'

Wallace beamed at me and said something folksy about the Lone Star State. He was glad I'd had a nice flight. He was real happy to meet me.

Wesley and I checked into the airport hotel, separate rooms on the eighth floor. I had a shower and a change of clothes, and it was nearly six when we rejoined Wallace in one of the downstairs bars. He was sitting by himself in the corner, reading a copy of the *Dallas Courier-Star*. Beside him, on the banquette, was an attaché case, deep red leather, with elaborate stitching and hideously oversized clasps. The glass on the table was empty, and according to the check lying beside it, Wallace was already three daiquiris down.

We drove to Fort Worth in Wallace's big maroon Lincoln, and I sat in the back watching Route 20 roll by, mile after mile of neon lights winking in the warm dusk. I was half asleep by now, exhausted after the crossing, but Wesley seemed unaffected, sitting in the front, rocking with laughter at some story Wallace was telling him.

In Fort Worth, we drove through the downtown area and finally stopped at a restaurant called El Mesón. When Wallace enquired whether we liked Tex-Mex cuisine, Wesley answered for both of us, saying fine, then he was out of the car, loping towards the restaurant entrance with his arm around Wallace's shoulders, a genuine tenderness. I followed them in from the street, wondering what had really happened between them the first time they'd met last month, the hotel in Geneva. Wesley wasn't the kind to hide what was wrong with him. Maybe Wallace was looking for a way out. Maybe he was desperate enough to see Wesley as the logical solution to his problems.

The latter had formed the basis for the notes I'd read on the plane. The details were complicated, but in Wesley's phrase it appeared to boil down to some kind of mid-life crisis, an overwhelming attack of conscience that had swamped decades of blameless service to the flag.

Wallace was an electronics engineer by training. He'd spent his twenties and early thirties working for a number of aerospace companies on the West Coast. He was numerate, dedicated and highly articulate – a rarer combination than you might think – and he'd been a key player in the application of laser technology to attack helicopters. Laser technology, according to Wesley, was a means of guiding missiles on to specified targets. You 'splashed' the target with lasers, and you developed missiles clever enough to recognize laser light from all the other surrounding junk. As long as the laser stayed on the target, the missile would home in on it. The principle, Wesley assured me, was simplicity itself, but the small print depended on specialist engineering. Which is where Grant Wallace came in.

At Extec, it appeared, they'd given him his head. They'd lured him to Dallas from the West Coast, and they'd set him up with a state of the art laboratory and a hand-picked team, and they'd asked him to fine-tune a missile they'd already codenamed *Scarab*. The point about *Scarab* was its weight. At 37½ lbs it was light enough to be man-portable. In test versions, it had a range of three and a half miles, ample for most battlefield applications. A specially shaped warhead could penetrate all known armour. For the provisional $98,000 apiece, it was a steal. Only the laser-guidance system remained a problem.

Wallace had worked on *Scarab* for eighteen busy months, commuting daily to the Extec laboratories on a Dallas science park from a rented house in the suburbs. A month before the Gulf War, he'd finally miniaturized the on-board electronics and developed a launcher small enough to be likewise man-portable. Within the industry, Wallace already had a reputation. Now they were saying he was a genius. The electronics were smarter than anything to come out of Japan. The thing was cheap, reliable and so user-friendly it was even, in Wesley's phrase, Arab-proof. For a company desperate to make a major killing, it was the perfect product.

By the time the Allied armies were liberating Kuwait City, the first *Scarab* tank-busters were rolling off the production line. But too late to join the mauling of the Iraqi Army. Extec executives had ordered cassette after cassette of video rushes from the broadcast organizations, determined to use the pictures to sell *Scarab*. The carnage on the Basra Road was the work of big, heavy laser-seeking missiles launched from helicopters and fixed-wing aircraft, but that didn't matter. On the contrary, it was the whole point. The video would go to a hundred Third World countries. Sales teams would shutter the windows, kill the lights and run the pictures over and over again. All this can be yours, went the pitch, for a zillionth of the price. No need for helicopters. No need for pilots. No need for all that First World sophistication. Just come to us. And spend a couple of million dollars. And let *Scarab* do the rest.

Wallace had been obliged to sit through the videos. His technical advice was deemed vital. What he'd seen had sickened him. Five months later, Extec's tame boffin at the Geneva conference, he'd met Wesley. Drink, loneliness, guilt and a long-suppressed homosexuality had done the rest. They'd talked and compared notes. They'd gone to bed. And only next day, when Wallace had realized the implications of what he'd said, had the conversations come to an end.

Now, in the restaurant, I listened to him talking to Wesley. He had small, chubby hands and they chopped the air as he leaned forward, making a particular point. Despite the air conditioning, there was a sheen of sweat on his forehead, and when the waiter arrived with the second round of cocktails, I realized that he was drunk.

According to Wesley, the pressures on him had been enormous. In the aftermath of the Geneva conference, Wesley himself had phoned and phoned, a missile of his own design, determined to penetrate Extec's protective screen of receptionists, secretaries and inquisitive corporate relations staff. At no point had he compromised Wallace, refusing to discuss the issue with anyone else, but he was determined to pursue the lead that the American had offered, and when Extec refused point blank to take any more calls, he'd plunged down another alley, pumping contacts on the

West Coast until he found someone who knew Wallace's unlisted home number.

He'd phoned him late at night, seven in the morning UK time, and the two men had talked for more than an hour. To Wesley's surprise, Wallace was glad to hear him. Rumours were spreading, friends were melting away, and since Geneva he'd been frozen out of a widening circle of management meetings. For weeks now, he'd done no work worth the name and a good night's sleep was barely a memory. But the more he thought about the conversation they'd had, back there in Geneva, and the harder he tried to analyse the morality of the thing, the more he was convinced that he must speak out. He'd been talking to one or two of the other guys. He'd been doing a little research. He had a couple of theories Wesley might like to test. Why not fly over? Stay a day or two? Kick the thing around?

'So what are we saying?'

Wesley frowned, still waiting for an answer, pushing a small mountain of *enchilada* to the side of his plate. A guitarist had appeared, Country and Western, perched on a stool beside a tiny dance floor. Wallace, totally oblivious, leaned forward.

'We're saying it's true,' he said. 'We're saying the thing was staged. Phoney. Make believe. Desert Sham.'

'Yeah?'

'Yeah.' Wallace nodded. 'You know how many US nationals we had out there in Saudi before this thing blew up?'

Wesley shrugged. For the first time in the evening, he was visibly exhausted. 'No,' he said.

'Twenty thousand. Twenty thousand US citizens, living in Saudi, working there, when Saddam went into Kuwait. That's how many we had.' He paused. 'There were Brits as well, of course. And the French. And some Spanish. And you know what happened to them?'

'No.'

'Evacuated. Ordered out by their own people. Your guys. British Airways laid on extra flights, right up to K-Day, right up to when the shit hit the fan.' He paused again. 'So what about our guys, eh? What about Uncle Sam?'

Wesley was leaning forward now, alert again. 'Well?' he said. 'What happened?'

Wallace looked at him for a moment.

'Nothing,' he said at last.

'*Nothing?*'

'Nope. Nothing. They all stayed. Not a single goddamn word from Washington. Nothing. Zilch. You know what usually happens? Situations like these? Third World situations? Civil wars? Insurrections? All that stuff? The State Department goes broody. Mother hen gets on the phone, and there's queues at the airport a mile long, like you've never seen. No one leaves the Third World quicker than the US. And that's not cowardice, my friend. That's just plain good sense. We care about what happens to our people. We hate uncertainty. We hate risk. We hate not knowing. So what made it all so different in Saudi, eh?'

Wesley nodded slowly. 'You knew,' he said, 'Uncle Sam knew.'

'Sure.'

'That there was no risk.'

'Right.'

'Because?'

'Because there'd be no real fighting, not the kind that would matter to our guys. There'd be public relations and scare stories and all those cute little maps with Iraqi tanks all over them, but that's about all. The rest of it was taken care of. Real well.'

Wesley nodded, leaning back in his chair, beaming with delight. I could see why he liked this little Texan so much. The way he put things smacked of Wesley himself, that same combination of fervour and mischief and contempt. Wesley glanced across at me, stoking up the fire, tossing on some timber of his own.

'You know that photo in my kitchen? On the pin-board?'

I nodded. Insects on a sandtray, I thought. Each one trailing its own little spoor.

'Tanks,' Wesley said, 'Iraqi T–72s. Filmed from one of the Russian satellites. The Soviets sold the picture worldwide and a paper down in Florida published it.' He looked at Wallace. 'You know about this?'

Wallace nodded. 'The *Times*,' he said, 'out of St Petersburg.'

'Spot on.' Wesley was looking at me again, teacher and pupil. 'The photo came from early on, August, the point when Bush was trying to put the shits up the Saudis. He wanted to ship US troops in. Marines, armour, planes, the lot, but the Saudis weren't that keen. So there had to be a threat, a credible threat, Iraqi tanks up there on the Saudi border, thousands of them, about to invade, about to head down from Kuwait.'

I frowned, following the logic, remembering the tiny dots on the pin-board. 'There were a handful,' I said, 'maybe a dozen or so.'

'Exactly.' Wesley nodded. 'And that was the reality. A light screen. Nothing awesome. Just a precaution.'

'And they showed the Saudis that photo? Is that what you're saying?'

'No, fuck no. They commissioned some alternative photos. Their own stuff. Right off one of the military satellites. They call them "overheads". They fetch them down and take them along to some little room or other in the Pentagon, and the guys in there get busy with their pens and their brushes and ... fuck me, thousands of the bastards, everywhere.' He beamed at me, delighted with his own exposition. 'Instant invasion, cooked up in Washington, courtesy of our friends in the White House.'

'You're saying they made it up? And the Saudis believed them?'

'Of course they did. Why else would they let in all those fucking infidels?' He glanced across at Wallace. 'Right, Grant?'

Wallace nodded. 'Right,' he said.

Wesley looked at me again, enjoying himself now, determined not to lose the initiative, his voice rising. 'Another thing,' he said. 'The MOD, your friends in London ...'

I nodded.

'They were running computer predictions. After K-Day, after our boys went in, all the data was coming back from Dhahran, real-time, as we pushed forward, and it went straight into the computers. You put stuff in one end, you get predictions out the other.' He paused for a moment, his eyes on a table beside the door. 'There were various predictions as the thing developed. One copy went back to Dhahran. Another went to Downing Street. The key figure was casualties, how many blokes we'd lose. It was meant to prepare the politicians for the worst. The military, too, for that matter.' He turned back to Wallace. 'I've never told you this. I had a contact on the analysis team. You know how many programs we ran? In the first forty-eight hours?'

'Nope.'

'Six.' He grinned. 'And not one of them put the body count below four figures. That's what logic said. That's what should have happened. *Thousands* of our guys. Blown away by the Iraqis. Curious, eh?'

Wallace nodded, reaching for his drink, giving a low whoop, partly glee, partly alcohol. He had moved on to beer now, most of his meal untouched. I glanced across at the table beside the door. There were two men at the table, both facing our way. One was black. The other had a small notepad beside his plate. They were well dressed in nicely cut dark suits. Neither was much interested in conversation. I looked at Wesley a moment and raised an eyebrow, and he acknowledged me with a small but perceptible nod. Wallace was staring at the wall. Wesley reached across to him.

'You mentioned a file,' he said, 'on the phone.'

Wallace looked at him, moist-eyed, and I began to understand what Wesley had meant on the plane by 'lost'. Whatever had happened to Wallace over the last month had taken an enormous toll. This wasn't the man I'd read about, the target for all those Extec dollars.

'It's in the car,' he said, 'in my attaché case.'

'Do I get to see it?'

Wallace said nothing for a moment, then picked up his glass. Wesley watched him drain it, then signalled to the waiter. Wallace was still looking at his hands when the man returned with a tray of fresh beers.

'You'd need channels,' Wallace said at last, 'surrogates. You want to do this thing, do it properly, that's what you'd need.'

Wesley leaned forward, distributing the beers, inching his chair to the left, blocking the view from the door.

'What thing?' he said softly.

'What thing?' Wallace looked up, echoing Wesley. 'The Desert thing, the Desert Sham thing.' He hesitated. 'You wanna orchestrate a war, you gotta have a script. Otherwise, it won't go right. You gotta agree when and where. Both sides. Both sides gotta know. Not everyone. Not all of them. But a tiny handful of guys at the very top. This many . . .' He held up his thumb and his forefinger, an inch apart, then closed the gap still further, 'Or maybe this many, no?'

Wesley nodded. 'Yes,' he said. 'That's what we said on the phone. Remember?'

'Sure. So,' Wallace shrugged, 'both sides have to nominate someone. Both sides have to decide who they're gonna send, who they trust, who ain't gonna drop the fuckin' ball. Not easy.'

'No.' Wesley looked at me a moment, one eyebrow raised, and I nodded, certain now, watching the table by the door. One of the two men, the taller one, had moved his chair. From where he sat, he could still see Wallace. Wallace was trying to get to his feet. Wesley reached up, restraining him. Wallace took his hand.

'The john,' he mumbled. 'You wanna go, too?'

Wesley shook his head. 'Sit down,' he said. 'We'll go in a minute.'

'Yeah?'

'Yeah.' Wesley paused. 'So two guys?' he said. 'You're saying two guys to do all the talking? One American? One Iraqi? Tight as that?'

Wallace nodded. 'Tight as that. So fucking tight you don't see daylight.'

'You *know* that?'

'No. I've just been doing a lot of thinking about it,' he said. 'This is an oil state. Extec runs on oil money. It's part of a conglomerate. The Texcal Corporation. Big bucks . . .'

'You think the American – whoever he is – you think he may have an oil connection?'

'I dunno.' He looked at Wesley. 'Yeah . . . maybe . . . something like that. Oil's big money. That's where it begins and ends. Has to.'

I kicked Wesley under the table. One of the men across the room was getting up. He walked to the bar and began to make a phone call. Wesley glanced round, understanding at once.

When he turned back, Wallace was staring at him. 'Something the matter?' he said.

Wesley pulled a face. 'Me,' he said briefly. 'I've got some pills in the car.'

'Sure,' Wallace began to get up. 'I'll fetch them.'

'No.' Wesley reached over again. 'Let Sarah. She knows which ones.'

Wallace looked at him a moment, then me. His car keys lay

on the table beside his plate. The man at the bar was still busy on the telephone. The other one had a lousy view. I picked up the car keys and my bag, aware of Wesley watching me. When I looked up, he was smiling, elbows on the table, forearms straight, fists clenched. Charades was never my game, but even I'm not that stupid.

'Usual stuff?' I queried.

'Please.'

'Sure you need it?'

'Positive.'

I looked at him a moment longer, then nodded. The rest rooms were in the far corner, at the back of the restaurant, away from the street. I walked towards them, smiling at the guitarist, pushing through the louvred swing doors. Another door, marked 'Señoras', was on the left. Inside, there were two cubicles and a couple of handbasins. There were fresh hand towels by the basins and small bottles of eau-de-Cologne. In a neat wicker basket were tiny packs of soap and half a dozen books of matches, each printed with the restaurant's name. I looked round. The only window, high on the wall, was barred on the outside.

Back in the passage, I tried the men's room. It was equally spotless, but this time there were no windows at all. I shut the door. At the end of the passage was a flight of stairs. I began to climb them. At the top of the first flight where they turned right, there was another door marked 'Exit'. In smaller letters, underneath, it read 'Alarmed. Emergency Use Only'. I hesitated a moment. Part of me wanted to push through it, to trust my luck and my sense of direction, to risk the alarm and hope that I made it to Wallace's car before our friends in the restaurant put two and two together and got there first. But another part of me, the bit that had more or less survived Northern Ireland, knew just how lousy a decision that would be. Tired or otherwise, I had to find another way. Wesley, and more importantly Stollmann, would expect it.

I went back to the women's room. Its cubicles, in keeping with the décor, offered two kinds of tissue. I selected the pink, pulling it off the roll in great handfuls, praying that no one else would come in. When I had what I thought was enough, I flushed the lavatory and left the cubicle. I put the plugs in both basins and turned on the taps. Then I took one of the books of matches and went out into the corridor.

A dozen yards of toilet tissue makes a brief but smoky bonfire. I lit it as close to the door to the restaurant as I dared, staying just long enough to be certain that it was well alight. Then I ran for the stairs, hearing the first of the basins beginning to overflow in the women's room, turning the handle in the emergency exit and putting my shoulder to the door. It gave at once, triggering a bell inches from my ear, and I pushed through, finding myself on a fire escape, a narrow alley beneath me. I clattered down the fire escape, and sidestepped through a line of dustbins. By the time I emerged on to the street, diners were beginning to appear from the restaurant, couples standing uncertainly on the pavement, men pulling on their jackets, women peering back through the big plate-glass windows. Of our friends by the door, or Wesley or Wallace, there was no sign.

I hesitated a moment, then walked across the street. Wallace's car was parked fifty yards away. I stood by the driver's door, feeling the key into the lock. The door opened at once. I slipped inside, stirring the engine into life, my eyes on the restaurant. Still no Wesley. Still no Wallace. I hesitated a moment longer, then the smaller of the two men by the door, the black one, appeared. He had a radio in one hand and he was looking in my direction.

I glanced down. The gear shift was automatic. I engaged Drive and floored the accelerator, and the big car surged out into the traffic stream. Passing the restaurant, I could see the black guy peering at the registration, talking rapidly into the handset. Miles away, faintly, I could hear the wail of a siren. Then another, much closer. At the first intersection, I swung left, away from the siren, accelerating as fast as I could, leaving the rest of the traffic behind. Three blocks down I took a left again, turning into a street flanked on both sides by tall office blocks. The street was empty, a long, glass-walled canyon, stop-lights receding into the middle distance. For half a mile or so, the lights were with me, a succession of greens. Then, at the first red, I pulled into the side of the road and killed the engine.

The trunk of the big Lincoln opened with the smaller of the two keys. Inside, under a travel rug, I found Wallace's attaché case. I looked at it for a second or two. Three blocks away, a car had appeared. I pulled out the attaché case, shut the trunk and began to walk quickly down the street. At the first intersection, I turned left. Across the street was a hotel. There was a big awning out over the pavement and a revolving door. I hesitated long enough to catch my breath and then pushed inside. The woman behind the crescent of desk looked up.

'Ma'am? May I help you?'

I smiled at her and asked for a room. She fingered a keyboard and offered me a single on the third floor. She took an imprint of my Amex card and pointed out the bank of elevators across the lobby. She gave me the key and hoped I'd have a real good night.

Upstairs, the room was enormous with two double beds, a sofa and a fridge stacked with drinks. I opened the fridge and poured myself a stiff vodka and tonic. Then I sat on the bed, staring first at the attaché case, then at the phone. The time on the digital display by the phone said 10.16. Back in the UK, it would be quarter past four in the morning. One of the two numbers Stollmann had given me was his home. I knew that because he'd told me. I'd phoned him from Gatwick while Wesley went to the loo, and he'd been quite explicit about procedures. Early morning calls on the o81 number would find him at home. If anything developed, regardless of the hour, I was to get in touch. I shook off my shoes and reached for the phone, draining the last of the vodka. Then I hesitated, my eyes returning to the attaché case, the huge mock-brass clasps, the personal monogram, the four-digit combination. For a full minute, I sat there, nursing the empty glass, debating what to do. Then I got up and went back to the fridge.

I found the metal bottle opener hanging on the inside of the door. I took it back to the bed and held the attaché case up to the light. Where the clasp seated on to the lock, there was a gap wide enough to insert the opener. I did so, levering the opener back against the bright metal. For a while, nothing happened and I was on the point of looking for something else when the catch snapped and the clasp sprung open. I did the same the other side, quicker this time, then laid the attaché case carefully on the bed and opened it.

Inside were a number of files, buff manila, the kind you get in legal offices. On top of the files was the copy of the *Dallas Courier-Star* Wallace had been reading at the airport hotel. I put the newspaper to one side, and I was still sorting through the files when I found the gun. It was an automatic, a Beretta, wrapped in a handkerchief. Beside it, nestling under an American Airways timetable, were three spare clips of ammunition and a folded invoice. I read the invoice quickly. It came from a Dallas company called Sun Valley Arms Corp. Using his own name, Wallace had paid $795 for the Beretta and the ammunition. I went back to the top of the invoice, checking the date. It was 8 October 1991. Just eight days ago.

I took the gun out, unwrapping it, weighing it in my hand, trying the slider at the top, thumbing the safety catch. It was fully loaded, fifteen rounds of 9 mm parabellum. I sat on the bed again, wondering why Grant Wallace should have considered the need for a handgun, and what, precisely, had taken him to the Sun Valley Arms Corp. Then my eyes went back to the newspaper, still lying on the coverlet. The paper had been folded over at a page near the middle, and there was a photo ringed in red Pentel. I looked hard at the photo. It showed a small group of men enjoying a conversation at some function in downtown Dallas. The caption beneath read '*City Chamber of Commerce Welcomes British Minister*'. I peered harder at the photo. The face on the left looked familiar: the slight stoop, the hooded eyes, the mirthless smile. Frowning now, the gun still in my hand, I scanned the accompanying story, looking for the name, finding it. 'Lawrence Priddy,' it said, 'promoting British trading interests.'

15

I phoned Wesley at seven next morning. I got the number of the airport hotel from the Southern Bell directory, and I'd drained the last of the travelling pack of Alka-Seltzer I had in my bag by the time I finally got through to his room. Stress and vodka give me headaches.

'Keogh,' he said.

'Me. Sarah.'

'Where the fuck are you?'

'Hyatt-Regency. Sixteenth and Commerce. What happened to you?'

'We got busted.'

'Who by?'

'The guys you saw.'

'Who were they?'

'FBI.'

'They take you back to the hotel?'

'Yeah.'

'And?'

He laughed at this point, that same mirthless cackle. 'We sat around and talked for a while. They were very reasonable. Either I took the deal, or I didn't.'

'What deal?'

He laughed again, then spelled it out. They had reason to believe he was HIV positive. As a visitor, that made him illegal. If he wanted to stay, he'd have to settle the argument by submitting to a test. The four days it would take to get a result, he'd be obliged to spend in custody. If the test proved negative, there were no problems. If the test was positive, he was looking at serious trouble. The US health authorities, keen to defend the nation against doses of foreign virus, were currently looking for guys to shaft. It was an unfortunate way of putting it, but Wesley might just be one of them.

I nodded, following the logic. 'And?'

'Plane leaves at eight.'

'Tomorrow?'

'This evening.'

'Ah.' There was a silence while I tried to think it through. 'You want me to come too?'

'No. You stay here. We have to meet before I go, but that could be difficult as well.'

'Why?'

'There's a guy outside in the corridor. And they'll be listening, too. Calls like this.'

'Great.'

It was all so obvious. The woman at immigration at the airport had made a phone call. I'd watched her do it. She had Wesley's name, flagged on her computer, doubtless culled from intercepted transatlantic calls for Grant Wallace. She'd have told somebody he'd arrived, and there'd be some kind of surveillance team in place, either waiting on the concourse, or already shadowing Grant Wallace. I thought briefly about Stollmann, whether he'd had anything to do with it, but I couldn't see the point. He'd already gone to extraordinary lengths to insulate our enquiries from outside interference. Telegraphing our arrival to the FBI would have been daft. I bent to the phone again.

'What about Grant?' I said. 'Where is he?'

'Dunno. They took him off in another car.'

'Under arrest?'

'No.' He paused. 'His own car had gone. Nicked. From outside the restaurant.'

'Oh?' I exaggerated my surprise, wondering whether Wesley was right about the call being monitored. 'Really?'

'Yeah.'

I looked up. A maid was at the door. I'd ordered coffee and Danish. I told Wesley to wait while I collected it.

Back on the phone, I finally got to the question that had been preoccupying me most of the night. 'So what about me?' I said. 'They knew about me? Being with you?'

'Yes.'

'My name? And what I do for a living? They knew about that, too?'

'No.'

'Ah.' I reached for another bite of Danish. 'So what did you tell them?'

'I told them you worked for MI5.'

'Nice. Thanks.'

'It's the truth, isn't it?'

'Yes, but—'

'Then there's no problem. In fact it's rather neat. Gives you a kind of immunity.' He paused. 'Medical term. They loved it.'

He laughed for a third time, and I was still wondering about all the loose ends – the restaurant, my bonfire, Grant's abandoned car – when he hung up. I was to come to the airport mid-afternoon. He'd be up in his room. It would be nice to have a chance to say a proper goodbye.

While I got dressed, I thought about Stollmann again. By now, he'd be waiting for a call. Given the photo of Priddy still looking at me from the top of Wallace's attaché case, that might not be a bad idea. I dialled the 071 number, presumably his new office, from memory. He answered on the second ring, someone else talking in the background.

'Sarah Moreton,' I said briskly, 'phoning from the States.'

He grunted something down the phone, then I heard him terminating the conversation in progress. There was a scrape of a chair and the sound of a door opening and closing. Then Stollmann was back on the phone. For the first time ever, he sounded flustered.

'Where are you?' he said.

'Texas.'

'I know that. Whereabouts?'

I gave him the number of the airport hotel. He was still reading it back to me, careful as ever, when I cut him short. 'They knew about Keogh already,' I said.

'Who?'

'The FBI. They were waiting for him.' I paused. 'They're deporting him later today. Did you know about that?'

'No.'

'But they've been on?'

Stollmann hesitated a moment, as reluctant as ever to share the script with me. 'Yes,' he said finally. 'This morning.'

'Checking me out?'

'Yes.'

'And you obliged? Vouched for me?'

'Yes. Of course.'

'Thank Christ for that.'

There was a long, transatlantic silence. Sitting on the bed, I could see myself in the mirror over the dressing table. Lately, I'd been experimenting with a new make-up, an Elizabeth Arden confection. In certain lights, I'd almost convinced myself that the scar was invisible. I reached up, touching it.

'Priddy's here, too,' I said, 'according to yesterday's paper.'

'Is he?' Stollmann sounded less than surprised.

'Yes,' I said.

'Doing what?'

I glanced down at the paper. 'Drumming up trade,' I said.

I read him the piece beside the photograph, a report on the reception organized for Priddy's visit. When I came to the two individuals responsible for sponsoring the hospitality, he told me to repeat the names. I did so, pleased to have stirred a little interest at last.

'Harold Beckermann, double "N",' I said, 'and a Daniel J. Curtis.'

'What do they do?'

'Doesn't say.'

Stollmann grunted, and I tried to imagine him adding my tiny dollop of intelligence to whatever mosaic he was trying to make sense of. For a while there was silence, and I found myself looking in the mirror again, having second thoughts about Elizabeth Arden. Maybe I should go back to the Aqueous Cream. Maybe the consultant had been wrong. Abruptly, Stollmann was back.

'Where are you going now?' he said.

'Back to the airport.'

'You're *leaving*? Coming back?'

'No,' I said, 'I'm staying. That OK?'

'That's fine.'

I eyed the open attaché case, the unread files, the butt of the Beretta tucked neatly into one corner. Then Stollmann was back on the phone again, checking the airport hotel number for the second time. I told him I'd be there mid-afternoon.

'I'll phone,' he said, hanging up.

It was half past two before I left Fort Worth and returned to Dallas. I'd spent the morning sorting myself out. A cab had taken me to a downtown shopping mall, and I'd bought a shoulder bag, heavy embroidery, an Aztec design of some kind, reds and blacks against a sand background. The bag was strong enough to carry the contents of Wallace's attaché case, and small enough to keep with me. Further down the mall, at a bookshop, I bought a Rand McNally *Road Atlas*, the big three-dollar version, one state per page plus city blow-ups, and a nearby Radio Shack sold me a tiny cassette recorder, with a facility for taping phone conversations.

Back at the hotel, late morning, I spent half an hour at reception with a young assistant manager called Karl. I needed a car, plus a $10,000 extension to my American Express card. The latter, for now, I was prepared to raise via my own bank, back in Devon, where my Irish compensation was still lodged in a deposit account. Now, at the reception desk, Karl confirmed the car. It would be a mid-range Chrysler. The rental firm would deliver at two p.m. He'd ring me in my room when it arrived.

I thanked him with a smile, squeezed his proffered hand and headed for the lift with my atlas and my new shoulder bag. I'd paid the bill for the hotel, and still had $1600 from the float I'd been given by Stollmann. With my rental car, my newly blessed Amex card and the deepening promise of Grant Wallace's still unopened files, I realized how free I suddenly felt. For the first time in a couple of years, I had no obligations, no awkward relationships, no hole-in-the-corner assignations, no frustration, no anger. I had questions to ask, answers to piece together and money to make it all possible. None of it would be easy, but the responsibility was entirely mine, and if I screwed up then I had no one else to blame. I felt safe. I felt busy. And above all, I felt strangely content. I was, in the exact sense of the word, a free agent.

My father, ten minutes later, did his best to prick the bubble.

'What's going on?' he said coldly, when he heard my voice.

'I'm in America. I've phoned to say hello.'

'Ruth's been round. A couple of times. Your mother's worried sick.' He paused. 'About you and Rory...'

He let the phrase expire, leaving me to pick up the conversation, put his mind at rest, tell him everything was fine, no problems, nothing to worry about. Instead, I lay back on the bed, my head against the wall, my eyes closed. Rory. Bloody Rory. Even that name, at four thousand miles, was enough to throw me.

'He's in Iraq,' I said carefully, 'isn't he?'

'No. He's back.'

'Have you seen him?'

'Yes. Last night, as a matter of fact.'

'How is he?'

'Not well. He had an accident. As you probably know.'

'No,' I said, 'I know nothing.'

'Oh.' My father hesitated. 'Well, he did.'

'What happened?'

'He fell off a mountain. He's broken his leg. He's over in Topsham at the moment. Ruth's looking after him,' he sighed, 'when she's not up here with your mother.'

I nodded, permitting myself a small, ill-intentioned smile. My pulse had returned to normal now, and I was looking down at the contents of Wallace's attaché case. The sight of the bundle of files gave me a curious strength. I wondered for a second or two about playing the innocent, but decided there was no point. My father had survived the Falklands, for God's sake. A helping or two of the truth wouldn't hurt him.

'Rory and I were lovers,' I said, 'for quite a while.'

'That's what Ruth says.'

'It's true.' I paused. 'After Christmas, I broke it off. I told him he should stay with his wife. I said we had no future. He agreed.'

'Oh?'

'But he came back. Last month. For about a week.'

'And?'

'We went to Scotland together.' I hesitated. Even now, even here, the memory of that trip made my stomach churn. However bumpy the landing, I knew those few grey days in the gloom of a Hebridean autumn were the closest I'd ever come to heaven. Room 7. The Cuillin View Hotel. My very own taste of paradise.

My father was back on the phone. Something else about Ruth.

'She's thinking of leaving him,' he said. 'She says she's had enough.'

'She's what?'

'Leaving him. Going off with the kids somewhere. New start. New life.' He paused, angry now. 'I told her not to be so bloody silly.'

'What about Rory?'

'I told him, too. Yesterday. The man's losing control. He says he wants to marry you. I told him you wouldn't dream of it.'

'You're right,' I said. 'I wouldn't.'

'Oh?'

I laughed out loud, hearing a new note in my father's voice, genuine surprise, the noise a child might make, wandering into some conversational ambush. He was confused, now, and slightly embarrassed.

'Sarah? Do I understand you correctly? You *wouldn't* marry him?'

'Marry him?' I grinned at myself in the mirror. 'I wouldn't share a bus ride with him. And you can tell him that from me.'

'Are you serious?'

'Absolutely.'

'About me telling him?'

'Yes.'

'Thank God for that.'

My father rang off several minutes later. I'd explained about the money, and the bank manager, and he'd promised to contact the man first thing. He asked me, *en passant*, about Dallas, what I was doing there, but he picked up the reluctance in my voice and sealed the conversation with a brisk 'good luck'. Before he rang off, I asked him again about Rory's accident.

'Seriously,' I said, 'how bad's his leg?'

'Seen worse. Simple fracture. Man's making a fuss. It's his head he should worry about, not his damn leg.'

'But he's in pain?'

'So he says.'

'Hmmm.' I nodded. 'Listen, give him a kiss from me as well, eh? Tell him . . .' I frowned, searching for a form of words, something to return us all to planet earth, 'tell him good game, no bad feelings.' I hesitated. 'Know what I mean?'

'No,' my father said grimly. 'I don't. And neither would you, my girl, if you had to sit and listen to bloody Ruth all day.'

He hung up at this point, telling me to look after myself, and I was left on the bed listening to the AT&T operator asking me whether I wanted any other numbers in the UK. For a moment or two, I thought seriously about phoning Rory. I had the Topsham number, and there were clearly no secrets to hide from Ruth any more, but in the end I shook my head and said I'd finished. She told me to hang up and I did so, reaching for the first of the files, making myself comfortable on the huge expanse of bed.

I was back at the airport by four o'clock. I parked the Chrysler half a mile from the hotel and walked to the nearest of the airport terminals. Inside, I wandered around until I found a bank of left-luggage compartments. I stowed my new bag and Grant Wallace's attaché case in one of them, locked it and ducked into a wash-room across the concourse. I taped the key to the inside of my knickers and then set off for the hotel. At reception, I paid my overnight bill and asked for the room key to collect my luggage. When the receptionist reached for my key, I saw a note beside it. She gave it to me. It was a telephone message. It read: 'Contact me soonest, Eric Stollmann'. I pocketed the message. The phrasing made me smile. Eric Stollmann, I thought. Not a man to waste words.

Up on the eighth floor, I found Wesley's room guarded by a tall, wiry-looking man in a lightweight Stayprest suit. He was heavily tanned, with an enormous Burt Reynolds moustache and I sensed at once that he knew who I was. I paused outside my room, inserting the key in the lock.

'Ma'am?'

'Yes?'

'Miss Moreton?'

'Yes.'

'A word?'

'Of course.'

I unlocked the door and began to turn the handle, but the man in the suit stepped in front of me, flipping open a small leather wallet. Inside the wallet was an FBI photocard and I paused briefly on the way past him, inspecting it. His name was Pedern-ales. I glanced up at him, managing a brief, cold smile, and went on into the room.

The room was a shambles. The bed had been stripped and the sheets were still bundled roughly on the floor where they'd fallen. The drawers in the vanity unit were all out and the inside of the closet, where I'd hung my handful of dresses, looked like a battlefield. Only my case, oddly enough, appeared to be untouched. I walked across and began to unlock it. I pack in a particular way, very methodically, bulky stuff like woollens at the bottom, knick-knacks on top. I opened the case and found myself looking at my one and only pullover, the one I'd brought over in case it got chilly.

'Who's been through this?' I said. 'You?'

'Ma'am?'

'This.' I nodded at the case. 'Your work? Friends of yours?'

I looked at him. Agent Pedernales had no intention of answering the question. Instead, he'd produced a clear polythene bag, the kind the scenes-of-crime people use. It was sealed at the open end, and he held it out between two fingers for my inspection. Inside, plainly visible, was a green book of matches. On the matches, embossed in gold letters, it said 'El Mesón'.

'We understand you're with one of those UK intelligence services, ma'am.'

'That's right, MI5.'

'Good.' The smile did nothing for the coldness in his eyes. 'Then you'll understand the rules of evidence.'

'Evidence?'

He nodded. 'Arson, ma'am. A Federal offence.'

He hesitated a moment, not bothering to qualify the phrase, then he turned on his heel and began to leave. When he got to the door, I broke the silence.

'You get what you wanted?' I said. 'From the case?'

Pedernales paused in the doorway, scarcely bothering to glance back. 'Only prints,' he said. 'But that's plenty enough.'

Wesley let me in on the first knock. Pedernales, his message delivered, had disappeared. I shut the door behind me and locked it. When I turned round, Wesley was standing on the carpet in his bare feet semaphoring a message about hidden microphones. He was wearing a pair of silk boxer shorts and a T-shirt. He looked like something out of Ethiopia. He was incredibly thin. I nodded, an indication that I understood about the microphones, and followed him into the bathroom. He turned on both taps in the handbasin, then the shower. When he was happy with the noise level, he shut the door. Through the steam, he looked paler than ever.

'You get Grant's case?' he mouthed.

I nodded. 'Yes.'

'What's in it?'

'Dunno.'

'*What?*' he peered at me.

I beckoned him closer, up on tiptoes, my mouth to his ear. 'Haven't read it,' I hissed, 'not all of it. Not yet.'

Wesley stared down at me, shaking his head. Then he opened a cupboard over the handbasin and took something off the top shelf. He gave it to me. It was grey, about three inches long, studded with push buttons. You use it in conjunction with a telephone answering machine, phoning your own number from wherever, and sending a special tone via a tiny speaker down the line. The tone does something magic to the recorded tape and the tape plays back to you. I have one myself, though I've never used it.

Wesley was still looking at me. 'You know what it is?'

'Yes.'

'You good on numbers? Remembering them?'

I nodded. 'Terrific,' I whispered. 'Years of practice.'

Wesley looked at me again, then grinned, wetting a finger, very theatrical, and writing a number in the condensation on the mirror.

'Got it?'

'Yes.'

'Good. I'll leave a message. As soon as I get back. Stuff you should know about. Names. Some more numbers.'

'Why not write them down? Give them to me now?'

'Too risky.' He shook his head, emphatic. 'These bastards'll search you. They've turned me over already. Twice. Grant, too, before they took him away.' He paused, frowning. 'Try and find him. Tomorrow.'

'OK.' Grant's address was in the attaché case, neatly typed on the Sun Valley Arms Corp invoice. I looked at Wesley. 'What else?'

'Nothing. Until I get back.'

His eyes returned to the mirror, and I took a final look, making sure I'd got it right, before reaching for the tiny wafer of soap in the basin. Wesley watched me working the lather carefully round the numbers. When they'd quite disappeared, he frowned.

'I was going to wipe it off,' he said crossly. 'I'm not that fucking ill.'

I smiled at him, reaching up again, kissing him on the cheek, genuine affection. There was still lots of condensation on the bottom of the mirror, more than enough for my brief message. 'I need to use your phone,' I wrote carefully. 'Yes or no?'

Stollmann, as ever, was brief. He gave me the name of a hotel in downtown Dallas and a room number. He told me to stay in the States as long as I thought it worthwhile and confirmed he'd cover my costs. Only at the end of the conversation did we return to the subject of the Dallas hotel.

'Room 891,' I mused. 'Who would that be?'

'What?'

'This hotel. The Statler.'

There was a brief pause. Then Stollmann was back. 'Your friend, of course,' he said. 'Our Mr Priddy.'

I stayed with Wesley until the time came to check in for the flight back. I laid him on the bed, coaxed him out of his T-shirt and retrieved my case from the room next door. In my wash bag, I keep a small selection of body oils, stuff I've picked up from here and there. I use them occasionally at Charlie's, trying to apply what little I've learned about physiotherapy and other hands-on treatments. There's a school of thought that says that body massage can sometimes help people like Wesley, toning flabby muscles, helping circulation, giving a little lift to the immune system. I explained the theory as best I could, ignoring his protests, reminding him that the journey back would be no joke.

'Got to get you into shape,' I said, kneeling over him. 'Got to get you fit again.'

Wesley looked up at me, one huge eye, his face flat on the pillow, shivering with cold despite the columns of hot air ducting up from the radiators. His flesh tone was awful, one shade off grey, and bones protruded everywhere.

'I was never beautiful,' he muttered, 'if that's what you're thinking.'

'No?'

'No. Fucking active. But nothing to look at.'

I bent over him, hands flat on his back, the tips of my fingers working the muscle paths away from his long spinal column.

'You sleep with Grant?' I said. 'In Geneva?'

'Sort of.'

'Properly?'

'No.' He shook his head. 'That wasn't what he wanted.'

'What did he want?'

He shook his head, not eager to tell me, and I left it at that for a minute or two, letting him make up his own mind, not pushing, not wanting to intrude.

At length he smiled, turning over, oblivious to the erection I'd stirred. 'He wanted a cuddle,' he said, 'nothing else.'

I looked down at him. 'And did you oblige?'

He nodded, gazing at the ceiling, thoughtful. 'Yeah,' he said, 'I did. Poor bastard. Felt sorry for him.'

'And you? Now?'

'Yeah,' he said again, 'if you're offering.'

16

Wesley's flight left at half past eight that night. From a distant parking lot, I watched the lights of the Jumbo lifting off, then I retrieved the bags from the lock-up, returned to the Chrysler and took the freeway towards Dallas. On the outskirts of the city, I found a tiny motel and booked in. I bought Chinese food from a take-away across the street and double-locked the door of the motel room. Cross-legged on the bed, a carton of noodles on my lap, I was ready, at last, for a proper trawl through Grant Wallace's files.

There were seven in all, six devoted to an analysis of the period between the Iraqi invasion of Kuwait and the chill, moonless night six months later when the first waves of Allied bombers took the war back to Saddam. Grant had organized the account with great care, one month per file. Each file was prefaced with a typed chronology, a day-by-day record of who was doing what. Attached to the chronology were thick sheaves of newsprint – cuttings from papers, whole articles from magazines, even the odd abstract from the weightier specialist publications – and these provided back-up, sourcing quotations, amplifying key events, offering glimpse after glimpse of the national mood as George Bush tugged America to war. As a feat of archival research, Grant's files were a revelation. His organizational skills were faultless. He seemed to have a natural eye for detail. He was scrupulous, painstaking and extraordinarily neat. Curzon House would have given him a job for life.

In the motel room, I spread the files on the carpet beside the bed, going through them one after the other, looking for the small print behind the headlines, the tiny bits of evidence that would tell me whether or not Wesley's thesis deserved any more of Stollmann's precious budget.

November, it seemed, had been the key date, the hinge on the door that led to war. August, September and October, the months immediately following the invasion, Bush had spent in furious consultation: with his allies abroad, with his cabinet, with his generals, with Congress. At first glance, the circle had seemed impossible to square. The State Department – the diplomats – favoured sanctions; the Pentagon argued for war, but with an overwhelming concentration of force. The latter would cost a fortune, both in money and in blood. The money, oddly enough, proved no problem. The hat went round the international community and came back brimming with foreign dollars. But the projected body count, the real cost to America, went up and up. As the Pentagon talked gravely about 'Iraqi capabilities' – their million-strong army, their world-class artillery, their stocks of chemical weapons, their ultra-modern air force – so the risks multiplied.

On 11 October, according to Grant Wallace, General Schwarz-kopf had sent his first attack plan back to George Bush in Washington. Phase Four of the attack, codenamed Night Camel, drove a three-pronged assault towards Kuwait City. US Marines would storm ashore from the east, US armour would push up from the south, while Egyptian units took on the Iraqis from the west. It was a textbook plan and it included a number of important footnotes. One of them anticipated heavy casualties from prolonged artillery duels. Success would mean the liberation of Kuwait City, but only at the price of 20,000 American deaths.

Bush rejected the plan, horrified, but there were other predictions, equally grave, each painstakingly detailed in Grant's files. On the best available information, Washington's Center for Defense Information was warning of 10,000 US deaths, with a further 35,000 casualties; the Brookings Institute, 10,000 deaths, with unspecified casualties; while the Pentagon itself, having taken another look at the Iraqis, talked of a worst-case figure of 30,000 Americans dying in just twenty days' fighting. This, Grant pointed out in a pencilled aside, would be a disaster of Vietnam proportions, a national wound too deep for any president to survive.

I looked again at the first file. There seemed little doubt that George Bush, early on, had made up his mind to go to war. On 15 August, with the crisis barely two weeks old, he'd begun to compare Saddam to Hitler. The parallels were clear. Both men had grabbed without asking. The lessons were therefore equally clear. Only force, in the end, would stop them.

Thus, within a month, there were thousands of US Marines in Saudi Arabia, plus fighter bombers, plus offshore carrier attack groups. A force of this size, Grant had noted, was certainly large enough to defend King Fahd, yet within weeks George Bush had accepted the need for more. On 25 October the Pentagon had requested nearly half a million troops. Five days later, at a meeting in the White House, Bush had said yes. Sanctions were now ruled out. The war would now take place at some point between 1 January and 15 February 1991.

I looked up a moment, memorizing the date of that crucial White House meeting, 30 October 1990. Bush had delayed making the decision public for a further week, not wanting to sour the mid-term congressional elections, but that wasn't the point. The point was what happened next. With the growing certainty of war, Bush had been left in no doubt about the lack of popular support. Within ten days, presidential approval was at an all-time low. American boys weren't ready to sacrifice themselves for cheap oil. 'No, no, we won't go' went the cry in a dozen big-city rallies, 'we won't die for Texaco'.

The vehemence of the protests sobered Bush. They might even cost him the next election. So how on earth was he going to pull it off? How was he going to launch a major war, hammer the Iraqis, liberate Kuwait and avoid spilling more than a thimbleful of American blood?

Wesley's answer was simple. Given the pressures, given the military odds, given the popular mood back home, George Bush would do what any politician in a corner would do: he'd look for a deal. Not in Washington. Not in Riyadh. But in Baghdad. This was the core of it. This was what we had to believe. This was what we'd been debating so endlessly. Wesley in absolutely no doubt about what had really happened. I thought about it now, cross-legged on the cheap nylon bedspread, trying to test Wesley's furious convictions against the cold facts listed in Grant's files.

By mid-November, Bush was half-way to assembling a huge striking force in the Persian Gulf. Regardless of all the hype about

Iraqi prowess, he knew that Saddam would be outgunned. He
wouldn't be helpless, he'd certainly fight back, there'd probably
be heavy casualties, but no way could he win. That was the
strength of the hand Bush had to play. Every week that passed,
every next planeload of troops and equipment that thundered
into Saudi Arabia, lengthened the odds against Saddam. Saddam
was no fool. Saddam knew those odds. So what would he do?
What would bring him to the table?

I smiled, thinking of Wesley again, wedged against the window
on the flight over, fuelled by three hours of steady drinking, his
dinner-tray untouched on the seat-back table. We'd talked about
a pre-war deal then, Wesley patiently explaining its merits. For
Bush, it was obvious. Even I could see it. He'd win. He'd be a
war hero. He'd keep his people behind him. He'd stay in power.
But what about Saddam? What was in it for him?

'Exactly the same,' Wesley had said, 'word for fucking word.'

I'd frowned at the time, not fully understanding the logic, but
now, thanks to Grant, it was infinitely clearer.

The proof, if that's what I needed, was in the back of the sixth
file. There was a whole section, marked POST WAR in carefully
formed capitals, very Grant Wallace. Inside, he'd simply detailed
what had happened at the war's end, 28 February 1991, the
wreckage still smouldering on the Basra Road, the flags out all
over Washington. While Bush had talked of drawing lines in the
sand and standing up to naked aggression, Saddam had simply
left the last word to Radio Baghdad. 'Iraq has fought, stood fast
and triumphed,' they announced, 'it was a victory for our
people, and for our President Saddam Hussein. Iraq is master of
the whole land, and leader of the Muslims in the whole world.'

I looked up a minute, my finger in the text, thinking about the
charred Iraqi faces in the Extec video. Victory? Triumph? Then I
remembered Wesley on the plane again, musing aloud about
Saddam and what the Americans had been able to do for him.
As far as the rest of the world was concerned, he'd stood up
against the big guys. He'd survived the most intense air campaign
in history, and when the ground war started, he'd survived that,
too. The most powerful alliance on earth had been sent to squash
him flat, and it had failed. He was back in Baghdad. He was
physically untouched. And even the Americans had to admit that

he was still – absolutely – in charge. The guy was alive and well and busy shooting his own people again. By surviving, he'd won.

'You think that's luck?' Wesley had asked me. 'Some fucking coincidence? You don't think they had a little chat beforehand? Sorted one or two things out? Saved themselves a lot of grief?'

'Maybe.'

'You don't think it's amazing? All those guys surviving? All those American kids? And then Saddam himself?'

'I don't know,' I said, 'and neither do you.'

'No,' he'd agreed, 'I don't. But it might be worth finding out. Don't you think?'

The memory of the end of that conversation had lingered. Wesley was half-way home now. Soon, I'd have to phone him. I glanced at my watch, trying to calculate the time in England, wondering when he'd be able to record whatever message it was he wanted me to pick up. Then I turned back to the litter of newsprint on the carpet, reaching for the last of the files. Unlike the other six, there was nothing on the cover, no date. I opened it. Inside, there was a single sheet of paper. It was headed HAROLD J. BECKERMANN. I paused, remembering the name from the newspaper piece about Priddy. Beckermann had been one of the two sponsors of the reception he'd attended. In the photograph, he'd had his back to the camera: bald head, thick neck and a rather loud jacket. I bent to the file again, realizing for the first time that I was looking at a press handout. At the bottom, beneath the copy, a discreet line of text read 'Extec. Excellence in Technology'.

I read the copy. Extec were announcing the retirement of Harold J. Beckermann. The tone of the piece was almost reverential. Beckermann had steered the company from oblivion to glory. He'd taken it from a back-lot computer software operation in deepest Alabama to the cutting edge of the American defence industry. En route, he'd won the affection of his workforce, the respect of his peers and a multi-million dollar take-over by the Dallas-based Texcal Corporation. Under the wing of Texcal, Extec had flourished as never before. In this giddy rise, Texcal's money had certainly been a factor, but the real laurels, said the handout, belonged to Beckermann. He was the one who'd raised the stakes in the laser-designation game. He was the one who'd prised open all those foreign markets. And he was the one who'd now put a large slice of the company's fortunes into *Scarab*. The latter already looked a winner, and in a closing quote Beckermann himself drew a folksy parallel between the new weapon and his own career. 'Takes one homing missile to recognize another,' he said, 'and I'm sure we're both on target.' Quite where Harold was headed next wasn't clear, but there seemed little doubt that he'd end his days in some style. As a parting token of their gratitude and affection, the Extec board had voted Harold J. Beckermann Honorary President-for-Life.

I put the handout to one side, wondering where it belonged in Grant Wallace's research. There was nothing else in the file, no pencilled notes, no magazine articles, just the bare bones of the man's career, larded with superlatives. I reached for the copy of the *Dallas Star-Courier* for a moment, and studied the photograph again. Priddy, I knew, was at least six feet, but Beckermann looked almost a clear head taller, wide shoulders, spare frame. Without seeing his face, it was difficult to form any other judgements, but Priddy, at least, looked impressed. He was laughing at some joke or other, and for once the smile seemed genuine, even eager.

I looked at it a moment longer, remembering the newspaper report I'd read back in the spring, the announcement of Priddy's promotion. Now, according to the *Dallas Star-Courier*, Lawrence Priddy was 'a high-flying young minister ... tipped for the top', and I tried to imagine him picking up the paper and tucking it into his briefcase, yet more evidence that he was heading, inexorably, for a seat at the cabinet table. That, I knew, was the motor that drove him on, and I was still thinking about it an hour later when, showered and changed, I finally dropped off to sleep.

Next morning, later than I'd planned, I phoned the UK number Wesley had made me remember. There were the usual clicks and buzzes, then I heard an answering machine engage. Wesley's voice came on the tape. He sounded tired to the point of exhaustion. He wasted no time on small talk, but addressed me by name, telling me to get in touch with a friend of his in Washington. The man's name was Jake McGrath. He was a working journalist who lived in a Washington suburb called Silver Spring. He knew a great deal about the defence industry, probably more than any other journo in DC. The guy was a mine of information and there was little that a bottle of bourbon and a little patience wouldn't unlock.

At the end of the tape, after McGrath's address and telephone number, Wesley instructed me to acknowledge. Once I'd picked this message up, there'd be others. It was a little piece of MI5 subterfuge. I was to think of it as our very own dead-letter box. I, too, could leave messages on the tape, and he'd pick them up by calling in. The number wasn't anywhere near Guildford, but he'd check it regularly. If I wanted to short-circuit the system, all I had to do when leaving a message was ask for Connie. Connie was monitoring all incoming calls. She could hear what was going down on the tape. She was a little gem. He'd trust her with his life. I heard Wesley stifling a tired laugh, then he was gone, leaving me to say I'd called.

'Bye,' I said awkwardly, 'hope you're OK.'

An hour later, dressed at last, I was back at the wheel of the Chrysler, picking my way through the Dallas suburbs, looking for Grant Wallace. I had the address from the Sun Valley invoice. Two attempts to charm his unlisted number from directory assistance had both failed, but in any case I sensed it would be better to talk face to face. I hadn't a clue what had happened to him after I'd removed his car from the restaurant but the least I owed him was an apology.

His house, when I found it, was bigger than I'd expected, a sprawling two-storey place, brick-built in half an acre of ground. Grass lapped the house at the front. At the far end of the drive, beneath a carport, was the Lincoln. It looked, thank God, undamaged.

I walked to the front door and rang a buzzer. Inside, bells chimed. I waited in the warm sunshine, rehearsing my lines. I'd return the attaché case. I'd admit to reading the files. But I'd do my best to avoid discussing the Beretta. Whatever else happened, it was definitely staying with me.

After a minute or two and another go with the bells, I heard footsteps. Then a voice, slightly querulous.

'Who is this, please?'

'Sarah. Wesley's friend,' I hesitated, 'from Tuesday.'

There was the scrape of bolts being withdrawn, two sets, and then the door opened. Grant was naked, apart from a towel. His face was wet, his shoulders too, and as he stepped forward into the light I saw that the left side of his body was purple with recent bruising, a line of strange raised welts, lacing his ribcage.

Grant blinked at me. He looked younger without his glasses.

'May I come in?'

He frowned a moment, his eyes on the street behind me, then nodded. 'Sure,' he said.

I stepped inside. The house was cool, sparsely furnished, bare walls. The only picture I could see was a photograph of a woman in her sixties, scowling out of a silver frame. I glanced back at Grant. He'd shut the door, pushing the bolts across, and now he was standing on the polished parquet flooring, two pools of water forming at his feet. He waved away my apology, finding him in the shower.

'Where is he?' he said.

'Who?'

'Wesley? What's happened? What did they do to him?'

I smiled, hearing the anxiety in his voice. I'm lousy at recognizing true love but I was sure, now, that I'd seen it in the restaurant. Grant wanted Wesley, whatever the consequences.

'He went home,' I said gently. 'They deported him.'

'*Deported* him?'

'Yes.'

'How come?'

'He's got AIDS . . .' I hesitated. 'I expect you knew that.'

Grant nodded. 'Sure,' he said. 'First thing he ever told me.'

'Well.' I shrugged. 'They knew, too. So they sent him home.'

Grant frowned, taking a tiny step towards me, looking up, no less concerned. 'And they never touched him? Only those boys can be rough . . .'

'No,' I said, 'they never touched him. Not once. Didn't even try.'

Grant nodded, turning away, and I wondered again about the welts on his body. I'd never seen marks quite like them. I was about to ask him what had happened, when he started up the stairs, calling back to me.

'Is he home yet?'

'Should be.'

'I'll phone him. After I'm dressed.'

Grant talked to Wesley from a room at the back of the house. The call must have lasted half an hour. Afterwards, he joined me in the kitchen, a round, neat, eager little man, perched on a stool nursing a glass of 7-Up. For the second time in forty-eight hours, I realized how much I liked him. I apologized about the car, and the attaché case. I had the case in the Chrysler. I said I'd fetch it in before I left. Grant shook his head, barely listening.

'He's well,' he said. 'Isn't that great?'

'Wesley?'

'You bet.'

'Any message,' I enquired, 'for me?'

'No.' He shook his head, grinning to himself. 'You know something, Sarah? About Wesley?'

I hesitated a moment, hearing his voice quicken, wondering what Wesley had told him on the phone, the way the conversation had gone. Wesley, as I knew to my cost, was far from straightforward. He laid bait. He set traps. He'd done it to me, the first time we'd met, that night in his flat, the audio cassette lying there beside the hi-fi stack, the little surprise he'd prepared to bring our evening to an end. The man looked for situations, adopted roles, played them with huge gusto. Grant, God bless him, would never have met anyone quite like it. Hence the spell.

'Wesley,' I said carefully, 'is pretty special.'

Grant nodded vigorously. 'Class of his own,' he said. 'Bet your life.'

'Quite.'

Grant beamed up at me, getting off the stool, swilling his glass under the tap. From time to time, the bruising made him wince with pain.

'You know something else?' he said. 'The guy's out of his time, a hundred years out of his time. You know when he should have been born? What period?'

I shook my head. 'No,' I said.

'Eighteen-thirties, eighteen-forties, in time for the big battles.' He paused a moment, drying his hands, staring out of the window. 'I've studied the Civil War all my life,' he said, 'and I never met anyone closer to Jebb Stuart than Wesley.'

'Who's Jebb Stuart?'

'Jebb?' He looked at me, surprised. 'Confederate brigadier.

Cavalryman. Helped lose the Battle of Gettysburg.'

'Lose?'

'Yeah,' he nodded, 'lose.'

I frowned, confused now. 'And Wesley?'

'Same kinda guy. Brave as hell . . .' he shook his head, 'and totally outgunned.'

He hesitated a moment, then he took me by the hand and led me towards the door. I was doing my best to balance my coffee cup. It was still half full.

'Where are we going?' I said.

'The den. The place I work.'

'Why?'

'You'll want to know about Beckermann.' He smiled fondly. 'Wesley's idea. Not mine.'

Grant's den lay at the back of the house. You stepped down into it from the hall. It was small, cluttered and cosy, and smelled of a certain kind of pipe tobacco. The walls were panelled in pine, tongue and groove, the wood stained a rich honey colour. There were a number of nicely framed lithographs on the wall, scenes from the American Civil War, and a long shelf over the desk was piled high with books. The books were mostly biographies – Ulysses Grant, Stonewall Jackson, Robert E. Lee – and in the corner by the window stood a large Confederate flag. The room had an almost shrine-like quality, and looking round, taking it in, I began to understand the kind of scholarship that had gone into the Gulf War files I'd read. The man was a born historian. God knows why he'd spent his working life designing guided missiles.

Grant shut the door, then bent to a big steel filing cabinet. The bottom drawer was full of files, the same kind I'd found in his attaché case. He pulled one out from near the back, pushing the drawer shut with his foot as he did so. Inside the file were a number of photographs. He sorted quickly through them, a smile on his face. Then he held one out.

'Harold J.,' he said, 'in his prime.'

I looked at the photo, recognizing the shape of the head, the thick bull neck. Beckermann was sitting behind a desk which looked too small for him. He was staring at the camera, his head tilted aggressively up, as if taken by surprise, one finger still

anchored on some document. He had a square, weather-rough-
ened, outdoor face and a brutally short crewcut. Despite the
setting, this wasn't someone who belonged in an office. I glanced
up at Grant. He was bending over the desk, filling his pipe. He
looked at me, the same eager smile.

'Some fella, eh?'

We talked about Beckermann for perhaps an hour. Grant had
known him by reputation before he'd joined Extec, and what
he'd found there had amply justified what he'd read and heard
about the man. He was, he said, a born leader. He hated bureauc-
racy and loathed committees. He never hid himself away. Everyone who worked for him was allowed one mistake, and until that
happened, he'd back you all the way. In short, he was exactly
the kind of entrepreneur the nation needed. Without men like
Beckermann, America was heading down the tubes.

'You liked him then?' I said drily, when Grant paused for
breath.

'Sure. Even if—' He broke off. 'Sure, no doubt about it.'

'Even if what?'

Grant shook his head, ducking the question, but after we'd
circled for a while, talking about Beckermann's early days, his
talent for spotting opportunities, his courage in taking on the
major players, we returned to the man I'd seen, back view, in
the *Dallas Star-Courier*, the older statesman, Mr Honorary
President-for-Life.

'You still see him?' I asked. 'At Extec?'

Grant glanced up, sucking on his pipe. He looked, if anything, confused.

'I guess Wesley didn't tell you,' he said at last.

'Tell me what?'

'About me . . .' he paused, 'and Extec.'

I shook my head.

'Well.' He shrugged. 'I don't work there any more, not since
last week, anyway. They fired me.'

I blinked. 'But you *were* Extec,' I said, 'as I understood it.
Scarab? Laser designators? All that?'

Grant sat on the edge of the desk, both feet off the floor.
'Beckermann's Extec,' he said. 'Always was. Always will be.'

'And?'

'I let him down.'

'How?'

'I don't know.' He shrugged, visibly miserable now. 'He never told me, never spelled it out. I guess it was my fault. I guess I just pushed a little too hard. Who knows? You wanna do something well, something you believe in, you wanna finish it.'

I gazed at him, hearing Wesley in the slow Texan drawl, same sentiment, same philosophy, almost word for word. 'I thought *Scarab* was finished?' I said. 'Ready to go?'

'It is.'

'Then . . .' I frowned. 'I don't understand.'

Grant looked at me for a long moment. Then he got off the desk and went to the filing cabinet by the door. He opened the bottom drawer again and stood to one side, letting me see the neat row of files.

'A year's work,' he said.

'About what?'

'Beckermann. I was writing his story. The story of his life. A little monograph. A tribute to mark his retirement.'

'He was *that* important?'

'Sure. Not to me. To the folks out there. To America. I told you. The day I met the guy, I knew he had it. The more I found out, the more I had to tell the story.'

'With his permission?' I paused. 'He knew about all this? He was helping you?'

'Sure. It was taking a little time, but yes, sure. He used to give me stuff,' he nodded down at the open drawer, 'lots of stuff, letters, memoranda, old contracts, everything he'd kept. Here, look, see for yourself.'

I nodded, not moving, believing him, trying to get the chronology clear in my head, what Wesley would call the time-frame.

'You started when? Exactly?'

'Two years ago. Back end of '89. I'd been up at Extec a couple of months. That's all it needed. Meet the man and you'll know what I mean.' He paused. 'I'm a single guy. I don't go out at nights. I don't watch television. I don't do drugs. I don't miss for company. You get to have a lot of time that way.' He peered at me, intense, determined to make me understand. 'I've been scribbling away since I was so high,' he said. 'I did it like other kids play softball. Or go fishing. It's a big part of me. A huge part of me. Talk to Wesley about it. He understands.'

'I'm sure.'

'So . . .' He shrugged. 'Writers need subjects. Even amateur guys, part-timers like me. Guy like Beckermann?' He looked away. 'Perfect.'

'And you've spent a year on it?'

'At least. Probably more. I was getting up to date when he fired me.' He shot me a quick, nervous look. 'Up to date in his life, I mean.'

'Right up to date?'

'More or less. Texcal bought the company in '79. That was the big change. I'd got as far as drafting '85. Research-wise, like I say, I was nearly up to date.'

I nodded. Eighty-five was right in the middle of the Iran–Iraq War. Eighty-five was when both sides started running out of stuff they needed to kill each other. Eighty-five would have been a tactful point to close the curtains on any half-honest account of Beckermann's life. Assuming, of course, he had anything to hide. I was still looking at the filing cabinet.

'Had he read anything you'd written?' I asked. 'Beckermann?'

'Yeah, lots. I used to send him drafts, for his comments. He'd tell me where I'd gone wrong.'

'And you'd change it? If he didn't like it?'

'Of course.'

'So what did he think?'

'Loved it.' He smiled, rueful now. 'Grade A loved it.'

'So what made him . . . ?' I frowned. 'I still don't understand.'

Grant said nothing for a moment. Then he crossed to the desk and opened a drawer, taking out an envelope. He slid a letter from the envelope and read it briefly.

'I'd been doing the research for Mr Beckermann's last few years,' he said, 'off on my own for once.'

'Where?'

'Newspaper offices mainly. Cuttings libraries.' He pulled a face. 'I guess it wasn't such a smart idea.'

'Why?'

He said nothing, passing me the letter. It was handwritten. In six brief lines, it demanded the return of 'all biographical materials'. The stuff was to be delivered to the office of a Dallas attorney by midday, a week hence. Failure to comply would incur legal action. I looked up at the top of the letter. The address read 'Fairwater Ranch'.

'Where's Fairwater?' I said.

'Out beyond Corsicana. About an hour and a half's drive.' He paused. 'That's where he lives. Big holding. Runs cattle.'

'You know the place?'

Grant nodded. 'Well. I was out there again this morning. I had to talk to him. I had to find out . . .' He shook his head. 'Letter like that, a year's work, hell . . .'

'You don't want to part with it?'

'No.'

I nodded. 'And Beckermann? What did he say?'

'He was out riding. Way over towards Two Rivers.'

'But you found him? You talked to him?'

'Sure.' He nodded. 'In the end, I did.'

'And?'

He looked at me for a long time. Then he crossed the room again, bent to the open drawer, straightened a couple of files, an almost maternal concern for neatness and good order. His precious child. His creation. Under threat.

'What happened?' I said again. 'Out at the ranch?'

Grant didn't look round. He appeared not to have heard the question. Then he sighed, easing the drawer shut, standing upright, his voice muffled, and I was suddenly back outside, standing in the warm sunshine, Grant semi-naked in the open doorway, his ribcage purpled with welts. Now, in the office, he glanced round. His eyes were moist.

'He had a bullwhip,' he whispered, 'and he lost his temper.'

17

By early evening, I was back at the motel.

I'd spent the rest of the afternoon in Grant's den, reading passages from his monograph on Beckermann. He'd fed me bits he felt especially proud about, and after a while I'd recognized a pattern in his choice. The stuff I was reading was all similar in tone: long passages of hero-worship, totally uncritical, a breathless, adolescent celebration of what women's magazines would call 'machismo'.

In this version, for page after page, our hero had been the US personified: vigorous, inventive, resourceful, fearless. To what degree this was a figment of Grant's imagination, I didn't know. The face in the photographs looked far from saintly to me, and the plain fact was that survival in the arms trade demanded sharp elbows and an eye for the main chance. But I could see at once why Beckermann had been so happy to co-operate with Grant's little hobby. A helping or two of this every week would appeal to anyone's ego, and if its author also found time to develop a world-beating missile, then so much the better. But why, so suddenly, had the love affair come to an end? What had Grant touched upon to warrant so brutal a divorce?

Before I'd left the house, I'd asked him exactly this question, and when he told me again that he didn't know, it occurred to me that he might be telling the truth. His conversations with Wesley, in Geneva and afterwards, were surely part of it. Someone in authority in Extec, someone highly placed, must have been notified that Grant Wallace was sharing sensitive information with a foreign journalist. That, after all, was why they'd put pressure on Aldridge, which in turn was why we'd become involved. The word would also have been passed to the US security authorities, which explained the attentions of our FBI friends.

But none of that need necessarily have reached Grant's ears. He'd been nervous, certainly, about company gossip. He'd felt isolated, a leper of his own making. But at no time, he said, had anyone spelled it out, and as far as the FBI was concerned, two nights earlier at the restaurant, it had been exactly the same story. Fully expecting trouble, he'd been surprised, and relieved, when they'd noted details of his missing car and simply driven him home.

This was a puzzle – why hadn't they questioned him about Wesley? – but what still confused me even more were the circumstances of his abrupt departure from Extec. As we left the house, I'd pressed him again. The two issues, I'd said, were surely connected. He and Wesley brooding about the Gulf War. Extec telling him to quit. Cause and effect. Yet even put this way, simple logic, Grant had shaken his head, totally emphatic.

'Completely different,' he'd said. 'No connection whatsoever.'

'What?'

'The stuff in Geneva. The stuff with Wesley. What we talked about over there in Fort Worth. All that,' he shook his head, 'nothing to do with Extec.'

'You don't think so?'

'No. Extec were simply instructed to bid. That's all. The rest of it stank, sure, but that was national business, Washington business, politicians' business. Beckermann's no politician. Ethically, the man would never have stood for it. Never.'

'Stood for what?'

'Any kind of pre-war deal. Any kind of fancy concert party. Us and the Iraqis. No, sir.'

'You're sure about that?'

'One hundred per cent.'

'So why did they fire you?'

He'd shrugged at this point, eager to end the conversation. 'It's the American way,' he'd said. 'I was hired to build them a missile. The missile got built. Job's over. Job's finished. We all move on.'

'And Beckermann? The stuff you showed me?'

He'd shrugged again, reaching for the door. 'Who knows? The upside's getting as far as I did. Knowing the man was a privilege. I just pushed too far. Hell, we all got a certain amount of patience . . .'

'Your fault?'

Grant nodded, loyal to the end. 'My fault. Anyway, this Iraqi thing's much more important. I realize that now, meeting Wesley, knowing him. We have to get to the bottom of it. Have to. You read all that stuff of mine? In the case?'

'Yes.'

'You see how it all fits?'

'Sort of.'

'There, then.' He'd paused, out on the lawn now. 'That stuff on the promotional tapes, the videos, Jesus. I'd had my doubts already but it was Wesley really made me see it. The arms business . . .' He'd shaken his head, tidying a pile of grass cuttings with his toe, 'who needs it?'

'Beckermann?' I'd suggested, heading for the car.

We'd parted friends, a handshake out on the sidewalk, but I'd realized then just what a shipwreck Grant had become. Much as I liked him, the man was hopelessly out of his depth. He may have been a genius in the electronics lab and he certainly had talents in the archival field, but emotionally he was marooned in early adolescence. I loved his eagerness, his passion, how trustful he was. He had so much to give. What made me sad was the kind of causes he kept adopting for all that guileless enthusiasm. First Beckermann. And now us. Grant Wallace, I concluded, was one of life's innocents, and watching him wave farewell in the rear-view mirror as I drove away, I'd whispered a silent prayer. People like him deserved to survive.

Back in the motel room, a day later than Stollmann would have liked, I phoned the hotel number he'd given me for Priddy. While the number rang, a phrase of Grant's kept settling in my head. '*I pushed too far*', he'd kept saying, '*I know I did*'. What did that mean? And where, exactly, had his conversations with Beckermann led?

The hotel number answered and I bent to the phone, asking for Lawrence Priddy. The hotel switchboard put the call through and there was a longish pause before a woman picked the phone up. An American voice, young. I asked for Priddy again.

'He's taking a shower.'

'Could he call me?'

'Of course.'

I left my name and the number of the motel and hung up. Half an hour later, the phone woke me up.

'Sarah? Sarah Moreton?'

I struggled upright. A recurring feature of my brief relationship with Priddy had been situations like these. Not once had I been in the driving seat. Not then. And not now.

'Me,' I agreed, rubbing my eyes.

'Here? In Dallas?'

'Absolutely.'

'And free this evening?'

I looked at my watch, thinking about the girl who'd answered the phone. Like most politicians, Priddy was rarely without company. And like most politicians, he was never averse to trading up.

'I'm flattered,' I said. 'I'll be with you about eight.'

When I got to the hotel, Priddy was already in the lobby, making a phone call from a booth beside the reception desk. He registered my arrival with the briefest nod, turning his back to me and taking his time with the call. He was wearing slacks and a beautifully cut lightweight jacket. He'd never been fat, but he'd lost a little weight since we last met and it suited him. The flesh on his face looked tauter, better toned, and hours by some pool or other had given him a fetching tan.

'Nice holiday?' I enquired when he finally crossed the lobby and extended a languid hand.

He smiled at my little quip, guiding me towards the elevator. Only inside, did I ask where we were going.

'Dinner,' he said lightly. 'Where else?'

The Skyline restaurant occupied most of the top floor of the hotel. From eighteen storeys, the view over Dallas was breathtaking. Priddy had reserved a table in the far corner. He ordered me a large Margarita and a bourbon on the rocks for himself. We toasted his promotion, but when I began to ask him how he felt about it, he shrugged the question aside. Of far greater interest, it seemed, was my own career. What on earth was I doing in Dallas?

'Just passing through,' I said. 'Stopped to see a couple of friends.'

'Old friends?'

'Good friends.'

'Friends who farm you out to a motel?'

'Had to.' I smiled at him. 'Two young kids. Tiny apartment.'

'Ah,' Priddy nodded. 'No room at the inn.'

I accepted the rebuke as I was meant to, with a certain grim amusement, changing the subject as soon as I could. I'd seen the piece in the local newspaper. I was intrigued to know just how demanding these transatlantic junkets really were. Priddy, true to form, ignored the question.

'How did you know where I was staying?'

'I phoned the Chamber of Commerce,' I said. 'I told them we were friends.'

'Ah, I was wondering.'

'About the hotel?'

'No.' He smiled. 'The other bit.'

The meal was quite beyond me. The house sirloin turned out to be larger than the plate, and the accompanying salad would have kept most rabbits going for months. Crunching my way slowly through the ice-cold radishes, I finally managed to stir the beginnings of a proper conversation. Priddy, it turned out, was heading a trade delegation, in the States for ten days. The schedule would take him and his buddies from Dallas, through the Sun Belt, to a handful of important get-togethers in the fleshpots of the San Fernando Valley. In parliamentary parlance, he was fact-finding. What that actually meant Priddy never specified, but I got the impression that his pals back in Westminster and White-hall would – at the very least – expect a report on likely sales outlets for key parts of the British manufacturing sector.

'Like arms sales?' I queried.

Priddy looked briefly pained. 'Must you?' he said. 'At this time in the evening?'

I shrugged. 'It's a third of what the country lives on, isn't it?'

'Something like that.'

'Then I just thought it might crop up.' I paused. 'That's all.'

Priddy studied me a moment.

'As it happens,' he said at last, 'it does.'

I grinned at him. 'So what's the commission? Two per cent? Have I got that bit right, too?'

Priddy looked away, saying nothing, wiping his mouth with his napkin. The smile I'd expected wasn't there.

'Joke,' I said, 'in case you were wondering.'

After dinner, we left the hotel and set out on foot for an open-air nightclub which Priddy had been recommended. The resident group evidently featured a talented slide guitarist and he thought I might enjoy it. I wondered for a moment whether he knew what a slide guitar was, but I decided I wouldn't pursue it. He'd never before expressed the remotest interest in what I might like, and I was impressed, as well as wary.

En route, at his suggestion, we made a three-block detour, emerging at a street corner beside a tall, pre-war building. Across the street was an area of grass, and further down, a railroad bridge. A train was crossing the bridge, an endless succession of freight wagons, and I was still watching them when Priddy touched my arm.

'Over there,' he said softly.

'Where?'

'There.'

I followed his pointing finger. Where the bridge crossed the road, there was a grassy hillock. The road curved away beneath it, disappearing under the clanking line of wagons. I glanced back at Priddy.

'Nineteen sixty-three,' he said. 'I don't suppose you were even born.'

'Barely,' I said.

He nodded. 'They shot Jack Kennedy from there,' he said.

I frowned, looking around again, newly curious. I knew as much as anyone my age about the Dallas assassination. I knew about Harvey Oswald and Jack Ruby. I knew, too, about all the conspiracy theories, the conviction in some quarters that the whole thing could have been cooked up by big business, or the Mafia, or the CIA. The authorized version said three bullets, in quick succession, from the building behind me. I looked up at it now, then down at the road again, measuring the distance by eye, trying to imagine the motorcade crawling past, the back of the president's head cross-haired in the telescopic sight. It all seemed feasible enough. I looked again at Priddy.

'Oswald, wasn't it?' I said lightly.

He glanced down at me, genuinely amused. 'No,' he said quietly, 'it wasn't.'

We went to the club. It was over-loud, phoney and awful, a honey-pot for out-of-town visitors with a taste for early deafness. Looking round, I could see no one under thirty, and after two numbers I suggested we could do better elsewhere. Priddy agreed. Our beers were barely touched. We left at once.

Back at the hotel, we went to the bar. By now, for the first time ever, I was beginning to enjoy Priddy's company. Away from London and the social strait-jacket of Westminster, he was almost human. Two or three times, his guard had begun to slip and although he never began to accept my story about friends and kids and passing through, he gave out a certain charm that wasn't simply the usual hunt for advantage. Now, with a gentleness I'd never suspected, he reached out and touched my face.

'Remarkable,' he said.

'What?'

'How little it shows.'

I gazed at him, astonished. 'What?' I said again.

'In your behaviour, I meant. How little it's affected you. I can see it. It's there. But you carry it well.' He paused. 'And that's a compliment.'

I looked at him, wanting to believe him. 'Carry it?' I said.

'Yes.' He leaned forward, across the table. 'Nasty incident. I'm amazed you survived at all.'

'You know about all that?'

'Second hand.' He nodded. 'Yes.'

'How?'

He shook his head, refusing to go into details. After a moment or two's close attention to his fingernails, he glanced up. 'So why are you really here?' he said.

'I told you. I'm on leave. Vacation.'

He nodded, smothering a yawn, not bothering to comment.

'That boss of yours,' he said. 'Eric Stollmann.'

I blinked. 'Yes?'

'He's either very brave. Or very foolish.'

I frowned. Neither word, in my experience, was remotely applicable to Stollmann. And anyway, who was Priddy to pass judgement?

'I'm not sure I like that,' I said. 'It sounds like a warning.'

'On the contrary,' he said, 'just a spot of friendly advice.'

'Why would I need that?'

'Because . . .' he sighed, toying with his second bourbon, 'these things can be more complicated than you might think. You're in deep enough as it is. Just be careful. That's all. I'd hate . . .' He touched his own face, just below his ear, a gesture rich in implications.

I chose the obvious. 'You're saying I'm in some kind of danger?'

'I'm saying you should keep your eyes open,' he smiled, 'and your powder dry.'

'But tell me . . .' I hesitated, only too aware of the rules of this curious game, nothing obvious, nothing attributable, just a handful of dust drifting innocently in the wind. Priddy was inspecting me from a distance, his fingers drumming some rhythm on the table top. The concern on his face looked close to genuine, and for a second or two I thought there was a real chance I might prise a little more from him.

'Listen.' I leaned forward. 'I'm not trying to tie you down but—' I broke off, staring at him. 'What's the matter?'

He was laughing out loud now, rocking in the chair. Finally, he mopped his eyes with a handkerchief and reached across the table, his hand covering mine.

'You tried that before,' he said at last, 'and I'm not sure it was entirely successful.'

In the lobby, saying goodbye, I thanked him for his hospitality. It had been a genuinely pleasant evening, and to my relief he'd not tried to end it in bed. He kissed me on the cheek and then began to shepherd me towards the waiting cab. By the door, he paused.

'Tomorrow,' he said thoughtfully. 'I didn't mention tomorrow.'
I looked blank. Tomorrow was Saturday. I was hoping for a little sunshine and an hour or so by some pool.

'What about it?' I said.

'I'm going out of town. To a barbecue. I thought you might be interested.'

'Why?'

He looked down at me, smiling. As ever, he'd saved the best line until last.

'Little place called Fairwater,' he said, 'Harold Beckermann's spread.'

When I finally coaxed Wesley to the phone, it was past midnight. I was back at the motel, a map spread beside me on the bed. Fairwater was down to the south. Priddy would pick me up at nine.

'Wesley,' I said, 'it's Sarah.'

'Hi,' he said drily. 'I thought we had an agreement.'

'We do. I need to talk to you.'

'That may be a problem.'

'Why?'

'Can't say. Not on this line.'

I smiled. 'Is that the problem?'

'Of course it fucking is.'

'Too bad.' I paused. 'There's a man called Beckermann. You obviously know who he is. I don't want details. I just want a one word answer. How much do we need to know about him?'

'Lots.'

'So how hard should I try?'

'Very.'

'Thanks.' I was still looking at the map. 'How are you, by the way?'

'Don't ask.'

'Classified?' I said. 'Or just bloody?'

'Bloody.' He paused. 'You get hold of our friend in DC?'

'Where?'

'Washington. D fucking C.'

'No.' I smiled again. 'He's next on the list.'

I sealed the conversation with a big, wet kiss and rang off. Wesley was probably right to believe that his calls were being monitored. Even Curzon House would have the wit to order a tap, though after Priddy's veiled asides about Stollmann, I'd begun to wonder quite what was happening. Stollmann was a high flyer. Of that I was certain. He was shrewd, painstaking and immensely dogged. But brave? Or foolish? I shook my head, still unable to find a place to file the comment, folding the map, beginning to wonder again about Beckermann.

Priddy had hired a car of his own. Typically, it was twice the size of mine, a big Cadillac with deep-stitched leather and tinted windows. Next morning we purred south at a steady fifty-five miles an hour, Otis Redding on the eight-speaker sound system,

Priddy at the wheel in jeans and a plain white shirt. For the second time in twelve hours, he took me by surprise: relaxed, cheerful and glad – he said – to have slipped the parliamentary leash for at least a day. Beckermann's barbecue was evidently a private affair, a few old buddies plus his nice new friend from England. There'd be plenty to eat, plus a bucket or two of ice-cold beers, and a little something to keep the boys amused. When I enquired about the latter, Priddy shrugged.

'God knows,' he said. 'I only met the man on Monday.'

For miles, we drove on across the flat, parched landscape, views that reminded me of the duller parts of South America. Finally, in the distance, I saw a white fence, miles of it, enclosing paddocks. There were horses grazing. There were trees beside a modest creek. And in the middle of it, there was a sprawl of buildings: a silo of some kind, a couple of barns, and a big L-shaped house, wooden, newly painted, the clapboard a brilliant white against the surrounding browns and greens.

We turned into a working drive, the big Cadillac soaking up the ruts and bumps. Outside the house, beside a line of sturdy four-wheel-drive runabouts, Priddy pulled the car to a halt. It was a hot day, hotter than Dallas, with a fitful wind eddying up from the creek. The wind smelled rich, of mud and silage. I paused by one of the four-wheel drives. It was white, a Cherokee Chief, brand new, with huge knobbly tyres and bull bars at the front. The windows at the back were curtained and it was impossible to see in, but there was something moving inside. On the back window, there was a tattered Reagan/Bush sticker, the colours bleached by the sun. The sticker must have been infinitely older than the Chief, a treasured relic from the elections of 1984.

I glanced across at Priddy, meaning to point it out, but he was already half-way to the house. There were steps at the front of the house, up to a long wooden stoop, and I recognized the figure standing there. He must have been six foot six, the big spare frame barely touched by his sixty-five years. He was wearing an old pair of jeans and a denim shirt, and the cowboy boots reached half-way to his knee. His eyes were narrowed against the sun and he had a spent match dangling from the corner of his mouth. Priddy was climbing the steps now, his hand already out, the working politician again.

'Harold,' he was saying, 'nice to see you.'

We had coffee and muffins inside the house, a big open kitchen, a gaggle of men around the table, not a woman in sight. The men were, by and large, Beckermann's age. They were loud, brash, and self-confident. They danced a kind of ceaseless attention around the brooding figure of Beckermann, quietening when he grunted some remark or other, laughing when he made a rare joke. Beckermann's voice was extraordinary, a low growl, part Hollywood, part hillbilly. When I first heard him, shaking his hand, trying to make sense of his gruff welcome, I thought he was sending me up, playing Lee Marvin to my Julie Andrews, but as the morning wore on I began to suspect that he really did believe this brutal, tough-guy persona. The way he moved, just crossing the room, was all part of the act, the slow cowboy lope, stooping to top up the big enamel mugs with fresh coffee, distributing dollops of maple syrup for the hot muffins.

His conversation was mostly body-language, too, the words few and far between, the eyes fixing on yours, a curious yellow. He had a face that belonged to another age, wind-burned, heartless, deeply seamed, a face I'd seen in half a dozen Hollywood Westerns, the guy who rides in from nowhere and throws his weight around, and an hour of his company was quite enough to understand his appeal. If you happened to be Grant Wallace, hero-starved and barely out of the egg, Beckermann would be truly awesome. If, like me, you belonged to the rest of the human race, he was weird and rather frightening. The bullwhip, I thought, as I watched him toying with Priddy, quarts of Jack Daniels appearing on the table, the laughter growing more coarse.

At noon, two young men appeared from the depths of the house. They were overdressed for the weather, heavy working jeans and thick sweatshirts, and one of them had leather chaps of some kind strapped to his forearms. They picked their way through the guests and one of them had a quiet word in Beckermann's ear. I was back with Priddy at this point, who was busy putting names to the faces around the big kitchen table. They were all, it seemed, from the upper reaches of the Dallas business world, weekend cowboys with Timberland boots and flabby, downtown faces. One of them headed a big insurance conglomerate. Another was vice-president of an oil company. A third owned huge swathes of Fort Worth real estate. Between them, Priddy confided, we were looking at a gross worth of not less than three hundred million dollars.

The money came out a few minutes later, hundred-dollar bills tossed on to the table, Beckermann up one end, licking the stub of a pencil, drawing careful lines on the back of a feed catalogue. As the pile of money grew, he went round the table, asking each man for a name, scribbling it down, making a note of the size of the wager. There were three or four names. One of them, as far as I could judge, was Mogul. The others I didn't catch. When he got to us, Priddy's hand was already in the back of his jeans, but when he produced his wallet, Beckermann waved it away.

'Guests go free,' he said. 'House rules.'

Priddy nodded, ever the gentleman, pocketing his wallet again. When Beckermann moved on to the next man at the table, I nudged him lightly on the knee.

He glanced across at me. 'No pay, no play,' he murmured. 'Thank God.'

'What's that mean? You understand any of this?'

'Yes,' he said, 'I think I do.'

He leaned forward, confecting a laugh at some joke or other. The Jack Daniels was going round again, hand to hand, and Beckermann was hauling in the money. There must have been at least five thousand dollars on the table, probably more.

I looked at Priddy again. 'Give me a clue?' I said. 'Just one?'

The men were on their feet now, heading for the door, and Priddy was getting up, too. He had one hand on my shoulder. He gave it a squeeze.

'No,' he said quietly. 'You'll find out soon enough.'

18

We walked down from the house to the creek. It was very hot by now, the kind of heat you associate with high summer, and the ground was bone-hard beneath our feet. The men sauntered down the dirt path. They formed a kind of loose cohort around Beckermann, joshing with each other, belly laughs at one-line jokes I never quite caught. Beckermann towered above them, grim-faced, oblivious, his face shadowed by a large stetson.

I was still with Priddy, hanging back a little. He'd managed to liberate one of the bottles of Jack Daniels from the kitchen table. Still half full, it hung from his hand. From time to time, he took a swig, offering me the bottle afterwards. I'm not over-keen on bourbon but I swallowed it just the same which, in view of what followed, was probably just as well.

When we got to the creek, the two youths I'd seen earlier were already there. They were both wearing the protective chaps now, with thick gauntlets and high rubber waders as well, and one of them was bent over a wooden crate. There was something in the crate, but I couldn't see what it was. The creek was barely ten yards wide, the sluggish brown water drifting slowly past. On our side, a crude chain-link fence had been erected around a shallow pit. The fence was chest height, and the pit was maybe two feet deep, old spadework, the sloping sides baked hard by the sun.

Peering in through the fence, I could see scuff marks in the loose soil at the bottom of the pit, and for the first time I began to suspect what we were in for. Priddy's phrase had been exact. Something to amuse the boys. I straightened up, reaching for the bottle, slipping it from Priddy's fingers. I took a long, scalding pull, then another, and when I'd finished I offered it back to him, but he shook his head. There was a strange look in his eye, a certain gleam, and it was a second or two before I realized what it was. The man was excited. Just like everyone else.

One of Beckermann's guests ambled over. He was lightly drunk, sweating in the hot sun. He beamed at me.

'Y'all from England?'

I nodded, dizzy already, glad of the intervention, glad of a chance to talk about something else.

'Yes,' I said.

'Ya got this kinda thing over there?'

I looked at Priddy, helpless. Priddy smiled.

'Yes,' he said, 'if you know where to look.'

'Anything like Mogul? Ya got anything like him? Ya ever *seen* anything like him?'

Priddy shook his head. 'I understand he's unbeaten?'

'Right.' The man leaned forward, one fat finger in the middle of Priddy's chest. 'Ya never saw anything that could live with that dog. Believe me, I know.' He nodded. 'Believe me.'

He turned on his heel, howling with laughter, his thumb going back over his shoulder, pointing at us. I watched him rejoining his friends. They thought it was pretty funny, too. Priddy looked briefly uncomfortable.

'What's Mogul?' I asked him.

He shrugged, nodding at the wooden crate, now being carried towards the pit. 'Look in there,' he said, 'and you'll see.'

The youth with the crate put it down beside me. I shuffled instinctively aside, still watching. I couldn't take my eyes off it. Another crate had appeared, too, on the other side of the pit. The men were gathering round, squatting on their haunches, spitting in the dust, acting tough. Beckermann was amongst them, his back against a stunted tree, the position of honour, top dog.

The youth beside me opened the cage. Inside, I assumed, was Mogul. A clever arrangement with a leash meant that the youth retained control when the dog threw himself out. The dog was a pit-bull terrier. I recognized it from a couple I'd seen back in Devon: the huge chest, the squat body, the thick neck, the long square snout. The youth beside me was restraining it on the leash, but only just. I looked at him.

'Mogul?' I queried.

The youth shook his head and muttered something I didn't quite catch. I looked at Priddy. 'Orders?'

Priddy offered me a thin smile. 'Hors-d'oeuvres,' he said. 'I think it's some kind of joke. The other one's Mogul, the one over in the other crate. There are obviously a number of fights. This is the first,' he smiled again, 'the appetizer.'

The dog was in the pit now, off the leash. It circled the enclosure, nose in the air, stopping from time to time to paw the ground. One of Beckermann's pals, drunker than the rest, had put his fingers through the fence, and I found myself looking at the dog, hoping he'd bite them off, one brief moment of glory before Mogul emerged from the other crate and tore his throat out.

I looked at Priddy. 'This is sick,' I said, my voice over-loud.

Priddy didn't seem to hear me. He was staring at the other cage. The youth in charge had one eye on Beckermann, waiting for some kind of signal. Priddy stirred, acknowledging me at last.

'This is supposed to be an honour,' he said, 'given to few. So we might as well enjoy it.'

'*Enjoy* it?'

A roar went up from the crowd. Across the pit, Mogul was straining at the leash. If anything, he was slightly smaller than the other dog, but he'd seen him now and he was up on his haunches, pulling and pulling, his teeth bared, his whole body quivering. His teeth were yellow, and every time he barked, flecks of saliva flew off into nowhere. The other dog was ready, plumb centre in the very middle of the enclosure, holding his ground. In a moment, the youth would lift the fence and slip the leash, and several generations of careful inbreeding would do the rest. I'd no idea how long these things took, but I didn't blame the dogs. Around the pit, the big sweaty faces were pressed to the wire, the eyes wide, the mouths open, animal voices howling for blood.

I shuddered, watching the youth stoop to the fence, lift it, then release Mogul. The other dog, in the middle of the ring, threw himself at the oncoming pit-bull. The two dogs met, and for a while it looked evenly matched, both animals snarling, lunging, tussling for advantage. Then, abruptly, blood began to gush from the flank of the bigger dog. The sight of it, or its smell, seemed to drive Mogul to greater frenzy, and he threw himself at the other dog's neck, his jaws clamping on to a fold of flesh, the huge shoulders tearing left and right until the wound was raw and open, exposing the other dog's windpipe. The other dog stumbled, lost his footing, fell on his side, and then Mogul was standing over him, the jaws sinking ever deeper, the flesh tearing apart, the loose dirt wet with blood.

The other dog was dying now, gasping for breath, each new heave of the lungs making the blood bubble and froth around the gaping wound. There was a sudden movement in the crowd, and then Beckermann was inside the enclosure, hauling Mogul off, forcing a stick of some kind between his jaws, kicking him in the flank, sending him back towards his handler. Then he bent to the other dog, scooping him up, like so much litter, glancing in the direction of the youth we'd seen earlier.

'Here,' he grunted.

He tossed the dog's body at the advancing youth, and the boy caught it, staggering backwards with the weight. The dog was limp now, and he held it out, away from himself, trying to avoid the blood still oozing from what was left of its throat. He pushed through the crowd of watching men, down towards the creek, and as he did so I thought I saw the dog twitch. The men closed around him, and I still had the bottle of Jack Daniels to my lips when the youth disappeared behind a low bluff.

I looked at Beckermann. He was standing by the wire, surrounded by his friends. He'd taken a wad of notes from the back pocket of his jeans and he was peeling off the bills, pressing them into outstretched palms, settling the wagers made earlier. I watched for a moment. Some of the notes were wet with blood from Beckermann's hands. I saw one or two of the men showing each other, pulling faces, laughing, pocketing the sticky bills. Across by the Cherokee, another crate had appeared. More livestock. Another throat for Mogul to tear apart.

I shook my head, numbed by the heat and the dust and the hot animal smells, and far too much bourbon. The last dog was still alive. I knew it. I looked at Priddy, giving him the bottle.

'Here,' I said, 'take it.'

'Where are you going?'

He half turned, trying to restrain me, but I was running now, back towards the house. In the kitchen, where we'd met Beckermann, there were guns. I'd seen them, a rack of three rifles, in the far corner. With luck, I'd find ammunition. With luck, I'd make it back to the creek in time to put the poor bloody animal out of its misery. It wouldn't begin to make amends, but it was something.

Looking back, it was a daft thing to do, adolescent and hysterical, and not at all in keeping with my Curzon House brief. But even now, I believe I had no choice. Given the same circumstances, I know I'd do exactly the same thing again. In the face of evil, as Wesley once said, you must act.

The house was a quarter of a mile up the hill from the creek. By the time I got there, I was beginning to suffer. My lungs felt like sandpaper, and every breath tasted of Jack Daniels. I pushed inside the house. The door clattered shut behind me. I stood absolutely still for a moment. In from the sun, the house was cool and dark. I felt my pulse begin to slow.

The kitchen lay at the end of the hall. I walked towards it, aware for the first time of a voice. Someone was having a conversation, maybe upstairs, I couldn't be sure. It was a man's voice, English rather than American. He must have been on the phone because there were gaps in the conversation when nothing happened. I paused for a moment, wondering what to do, then the rage and the frustration came flooding back, and I slipped through the door at the end of the hall and into the kitchen.

The kitchen was empty. The guns lay against the far wall. One of them was a bolt-action Ruger 77, a good, solid weapon, easy to use. It had a Redfield telescopic sight, 4 × 40, and a scuffed leather sling. I began to look for shells. In the third drawer I opened, I found a box of fifty, 7 mm, soft-nose game rounds. Perfect. I took a handful and lifted the rifle from the rack. Hearing the door open behind me, I turned round.

A young man was smiling at me from the hall. He was wearing slacks and a blazer. He was tallish with curly blond hair, neatly cut. He had the face of a male model, with regular features and wonderful teeth. He must have been my age, maybe slightly older. There was a dog beside him, a spaniel/collie cross, friendly, domesticated, intact. With his dog and his blazer, he looked like a full-page spread from *Country Life*. Even the voice was perfect, nicely modulated, discreet public school accent, very definitely English.

'Can I help at all?'

'No.' I shook my head. 'I'm fine.'

'You're English? Over from the UK?'

'Yes.'

'You wouldn't be a friend of Harold's, by any chance?'

I shook my head again. 'Friend of a friend,' I said. 'Come to share the fun.'

He gazed at me a moment, speculative, picking up the irony.

'I called by on the offchance,' he said at last. 'Am I missing something?'

'No.' I looked at the dog. 'Quite the reverse.'

'What's going on then?' He glanced over at the table, still littered with empty bottles of Jack Daniels. 'Harold having some kind of party?'

'Yes.' I nodded. 'I suppose that covers it.'

'I see.' He pulled a face, then shrugged. 'Just my luck to miss it I guess.'

'On the contrary,' I said, slipping the rifle over my shoulder, pushing past him, out into the bright sunlight.

I began to run again, glancing back towards the house. There was no sign of the young man with the dog, but for the first time I saw the car amongst the untidy line of four-wheel drives. It was a Jaguar saloon, low-slung, dark blue, left-hand drive with tinted windows. It definitely hadn't been there when we'd left for the creek.

The path dipped to the right and I lost sight of the house. Ahead of me, already, I could see the men pushing up against the enclosure fence, urging on the dogs, another fight in progress. Beckermann was clearly visible, head and shoulders above the rest, but Priddy I couldn't see.

I left the path and began to track through the low scrub, hurrying on, trying to avoid the low clumps of thornbush and the termite mounds. Ahead, I could see a thin line of trees. There were crows in the trees and other birds I didn't recognize. The men were baying now, a deep animal roar. I paused a moment. The enclosure was hidden by a small bluff. I hesitated a moment longer, knowing that finding the creek offered the best route to where the dog probably lay. By the trees, I'd find the water.

A minute later, I was there. The creek was wider here, the muddy water dimpled with flies and midges. There were animal bones on the baked earth by the water's edge, bleached white by the sun, and further upstream I could see the empty skull of what must once have been a cow. I peered at the water, wondering whether the dog might have been thrown in, but there was nothing. I began to walk slowly back towards the enclosure, still hidden from the men, my eyes quartering the water, the way they'd taught me to do it at Hereford. Top left. Top right. Bottom left. Bottom right. I stopped again, the rifle cradled in my arms. The sun was hotter than ever. I could feel the heat bubbling up from the ground beneath my feet and the slow trickle of sweat down the middle of my back. The fight, much longer than before, was definitely coming to some kind of climax.

I began to climb the bluff, keeping my body low, advancing at a half-crouch. The top of the bluff was dotted with thornbushes. I chose the biggest of them, and for the last ten yards or so, I crawled forward on my elbows and knees, oblivious now of the thorns tearing at my shirt. Flat on my belly, hidden by the thornbush, I peered down through the coarse yellow grass. The enclosure was perhaps a hundred yards away, the men pressed to the wire, a blur of bodies snarling and yapping in the pit. It was too far away to judge where the contest had got to, so I put the rifle to my shoulder, bending to the telescopic sight, adjusting the lens to my eye.

Mogul was once again the smaller of the two dogs. His head and shoulders were covered in blood and he had the other dog on the ground. Belly up, the other dog was using its hind legs to try and prise Mogul away, but Mogul's jaws were buried in its throat and he wasn't letting go. From time to time, he'd back across the pit, pulling the other dog after him, then shake his head, ripping left and right, more blood.

I eased the rifle to the left, away from the slaughter, sickened again. The third face I found belonged to Beckermann. He was in half-profile, intent on watching the dogs, his eyes narrowed, most of his face in deep shadow. The stetson had gone. In its place he now wore a blue baseball cap. Across the top, above the peak, it read 'USS New Jersey'. I held the sight on his face a moment longer, fascinated by this man, by the intensity of his concentration, his mouth slightly bared, the spent match between his teeth, the big jaws slowly working. I shuddered, still watching him, hearing the long collective whoop of the men around him, the smack of flesh on flesh, big meaty handshakes when the fight was finally over.

I moved my body slightly, the rifle still to my shoulder, trying to find a new position, wondering about the creek again, the body of the first dog, the chances of finding him alive. Then, abruptly, I felt a shadow fall over me. There was a smell of bourbon and a voice in my ear.

'Don't,' Priddy murmured.

I lowered my head from the gun. Priddy was lying beside me in the grass. His shirt was ripped, high up on the left arm. He must have crawled up the bluff behind me.

'Why not?' I said.

'Because he's worth a fortune to us.'

'Who is? Beckermann?'

'Yes,' he nodded, 'and the bloody dog, too.'

'The *dog*?'

'Yes.'

I frowned, looking at Priddy, realizing how drunk he was. 'Why?' I said.

Priddy didn't reply. He was eyeing the buttons on my shirt.

'Why?' I said again. 'Why should we care about the dog?'

Priddy reached out, his fingers on my face. I pushed him away. He smiled, his eyes glassy, his tongue moistening his lips.

'You know who that dog belonged to? Before Beckermann got hold of it?'

I glanced down at the pit. Mogul was back beside his crate, panting in the heat.

'No,' I said. 'Tell me.'

I looked back at Priddy. He was shaking his head, changing the subject, asking me to give him the gun. I put the question a third time, who had owned Mogul, but he ignored me, easing the gun out of my hands, the way you'd treat a madman or a sleeping child, great caution, elaborate care. I hesitated a moment, wondering how far to push it. Then I shrugged, handing him the rifle.

'It's not even loaded,' I said, 'more's the pity.'

We took the same path back to the house. Priddy had spare clothes in the trunk of the Cadillac, and got changed in the bathroom upstairs. I returned the rifle to the rack in the kitchen. The Jaguar was still parked out front, but of the young man I'd met earlier there was no sign.

When Priddy came downstairs again, I was sitting on the stoop in the sunshine fingering the worst of the tears in my shirt. I could smell the roasting flesh from the barbecue, and I could hear Beckermann and his friends returning from the creek. Coming back to the house, Priddy had been insistent about not leaving too soon. Beckermann wasn't someone you simply walked out on. For an hour or two, at the very least, we were obliged to play the grateful guests. I'd told him then that I was going back to Dallas. If I had to walk, so be it. Beckermann and his friends disgusted me. There wasn't enough Jack Daniels in the world, I'd said, to make me stay a moment longer. Priddy had listened, the same faint smile, confirming that we had no choice. There was a certain protocol in these things. Like it or not, we had to stay.

Now, for the first time, Priddy saw the Jaguar. He glanced quickly around, frowning. The advance party from the creek was in sight now, sauntering back up the path. Of Beckermann there was no sign. Priddy looked down at me. The keys to the Cadillac were already in his hand.

'Shall we?' he said.

'Shall we what?'

'Move on?'

'I thought you wanted . . . ?' I started again: 'Isn't there some kind of barbecue? Aren't you worried about . . . ?'

Priddy was already clattering down the wooden steps, heading for the car.

'Not at all,' he said briskly, glancing back at me. 'Needs must.'

'Needs?' I said. 'Whose needs?'

'Yours, my dear.' He smiled, unlocking the car. 'Hate to spoil that vacation of yours.'

We hardly spoke at all on the journey back to Dallas. Priddy had found some aftershave from somewhere and the smell of it filled the car, a thick curtain drawn across the day's events. Neither of us felt much like a post-mortem, and instead I found myself trying to work out the real reason for our abrupt departure. One moment, he'd forbidden me to leave. Next minute, he was telling me to get in the car. So what had happened in the mean time? What had made him change his mind? These weren't the kind of questions Priddy would ever welcome, but by the time the long smudge of Dallas appeared over the horizon, I thought I had the answer.

'That Jaguar,' I said, 'whose was it?'

'That what?'

'Jaguar. The car. At the ranch. You must have seen it. I know you did.'

'Ah,' he nodded, 'the Jaguar.'

'So who does it belong to? An English guy? Blond? Young? Good looking?'

Priddy glanced across. 'Are you telling me, or asking me?'

'Asking you.'

'Then I've no idea.' He smiled. 'Should I?'

I looked at him for a long moment, knowing he was lying. 'You didn't expect him to be there, did you?' I said at length.

'I'm sorry?'

'Our English friend . . . bit of a surprise, wasn't it?' I paused. 'He said he'd come on the offchance, but he knows Beckermann. Must do. Uses his phone. Calls him Harold. Friends, probably. Partners, even.'

Priddy was studying the mirror, playing dumb. 'This could have been very simple,' he said at last.

'What?'

'You and me.'

'And Beckermann?'

'No. Just you and me.' He paused. 'A couple of days on our own. Away from it all.'

'All what?' I looked at him, half expecting an answer, getting nothing more than a faintly reproachful smile. 'Listen,' I began, 'the English guy I met. You know who he is. Just give me a name. That's all I want.' I looked at him. He didn't even bother to shake his head. I shrugged. 'There are other ways of finding out,' I said quietly, 'as you well know.'

Priddy nodded, looking at me across the car. 'Then I suggest you use them,' he said, 'if it's that important.'

Priddy dropped me at the motel half an hour later. After a long, hot shower, I phoned Stollmann. In London, it was nearly Sunday.

'News for you,' I said, when the number answered. There was a long silence. When Stollmann finally remembered my name, it sounded like he'd forgotten to put his teeth in.

'Sarah?'

'Me.'

'Long time,' he said, more coherent, 'no hear.'

'I've been away. With Priddy.'

'That's hardly the point.'

I waited for guidance, but it never came. I knew he wanted to scold me for not phoning sooner, but somehow he couldn't put it into words. Instead, I told him briefly about Priddy, where we'd been, who we'd met.

'Beckermann?' he said.

'Yes. And someone else. Someone English. I never got the name. Drives a Jaguar. Blue thing.'

'Harold Beckermann?' he said again. 'The one you mentioned? From the paper?'

I recognized a lift in the voice, a new tone, the closest Stollmann ever gets to excitement. 'Yes. Harold J. Runs Extec. Priddy knows him well. As of this week.'

'Is that a joke?'

'Not really. It's what Priddy says. If we believe him.'

'And do we believe him?'

I hesitated a moment. 'Yes,' I said at last, 'I think I do.'

'You ask him about this friendship of theirs? This relationship?'

'Yes.'

'And what did he say?'

'Not much. He just said they'd met on Monday and now they were good friends. That kind of thing happens in America.' I paused. 'There was this English guy, too. I got the impression Priddy wasn't keen on me meeting him.'

'You seeing Beckermann again?'

'Not if I can help it.'

'What?'

I frowned. The miracle of satellite technology wasn't doing much for me and Stollmann.

'This English guy I mentioned,' I began again.

'Have you upset him?'

'Who?'

'Beckermann.'

'I don't know.' I thought about our abrupt departure, wondering whether men like Beckermann took that kind of thing personally. 'Maybe,' I said at last, 'but that's not the point. The point is this English guy—'

'Sarah?' Stollmann was insistent now, his voice raised, a rare event.

'What?'

'Listen to me. Did Priddy take you back tonight? Drop you off? Wherever it is you're staying?'

'Yes.'

'OK. So what's the time? Your end?'

I peered at the bedside clock. 'Six twenty-seven.'

'Good. Then move. Change hotels. Cities, if possible. Doesn't matter how. Just do it.' He paused again. 'Do you have access to a weapon?'

'Yes.'

'Then take it with you. And for God's sake make sure it's loaded.'

I looked at the phone, speechless, a thousand questions forming in my pea-brain. By the time I'd got as far as putting the first one into words, Stollmann had gone. Hotels? *Cities?* I shuddered, thinking of the afternoon again, the hot muddy smell of the creek, the men's faces pressed to the wire, the death throes of the dog I'd wanted to shoot, the taste of the bourbon in my mouth.

I reached for the Rand McNally, then changed my mind and dialled another UK number. When it answered, I listened for perhaps half a minute, hearing Wesley's voice, the latest recorded message. Then I smiled.

'Nice idea,' I said slowly, leaving a message of my own.

19

It took me two days to drive from Dallas to Washington.

I went by car for two reasons. First, I was keen to get my head into some kind of order, and second, I was even keener to hang on to Wallace's automatic. Flying to Washington was obviously the quickest way, but trying to smuggle a handgun on to an American airliner was a high-risk occupation. Chances were, I'd get caught by the X-ray machine or the body-search, with the subsequent loss of the gun. The Beretta, I'd begun to suspect, was now more important than ever. Thus, thanks to Stollmann, the thousand-mile drive.

I spent the first night in a motel in Arkansas. After dark, America becomes a succession of roadside neon lights, but by the time I finally pulled in they'd thinned considerably, miles of nothing but the interminable pale grey asphalt. The motel I found was seedy – the middle of nowhere – and the rooms were even worse. The carpet was cratered with cigarette burns and the nylon sheets had seen a great deal of action, and when I turned off the light and tried to sleep, the air conditioning kept cutting in, whining and squeaking. I looked everywhere for a plug or a switch but found nothing. Finally, numb with exhaustion, I severed the only lead I could find with a pair of nail scissors. The rubber soles on the Reeboks I'd slipped on took the worst of the shock and I left at eight next morning, before the owner had a chance to talk compensation.

By Sunday evening, exhausted again, I was six hundred miles further north-east, an hour or so into West Virginia. The day had seemed like one long Country and Western festival, and I'd set the cruise control to 55 m.p.h., letting the endless ribbon of freeway unwind before me, singing along to Dolly Parton and Tammy Wynette, watching the landscape slowly soften. In Tennessee, for the first time, it was visibly autumnal, the trees flamered at the roadside, and as I crossed into Kentucky, I could see the first blue shadows of the Appalachian Mountains up ahead. By the time I got to West Virginia it was dark again, and I peeled off the interstate at a place called Friendship. Washington, according to the roadside boards, was still three hundred miles away, a six-hour drive which would take most of tomorrow.

I phoned Wesley's friend from the first motel I found. It was a tiny place, smaller even than last night, but there were fresh flowers in the lobby and someone had bothered to give the room a proper airing. I dumped my bags beside the bed and started on a six-pack of Michelob I'd bought from a store up the road. Later, if I was still awake, I'd find a place to eat. For now, while I was still coherent, I'd introduce myself to Wesley's friend.

On the message he'd left on the answerphone tape, Wesley had told me very little. All I knew was that the man was a working journalist, a specialist on defence affairs, and that Wesley rated him very highly indeed. He knew the industry inside out. He knew who was hot, and who wasn't. He knew where most of the bodies were buried. And, most important of all, he'd managed to keep his distance from the lobbyists and the free lunches that had corrupted so many others. Quite how he'd done this, Wesley hadn't explained. But it was, he'd said, the key to the man. He had what few of us ever achieve: real independence. That, at least, was Wesley's version.

McGrath answered the phone while I was still emptying the first can of Michelob. He had a deep voice, richly American, but with a strange, slightly breathless intonation. I was still apologizing for phoning so late when he interrupted me.

'You're Sarah,' he said. 'Wesley Keogh's friend.'

'Yes,' I nodded, impressed, 'I am.'

'You're coming to see me tomorrow?'

'Yes.' I hesitated. 'Will that be OK?'

'Sure.'

'You won't be out?'

There was a moment's silence. Then I heard him laughing. 'No,' he said at last, 'I won't be out.'

He told me to get a pencil, and gave me directions while I scribbled on the back of the phone directory. Then he told me to read them back. I did so, picking my way through Washington's northern suburbs. When I got to the top of his road, he told me to stop.

'Van outside,' he said. 'Big red camper. Ring the doorbell at the front of the house. And don't let Nghien fool you. He understands everything.'

'What?' I said, hearing the line go dead. 'Who?'

Next morning, none the wiser, I left Friendship and rejoined the interstate. A good night's sleep had done wonders for my nerves and I spent infinitely less time inspecting the rear-view mirror. After three years at Curzon House, I knew a great deal about surveillance and I was absolutely certain that since Dallas, I'd left no tracks worth following. If they found me now, whoever they were, it would be pure luck. By noon, a hundred or so miles south of Washington, I was even confident enough to slip the automatic into the glove compartment, rather than leaving it under a fold of newspaper on the seat beside me. The traffic, after all, was light. The sun had burned off the last of the morning mist. The mountains were glorious. Why let my baser instincts wreck it all?

Washington is circled by a multi-lane racetrack called the Beltway. I left it at the junction with Interstate 95, following McGrath's instructions. Ten minutes later, I was on the northern edges of Silver Spring, easing the Chrysler through the endless suburban sprawl, looking for Marion Street. When I found it, I pulled in for a moment, surprised by the small, single-storeyed clapboard houses, the weeds greening the cracked asphalt, the air of faint decay. McGrath's house was at the end, the red camper parked beside it. The street was a cul-de-sac and I stood on the sidewalk for a moment or two, savouring the air. There was little warmth in the pale autumn sunlight, and for the first time since I'd arrived, I could smell the coming of winter.

I ducked inside the car and retrieved Wallace's files. These, I'd decided, would shape our afternoon. If McGrath was the expert Wesley had described, then I wanted – above all – a second opinion. I pushed through the gate and walked to the front door. Beside the step was a concrete ramp. I was still wondering about it when the door opened. Half expecting McGrath, I found myself looking at a small, middle-aged Asian. He was wearing denim cut-offs and a very old T-shirt. The T-shirt was splattered with blood. He had a cleaver in one hand and a kettle in the other. He was grinning.

'You Sarah?'

I nodded. 'Yes,' I said.

'Come.'

I followed him into the house. It smelled, at once, like Wesley's place: bleach and antiseptic, plus flowers of some kind, maybe honeysuckle. At the end of the narrow hall was an open door. Beyond the door was a tiny kitchen.

'Please?'

The Asian gestured me into the kitchen. There was more blood on the floor and feathers everywhere. In the washing-up bowl was a half-plucked chicken. Its head, newly severed, lay on the draining board beside a rack of plates. I side-stepped the biggest pool of blood, remembering the phone conversation, trying to recall the name.

'Nghien.' The Asian beamed, pouring the contents of the kettle over the chicken, then wiping his hands on his T-shirt. 'Please . . . with me.'

We left the kitchen again. Down the hall, on the left, was another door. Nghien went in without knocking. The smell of bleach became stronger. I waited a moment in the hall, hearing another voice inside, an American voice, slightly breathless, the voice on the phone.

'Sarah?'

I went into the bedroom. It was bigger than I'd expected, and very bright, the sunshine flooding in through a huge window. There was a skylight, too, and a hanging basket overflowing with flowers. Beneath the skylight was a bed. In the bed, propped up on several pillows, lay a man of about forty, maybe older. His head was turned towards me, and a smile was spreading upwards from his mouth as he listened to Nghien. The Asian was speaking in a low, urgent voice, a foreign language I didn't recognize. At length, still watching me, the man in the bed nodded.

'You don't mind chillis?' he said to me. 'With fresh chicken?'

'Delicious.'

His eyes turned back to Nghien and he said something brisk in the same language. Nghien hesitated perhaps half a second, then darted past me. I heard the kitchen door slam shut, then, seconds later, a furious chopping. I still had the files. I looked at the face on the pillow.

'Mr McGrath?'

'Jake.'

'Sarah Moreton.' I held out my hand. Nothing happened. At length, I withdrew it. 'I'm sorry about this,' I muttered. 'Wesley never told me.'

'Told you what?'

'That you . . .' I nodded at the bed. A device of some kind was suspended from the ceiling. It looked like the top half of a music stand, the bit where you put the score. Beside it, on a swinging arm, was a mouthpiece connected to a rubber tube. Quite what you did with it, I didn't know, but Jake McGrath was plainly no ordinary journalist. 'I'm sorry,' I said again, 'I'm not doing very well, am I?'

McGrath smiled and then nodded at a chair across the room. I fetched it and sat down, beginning to realize already why it was that Wesley held the man in such awe. He had an instant presence, at once commanding and purposeful, yet relaxed and easy-going as well. He must have handled scenes like this for years. The embarrassment was entirely mine.

'Sunshine too much for you?'

I began to say no, but the head was already off the pillow, the lips reaching for the mouthpiece. He took three little sips of air, then blew twice, some private signal that the blinds, at least, understood. They clattered down over the window, softening the light in the room.

'Enough?'

'Fine.'

'You too warm? Shall I turn down the heat?'

'No. Truly. It's fine.'

'OK.'

The head was back on the pillow, the eyes watching me. I put the files carefully on the bed, where I could reach them, and pulled the chair a little closer. Beneath the thinning hair and the pale complexion, McGrath's face had a beautiful bone structure, and I was still trying to visualize what he must have once looked like when the door burst open and Nghien returned. He had two glasses with him. Mint tea. I turned back to McGrath. There seemed little point in small talk.

'You're paralysed?'

'From the neck down,' he nodded, 'yes.'

I looked at him a moment, understanding now why his breathing was so shallow, trying to pick my way as tactfully as I knew how. 'Must be strange,' I said, 'everything happening at mouth level.'

'You get used to it.'

'I'm sure.'

'No, you're not.'

I looked at him again, startled by his directness. Then I nodded, returning the compliment. 'You're right,' I said. 'I'm not.'

'Does it upset you? All this?'

'No,' I said truthfully. 'It's just Wesley.'

'What about him?'

'He might have said something. Told me . . .' I shrugged. 'It might have been easier, that's all.'

McGrath eyed the mint tea a moment. Then he smiled.

'Wesley lives in outer space,' he said. 'To him, I'm probably normal.'

We talked all afternoon. McGrath had an extraordinary gift for communicating, for reaching out. He did it at once, reducing the situation to eye-contact, stripping away the inessentials – the body-hoist in the corner, the bank of TV monitors, the adapted computer keyboard, the draped trolley beneath the window with its cargo of half-concealed medications. He sensed, with great precision, the exact depth of my embarrassment, or perhaps my curiosity, and told me just enough about himself to put me at my ease.

Twenty years back, he'd taken a fall on a motorcycle. He'd collided with unmarked repair works on a quiet suburban road and broken his neck. The break, he said, had been high, C4 Quad, and that meant lifelong paralysis below the neck. Apart from his face and his neck, most of his body was dead. He couldn't feel, or do, anything. In the immediate aftermath of the accident, he'd spent untold months in hospital, and there'd been a year or so of trying to come to terms with it all. His marriage had gone and his youth with it, but as he'd finally begun to adjust, there'd been definite compensations.

The last fifteen years, with the help of a large damages settlement, he'd been able to buy himself a new life. Money was the bottom line. With money, he said, you could do anything. It had bought him nursing care, transport and a driver who knew the right moves. He'd taken a Master's in journalism and learned a handful of languages, and for the last five years he'd earned a good living specializing in defence affairs. Anything published in the languages he understood could be delivered to the house. It came in by fax or by post. He had a secretary to load the overhead lectern and there was a neat little electronic device for turning the pages. He had a series of mouthsticks for the computer keyboard, and a database that was now the envy of several newspapers. From his bed and his wheelchair, he was as well placed as any journalist to monitor the follies of a fast-disintegrating world. The last year or so, especially, had almost been scripted for him.

I frowned at this, not quite understanding, and he smiled at me, nodding at the row of televisions mounted in a rack at the end of the bed.

'CNN,' he said, 'CBS, NBC, you name it, the Pentagon's wised up. Never begin a war until the cameras are ready. Never advance till the man yells "Action". It's not West Point any more, it's Disney.' He paused, looking at me. 'We'll be talking sponsorship soon. Maybe we already are.'

I laughed with him, understanding again the kinship with Wesley, the same black sense of humour and the same contempt. A little later, his story up to date, I told him Wesley had sent his love. He nodded, saying nothing for a moment or two.

'He's crazy,' he said at last, 'that boy. I love him too, but he's mad. This . . .' his eyes revolved slowly round the room, 'was an accident, nothing I had planned. But Wesley,' he shook his head, 'Wesley went out and *looked* for it. That takes something special. Either madness, or folly.'

'He didn't care,' I said. 'He knew the odds and he didn't care.'

'You believe that?'

'Yes.'

'Then he *is* mad.'

'Maybe.'

'And dangerous.'

'Yes.' I paused. 'But is he right?'

McGrath didn't answer. He was looking at the files now. I'd picked them up off the bed, trying to find the first one. '*Show him,*' Wesley had told me, '*tell him you're here to listen. Tell him it's his to call. Show him everything.*' I slipped Wallace's carefully typed chronology out of the August 1990 file and rested it on the overhead lectern. McGrath was already reading it, his eyes scanning quickly down the page. By the time I'd sat down again, he wanted a new sheet. I obliged, pausing at the bedside, looking down at him.

'You know Grant Wallace?'

'By reputation.'

'And?'

'He's a gimp. Like me. Different reason. Different history. But still a gimp.'

'Meaning?'

The eyes left the lectern a moment. 'Brilliant designer. No question about it. Light-years ahead of the field. But the rest . . .' He shook his head. 'Ask Wesley. He pretty much summed it up.'

'What did he say?'

'Thinks the guy should be in nappies. And he's right. The man's helpless. Arrested development. You ever read Spock?'

I smiled, not answering, trying to mask my shock. I'd seen Wesley with Grant Wallace. I'd seen the fuss he made of him, the arm around the shoulders, the public shows of affection. Was all that make-believe? A tease? A hook to extract as much information as he could? Was Wallace just another source? *Everyone's* fall guy?

McGrath had finished with August. I reached for the file marked 'September'.

'What's your judgement,' I said, 'so far?'

McGrath said nothing, that same quiet smile. Then there was a knock at the door and I glanced around, expecting Nghien, finding a woman in her early twenties. Seeing me by the bed, she apologized at once in a southern accent, warm, informal, friendly.

'Hey, guys,' she said, 'I'm sorry.'

McGrath looked up. 'Cathy,' he nodded at me, 'Sarah Moreton. A friend.'

'... of a friend,' I said, getting up.

McGrath scowled. I'd never seen him scowl before. It altered his whole face, a cloud that masked the sunshine.

'No,' he said firmly. 'A friend.'

I nodded, not arguing, glad to accept my new status. Cathy was looking meaningfully at her watch. 'You want me to come back later?' she was saying to McGrath.

'No.' McGrath looked at me. 'You mind if I get dressed?'

'Not at all.'

Cathy hesitated a moment, then shrugged, hanging her shoulder bag on the back of the door. McGrath waved away the September file and told me to start reading through October. He'd listen, while Cathy dressed him. Cathy was already bent over the trolley under the window. She obviously knew the routines backwards, quick, deft, practised movements. I picked up the file and began to read, half wondering whether this was simply a clever ploy to keep my eyes away from the bed. McGrath would know all this by heart, must do.

'First of October,' I began, 'the Iraqis make contact with the French Government in Paris. They're desperate for friends amongst the Allies. The French have done well out of the Iraqis. Only a year earlier, they've begun negotiations to sell Saddam an entire aerospace industry on a keyturn basis. They called it the Fao Project. It went through de l'Estoile, at Dassault. They were near closing the deal at the Mirage 2000 chalet in Vaucresson. The French stood in at six and a half billion dollars. Chevènement, the French Defence Minister, was especially keen—'

McGrath interrupted me: 'Very pro-Iraqi, Chevènement.'

I looked up. McGrath was lying naked on the bed. A tube ran from a condom in his groin to a bag taped to the frame of the bed. Cathy was bent over him, examining every part of his body, checking it quickly, eyes and fingertips, and I remembered Wesley's line about being on patrol, day and night, trying to judge which bit of you might give out next. I'd read a little about paralysis, about the dangers of bedsores turning into gangrenous ulcers. This woman, Cathy, was McGrath's defence. She was the one on patrol. It was her job to keep him in one piece.

'He founded the Franco-Iraqi Friendship Society,' McGrath was saying. 'You listening?'

'Oh, yes.' I reddened. 'I'm sorry.'

'You want more on that?'

I shook my head, still scarlet, returning to the text. Cathy was back across the room now, selecting clothes from the closet, holding them up, one by one, while McGrath chose what to wear. A loose pair of cord trousers got a firm yes. There was a wheelchair beside the trolley. The trousers went on to the wheelchair.

'October the fourth,' I read, 'French President, François Mitterrand, puts a peace plan of his own to King Fahd in Saudi Arabia. Fahd likes it . . .'

I looked up. Cathy had disconnected the tube from the urine bag and begun to work the trousers up McGrath's legs. His legs were thin and hairless, the muscles wasted, the flesh pale. I bent to the notes again, more about the French, and I was still in mid-October when Cathy started to wind a thick corset around McGrath's stomach. A strip of Velcro bound it tight. McGrath glanced across at me.

'You wanna watch this?' he said. 'Only Cathy's world class.'

I stopped reading, putting the file down while Cathy drew the wheelchair towards the bed, readying it for McGrath's body. Then she turned back towards him, working her hands inside the corset, pulling McGrath gently upright until his body was perfectly balanced. She hesitated a moment, taking the shallowest of breaths, then she lifted him off the bed, a single easy movement, transferring him on to the wheelchair. I got up, pure instinct, thinking she needed help, but she shook her head, aware of me by the bed, McGrath's body sagging over hers, thin, pale, floppy, doll-like, only the eyes moving, ever-watchful.

In the chair, she folded his hands in his lap and arranged his feet on the metal foot supports. Then she opened his trousers and re-connected the tube to the condom, and as she did so I had a sudden vision of the way it would probably be with Wesley, once the virus got past the last of his defences, leaving him helpless, a list of jobs that someone else would have to do while he waited to die. I looked away a moment, knowing with absolute certainty that it would be me in Cathy's place, me with the comb, me with the mirror, me with the bright smile and the tuneless whistle. Wesley, back in the Guildford flat the first time we'd met, had been spot on. None of the rest of it mattered. Not, at least, compared to this.

I shook my head, trying to concentrate again. McGrath was looking at the files in my lap. He sounded thoughtful.

'Wallace has a point about the French,' he said slowly. 'That had occurred to me, too.'

Later, Cathy gone, I wheeled McGrath down the ramp beside the front door and along the concrete path that skirted the side of the house. At the back of the house there was half an acre or so of cultivated garden. The ground was carefully turned, neat rows of zucchini and maize, a stand of runner beans, a fenced-off chicken run. In the far corner, nicely sheltered, was a magnificent cannabis plant. I brought the wheelchair to a halt beside the latter. We'd been talking about Wallace again. I reached for one of the cannabis leaves, and broke it off, rubbing it between my fingers, then holding them beneath McGrath's nose. He said he smoked regularly. He said it often helped.

'Wallace . . .' I said. 'Did you know about his little project? The stuff he's doing about Beckermann?'

McGrath nodded. 'Wesley told me. And one or two other guys. Beckermann humours him. He does it to keep him on the team. Guy's far too valuable to lose.'

'But they've just sacked him. Wesley tell you that, too?'

'What?' McGrath's head jerked up. I'd seen the reaction once or twice before, back in the bedroom. It meant that something was bothering him.

'Sacked him,' I said again. 'Wallace got fired. A few days ago.'

'Who by?'

'Beckermann.' I frowned. 'I think.'

'Why? He tell you that?'

'No. He said it had to do with the business. Routine thing. The work ran out. He was very philosophical about it. A real stoic.'

'That's nonsense. There's work there for as long as he wants it. *Scarab*'s going longer-range. There's an enhancement programme. They'll need him for that.'

'Too bad,' I said. 'He's gone.'

I pushed the wheelchair on. We stopped by the chicken run.

McGrath asked me to toss in some handfuls of feed from a hopper by the water butt. I threw in the grain. The chickens bustled around, a blur of pecking heads.

'Do you know Beckermann at all?' I said.

'No.'

'Seen him on TV?'

'Of course.'

'So what do you think?'

'Think?' He looked up at me. Beyond a certain angle, his head wouldn't go up any more. I circled the wheelchair, giving him a better view.

'Well?' I said.

There was a long silence. I could hear Nghien in the kitchen. He was singing.

'Wesley volunteer me for this?' McGrath said at last.

I smiled, trying to soften the question. 'He said you might help,' I murmured, 'that's all.'

'Why?' he said. 'Why does he think that?'

'I don't know.' I paused. 'Except that he admires you a great deal.' I smiled again. 'He thinks you're straight. He thinks you care.'

'That's not an answer.'

'To Wesley, it probably is.'

'Yeah.' McGrath nodded, grim-faced. 'You're right. That's his problem. Doesn't know the difference between morality and good sense. Blacks are blacks, the way Wesley sees it. Whites are whites. Very neat. Very straightforward.' He looked up at me again, squinting in the low sunlight. 'Don't get me wrong. I've heard the theory. I know what he thinks. I know what he's after, from me. But some things just ain't that simple . . .' he paused, 'and one of them's Beckermann.'

I nodded. 'Wesley says he's highly placed.'

'Wesley's right.' He fell quiet for a while, a long, brooding silence, his body held upright in the wheelchair by a thick retaining strap around his chest. At length, the head jolted up again. 'Everywhere there's a middle to it all,' he muttered, 'an inner circle. My country. Your country. Everywhere. It's not something you can see. Or photograph. Or hold to account. Or even vote for. But it exists, believe me. Here, the last ten years, it's been pretty much the same people. Oil people. West Coast people. Newish money, looking for a home.'

'And Beckermann?'

McGrath fell silent again. 'Beckermann's part of it, sure,' he said at last.

I waited, wanting him to elaborate, but nothing happened. I was still thinking about Wallace, the files in his office, the precise point when his crush on Beckermann took him into dangerous territory. What had he asked the man? Where was he headed?

McGrath was looking at the chickens again. When he spoke, his voice was low. 'Wesley gets some funny ideas,' he said.

'You don't think it's true?'

'I don't mean that. I'm not talking about that. I'm talking about me. All this . . .' He paused, his chin on his chest. 'I guess he thinks I'm braver than I really am. You know what I'm trying to say?'

'Not really.'

There was another long silence. Then Nghien appeared in the garden, a phrase or two of Vietnamese. McGrath blinked, answering him at once in his own language. He'd acquired Nghien through one of the Veterans Hospitals. Nghien had been a marine in the South Vietnamese Army. He'd been injured in the fall of Saigon and helicoptered out. McGrath said the two of them were very close. Now, McGrath had evidently said something funny. Nghien ran back into the kitchen, cackling with laughter. McGrath fell silent again.

At length, he sighed. 'Wesley thinks I've nothing to lose,' he said, 'that's what he really thinks. He thinks I'm so far down the road, nothing else is gonna make much difference.' He paused. 'He's wrong. If you end up with nothing but your head, you get pretty damn careful about keeping it in one piece. Years ago—' he broke off.

I bent towards him. 'Yes?'

'Years ago,' he began again, 'at the start of all this, I made a decision. I decided to end it. I'd nothing left. Nothing. No wife. No body. No prospects. Nothing. So . . . endgame . . . zappo.' He smiled, rueful. 'Problem was, how to do it?' He looked up. 'You with me?'

'Yes.'

'So, OK, I had a wheelchair, an electric wheelchair. The front door of the place I lived in, they kept it locked. One day, I found it open. I took the chair out on to the porch. There were steps from that porch down to the sidewalk. I'd counted them. There were seventeen. Seventeen steps. That was enough to kill me. No question. I'd just hit the toggle with my chin and zap. Finito.' He shook his head, the faintest whistle of breath leaving his thin body. 'And you know what stopped me?'

I shook my head. 'No,' I said.

'The thought that I might screw up. That I might only half do it. That I might end up even worse than now. My head ... the inside of my head. Can you imagine that? Being brain-damaged? Not being able to speak or hear? But having just enough cells left to realize how *lucky* I'd been? The way I am now?' He smiled again. 'Interesting thought, eh? Me? Now? *Lucky?*'

I looked down at him, following the logic, wiser now about how cautious he'd become.

'You think Beckermann might ... ?'

The head jerked up. 'He's a powerful man. He has a lot to lose. So do others, including me. There's not much left to damage. But it's all I've got.'

'And Wesley?'

'Wesley's a goner. Wesley's past tense, and he knows it. That's what makes him so dangerous.'

'But do you think he's right? About the war?'

McGrath looked up at me again. There was a bleakness in his eyes, and I knew that was the closest I'd get to an answer. I hesitated a moment. There was a clatter of plates from the kitchen. The conversation was nearly at an end.

'There's an Englishman I met at Beckermann's place,' I said quickly. 'He's about thirty. Drives a Jaguar. We were never introduced. I think he must be a friend.' I paused. 'Know who I mean?'

McGrath frowned for a moment. 'Beckermann's line of business? Arms sales?'

'Maybe.'

'Blond? Six one? Six two?'

'Yes.'

'And English, you say?'

'Yes.'

I knelt beside him, scooping another handful of corn from the hopper, waiting for a name. The chickens had nearly finished by the time it came.

'Peter Devlin,' McGrath said quietly. 'I'd have thought you'd have guessed.'

20

I phoned Wesley from a call box in a large shopping mall on the edge of Silver Spring. It was half past eleven at night and the place was quite empty.

'Devlin,' I said, when he answered.

It took him a second or two to sort himself out. For half past four in the morning, I didn't blame him.

'What?'

'Devlin. Peter Devlin.'

'What about him?'

'He's out here. In Dallas. He's working with Beckermann. He's part of it all.'

I paused, trying to picture Wesley in the darkened flat. Eight hours in McGrath's company had given me a new perspective on AIDS. Maybe, after all, there were worse things than dying. Wesley came back on the phone. He sounded awake at last.

'What made you phone here?' he said. 'I told you not to.'

'Devlin,' I repeated.

'Listen—'

'Devlin,' I said for the fourth time.

There was a silence. Then, reluctantly, he acknowledged the name. 'Polly's son?' he said. 'In Dallas?'

'Yes. I've got an address.' I fumbled in my bag. 'Devlin, Coffey and Sweetman. That mean anything?'

'No.' he paused. 'But why are you phoning here? What's wrong with the other number?'

'Nothing,' I lied, 'except it's always engaged.'

'Try again, then,' he said, 'and stay on the fucking case.'

The phone went dead and I backed slowly out of the call box, still uncertain whether the name had really registered or not.

'Polly' Devlin was a cabinet minister. His real name was Anthony but people in the know, people like Wesley, called him Polly because of his closeness to his ex-leader. For years, clambering up the ladder, he'd faithfully parroted her views. What she believed, he believed. In due course, to no one's surprise, he'd earned his rewards. First, he'd become a junior minister, non-cabinet rank. Then, after a major reshuffle, she'd led him to the bridge and given him a turn at the wheel. Secretary of State at the Department of Trade and Industry. One of the UK's key posts.

I walked slowly back across the car park. For whatever reason, I'd never made the connection. There'd been whispers about Devlin's son, certainly. I'd heard them in the usual ebb and flow of Whitehall chit-chat, rumours and counter-rumours that washed around the great bureaucracies. One or two had even ended up in the Curzon House files: stories about commodity deals in Central America, information from a British businessman about a hushed-up Customs arrest in Miami, even a whisper linking Peter Devlin to the Fort Lauderdale arm of a Mafia cocaine cartel. None of this had ever been substantiated, and in the political culture of the late eighties, much of it had done him no harm at all. On the contrary, it was proof positive that young Devlin had the wit and the footwork to mix it with the best of them. But arms dealing? With Beckermann? And the Iraqis?

That, with some reluctance, had been McGrath's contribution. Over dinner, while Nghien fed him spoonfuls of chopped noodles and shredded chicken, he'd taken me as far as he was prepared to go. Peter Devlin, he'd said, had recently established a base in Dallas. Like many businessmen, he'd recognized the end of the Iran–Iraq war as an enormous opportunity. Iraq needed re-equipping. She had oil money. She had limitless ambition. And so Devlin had joined the immigration queues at Saddam Hussein Airport, focusing his energies on feeding the voracious Iraqi war machine.

And it hadn't stopped there. The Persian Gulf was full of the kind of tensions that only big money can generate. The one, McGrath had pointed out, fed off the other, a neat symbiosis. Wherever you looked – Kuwait, Saudi, Oman, the Emirates – there were ruling families desperate to swop a little of their wealth for another few years in the sun. That meant weapons, the best

stuff off the shelf, the latest armour, the smartest bombs, prefer-
ably a bigger helping than the next guy down the Gulf. In the
supply of all this hardware, there were problems, sure, but
nothing that money and influence couldn't sort out. If item A
was deemed off-limits for the Middle East, then it was simply re-
routed via another destination. At every stage, there'd be kick-
backs and commissions, but what mattered was that the stuff still
got through. The Middle East was a giant bazaar. With the right
word in the right ear, the Arabs could buy anything.

But Devlin, I'd said. What about Peter Devlin?

McGrath had pondered the question, signalling Nghien for
more rice wine, watching the little Asian dancing round the table
with the carafe. The carafe had a long glass spout. He held it
above McGrath's open mouth, inch-perfect with the pale gold
stream.

'Devlin,' he'd said at length, 'brought blessings.'

'Blessings?'

'Some of the UK stuff was embargoed. It was politically sensitive. Clients would need to be assured it would arrive . . .' he
smiled, 'regardless.'

I'd nodded, remembering all the fuss about Clive Alloway, why
it had happened, where it had led.

'And Devlin brought that assurance?' I'd said.

'He *was* that assurance.'

'Because of who he was?'

'Of course.'

'For money?'

'You bet.'

'And Beckermann?'

'Beckermann's taken him on. He works for Texcal now, the
parent company. He's more than useful to them. Bet your life
on it.'

'No conflict of interest?'

'I doubt it,' he'd said thinly. 'Half a million dollars is a lot
of money.'

'You mean he's on the payroll? As crude as that?'

'No. He has a consultancy. Devlin, Coffey and Sweetman. The
half million's a retainer. There's money on top, of course. For performance.'

Now, as I crossed the shopping mall car park towards the Chrysler, I thought again of the young Englishman I'd seen so briefly out at Beckermann's ranch. The more McGrath had talked, the more I was convinced it had to be Devlin. Another reason his father was called Polly was his looks. Devlin senior, according to most women's magazines, could have made his living in the fashion world. He was the perfect clothes horse. The face I'd seen at Beckermann's had come from the same mould: same hair, same bone structure, same ability to smile at a total stranger without the faintest trace of insincerity. That made him Pretty Polly's son. No question.

And Priddy? I shook my head, getting back to the car at last, realizing just how slow I'd been. Priddy, at the DTI, worked for Polly Devlin. Before his recent promotion, he'd been hand-picked to be the Secretary of State's PPS. Now he was himself a junior minister, a key part of the Whitehall sales team, pitching for what Wesley called 'UK Ltd' or 'The Firm'. That meant, of course, that he'd know Peter Devlin. That explained the invite to Beckermann's ranch, the hand extended from the inner circle. But why, then, had Priddy invited me to join him out at Fairwater? Why had he taken the risk? Lust? Pride? Some male fantasy about getting it right? After our last disaster?

I shook my head again, unlocking the car door. I got in and reached for the ignition. Then I stopped, aware at once of a terrible, terrible smell, an animal smell, a smell so heavy it was almost tangible, a physical presence. My eyes went to the mirror, but hard as I looked I could see only the pale empty spaces of the car park. I reached slowly for the glove box. I eased it open, feeling inside, but after a second or two I knew it was pointless looking any further. Grant Wallace's gun, my precious Beretta, had gone.

I swallowed hard, forcing myself to breathe properly, forcing my pulse back to normal. Then I looked round. The car was empty. I leaned back, bending over the seat, peering down at the floor, half wanting to use my hands, feeling for whatever it was that smelled so hideous, terrified now of what I might find. After a while, certain there was nothing there, I got out of the car again, looking around, aware of how exposed I was. I went to the boot and unlocked it, standing back and letting it open on the spring. For a moment or two, I did nothing, knowing now that I'd found the source of it. The boot open, the smell was overpowering. Finally, I stepped forward, my body shadowing the inside of the boot. All I could see was my case. I reached inside the boot and opened the case, aware of something bulky jammed inside. Then I moved slightly, letting the light in, recognizing the huge shoulders, the square head, the teeth bared in a final snarl, the throat torn open, the huge wound still crusted with blood. I steadied myself against the car, my hand to my mouth. Mogul's first victim. The dog I couldn't find in the creek.

Half an hour later, I was back outside McGrath's place. By now, I was as sure as I could be that I wasn't being followed. Coming out of the car park at the shopping mall, I'd driven classic anti-surveillance patterns, a succession of lefts, then rights, then a couple of U-turns, watching all the time for movement. But there'd been nothing, just the endless grid of suburban streets, the parked Volvo estates, the shadowed gardens, the cold blue flicker of TV sets, curtained from the world outside. At a major intersection, glad of the occasional traffic, I'd pulled on to the sidewalk and opened the boot. I had no gloves, not even a piece of rag. Everything I had was in my case, and on top of everything lay the rotting body of the dog. I had no choice, therefore, but to use my bare hands, and I reached in and lifted the dog out, leaving him curled by the roadside. The body was heavier than I'd expected and slippery with something I tried hard not to think about, and afterwards, I'd knelt on the verge, wiping my hands on the dew-wet grass. But they still felt sticky, even now, a minute past midnight, parked in the darkness at the end of McGrath's cul-de-sac, wanting to go in, knowing I shouldn't.

The light was still on in the bedroom. I could talk to him, warn him, apologize, but the more I chased the conversation around in my head, the more I knew that it was a conversation we shouldn't have. The man was hopelessly vulnerable and I'd exposed him already. By simply arriving, by parcelling up all Wesley's questions, knocking on his door and inviting him to admire this dangerous new toy, I'd made him part of it, one of us. That, he didn't want. He'd been prepared to talk about Devlin, but the rest was off-limits. The stuff that Grant had done was fine, he'd said, as far as it went, but a chronology as loose as that could support a thousand interpretations. If Wesley could make a case for George Bush fixing the war ahead of actually fighting it, then so be it. It was a neat theory. It might even be true. But either way, McGrath was wholly agnostic. He said he didn't know. And he said he wouldn't guess.

I'd mentioned Beckermann again, at this point, one last attempt to coax at least a hint from him. I'd described my afternoon out at the ranch, the scene down by the creek, the pit-bulls. At the mention of the dogs, McGrath's head had jerked up, and I'd paused there, asking him what he knew. I'd described Mogul, the top dog, the killer they'd all come to see, and he'd nodded, evidently recognizing the name, but saying nothing. Later, back in the bedroom, before I'd left, he came close to offering me an apology. I was getting myself into a war, he'd said. I was tangling with serious money, and honourable though my cause might be, he was remaining strictly non-combatant. Nothing personal. Nothing unduly heavy. Just an understandable urge to hang on to what little he had left.

I sat in the car in the darkness, knowing now how right he'd been. Blood had been shed. Not mine. Not yet. But blood, none the less. I checked the mirror again, certain before I did so that it would be empty. Looking for the obvious was pointless. These guys, whoever they were, were infinitely better than that. They didn't lumber round America, a hundred yards behind you, an obliging dot in the mirror, a face behind a wheel. No, it was altogether more subtle than that and altogether more menacing.

I reached for the ignition key and started the engine. Backing the car slowly up the cul-de-sac, I opened the electric windows, oblivious of the cold night air, determined to get rid of the smell. Twenty minutes later, freezing, I was out of the suburbs, heading north, away from Washington. When the houses stopped and there was nothing but darkness, I checked the atlas again. Beyond Wheaton, according to my Rand McNally, there was a big reservoir. I guessed the distance at no more than ten miles. After a while, I saw a sign. Then another. I took a right turn off the road and bumped down a rutted country track. There were trees up ahead, and then the ground began to fall away, a gentle slope, cropped grass, the shadows of fleeing sheep and the inky blackness of water beyond.

I drove as far as I dared across the grass and then stopped. I kept the car headlights on, retrieving my case from the boot and walking down the lit path to the water's edge. It was a cold, still night. I laid my case on the wet stones, and began to sluice the inside of the lid with water, rubbing hard with my knuckles, trying to get rid of the slime. When I'd done as much as I could, I pulled everything out, garment after garment, lifting them to my nose, trying to judge what stank, what didn't. The pile of 'Don't knows' grew by my side, and in the end I gave up, and stripped off the clothes I was wearing, one by one.

Stark naked, I waded into the reservoir, catching my breath at the cold, feeling mud oozing up between my toes. Up to my waist in freezing water, I washed myself all over, using soap from the last motel, lathering as hard as I could. Dripping wet, I used a towel from the bottom of the case, rubbing the hard nap against my skin, returning a little warmth. Then I got dressed again, jeans, a vest, a sweatshirt on top, stuff I'd packed deep in the case. It was a scene that would have made my father proud of me, but what I still smelled like, I shuddered to think.

Back in the car, I pulled the Chrysler in a tight circle and bumped back up towards the trees. I'd left the clothes I'd been wearing in the reservoir, weighted down with rocks from the water's edge. Ditto the suitcase and stuff I knew was beyond salvation. Some day, maybe, they'd come to light. But by that time, God willing, I'd be back in the real world.

An hour later, no questions asked, I was standing in front of a mirror in Room 17 of the Days Inn, just south of Leesburg. The shower was waiting for me and I'd found some Ella Fitzgerald on the bedside radio. Four miles down the road was Dulles Airport, and from Dulles Airport, according to the Puerto Rican woman behind the reception desk, there were plenty of transatlantic flights. Tomorrow, I thought, I can end this madness.

I glanced at my watch. It was nearly half past three in the morning. I looked at the telephone a moment. McGrath had told me he usually read most of the night. The least I could do was say goodbye. I lifted the phone and dialled his number. He answered almost at once, God knows how.

'It's me,' I said, 'your little English friend.' I paused. 'Homeward bound.'

'Sarah?' I caught the rising tone in his voice. Just as well I'd phoned.

'What's the matter?' I said.

There was a moment's silence. Then he was back. 'The FBI have been on,' he said, 'an Agent Pedernales.'

'And?'

'Nothing specific . . .' he gave a little cough, '. . . but I gather they're watching international flights.'

American Airlines run two non-stops from Washington to Dallas every day. I was on the first, a window seat at the back of the aircraft, the one and only time I've ever volunteered for a smoking seat. Smokers, I told myself, have no sense of smell.

By mid-afternoon, I was back at Dallas/Fort Worth Airport. I took a cab to Grant Wallace's house. En route, I asked the driver to find a shopping mall where I could buy clothes. When he raised an eyebrow at my estimate that I'd be half an hour at the mall, I gave him a hundred-dollar bill and told him to wait. There'd be another one for him when we got to Grant's place. Under the circumstances, money was the least of my problems.

At the mall, I replaced the bits and pieces I'd left at the reservoir. I bought a simple two-piece, skirt and jacket, formal enough to get me through most social occasions. I found a couple of nice shirts, two pairs of jeans and three sets of underwear. I also bought a case to put it all in and a new pair of Reeboks.

Back in the cab, we drove to Grant's. One of the favours I wanted from him was a little privacy – an hour or so to soak in the tub and wash my hair, and make myself look half-respectable. Another, given my reluctance to risk a flight home, was a fresh look at the material he'd compiled on Harold Beckermann. By now, in my head, I'd turned an important corner. Whatever I'd got myself into, I told myself, wasn't going to go away. Quite what it had to do with the Gulf War was anybody's guess, but it was better – whatever happened – to confront it. Both for Wesley's sake and, in some curious sense, my own.

The cab dropped me outside Grant's house. There was another car in the drive, parked behind the big Lincoln. I looked at it for a moment, wondering if this was such a good idea. Then I dismissed the thought and followed the path to the front door, rang the bell. Nothing happened. I rang again. Finally, there were footsteps and the sound of a dog yapping. The door opened and a small, thin woman peered out. I recognized the face at once from the photograph behind her on the wall: the grey perm, the beaky nose, the hard, baleful expression. Grant had put a name to the face the last time I'd been here. 'Mom' wasn't a word that had come easily to him.

'Mrs Wallace?' I said.

'Yes?'

'My name's Sarah Moreton.' I paused. 'Friend of Grant's.' She looked at me, saying nothing. The poodle at her feet began to bark again. Then she frowned, her eyes on something by the gate. 'Squirrels,' she said briskly, 'darn things.' She looked back at me. 'Suppose you'd better come in.'

I followed her into the house. There was something different about it I couldn't quite place. Then I had it. The smell of flowers. I looked around. There were bunches of them everywhere, stacked carelessly in vases, no attempt at an arrangement, or an effect. Typical, I thought. Men.

I paused at the foot of the stairs. Grant's mother was looking pointedly at my suitcase. For the first time, it occurred to me that she might be alone.

'Is Grant out?' I said.

Mrs Wallace frowned at me again, shaking her head. 'No,' she said, 'he's dead.'

She made me coffee in the kitchen, matter-of-fact, impatient, a woman untouched by grief or mourning. First she'd heard was a call from the state police, three days ago, Saturday morning. She lived across the city in a suburb called Sunnyvale. The trooper had said there'd been some kind of accident. A friend of Grant's had phoned in. It all looked pretty straightforward, but there was the question of formal identification. He was sending a car. He'd said he was sorry.

I nodded, listening. 'You saw Grant a lot?'

'Very rarely. Not since Christmas, matter of fact.' She paused. 'You want the rest of it?'

She'd gone to the city morgue. Grant was tucked up there in a fridge. He'd been shot in the head. The attendant at the morgue had told her it would have been painless. He'd known exactly what he was doing. It was as simple as turning off the light at night. He wouldn't have felt a thing.

I frowned, still nursing the coffee. 'He?' I said.

Mrs Wallace reached for another cigarette. The pack at her elbow was three quarters empty. 'Sure,' she said, 'he did it himself. Suicide.' She paused. 'Just as well it worked, too. His father would have been mad as hell.'

'But whose gun was it?'

'His own gun. They showed it to me. New one. I don't know . . .' She shrugged. 'He'd just bought it. They had the sales slip. And the box it came in. They found the box in that hidey-hole of his.'

We went to the den. Someone had been through it since I was last there. Grant's desk was a mess, papers everywhere, totally out of character.

'So where did he do it?' I said.

Mrs Wallace was standing in the doorway. There were steps down into the den, and the extra height made her look even more formidable. She had one arm folded across her body. The other hand tapped ash on to the carpet.

'There. On the sofa. I saw the photos.'

'And the gun?'

'In his hand.'

I nodded, saying nothing. Then I crossed to the big filing cabinet, aware of Mrs Wallace looking down, following my every movement. I knelt quickly, half expecting the cabinet to be locked. it wasn't. I pulled open the bottom drawer, the one where he kept the files on Beckermann. It was quite empty. I looked up. Mrs Wallace was stifling a yawn.

'Happy now?' she said.

Book Three

2 1

The next few days were critical. They marked the moment when circumstances eased the baton from other hands and passed it to me. So far, like the good trooper I'd always been, I'd taken my orders, respectively, from Stollmann and from Wesley Keogh. For reasons that will become clearer, these chains of command were about to disintegrate. In Stollmann's case, the story is complicated and had yet to unfold. Wesley's situation was infinitely simpler. By late October, he was dying.

I spent three solid days effectively in hiding, trying to raise him on the phone. Grant's death, on top of the Washington incident, had certainly affected me. The polite term would have been 'unnerved', though I'm sure Wesley would have found something a little more colourful. Either way, it was at this point that I thought it wise to adopt a new identity, Frances Bevan, an alias that was easy to remember because it was my mother's maiden name.

In the US, performing this little conjuring trick isn't as simple as it sounds. Most people use credit cards to settle their bills and credit cards are an instant giveaway if you're trying to pretend you're someone else. I, though, had still got a hefty reserve of cash, and as soon as I knew I'd be staying a little longer, I drew more. Cash is increasingly suspect in most American transactions, but the kind of places I was now checking into didn't ask too many questions. As the laconic black student behind the desk at the Patriot Motel put it, 'A dollar's a dollar, ma'am. That's where the rubber meets the road.'

I stayed at the Patriot for four nights, wrapping myself in the anonymity of my new name. I put the Chrysler in a lock-up around the corner, and didn't go out at all, except for brief, after-dark excursions to the K-Mart across the street. I didn't believe for a moment that Grant Wallace had taken his own life, and if they'd got rid of him with such brisk efficiency, then I saw no reason why I shouldn't be next on the list. The fact that they'd even gone to the trouble of retrieving the gun they were going to pass off as the so-called 'suicide weapon', the Beretta that had disappeared from my car, simply added to my paranoia. Not only were these people dangerous, they were also bloody clever. And not only were they clever, but they were also well connected. The police ballistics report must have ruled out Grant's Beretta. Yet the cause of death remained 'suicide'.

But I couldn't find him. The Guildford number, hard as I tried, wouldn't answer. And when I began to dial the answerphone as well, expecting – at the least – to find some kind of message waiting for me, there was nothing. Just the ring-ring of the number at the other end and the hollow transatlantic spaces in between. Calls to Stollmann got me no further, either. For reasons I didn't begin to understand, he, too, wasn't answering.

In the end, day two, I rang Derek Aldridge. By this time, I'd mastered the little recording machine I'd bought at the Radio Shack and I was taping everything. Listening to the tapes now, I can hear how guarded he was, though at the time just the sound of an English voice was enough to bring a smile to my lips. I explained I needed to talk to Wesley. I said it was urgent. I said I couldn't find him. Might there be a number I hadn't tried? Aldridge gave the question a second's thought and then asked for my number, saying he'd call back. I said no. I'd ring again in ten minutes. There was a moment's silence at this and then he laughed.

'Moscow rules?' he murmured, before ringing off.

Ten minutes later, I was back on the line. He said he had a number. He read it over to me. I stared at it. It was the same number I'd been ringing for the taped messages, the electronic dead-letter box Wesley had been so proud of.

'Where's this?' I said.

'Southend.'

'Whose is it? Who lives there?'

'His mother.'

'Ah.' I nodded, wiser now. 'Connie?'

'Yes.' He paused. 'And she's there now. I just talked to her.'

I phoned the number. A woman answered. She sounded old and a little vague, a flat, ugly East London accent, Wesley without the voltage. I asked for her son.

'He's ill, dear. You a friend of his?'

'Yes.' I paused. 'How ill?'

'He's in that hospital again. The same one. The one in Paddington. St Mary's.'

'Which ward?'

'I dunno.'

'Do you go and see him?'

'Yesterday, I did.'

'Is it upstairs? Downstairs?'

'What, dear?'

'The ward. The ward where they're keeping him . . .' I paused again. 'The place where the bed is.'

'Upstairs. Top of the stairs. It's the one with all those poor young men in. You go into the old building. He's in the bed at the end on the left. Next to the window. Are you going tonight? Only—'

'No,' I said hastily, 'no, I'm not.'

I got the number of the hospital from the international directory. Wesley had already told me about St Mary's. He'd been there before, the time he'd contracted TB. I knew he had no great affection for the place, but I knew too that they went out of their way to make life bearable for AIDS patients. That included access to telephone callers. When I got through, I gave Wesley's name to the admissions clerk, plus a brief reprise of his mother's directions. Thirty seconds later, after a word with the ward sister, there was another voice on the phone. He introduced himself as Mark.

'Mark?' I said blankly.

'Friend of Wesley's.'

I hesitated a moment, then remembered. Mark had been an old flame, the young actor who'd nursed him the last time round.

'It's Sarah,' I said. 'Tell him it's Sarah.'

'I can't.'

'Why not?'

'He's . . . asleep.'

'You mean that?'

There's a silence at this point, another of my little tapes. In the
background, you can hear hospital noises. Half-buried amongst
them, but still audible, is Wesley. He's wanting to know who it
is. He definitely isn't asleep.

'Mark—' I begin.

'Sarah, listen. This isn't as simple as it—'

'No. You listen. Put him on. Just put him on. OK?'

'Sarah, I—'

'Just do it. Please.'

'OK.'

There's a pause here and a scuffling sound, the phone passing
from hand to hand, or perhaps Mark joining Wesley on the bed,
holding the phone to his ear. God knows.

'Wesley?'

'Yeah? Who's that?'

I remember gazing at the phone. He sounded about ten million
years old.

'It's me, Sarah. Listen, how are you?'

'Fine . . . fine . . . just fine. Sarah?'

'Me. Yes. Look—'

'You coming up to see me? Only . . .'

The voice falters and gives way to a strange whooping noise.
Then Mark's back. He sounds upset and a little angry.

'Please,' he says. 'You see what I mean?'

'How is he?'

'He's ill, Sarah.'

'How ill?'

'I can't say. Not here.'

'Give me a number.'

'OK.'

Mark gave me a number, the flat where he lived. I wrote it
down and he told me to phone in a couple of hours. When I did
so, I told him how sorry I was. Not about Wesley, but for being so
difficult earlier. The last thing either of them needed was some
idiot woman pretending to be Florence Nightingale. Mark
accepted the apology with a quiet laugh. He sounded tired. Wesley
had been taken into hospital the day I'd returned to Dallas from
Washington. The hospital still had his number on Wesley's file
and had phoned him. He'd been pretty much living there ever

since. Now, on the third day, Wesley's temperature was still nudging 104°. When he was lucid, he complained of a terrible headache and pains behind his eyes, but most of the time he was barely conscious. The last twenty-four hours had been especially bad although, oddly, he'd been able to put together the odd word for my benefit. I'd asked him what he'd said afterwards, once I'd hung up. Had he mentioned anything specific? Was there a message of some kind?

'Sarah,' Mark had said gently, 'he hasn't a clue who you are.'

'You mean that?'

'Yes.'

'And his mother? Connie?'

'Another stranger.'

'And you?'

'God knows.'

I'd ended the conversation at this point, both of us too upset to take it any further. The only additional information I gathered was about his treatment. They were giving him massive doses of sulphadiazine and pyramethamine, the surest sign that they'd diagnosed cerebral toxoplasmosis.

'Toxo' was the infection that Wesley had been fearing for months. It's an organism that invades the central nervous system, and causes abcesses in the brain. It's sometimes found in cats, and most of us are never infected, but if your immune system's down then you can end up paralysed and half mad, and even if you respond to treatment and get better, there's no telling when you'll relapse again. Once infected, you're infected for life, and thinking about it, I couldn't help wondering whether Jake McGrath hadn't been right about Wesley's death wish. Living with a cat like Scourge was asking for trouble. The odds again. And Wesley's determination to ignore them.

Before I went to sleep that night, I phoned Wesley's mother. I didn't know what to say, except that I was sorry, but it was obvious that she hadn't a clue what the problem was. She talked vaguely about chickenpox, and said how funny it was that she couldn't see any spots, but when I probed a little further, she began to complain about the trains. Maybe, on reflection, Wesley was right not to have let her into his little secret. There can't have been much room in her life for that kind of complication.

Next morning returned me to my own nightmare. Still depressed about Wesley, I rummaged through Yellow Pages, looking for the section on private investigation agencies. I'd decided by now that I'd have to buy the help I needed. There were various clues I knew I should pursue, but doing the work myself would mean breaking cover in the most obvious places. Although I'd returned the sales invoice for the Beretta to Grant, I could remember the name of the supplier, the Sun Valley Arms Corp. Their address was in the phone book, and it would be interesting to know who might have been enquiring about similar guns in the last few days, but these kinds of questions I couldn't afford to put myself. If they could find the Chrysler in a Silver Spring car park, a thousand miles away, they'd have no difficulty staking out the Sun Valley Arms Corp, waiting for little me to turn up.

The first three agencies I phoned responded to my initial enquiries in exactly the same way. They asked me for a domicile address and a credit reference. When they established that I was non-resident, a visitor, they quoted me an hourly rate and warned me that any work would be contingent on a sizeable deposit. The deposit, as it happens, was within my means, but that, somehow, wasn't the point. The point was that I had to know these people. I had to trust them. I had to be sure that they were honest and wouldn't simply sell or pass the information on. Whether or not that kind of thing ever happened, I'd no idea. But I needed more reassurance than a brisk conversation about hourly rates.

In the end, after some thought, I came up with a solution. It was far from perfect, but it offered a logical way forward. It was also, I told myself, a move of which Wesley would approve.

According once again to Yellow Pages, there were four newspapers in the Dallas/Fort Worth metropolitan area. Since the *Courier-Star* was the only one I'd ever heard of, it seemed a logical place to start. I phoned the switchboard and asked for the crime correspondent. His name, the woman told me, was Raoul Delahunty. When he picked up the phone, he sounded younger than I'd expected. I gave him my false name and told him I had a story I wanted to discuss. He asked me for details, but I said we had to meet. He told me he was busy, but there was maybe a chance we could get together later. Around five o'clock, after the deadline for the paper's final edition, I could find him in a bar called the Mission Bell. If I gave my name to the barman, he'd locate me. I was still scribbling the address of the bar when he hung up.

I spent the rest of the day in the motel room, watching television between abortive calls to Stollmann. For whatever reason, he still wasn't answering. At five, I ordered a cab. I was wearing the semi-formal two-piece I'd bought on my return from Washington, plus a tacky pair of sunglasses I'd found across the street at the K-Mart. Studying myself in the mirror, waiting for the cab, I was amazed how quickly I'd acquired the local disguise. Take away the scar, I thought, and I looked just like any other female Dallas executive: hollow-cheeked, hard-faced, brisk, watchful.

The cab dropped me outside the bar at half past five. The Mission Bell was tucked between an insurance building and a branch of Texas Realty Inc. There were lights on behind the smoked glass and discreet posters advertising a forthcoming evening with a jazz saxophonist. Inside, it was much warmer than I'd been used to. There were circular tables around a long crescent of bar, and a light-fingered pianist in the corner was doodling with a version of 'Ain't Misbehavin''. The place was busy, mainly men in suits, and there was a comfortable hum of conversation. I went to the bar.

'Frances Bevan,' I said, 'for Raoul Delahunty.'

The barman nodded, but said nothing. Seconds later, I felt an arm on mine. Raoul Delahunty was tall and thin, straggly blond hair, sharp features, no more than thirty years old. His eyes were the palest blue, the colour of a certain kind of china. My mother has a whole teaset in it, seldom used.

'Pleased to meet you,' he said, shaking my hand.

I followed him back to his table. The bar, it turned out, was L-shaped and the alcove around the corner gave us a little privacy. I sat down and he signalled the waiter.

'You wanna beer?'

'Please.'

He gave the waiter the order. He had a strange manner, at once terse and playful, as if he was trying to keep me permanently off-balance.

'You're English?' he said.

'Yes.'

'OK.' He nodded. 'So why the call?'

I looked at him for a second or two. I'd rehearsed this moment a number of times in my head, back at the motel, but now I wasn't at all sure it was such a good idea. Maybe I should ask him about hourly rates. Maybe money had its uses after all.

'I'm after advice,' I said carefully, 'and maybe a little help.'

Raoul gazed at me, saying nothing, then a smile flooded his face and he leaned forward, taking off my sunglasses.

'Bad mistake,' he said. 'Makes you look like some gangster's bimbo.'

He was holding the glasses up, examining them, Exhibit A. I began to blush. The beers arrived. Raoul proposed a toast, consigning the glasses to the ashtray.

'Lovely eyes,' he said, 'why hide them?'

I sipped the beer, feeling strangely naked. Raoul leaned forward over the table again. He hadn't once looked at my scar.

'So why the call?' he said. 'Why me?'

I hesitated a moment, then told him about Grant Wallace. The man had been a personal friend. I'd flown over to see him. He'd seemed perfectly normal, no more stressed than usual, certainly not depressed. I'd gone away last week. I'd returned a couple of days later, only to find him dead. Raoul was toying with his beer. The word had barely registered.

'Dead?' he said.

'Yes.' I paused. 'Suicide.'

'Oh,' he nodded, 'and you have a problem with that?'

I said nothing for a moment, knowing the conversation was about to turn an important corner. From here on in, I had to trust him. If I got it wrong, the consequences could be less than pleasant. Raoul was still watching me. He had a notebook out now. It lay on the table beside his glass, a statement of intent. Hourly rates, I thought again. Information, instead of money. I smiled at him and took a sip of my beer. Everything in America had a value. Including this man's time.

'My friend shot himself,' I said carefully, 'with a gun that wasn't there.'

'How do you know?'

'I had it with me. In Washington.'

'You can prove that?'

'No.'

'Why not?'

'Someone stole it.'

'When?'

'Monday night.'

'And when did your friend . . .' he frowned, 'die?'

'Two days earlier.'

'Who says?'

'The state police. They phoned his mother. A friend reported him dead on Saturday morning.'

Raoul was writing now, a series of lazy scribbles, his long body slouched in the chair, one hand still nursing his beer. He looked up.

'They say it was his gun? The police? Specific make? Specific model?'

'Yes. According to his mother.'

'And you say it couldn't have been his gun?'

'Yes. Unless he'd bought another one. Same model. Same shop.'

'Have you checked that out? At the shop?'

'No.'

'Why not?'

I looked at him, saying nothing, and for the first time I saw signs of real interest in his eyes. He was smiling again.

'Why not?' he said again.

I shook my head. 'I can't say. Not now.'

'You want me to check it out? Whether he bought another gun?'

'Yes, please.'

I gave him the name of the shop and the make and model of the gun, and he made another note. Then he frowned.

'I get this right?' he said. 'Some guy comes in? Shoots your friend? Identical gun? Leaves it there? Makes it look like suicide? That the way the story goes?'

'Something like that,' I nodded, 'yes.'

'He have any enemies? This friend of yours? Any . . .' he shrugged, 'business problems?'

'Not really.'

'Emotional problems? Any particular relationship?'

'He was gay.'

'Boyfriends?'

'Not to my knowledge. No one special. No one who'd . . . you know.'

'Who then? Who could it have been?'

I shrugged, telling him I didn't know, couldn't guess. Then, as casually as I could, I frowned. A passing thought. Plucked out of the air.

'He *had* just been sacked,' I began, 'though I don't know whether—'

'Sacked?'

'Fired.'

'Who by?'

'Extec.'

'He worked for Extec?'

I nodded, watching his eyes again, that same small spark. He reached for the pen and I obliged with more details, what he'd done at Extec, who he'd worked for. The pen stopped.

'Beckermann? Harold Beckermann?'

'Yes.' I frowned. 'You know the name?'

'Sure.' He nodded. 'Sure.'

The pen began to dance across the page again. I reached for my beer. The frosting of ice on the glass had melted, leaving a small, round puddle on the table.

'This Mr Beckermann,' I began, swallowing the last of the beer. 'You know him personally?'

'Me?' He looked up, smiling again. 'I've met him, sure. But no, ma'am, can't say I'm a friend.' He paused. 'Why?'

'Oh . . .' I shrugged. 'I just wondered.'

'Why?' he said again.

'Grant thought the world of him, that's all. You know, real hero figure. In fact, he was putting together a little book about him. Nothing enormous. Just . . .' I trailed off, sure now that I had Raoul's full attention. Even the way he was sitting had changed.

'Book, you say?'

'Yes.'

'You see any of it?'

'Yes.'

'You *got* any of it?'

'No.' I shook my head, regretful. 'That went missing, too.'

I was back in the motel by seven o'clock. Raoul had pressed me in the bar for more details about Grant, but I'd been vague and apologetic, telling him I was sorry to have wasted his time. I was a stranger, I said, and I was worried. I wasn't brave enough to make a fuss and go to the police, but in the UK a good journalist was the next best thing. The latter remark had brought another smile to Raoul's face and I'd ended our little chat by reclaiming my sunglasses from the ashtray and standing up. I'd thanked him for the beer. I'd apologized again for phoning out of the blue. Then I'd shaken his hand and left. He'd caught up with me in the street outside while I was still looking for a cab.

'Where do I find you?' he'd said. 'Where are you staying?'

I'd smiled at him. 'I've got your number. I'll phone you in a couple of days.'

Now, back in the motel, I dialled Grant's house, looking for his mother. We'd never discussed the arrangements for Grant's funeral, but I assumed it was imminent. Attending in person would have been foolish, but the least Wesley would have expected from me was something flamboyant in the flower line.

After a while, the number answered. Mrs Wallace's voice was as cold as her smile. I asked about Grant's funeral.

'I just need a date,' I explained, 'and a place.'

Mrs Wallace grunted something graceless about the will. Evidently Grant had made specific provisions for the disposal of his body. He wanted to be buried in a graveyard north of Front Royal, a town in West Virginia, and he'd long ago made the necessary arrangements. The plot overlooked the Shenandoah River. It was close to Stonewall Jackson's headquarters.

'Do you know how far that is,' she said, 'in airfreight charges?'

I mumbled something about what it must have meant to him, hearing her tallying up the bill. When it got past $3000, she stopped.

'If he'd ever mentioned it to me, I'd have told him not to be so damn stupid,' she rasped, 'and that's a fact.'

'I'm sure it is.'

'So what's wrong with cremation? Anyone explain that to me?'

'Maybe he felt—'

'Too common, too obvious, that's what he felt,' she snorted, answering her own question. 'Show Grant a T-shirt, he'd put the damn thing on backwards, just to be different. That's the kind of child he was. Awkward. Never changed. Never grew up. Talk to his father some time. If you want the truth of it.'

She rang off soon afterwards, still ranting about the costs of shipping her dead son north, and I was left with the name of the tiny country churchyard where he was to be buried, scribbled on the back of the week's TV listings.

An hour later, when I was still wet from the shower, there was a knock at the door. I glanced at my watch. It wasn't the kind of place where the management bothered with anything but the bill. I went to the door. A lot of me wanted to turn off the light and the radio and pretend I was out for the night.

'Who is it?'

'Raoul Delahunty.'

I opened the door. Raoul was standing in the corridor. He'd changed since the bar, jeans and a leather jacket instead of the suit, and there was another man beside him, short and squat, with a flat, wide face, sallow complexion and Mexican features. Raoul indicated him with a slight tilt of the head. There was a powerful smell of aftershave.

'Luis,' he said. 'Friend of mine.'

He said something in Spanish to the Mexican. Luis nodded, and disappeared towards the reception area. Watching him go, short legs, a curious, flat-footed walk, I realized I'd seen him before, only a couple of hours ago, on the street outside the Mission Bell. Raoul was looking beyond me, into the room.

'You been here long?'

'Yes.'

'You should move. Every day.'

'Why?'

He glanced down at me, not bothering with the smile any more. 'Home truths?' he said. 'Or more bullshit?'

22

I flew back to Washington the following day, the recorder on my lap, playing and replaying the tape I'd made the previous evening.

Raoul Delahunty had stayed in my room at the motel for a couple of hours. The first part of the conversation's missing from the tape because until he'd gone to the bathroom, I'd no chance to set up the machine, but once it was running, you can still hear the occasional impatience in his voice. He plainly didn't believe my line about being a visiting tourist. I suspect he'd made a couple of calls since the Mission Bell, and what he'd discovered about Grant Wallace had been enough to convince him that I knew a great deal more than I'd so far let on. Neither of us, to be fair, was telling the whole truth, but we both had powerful reasons for pursuing the conversation as far as it might go.

Amongst all that, I like to think that there was also room for one or two other things. Raoul was extraordinarily candid about his attraction to large-breasted redheads, and a couple of times he suggested it might be a neat idea to fuck. I turned him down on both occasions, but the more we talked, the more attractive the proposal began to seem. He was shrewd, amusing and thoughtful, and when he said he was worried about something he termed my 'physical integrity', I believed him. The aftershave, thank God, belonged to Luis.

Luis, incidentally, turned out to be Raoul's bodyguard. He'd overseen our chat at the Mission Bell, and afterwards he'd followed my cab to the motel. Hence Raoul's surprise arrival. Quite why a journalist on a respectable Dallas paper should need a bodyguard Raoul never made entirely clear. In some parts of America, Luis would be pure set dressing, a kind of designer accessory, but the more I listened to Raoul, the more I began to understand why the need might, after all, be genuine. One reason was the stable of petty criminals and corrupt policemen he was obliged to maintain as off-the-record sources. Another, amongst an assortment of bigger names, was Harold J. Beckermann.

We were talking about Beckermann's position in Dallas society. I was doing my best to steer the conversation towards pit-bulls. By this point, we were both on the bed, Raoul sprawled across the bottom, me propped up against the wall, supported by a couple of pillows. Beckermann, it seemed, was big on 'giving'.

'Giving?'

Raoul nodded. 'Charity stuff. He's a major benefactor in the city. Mainly in the health field. There's a hospital out towards the university. He organized donations for a new surgical unit. Came on stream last year. Bells, whistles, you name it, the place has everything.' He paused. 'They love him out here, believe me. Yessir, Mr Generous.'

'How much?'

'Ten million on the first hit. Another five for the second. Plus regular bucks from an update fund. For that kind of money you get your name up there in lights. The Harold J. Beckermann Cardiothoracic Center. A citizen's gift to the people of Texas. From the man with the big heart.'

'Was that the headline?'

'You kidding?' He laughed here, a soft sound, genuine amusement. 'No, ma'am.'

'No?'

'No.' He'd shaken his head, picking at loose ends from the pattern in the bedspread. 'Anyone ever tells you America ain't deferential, they're wrong. What we love, what we respect, what matters, is money. Beckermann is money. Big money. Money doesn't come bigger than Beckermann. That's how the class system works out here. Guys like him, high rollers, self-made guys, billionaires, Jeez, they're the living proof the whole fucking system works. We don't have royalty, we don't have a king and queen, but I guess that's because we don't need it. What we do most of the time is make money, and what we end up with is guys like Beckermann, and other guys like your friend here . . . Grant Wallace. Guys like him. Guys who believe it, and write it all down, and get dead in the process.'

'You think he was killed? You think that possible?'

'Possible? Sure. Did it happen the way you tell it? I dunno.'

'But Beckermann?'

'Beckermann's money. Big money. Plus everything that goes with it.'

'Like what?'

'Like influence. You ever hear of the fraternity clubs we have? Those little masonic outfits? Skull and Bones? Bohemian Grove? Any of that?' He'd paused, favouring me with an enquiring stare, unsure again whether my ignorance was real or not. 'You don't know about these people?'

'No.'

'Well, I guess it's obvious enough. You get to be important, a big hitter.' He'd shrugged. 'Commerce, showbusiness, politics, whatever. You get to the top, and then you get to be pretty selective about who you spend time with.'

'Your spare time?' I'd queried. 'Friends?'

'Shit, no. Friendship ain't worth a damn. What matters is money. The bigger the bucks, the higher the profile, the more you limit the exposure. Believe me, it's an interesting test, the real high-rollers . . .' He'd sighed. 'Fucking sub-human.'

'Beckermann?'

'An animal.'

'You mean that?'

'Sure I mean it. With most of these guys, it's the same. They lose touch with planet earth. They're all out there somewhere. Deep space.' He'd fallen silent for a moment, looking at me. 'Tell me something.'

'What?'

'In your country, what do you call it when a guy makes, say, really serious money? On a deal? Millions? Zillions?'

'*Call* it?'

'Yeah. You gotta phrase? A saying? Over there? Lil old England?'

I'd looked at him a moment, not understanding. Then I'd seen the drift. 'A killing,' I'd said at last, 'we'd call it a killing.'

'Sure,' he'd said quietly, 'that's what we say, too. Real neat little phrase. Except some of these guys mean it.'

'Like Beckermann?'

'Sure.'

'And he's in these . . . fraternity things?'

'Sure. Him and a handful of other guys. Pols. Business guys. Republicans, mostly.'

'Names I'd know? Washington names?'

'Yeah.' He'd smiled, 'Power. Money. Influence. The Holy Trinity. Sucks, doesn't it?'

I'd not answered him, lying back against the pillow, staring at the whorls of plaster on the ceiling, remembering the faces of the men round the pit, the hot, muddy smells drifting up from the creek.

'You ever hear any rumours about dogs?' I'd said carefully.

'Dogs?'

'Fighting dogs? Bets? On pit-bulls?'

'Regarding Beckermann?' I'd nodded. 'Sure. Goes on a lot in these parts. And not just him, either.'

'But he's in it? Involved?'

'Yeah. Goes with the territory. Power, money, influence . . .' he'd shrugged, 'blood.'

'And he's got a lot of dogs? Owns them?'

'Yeah, I guess so.' He was frowning at this point, watching me carefully. 'You have a dog in mind? A particular dog?'

'Mogul,' I'd said, 'a dog called Mogul. You've heard of a dog called Mogul?'

Raoul had hesitated a moment, then nodded. Mogul was a newcomer, he'd said, as yet unbeaten. Beckermann had acquired him from someone else. To date the dog had killed a dozen times, earning Beckermann a small fortune in side bets. That, at least, was the rumour.

'So who was the previous owner?'

'I don't know.'

'You're sure?'

'Yes.' He was staring at me, speculative, trying to work it out. 'You interested in all that stuff? Fighting dogs? Pit-bulls? Is that it?'

'No, I just . . .' I'd shaken my head. 'No.'

There was a long silence here on the tape. Raoul was still looking at me. From time to time, he'd been stroking my ankle, a light touch, the tips of his fingers, neither unpleasant nor menacing. Quite the contrary, in fact. Now, he'd withdrawn his hand.

'What's the matter?' I'd said at last.

'You.'

'What do you mean?'

He'd shaken his head, refusing to answer, and when I'd asked the question again, he'd turned over, lying on his back, his hands clasped behind his head. 'It doesn't end there,' he'd said softly. 'You should know that.'

'Where? Doesn't end where?'

'With the dogs.' He'd looked at me sideways. 'You know what matters about Texas? Really matters?'

'Tell me.'

'Mexico. We have the longest border with Mexico, El Paso to the Gulf. And you know something else? About Mexicans?'

'No.'

'Lots of them want to be Americans. That's why they're forever trying to get in. Most of them we catch and ship right back. Some get through, couple of hundred a month maybe. Then there are the others.'

'Others?'

'Yeah. Not many. But enough . . .'

'I don't understand.'

At this point, Raoul had got up on one elbow again. Luis was out in the car park, playing sentry. Every now and then, he'd tap lightly on the window and whisper something in Spanish. He was doing it now and Raoul had frowned, acknowledging him with a grunt, irritated at the interruption. He turned back to me, his interest in my ankle entirely gone.

'To settle in the States, do it properly, you need citizenship,' he'd said. 'We call the Mexicans "wetbacks". If you're a wetback, citizenship's worth more than gold.'

I still hadn't understood. 'And Beckermann?' I'd said.

'Beckermann can fix anything. Including citizenship. For a price.'

'Money?'

'No.'

'What then?'

There was another long silence. I was back at the ranch again. The big Cherokee Chief parked outside the house. The one with the carefully curtained body. Something large inside. Something moving.

'Are we still talking about dogs?' I said.

'Shit, no.'

'Something else, then?'

'Yeah.'

'What?'

'Men. We're talking men. Men fighting men.'

'For money?'

'For bets, sure.'

'Long fights?'

'Sometimes.'

'Stand-up fights?'

'At first.'

'Until . . . ?'

He'd shrugged, not answering, rolling over again, closing his eyes. 'I'm sorry,' he'd said at last, 'I thought that's where we were heading. I thought that's what all this was about.'

On the plane, circling Washington, one wing dipped for final approach, I replayed this final sequence for the third time. As we flew down the Potomac, I listened to Raoul's voice again, the long silences between us, the way he tried to coax me to part with information I didn't have, the way the conversation drifted remorselessly back to that final moment when it dawned on me what we were really discussing. Men fighting men. To death. The loser buried, or burned, or ground into pieces and fed to the cattle. The winner declared an instant American.

Before he left the motel, Raoul had sworn me to secrecy. He'd been working on the story for months. He'd assumed I'd had a contribution. Knowing now that I hadn't, he'd willingly meet the conditions for my silence. He'd talk to the Sun Valley Arms Corp and he'd make some discreet enquiries about the circumstances of Grant Wallace's death amongst his police contacts. They, if anyone, would know about a cover-up. More than this he couldn't do. And more than this I didn't expect. I was still listening to the tape when the White House slid beneath the wing and the landing gear began to rumble down. The heat, I thought, and the smells, and the sweat on the men's faces, watching.

I made the day's first phone call to Stollmann from a booth at National Airport. For a moment or two, because of the noise, I didn't realize he'd answered. Then I recognized the flat, dry voice.

'Sarah,' I said briskly. 'Is the phone secure? Your end?'

'Yes.'

'OK.'

I bent to the phone, shielding the conversation with my body, paranoid, already. I explained that Grant Wallace was dead. I told him the way it had happened and I said I'd gone to ground. I was about to brief him on Beckermann, and Polly Devlin's son, when he interrupted.

'Come back,' he said, 'tonight.'

'I can't.'

'Why not?'

I explained about the FBI watch on international flights. They had my name. My name was on my passport. My new persona, Frances Bevan, would get me as far as the first emigration check. After that, in Wesley's phrase, I was dead meat. Stollmann grunted and told me to get a pen. Then he dictated a Washington telephone number.

'The name's Eddie Cassidy,' he said, before hanging up. 'Give me an hour to sort him out.'

I put down the phone, still staring at the name. Stollmann, as ever, was being careful with the extra details. I left the booth and took my bags outside to the cab rank. By the time I got to the front of the queue, it had started to rain. The first three cabs I donated to people behind. The driver of the fourth, at last, was black and more likely, I thought, to turn a blind eye to the next half-hour or so. I got in, struggling with my cases.

'Pharmacy,' I mumbled. 'I need a syringe.'

The driver studied me in the mirror, totally impassive. 'And after, ma'am?'

'Silver Spring.'

We drove across the city and up through Rock Creek Park. Three blocks from the Walter Reed Medical Center, we stopped at a parade of shops. The one on the end was a pharmacy. It took me less than a minute to buy a pack of five disposable syringes and a $1.50 box of Bandaids.

Back in the cab, I gave the driver an address. '9 Marion Street,' I said, 'and I'd like you to wait.'

'How long?'

'Not sure. Depends.'

'You know the rate?'

'Of course.'

'OK,' he shrugged, 'ma'am.'

We set off again, skirting Silver Spring. I had my jacket off by now, and I was undoing the cuff of the blouse I was wearing underneath. I could see the driver's eyes in the mirror, flicking up and down, uncertain what to do. National Airport to Silver Spring, I told myself, was a good fare. Add the extra he'd get for waiting and the man was looking at a hundred dollars, probably more. A hundred dollars was serious money. Too serious to risk losing.

We were slowing for lights now. I rolled back the sleeve of the blouse, exposing my forearm. The car stopped and I extracted the needle of the syringe from its tiny plastic scabbard, clenching my fist and massaging the biggest vein I could find. Then I drove the needle into the knotty blue vessel, feeling it slide in, easing the handle of the syringe out, watching it fill with blood. The blood was a deep scarlet, and when the syringe was full, I pulled it out, covering the wound with my thumb, fumbling for a plaster, stemming the trickle of blood. We were off again by now, traffic everywhere, the driver still looking at me in the mirror, big white eyes, slow shakes of the head.

In Marion Street, I told him to turn round and park. Then I wrapped the syringe in a Kleenex and got out.

'Fifteen minutes,' I told him, 'maybe longer.'

'You paying me now?'

'No.'

'You leaving yo' bags?'

'Yes.'

'OK.'

I set off down the street. McGrath's red camper was still parked beside the house at the end. I knocked on the door, hearing Nghien running down the hall. When the door opened, he was obviously pleased to see me.

'Miss Sarah,' he said.

He let me in, still beaming, leading me straight to McGrath's bedroom. According to the calculations I'd made in the plane, Cathy wasn't due until mid-afternoon. With luck, McGrath would be alone. Nghien pushed the door open. McGrath was lying in bed watching television. The room, thank God, was empty. I turned round to thank Nghien, but he'd gone. McGrath was watching me from the bed. He wasn't smiling.

'Surprise me,' he said drily. 'You're back for more.'

'Only one thing.' I paused. 'Then I'll go.'

'I've told you everything I can,' he said. 'There's nothing more.'

I smiled at him, drawing up a chair, wondering whether Nghien would be back.

'All I want is a name.' I paused, leaning forward. 'Remember we talked about the dogs? The pit-bulls? Down at Beckermann's place?'

McGrath's eyes flicked towards the window. The closest he got to acknowledging the question was a tiny pursing of the lips. I got up quickly, anticipating the tiny lunge he made for the gooseneck, pushing the mouthpiece away, catching his head as it tried to hinge forward. He felt thin and frail. His eyes were an inch from mine.

'You wanna hurt me,' he muttered, 'you're gonna have to work at it.'

I ignored the gibe, laying him back against the pillows, adjusting the gooseneck so it was beyond his reach. Then I took the little parcel of Kleenex from my bag and began to unwrap it. The sight of the syringe full of blood made McGrath frown. I laid it carefully on the bedside table.

'Wesley,' I said carefully, 'sends his regrets.'

McGrath blinked. He wasn't slow on the uptake. 'Where is he?'

'Downtown. In a hotel. Sick.'

'And that . . .' he indicated the syringe with the merest tilt of his head, 'is his?'

'Yes.'

'You're lying.'

'OK.' I shrugged, picking up the syringe. 'So maybe I am. Is that a risk you want to take? Or would you prefer to hear the question first?'

I looked at him a moment, expecting a reply, but he didn't say a word. He couldn't take his eyes off the syringe. Every time I moved, he was there with it. I reached across as gently as I could with my free hand and pulled back the sheet. McGrath's arm lay dead on the crisp white cotton. I began to massage the pale flesh, searching for a vein.

'I need the name of an owner,' I said, 'of Mogul. Remember Mogul? Top dog?'

'Beckermann owns Mogul.'

'I know. But where did he get him from? Who owned him before? Before Beckermann took over?'

McGrath looked up at me. He was sweating now. I could smell it. He shook his head. 'Can't say,' he muttered.

I smiled, asking the question again, mopping his forehead with a wipe from the drawer in his bedside cabinet. When he shook his head for the second time, I used another wipe on his forearm.

'You can't feel this,' I said, 'but it's best to stick to the rules.'

'What rules?'

'Hygiene.' I paused. 'Please, listen, I mean it. You have the name. I need the name. No one will know where it's come from. I'll be out of your life. Wesley, too. No phone calls. No visits. Nothing. I promise.'

McGrath was staring up at me now, his eyes wild. 'Have you done it?' he said.

'No.'

'You're sure?'

'Truly.' I held up the full syringe.

'Shit . . .' he shook his head, side to side. What little colour there'd been in his face had quite disappeared.

I began to lower the syringe again, until it dropped beneath his eyeline. From here on in, he'd have to rely on his imagination. I narrowed my eyes, concentrating on his forearm, hearing his throat clearing, the name stuck somewhere in there, struggling to get out. Priddy, drunk, had told me how important Mogul was. Find the name of the previous owner, he'd implied, and the story starts to unravel. McGrath knew the name. And it was nearly more than his life was worth to pass it on. I looked at him now, my face an inch from his.

'Ghattan,' he whispered at last.

I lifted my head. His eyes had closed. 'Spelling?' I said.

'G . . . H . . . A . . .'

I wrote it down. 'First name?'

'François.'

'Thank you.'

I kissed him on the forehead, squeezing his dead arm. Then I stood up, turning on my heel, heading for the door. Outside, in the street, the cab began to back towards me.

I phoned Stollmann's friend from a hotel near Du Pont Circle. I'd checked on flights out of Dulles Airport and made reservations on two of them in my false name. That way, whatever happened next, I knew there were two empty seats, eastward-bound. The number I had took me directly to Eddie Cassidy, no secretaries, no switchboard.

He was even brisker than Stollmann. 'Where are you?'

'Holiday Inn. Rhode Island and Seventeenth.'

'Go sit in the bar. I'll be there in fifteen minutes.'

I did what I was told, ordering a plate of ham sandwiches. I was still eating them when Stollmann's friend arrived. He was wearing a very loud jacket in electric blue. Booze had reddened his face and his hair looked prematurely grey, but the smile seemed genuine enough.

He sat down beside me, waving away the offer of a sandwich.

'This is kinda complex,' he began, 'and somewhat irregular.' He produced a long, white envelope. On the top left-hand corner, blue script, it said 'US Customs and Immigration'. He opened the envelope with a perfectly buffed nail and shook the contents on to the table. The first thing I picked up was the British Airways ticket. It had my name on it. Sarah Moreton. I showed it to him, shaking my head.

'There's a problem,' I said. 'You may have heard.'

'Yeah.' He looked at me. 'That's why I'm here.'

He hesitated a moment, on the point of asking me a question, then he changed his mind and began to brief me on the arrangements he'd been able to make. I was to take a cab to Dulles Airport. I was to go to a public phone on the concourse and dial a certain number. A colleague of his would come down and collect me. In due course, I would find myself aboard BA 222. Eight hours later, all being well, I'd be home. I stared at him. It sounded absurdly simple, a sleight of hand, a transatlantic conjuring trick.

'How come,' I said, 'it's so easy?'

Cassidy looked at me for a long time. Then he shook his head, standing up, reluctant to extend the relationship a moment longer.

'Eric's a very good friend of mine,' he muttered, 'so let's make sure he fucking survives all this.'

23

We landed at Heathrow at half past seven next morning, bumping down through layer after layer of cloud to a cold,
wet dawn. I took the tube into London, sitting beside my cases
in a near-empty carriage, reading a copy of that morning's *Sunday
Times*. One headline announced a seventy per cent pay increase
for some captain of industry. Another speculated on the possibility
of three million out of work. A secure job, ran the latter story's
opening paragraph, has now become a thing of the past. Some
people are frightened, others just resigned. Looking at the
occasional face on the platforms heading east – pale, slack,
expressionless – that seemed about right.

Back home, at the flat, I piled the post on the television, had
a bath and tried to take stock. I'd brought back everything I
could – tapes, names, addresses, impressions, detailed notes on
individual encounters – and I'd spent half the night on the plane
trying to get all this material into some kind of order. The result
was a dozen or so pages of squiggly longhand, a day-by-day
account of exactly what had happened, and I knew that one of
my first jobs would be to convert it all into a formal source
report, including the all-important 'field comment', my own views
on the value and implications of what I'd brought back.

One of the joys of working for Stollmann was his obsession
with presentation. Whatever you did, however long it took,
source reports had to look sensational. Time, therefore, to ask
him to find me a decent word processor. The first two calls to
the private numbers I'd been using from the States got me
nowhere. The numbers rang and rang, but nobody answered.
Thinking he might be at work, even on a Sunday, I rang his direct
line at Curzon House, but when the connection went through all

I got was the unobtainable signal. Puzzled, I phoned the main switchboard, asking for him by name.

'Who is this, please?'

'Sarah Moreton.' I paused. 'Registry.'

'A moment, please.'

There was a long silence, then a man's voice I didn't recognize. He sounded old and rather distracted, as if I'd interrupted something infinitely more important. 'You're after whom?'

'Eric Stollmann.'

'Then I'm afraid we can't help you.'

'Why not?'

'He ... ah ... no longer works here.'

'Since when?'

'Last week, I believe.'

'Has he been transferred?'

'No, I believe not.'

'What, then?'

'Ah ... reassigned, I think, would cover it.'

'Oh.' I frowned. 'So where is he?'

I waited for an answer but the phone went dead in my ear, and I sat on the sofa for a moment or two, a towel wrapped round my head, wondering what on earth might have happened. On the phone, the times I'd called from the States, Stollmann had sounded even flatter than usual. But *reassigned*? What in God's name did that mean?

Late morning, none the wiser, I set out for the hospital. A call to Mark, Wesley's boyfriend, had drawn yet another blank, but the people at the hospital had told me on the phone that visiting hours were unrestricted, so I went regardless.

St Mary's Hospital is a big medical complex in West London. Paddington Station lies at one end, and there's a brand new wing that overlooks the Grand Union Canal. Wesley, according to the admissions clerk, was in Victoria Ward, part of the original hospital.

I arrived just after midday, realizing how nervous I was. My counselling work at Charlie's had always stopped at the hospital gates. After our clients were diagnosed as having full-blown AIDS and admitted to a hospital or a hospice, other people took over. What would I find? How much difference would a couple of weeks have made?

Victoria Ward was on the first floor, a long, cluttered, neon-lit room with a dozen or so beds. There were nurses in loose green overalls, and a handful of visitors. It was extraordinarily quiet, only the low murmur of bedside conversations, even the big television in the middle turned down to a whisper.

I hesitated for a moment in the corridor, peering in at the rows of beds. Some of them were curtained off, and I began to wonder if I'd chosen a bad moment when I recognized Wesley down the far end. He was occupying a bed by the window, exactly where his mother had described. He was propped up on a bank of pillows, enveloped in a pair of red pyjamas, pointing something out in a newspaper to a visitor sitting beside him. Infinitely more important than anything else was the expression on his face. As far as I could judge, he was smiling.

I walked down the ward, avoiding a traffic jam of drip trolleys. When I got to the foot of the bed, the visitor glanced up. He was younger than Wesley, mid-twenties. Under the tan he looked exhausted. I smiled.

'Mark?'

He nodded, nudging Wesley. Wesley lowered the paper, the eyes even bigger in the hollowed spaces of his face. When I'd left him, at Dallas/Fort Worth, he'd been thin. Now, he was skeletal.

'Fuck me,' he whispered. 'You're back.'

Mark made space for me beside the bed. We had tea from a passing trolley. A nurse found a vase for the roses I'd brought. After the chaos of the last week or so, it was an extraordinarily peaceful moment, the weak sunlight puddling on the buffed lino-leum, Wesley seemingly back from the dead.

After a while, Wesley told Mark to get his temperature chart from the foot of the bed, and he took me through the story of his last few days, pointing out the peaks and troughs, still shud-dering at what little he could remember. At times, he muttered, he'd wanted to give up completely, surfing up and down through semi-consciousness, keen for the whole wretched business to be over. He'd had the sweats again, even worse than last time, and diarrhoea, too, so badly that he said he'd been able to feel his insides melting away, the muscles shredding off the bone, yards and yards of viscera just emptying down the pan. One last push, he'd thought, just another minute or two, and I'm gone.

Listening to him go through it again, I realized how much he'd changed. His conversation was slow and halting, the voice weak, and he'd plainly been badly frightened by the whole experience. His mortality had come home to him, a thing of flesh and blood, and the last few days had taught him, above all, that there was absolutely nowhere to hide. Booze wouldn't do it. Nor any other drug. He'd tried everything else, every mind game he could think of, but nothing had helped. In the end, it was just you and the virus. Endgame.

'Rough,' he said at last, 'fucking grim.'

Later, Mark gone, I told Wesley most of what had happened in the States, day by day, picking up at the point when he'd left me at Dallas/Fort Worth. I told him about my visits to Grant's place and his death, and I showed him a page or two of the chronology I'd brought back. I described the drive north up to Washington, and I said how thoughtful he'd been to spare me any kind of warning about Jake McGrath. Why hadn't he mentioned the man's state of health, for God's sake? Why hadn't he told me he was paralysed? At this, Wesley's eyes rolled towards me.

'He OK?' he said.

I blinked. 'Yes,' I said, 'considering.'

'Considering what?'

'His state of health.' I bent towards him, the way you would to a naughty child, someone you loved, someone you had to scold. 'You should have told me,' I repeated. 'It would have saved me a lot of embarrassment.'

Wesley was frowning now, trying to concentrate. 'What?' he kept saying. 'Told you what?'

'His paralysis,' I explained patiently, 'the fact that he can't move. I didn't know. It would have helped.'

Wesley's frown deepened. 'You talking about Grant?' he said helplessly. 'Some kind of accident?'

I looked at him for a long moment, then away down the ward. First impressions were worst impressions. Wesley wasn't better at all.

'Jake,' I whispered to him, turning back, 'in Silver Spring.'

Wesley peered up at me. I could see how hard he was trying to follow me. 'Jake?'

'McGrath.'

'Ah . . .' he nodded at last, 'Washington.'

I skipped on trying to pretend nothing had happened, taking the story back to Dallas and Grant's death. I told him about getting in touch with Raoul Delahunty when things got really tricky. I passed lightly over the fact that Raoul was a fellow journalist, but Wesley caught the word and stopped me.

'Journo?' he whispered.

'Yes.'

'And you gave him the story?'

'Not much of it.'

'But some of it?'

'A little,' I nodded, 'yes.'

Wesley was silent for a moment, his head back on the pillow, his tongue moving slowly over his lips, moistening them. His lips were dry and cracked and a little swollen.

'Scum,' he said at last.

'Who?'

'Journalists.'

I reached out, patting his arm, trying to reassure him, telling him how clever I thought I'd been, explaining again how little I'd actually told the American and how much he'd given me in return. For the first time, Wesley's face came alive, some nerve in perfect working order, some deep instinct, out of reach of the virus.

'Mexicans?' he asked, incredulous. 'Killing each other? For citizenship?'

'That's what Raoul says.'

'No bullshit? He can stand it up?'

'So he says.'

'Christ!' He shook his head on the pillow, bright-eyed. 'Unreal.'

Encouraged, I began to tell him about Peter Devlin, the smiling young Englishman I'd met out at the ranch, the minister's son. This, I said, was surely the heart of it, Peter Devlin, the conduit, the backstairs channel for all that embargoed hardware. People in the know said he was. Jake McGrath had told me so himself. I looked at Wesley. His eyes were closed again.

'Old story,' he whispered at last.

I frowned, engaged now. 'What's an old story?'

'Devlin. Peter. Polly. The Texcal consultancy. It's been doing the rounds for ever, but no one's had the bottle to see it into print. Old hat. Believe me . . .'

'But if it's true?'

Wesley opened one eye, looking up at me.

'So what?'

'So *what*?'

'Yeah, so what? These spivs have been at it since '79. Fingers in the till. Everyone knows they have. The whole fucking world knows it . . .' he paused, out of breath, '. . . and fuck all ever happens.'

He closed his eyes again, shaking his head, and I reached for him, the way you do to someone you want to shake awake, the house on fire, something terrible about to happen.

'Wesley,' I hissed.

A patient on the other side of the ward glanced our way. I gave him an uncertain smile, lowering my voice, withdrawing my hand. Wesley was looking at me once again. The expression on his face suggested he'd found another story, infinitely more personal, infinitely more important. I smiled at him. One last try, I thought. Just one.

'Your friend gave me a name,' I said, 'but I'm not sure where it fits.'

'Who?'

'Jake. Jake McGrath. He wasn't keen on telling me but . . .' I shrugged.

Wesley was still looking at me. I think he was nearly asleep.

'What name?' he said.

'François,' I said, 'François Ghattan.'

Wesley frowned, a heroic effort of concentration.

'Ghattan?'

'Yes.'

'And Jake told you that?'

'He told me that the two of them were close. This François and Beckermann. They were both into pit-bulls. In fact Ghattan used to own this Mogul creature I told you about.'

Wesley nodded, and then gave a deep sigh, his eyes starting to close. I touched him lightly on the face, then got up and began to apologize for banging on so much. Wesley's hand found mine.

'Ghattan's dead,' he said. 'Jake tell you that, too?'

'No.'

'He died a couple of months back. In the summer.' He frowned. 'In Dallas, I think.'

'Oh?' I sat down again. 'What was the matter with him?'

There was a long silence. Then the eyes flickered open. 'I'm not sure,' he said vaguely, 'but I think he had a heart problem.'

I left ten minutes later, Wesley asleep. I took another cab back to the flat, exhausted myself, and was on the point of getting into bed when the phone rang. I went back into the living room. It was Stollmann.

'Good flight?'

'Fine . . .' I yawned, 'thanks.'

'Eddie phoned. Said you were safely away. We need to meet.'

'Now?'

'Yes.' He paused. 'Please.'

I said nothing for a moment, remembering the call I'd made to Curzon House, the news that Stollmann had, in the office parlance, been 'reassigned'.

'Where are you?' I said. 'As a matter of interest?'

'At home.'

I nodded. According to rumour, Stollmann lived out in the sprawl of suburbs around New Malden. No one had ever been to his house, invited or otherwise, and no one had a clue whether he shared his life with anyone else. I stifled another yawn. According to the digital clock on the video recorder, it was half past five, though it felt closer to midnight.

'Where?' I said numbly. 'And when?'

I met Stollmann at a café at the bottom of Kingsway an hour and a half later. He was sitting at a table at the back. He was hunched over a cup of black coffee and he still had his coat on. His face, when he glanced up, was grey. He looked terrible.

I sat down without saying anything. For the first time in our relationship, I realized I felt sorry for him. Something had been taken away from him, something had gone and the evidence was there in every movement he made. Whether or not I managed to type up the source report, I suspected, was now academic.

At length, he sat back, examining me across the table.

'You've been reassigned,' I said.

'Yes.'

'What does that mean?'

He looked at me a moment longer, then shrugged. 'It means they've moved me. Physically, I no longer work at Curzon House.' He paused. 'The job's gone, too. As of yesterday. My decision. Not theirs.'

I nodded, saying nothing. Exactly where Stollmann figured in the pecking order, I'd never quite worked out. He'd certainly been my boss for a while, but his other responsibilities seemed to have cut across some of the more traditional boundaries. In MI5 terms, that made him inter-departmental, a hybrid, an object of instant suspicion.

'Why?' I said at last. 'Why did they do it?'

'Is that a serious question?'

'Yes,' I nodded, 'if you don't mind me asking.'

'Not at all.' He offered me a thin smile. 'It's your head, too, as it happens.'

'Oh?'

'Yes. They'll get round to writing to you sooner or later.' He paused. 'Here,' he said, 'before I forget.'

He took a buff envelope from his pocket and gave it to me. I opened it. Inside, made out in my name, was a cheque for £4516.98.

'What's that for?' I said.

'Your American expenses. It's a guess, I'm afraid, but it should help.'

'It's more than enough,' I said. 'What about the receipts?'

'Submit them as usual.'

'And what about the difference?'

I looked at him. Mentally, I'd calculated my American expenses at just under four thousand pounds. That included hotels, hire car, air tickets and one or two extras.

Stollmann shrugged again. 'Put it down to wear and tear,' he said grimly. 'Call it combat fatigue.'

He signalled the waiter and ordered beans on toast. When they arrived he dribbled a large X of Brown Sauce across the top while I finished telling him most of what had happened in the States. In between mouthfuls, he drank more coffee, listening in silence while I described events in Dallas. When I got to the bit about Peter Devlin, he nodded, mopping his plate with a slice of white bread.

'You talk to him at all?'

'No. Not really.'

'Priddy mention him?'

'No. Refused to discuss it.'

'But you tried?'

'Yes.' I nodded. 'Of course.'

I hesitated, awaiting more questions, but Stollmann pushed his plate carefully to one side and told me to go on. When I finally got to the end of it, he was studying the menu.

I looked at him a moment. A great deal of stress and a bad case of jet lag weren't doing much for my temper.

'So you're out on your own?' I said drily. 'Free agent?'

'Hardly.'

'No?'

He gazed at me a moment, not answering. Then he glanced round, signalling the waiter for the bill, reaching for his wallet.

'Let's walk,' he said.

We left the café and stood at the kerbside a moment. The last of the rush-hour traffic was swirling down Kingsway and there were little squads of theatre-goers bustling towards Covent Garden and Leicester Square. I glanced at Stollmann. He was hunched inside his thin, black raincoat. One corner of his mouth was still smudged with brown sauce.

We walked south, along the Strand, then down by Charing Cross Station. On the Embankment, the shadows hid a ragged line of cardboard boxes. There were bodies inside, already asleep, huddled in newspapers. We climbed the steps to the pedestrian bridge beside the railway line that crosses the Thames. The water was black beneath us, the trains clattering past.

Half-way across the bridge, Stollmann stopped. Turning his back on the railway, he leaned against the parapet, his elbows on the top, gazing out at the lights downstream. One or two commuters hurried past, heads down, then an old tramp. The tramp asked for money. Stollmann gave him a pound. The man lurched off, muttering to himself. It was a cold, raw night, the cloud mostly gone, a bitter wind off the river.

'You'll have gathered most of it,' Stollmann said at last, 'if I'm any judge.'

'You mean Priddy?' I said.

'Yes.' I nodded. It all seemed logical enough. Priddy had doubtless been encouraging exports into Iraq. Stuff that should never have got through. Thus the Dallas links with Peter Devlin and Beckermann.

'We're on to him?' I said. 'Priddy's under investigation? Is that what we're saying?'

Stollmann looked at me a moment. 'We?' he said bleakly.

I gazed at him, beginning at last to understand. MI5 had been off-limits to the politicians for years, one of the few government agencies they couldn't control. Now, it seemed, they were putting the record straight. Starting with Stollmann.

'Is that why they've sacked you,' I said, 'for going after Priddy?'

'Effectively,' he nodded, 'yes.'

'For asking the wrong questions? Upsetting our masters?'

'Yes.'

'No backing? No authority?'

Stollmann said nothing for a moment. A woman with a cello case walked past.

'I come from Customs and Excise,' he said at length. 'Wrong pedigree. No chums. In this game, it pays to have chums.'

I nodded again, remembering the day I'd trailed Stollmann to the Westminster Baths, the image of him still fresh in my mind, the stiff, driven figure, forcing his way up and down the pool. Stollmann had made no friends at Curzon House. He was too serious, too diligent, too stern. He was looking at me now. His eyes were very black.

'As a matter of interest,' I said, 'what do you think about the other thing?'

'Other thing?'

'Wesley Keogh's little theory. The war that never was. All that.'

Stollmann frowned. 'I think it's a fantasy,' he said at last, 'and I think it's irrelevant.'

'So why did you give me the file in the first place?'

'To get you to Dallas. Alongside Priddy.'

'You knew he'd be there?'

'Of course.'

'And you knew Wesley was going?'

'Yes. I'd seen the brief from Aldridge. I knew Wallace was the prime source. Wallace lived in Dallas. Sooner or later, Keogh would meet him. All I had to do was check the bookings.'

'The airline bookings?'

'Yes.'

'Knowing you could send me, too? Using Wesley as cover? When Priddy was there?'

'Yes.'

I stared down at the water. A tug had appeared beneath us, pushing hard against the flood tide. Behind, one by one, a string of barges.

I turned back to Stollmann. 'I don't understand,' I said. 'Why didn't you simply tell me? I could have gone to Dallas in any case, just for Priddy. I could have done the whole number on the man. No Wesley. No Gulf War. Just me and him.' I paused. 'So why dress it up?'

For the first time, Stollmann smiled. 'You think that was for your benefit,' he said grimly, 'all the games about Keogh? You think that's why they've—'

He broke off, his rage for once running away with him. He turned on his heel, beginning to walk again. I caught up with him, angry myself now, my head full of questions I should have asked far earlier. I grabbed his arm, a clumsy gesture, but effective. He stopped, shaking me off.

'They?' I said. 'Who're they?'

'Who do you think?'

'We talking about Five? Curzon House?'

He looked at me, saying nothing, a silence that affirmed my every word. He began to walk again, but I stood in front of him, knowing he'd have to stop, knowing that the very awkwardness of the scene would force him, in the end, to talk.

'Why they've what?' I said. 'Tell me.'

He shook his head, his elbows back on the parapet. At the end of the bridge, where the steps dropped down to the South Bank, I could see another tramp heading our way. News of Stollmann's largesse must have got around. Time was short.

'You're after Priddy,' I said, 'and they've stopped you. They've stopped you because they're the masters now, they're in charge.' I paused. 'Am I right?'

'Masters?' he asked. 'Who?'

'The politicians. HMG. People like Priddy.' I bent close to him. 'The spivs. Just tell me, am I right?'

Stollmann looked at me for a second or two. 'Yes,' he said softly.

I nodded, determined not to lose the initiative, determined to squeeze Stollmann dry while time and his own resentments allowed.

'So they've seen through Wesley and Aldridge and Extec and all the rest of it. They've seen through all the smoke and mirrors, all your little alibis, and now they've dragged you off.'

'Yes.'

'Before it gets too awkward?'

'Yes.'

'For Priddy?'

'Yes.'

'And Devlin senior?'

'Yes.'

'And one or two others?'

'Of course.'

'Because now even Five does their bidding?'

Stollmann nodded, looking away again. There was a long silence. Another train was on the way.

'Exports,' he said at last. 'They think we're part of the export drive. That's the rationale. That's the line they take. Every shoulder to the wheel. Including ours.' He gazed downriver, towards St Paul's and the fairy lights of the City of London. 'There's no one left in this country who isn't trying to sell something,' he said bitterly. 'You know that?'

We walked to Waterloo Station. The bars were still open and I suggested a drink. Stollmann shook his head, his hands plunged deep inside his coat pockets, his eyes already scanning the departures board, looking for the next train home.

'I've got a couple of interviews tomorrow,' he said. 'Pays to have a clear head.'

'Interviews?' I stared at him. 'Already?'

'Yes.' He offered me his thin smile. 'I was once an accountant, believe it or not. I think I might go back to it. There's still lots of work around . . .' the smile widened, 'mainly in liquidations.'

I nodded, thinking again about the contents of the file this strange, solitary man had handed me, all those busy weeks ago.

'You really think all the Gulf War stuff's a fantasy?' I said. 'You really think that?'

'Yes.'

'Then you're blind,' I said quietly. 'All you see is Priddy and Devlin. The little guys. Trees in the wood.'

Stollmann stared at me. His voice was sharp again, a brief gust of anger. '*Little* guys?'

'Yes. Wesley started the other end, with the big picture. That's the way journalists work. Go for the big theory. The headline. Then set about proving it.' I smiled, my hand on his arm. 'Don't believe me?'

Stollmann looked at me a moment longer, back under control. Then he shook his head, turning away, one eye on the big overhead clock.

'Not a word,' he said. 'But good luck.'

24

Wesley stayed in hospital for the next month. I visited most days, spending an hour or so at his bedside, expecting always to find him better, the old Wesley, that extra-special mixture of earnestness, outrage and high camp.

His moods swung wildly. Sometimes, he'd barely bother to stay awake, just a face on the pillow, the ghost of a smile at this story or that, a grunted request for a different station on the bedside radio, or a cup of tea from the passing trolley. Other times, he'd be sitting up in bed, alert again, engaged, passing on bits and pieces of ward gossip, asking me questions about the States, what I'd made of Jake McGrath, of Grant Wallace, of Raoul Delahunty, whom he now referred to, in his brighter moments, as 'my Dallas screw'. All this I ended up telling him three or four times, simple repetition, nothing added or embellished, and after a week or two I'd begun to suspect the worst.

I put the thought to Mark, his faithful boyfriend. We'd worked out a rota between us for visiting times. Sometimes we overlapped, sharing a table at the Towpath Coffee Shop in the new part of the hospital across the bridge, comparing notes.

'He's different,' I said. 'Something's gone. Something's missing.'

Mark was nodding. 'I know. I've thought about it a lot. If he was a radio, you'd do something about it. You'd give him a shake, tune him in properly.'

'Maybe it's a lousy reception area.' I smiled. 'Have you thought of that?'

He said nothing for a moment or two. His patience, I knew, was wearing thin. Wesley had always pushed him to the limit and now was no different. Except the compensations had gone:

the laughter, the energy, the mischief in the man. Mark sipped at his cappuccino.

'They'll discharge him sooner or later,' he said quietly. 'He won't be here for ever.'

'I know.'

'He wants me to look after him. He can't stand buddying. Strangers. Charity. All that.'

'So I gather.'

Mark looked away a moment. The more I got to know him, the more I liked him. He was quiet and kind and shy, not at all Wesley's style, and the fact that he was HIV positive himself made the whole thing hideously complicated.

'Could you cope?' I said slowly. 'Full time?'

He glanced across at me, wall-eyed. 'No,' he said at last.

I nodded, understanding the realities behind the muttered, one-word answer. The experience of everyday life in Victoria Ward had unnerved him, but the changes in Wesley had made it infinitely worse. Wesley had pitched his tent in the no man's land between HIV and the last rites, and what Mark had seen so far had terrified him.

'His brain's going,' he said, 'I know it is. There's stuff he can't remember any more. Simple stuff. Places we've been. Things we've done. Music. Clubs. Even his mother's second name. They passed on a message from her the other day. On the phone. He couldn't work out who she was.'

He looked at me. His eyes were moist.

'But there are other times,' I put my hand over his, 'when he's back on form.'

'I know. I know.' He shook his head, fumbling for a Kleenex. 'Believe me, I know.'

'So he might get better . . . mightn't he?'

'That's not what they say.'

'Who?'

'The doctors. The consultant. The one with the limp.'

'You've talked to him?' He nodded. I'd bumped into the consultant a number of times. He was a small, thin Indian with a withered leg and a permanently doleful expression, not one of life's optimists. 'What does he say?'

'He says he's got abcesses on the brain. Scars. You can see

them on the X-rays. He showed me. White marks, four or five of them, so . . .' he shrugged, blowing his nose again, 'I imagine that explains it.'

'Are they permanent? These scars?'

'Yes. So I'm told.'

'No chance of getting better?'

'Not short term.'

'Long term?'

Mark glanced up at me, a strange look on his face, at once despairing and reproachful. 'There *is* no long term,' he said softly. 'That's the whole fucking point.'

I went home that afternoon, knowing exactly what I should do. Looking after Wesley would be a full-time occupation, no question, but two phone calls from the personnel department at Curzon House had already convinced me that time wouldn't be a problem. MI5 was evidently confronting a major reorganization. Establishment costs were being slashed right across Whitehall. The woman in the personnel department had a word for it. She called it 'downsizing', and the way she used the word suggested that the loss of jobs – including mine – was simply a sensible piece of management reform.

I, though, knew different. I'd listened to Stollmann. I'd heard the anger and the contempt in his voice. And I knew that the politicians, after decades of frustration, were finally in the saddle. Employees who didn't toe the party line were out. MI5 had become simply another arm of Smith Square, an intelligence machine dedicated to buttressing the doubtful gains of thirteen troubled years.

I arrived back at Fulham to find a letter on the mat. The letter confirmed that my employment with MI5 was being terminated, effective at once. There was a consolatory message from my Group Controller, a new appointee whom I'd never met, and a separate sheet of paper detailed the arrangements the service had made for my redundancy payments. This money would not, I was assured, be subject to tax.

A few days later, back at Wesley's bedside, I gave him the good news.

'I'm a free woman,' I said, 'your future's secure.'

He eyed me from the bed without enthusiasm. Sometimes, like now, he was as alert as ever, the old Wesley.

'What future's that?' he said.

'Convalescence. When they let you out.'

'What about Mark?'

'Mark's been offered a play,' I lied, 'in Glasgow.'

Wesley said nothing, turning his face to the wall. He'd never been one for the normal rules of conversation – question, response – but since I'd come back from the States he'd developed a habit of lapsing into total silence. If he didn't like what he heard, he simply ignored it. I leaned forward. The drugs he was taking gave his breath a sweet, slightly cheesy flavour.

'It'll be fine,' I told him. 'It'll be good. You'll need someone around for a bit. Plus we can try and make sense of . . .' I smiled, 'you know.'

'What?'

'The war. All that.'

Wesley's face turned towards me on the pillow. One yellow eye opened. 'Yeah?' he said.

The morning before Wesley was due to leave hospital, late November, I arrived earlier than usual. The bus had fooled me by turning up on time and I had half an hour in hand. Because I was scrupulous about keeping to the visiting schedule we'd agreed, I waited downstairs, in the big entrance hall, sitting on a bench beside the staircase. I was still on the *Guardian*'s front page when someone stopped beside me. I glanced up. It was Derek Aldridge.

'Long time,' he said pleasantly, extending a hand, 'no see.'

We went outside, into the thin winter sunshine. Aldridge had called by on his way to an interview at the British Forces Broadcasting studios, half a mile north, across the Grand Union Canal. He needed to be there by eleven. We began to walk.

'What do you think?' I said. 'How is he?'

Aldridge said nothing for a moment, buttoning his coat. Only when we were climbing the steps to the canal bank did he answer my question.

'Changed, hasn't he?' he said. 'Changed a lot.'

I nodded. 'Yes.'

'Lost the sharpness. The edge.'

I looked at him. 'It's called AIDS,' I said, 'you may have heard.'

'I know, I know. It's just . . .' He paused.

We were on the towpath now, beside the canal. There was a

narrowboat moored beside the further bank. Smoke curled from a stove-pipe chimney near the bow. Aldridge was still frowning, still hunting for the right word.

'Sad?' I suggested.

'Sure, sure, but something else, too.' He shook his head. 'I can't pin it down, can't put my finger on it. He was always so . . . bloody stroppy. Even that seems to have gone. He's just . . . flat. There's nothing. Absolutely nothing. Just a vacant space. I never thought I'd see it. Never. Not him. Not Wesley.' He looked at me. 'It's as if he's gone already. You know what I mean?'

'Yes,' I said bleakly, 'I do.'

There was a long silence. Gulls swooped over a neat row of council refuse trucks parked opposite. Aldridge, after another look at his watch, seemed in no hurry to move on.

'What's the interview about?' I said idly.

Aldridge pulled a face. 'The Saudis.'

'What about the Saudis?'

'There's a big arms deal. You may have read about it. Al Yamamah. It's huge. Really huge. We've delivered a couple of billion's worth so far. There's another ten billion to come.'

'And?'

'There may be a problem. Nobody really knows. The Saudis are making all the right noises, and we certainly did our bit in the Gulf, but the Americans have their noses in the trough, too.' He paused. 'These things are always trickier than they seem. As you may have gathered.'

He looked down at me a moment, smiling, an invitation to share my tiny secrets, but I didn't respond. Instead, I turned my back on the canal and leaned on the balustrade, looking across the road towards the hospital.

'How are you and Extec?' I said. 'Friends again?'

Aldridge nodded. 'Yes,' he said, 'as a matter of fact.'

'Didn't pull their advertising in the end? Make life hard for you?'

'No, not at all.' He smiled again. '*Au contraire.*'

'Business as usual?'

'Yes, plus some.' The smile became a grin. 'Rather encouraging, actually.'

I hesitated a moment wondering whether to pursue it, then

shrugged, deciding there was no point. The thing was history. What mattered now was Wesley.

'Good,' I said, offering him a bright smile of my own, 'nice to hear someone's making it.'

Wesley left hospital a couple of days later. He wore the clothes he'd arrived in, newly laundered, and they enveloped his shrunken frame. I'd brought my car over from Fulham, and I helped him out of the door and across the pavement to the kerbside. I'd packed enough clothes of my own to last at least a week. I'd no idea when I'd be back.

We drove south, across the river, out through Battersea and Wandsworth. The traffic on the A3 was light, the rush hour come and gone, and we were out of London within the hour. Just past the junction with the M25, Wesley spotted a sign by the roadside. It said 'RHS Gardens, Wisley'. He nodded at it.

'You mind?' he said.

I pulled the car off the road, following the signs, glad to have found a response at last. So far, he'd said virtually nothing, sitting beside me, the roll-up on the dashboard unlit, the huge eyes staring ahead, unblinking.

We parked the car and began to walk. It was a lovely day again, but there was a cold wind from the east and I made Wesley wear my anorak. What should have looked absurd, didn't. In fact, it fitted him rather well. We walked for maybe a quarter of a mile, very slowly, my arm through his. Then he sank on to one of the slatted wooden benches that line the path. His face was pale and sweaty and he was having trouble getting his breath, but he leaned away from me when I tried to zip up the anorak.

We sat in silence for a minute or two, gazing around. The gardens were magnificent, no one else to be seen, the huge trees ablaze with autumn. Down the bottom of a slight hill, I could see ducks on water, the sunlight splintering as one of them took off. I turned to Wesley, pointing it out. Tears were pouring down his face.

'What's the matter?' I said.

He shook his head. 'Nothing.'

'Please, tell me.'

'It's nothing. Nothing.'

'Wesley?'

I reached across and touched his face. The flesh was ice cold. He didn't move.

'Favourite season, this,' he said at last, 'always was. Never understood why.'

'Autumn?'

'Yeah. Mists. Mellow fruitfulness. Decay...' He sniffed. 'Death.' He looked at me. 'That sound about right?'

I smiled, trying to comfort him. 'It's beautiful,' I said, 'and so are you.'

'Bullshit. I'm dying. There's nothing beautiful about that. It's dull as fuck.'

'You're not dull.'

'No, but dying is. Believe me.'

He lapsed into silence again. Then a squirrel hopped into sight, bobbing across the grass towards us. It stopped no more than a yard away, head up, tail arched, looking Wesley in the eye. Wesley studied it for a moment. Then he produced a coin from my anorak pocket and tossed it towards the squirrel. It was a new twenty-pence piece. It gleamed in the sunshine. The squirrel didn't move.

'It wants bread,' I said, 'something to eat. The idea is you feed it.'

Wesley was still watching the squirrel. He couldn't take his eyes off it. Finally, for the first time that morning, he mustered the beginnings of a grin. It spread across his face, bringing it to life.

'Bollocks,' he said quietly. 'Bet the little fucker's on the take.'

When we got to Wesley's flat, it had been redecorated. I stood in the lounge, astonished at the transformation. White walls. Sage for the skirting boards and the picture rails. Even a new pair of curtains, scarlet velvet lined in a glorious deep blue. Professional job. Tastefully done. I gazed round. It was even warm.

'Who did all this,' I said, 'the tooth fairy?'

Wesley smiled. Physically, the journey had wrecked him, but he seemed much more cheerful. 'Aldridge fixed it up,' he said. 'The last couple of weeks. He dropped by this morning, too. Switched on the heating. First thing.'

'*Aldridge*? Why?'

'Conscience. Plus he was embarrassed to bring his women here.

Appearances mean a lot to Derek. You probably noticed.'

'So he got the decorators in?'

'Yeah. Little surprise.' He frowned, unsure about the final effect. 'What do you think?'

'It's nice. I'm amazed.'

'So am I.'

He walked across the room, very slowly, an old, old man. Then he sank into the armchair beside the fireplace. I looked round, knowing something was missing.

'Where's Scourge?' I said. 'The cat?'

Wesley said nothing for a moment. When we'd flown to Dallas, he'd mentioned something about 'arrangements'. I assumed, like me, that he'd put the animal into the local cattery. But now he shook his head.

'He went,' he said.

'Went where?'

'Away.' His eyes revolved upwards. 'The big duvet in the sky.'

'You had him put down?'

'Yes.'

'Why?'

He looked at me for a moment. Then he smiled.

'Get things ready,' he said, 'for little me.'

Wesley was in bed by six o'clock. I made him as comfortable as I could and spent the rest of the evening in the living room, curled up on the floor under a blanket. Twice I tried to phone Raoul in Dallas, but both times he was out. By ten o'clock, I, too, was asleep.

I awoke to total darkness, unsure for a moment where I was. It was stiflingly hot and I rolled over, fanning the blanket to get some air. Beneath the door was a thin strip of light. Going to bed in the tiny spare room, I'd switched off all the lights, I was sure of it. It was an old habit, acquired from my father. I frowned, up now on one elbow, aware of something else, notes, music, something familiar picked out on a piano with agonizing slowness. I listened hard, trying to recognize the piece, the right hand picking its way softly down the keyboard, falling chords with the left, an inexpressible sadness.

I slipped out of bed. There was a piano next door, in the corner, away from the window. I'd never seen Wesley play it and we'd never discussed music at all, but if there was another way of expressing what he'd tried to say earlier, in the gardens at Wisley, then this was it. Rachmaninov. Second Piano Concerto. Wesley's kind of music. One hundred per cent over the top.

I opened the door, shrouded in a blanket, and tiptoed down the hall. The door to the living room was ajar an inch or two, enough for me to peer in. Wesley was sitting at the piano. He was wearing Mark's silk dressing gown, three-quarter length, and he was playing without music. From time to time he stopped and recapitulated the theme, tugging it out, again and again, note-perfect. There was a candle stuck in a saucer on top of the piano and the guttering light played on the planes of his face, softening the harder angles, filling the deeper hollows. His eyes were closed and his head dipped and swayed with the music, and after a while I crept back to bed, knowing I'd trespassed.

Next morning, I didn't mention the incident. When Wesley asked me if I'd slept OK, I said yes. He seemed rested and a lot more peaceful. In the living room, when I went to tidy up, there was no evidence of the candle, except the smell.

At ten o'clock, Wesley still in bed, I said I'd go out shopping. There was no food in the house and supplies of stuff like bleach and washing powder were pretty low. Wesley gave me directions for the nearest supermarket, and said he'd be up when I got back. He needed a bath. He felt much better. He'd even join me for a little light lunch. I took the car to the supermarket. I had a list of foods from the people at the hospital and I supplemented it with lots of the other stuff we always recommended at Charlie's. By twelve o'clock, I was back outside the flat, unloading the cardboard boxes from the boot.

I knew something was wrong the moment I got to the side door. I could hear the sound of water falling. It seemed to be coming from the downstairs flat. I peered in through the nearest window, but the curtains were pulled. I fumbled for my keys, opening the door to Wesley's flat. Upstairs, the bathroom door was open. I looked inside. The bath was full of water, both taps still on. Wesley was lying full-length, his feet towards the taps, only his nose above the surface. I bent towards him, thinking the worst, understanding now about the Rachmaninov, his requiem, his personal goodbye. I reached down, my hands under his armpits, and hauled him upright. Water spilled out of his mouth. I patted him hard on the back, the way you do it to a baby after a feed, and he began to choke. After a while, no more water came out. One eye opened. He was very drowsy. He looked at me, uncomprehending.

'Yeah?' he said.

I began to say something foolish, a mixture of anger and relief, but I thought better of it. I turned off the taps and pulled out the plug, helping him upright. There was water everywhere. It had spilled across the lino and poured down between the floorboards. I could still hear it falling into the flat beneath and there was a smell, too, something acrid, something electrical. Wesley was hanging on to me now, groaning. He said he wanted to be sick and I bent him over the lavatory bowl, forcing his mouth open, inserting my index finger, trying to remember just how many tablets they'd given him at the hospital dispensary to take away. Some of them, if you took enough, would kill you. No question.

Wesley was being sick now, a thin stream of vomit, yellowish, almost viscous. It smelled odd, no food of any kind and I knew then that I'd been right. God knows how many tablets he'd swallowed, but with luck – if I could empty his stomach – he'd survive. The huge head came up, gasping for air, the veins knotting in his neck, and I waited a second or two before walking him back to the bath. I began to refill the bath, and forced his head down, his mouth underwater.

'Drink,' I told him. 'Drink the stuff. As much as you can.'

He nodded, his head still down there, swallowing mouthful after mouthful, a primitive kind of stomach pump, and then I brought him up again, in time for the stuff to spill back out, thinner this time, his whole body wracked by spasms.

'Jesus,' he kept saying, 'Jesus Christ!'

Finally, minutes later, I knew there was nothing else I could do. He'd stopped being sick, except for a dribble of green bile, and if he died now it would be from exposure. He was icy cold, his body wrapped in a thin bath towel, the first thing I'd managed to lay my hands on. I helped him back to bed, drying him with fresh towels, rubbing the warmth back into his thin body, dressing him in a sweatshirt and a tracksuit from my own case. The electrical smell was much stronger now and I could hear a fizzing noise, somewhere in the flat below. I mentioned it to Wesley, tucking him in.

'Mosquitoes,' he mumbled vaguely, staring at the wall.

I went downstairs again. The entrance to the ground-floor flat was at the front. I rang the bell. Then again. There was no reply. Alarmed now, I went back round the side, trying each window as I passed. They were all shut. Finally, knowing there was no alternative, I chose the smallest piece of glass I could find and smashed it with a half-brick from the garden. Standing on the windowsill, knocking the glass inside, reaching through, I felt my way to the catch on the big window, slipping it up. I knew now that, at the very least, I'd found the source of the smell. It came from this very room. I could swear it.

I opened the window and stepped inside, through the heavy curtains. The floor was awash, the carpet soggy underfoot. I felt my way towards the door, meaning to find a light switch, then I had second thoughts, nervous about the electrics. Instead, I returned to the window and pulled back the curtains. Daylight flooded into the room and I looked round. The room had once been a small lounge of some kind or perhaps a study. Now, though, there were racks of recording equipment lining the far wall, professional stuff, Revox quarter-inch two-reel machines, monitoring scanners, the lot. I stared at it all, the carefully taped cables looping up into the ceiling, spike microphones driven into the plasterboard, more cables running towards the door. Ignoring the smell now and the fizz of a short circuit, I followed the cable paths into other rooms. Everywhere I went in the flat the ceilings were wired for more microphones, and I began to count them all, recognizing the handiwork, the careful grid of listening electronic ears, every inch of Wesley's flat wired for sound.

I splashed back to the room I'd broken into. This, it seemed, was the heart of the operation. There was a table in the middle with a pile of ring binders. Opening the top one, I saw the master schedule, a list of audio cassettes carefully logged alongside a time and a date. I looked up. On a shelf beside the rack of recording machines was a matching line of audio cassettes. Each one had been indexed, the letters and numbers corresponding with the written log. On the floor, beneath the shelf, was a cardboard box. I opened it. Inside, miraculously dry, were dozens more cassettes. I took out a handful, examining them. These, it seemed, had been edited. One of them, to my amusement, was labelled 's. MORETON. TRANSATLANTIC CALLS. OCTOBER '91'.

I stood in the room a moment longer, debating what to do. The set-up was all too familiar, a Section A job, one of the operations run from a suite of offices off Wilton Street, and I remembered the scene on one of my first visits, all those weeks ago, the estate agent and the new tenant on the lawn, taking down the 'For Sale' sign. They'd moved in then. They'd been running the operation ever since I'd arrived. Checking again, I even recognized the handwriting in the ring binders. I'd seen output like this in Registry, photocopies that came through to us for filing. Given a couple of phone calls, I could even come up with a name, Sweeney or Campbell or Blundy, any one of the familiar cyphers who spent their working lives supplying us with other people's conversations.

I went back to the hall. The electrics in the flat were old, and the fuse box over the front door was smouldering. I got a chair and stood on it, and took a risk with the switch that controlled the main supply. I turned it off, glad to avoid a shock, knowing now that the place – at the very least – wouldn't burn down.

Back in the control room, I began to sort carefully through the box, taking everything I could find, every recorded cassette. In the kitchen, beneath a pile of tinned food, I found some carrier bags. I put the cassettes in the bags. There were two bags, at least a dozen cassettes in each. The control room emptied, I picked up the log books and returned to the hall. Stollmann, I thought grimly, might have been a little more explicit. He'd obviously discovered the operation. That's what he'd tried to tell me. This was the grubby little secret he'd so very nearly shared. But why hadn't he gone the whole way? Why had it taken a suicide bid to lead me to the truth?

I shook my head, angry again, opening the front door, stepping outside. Sooner or later, our neighbours would return. What they'd find – sodden carpets, stained ceiling, broken window, missing tapes – would tell its own story. Even MI5 couldn't fail to join this particular set of dots.

I found Wesley where I'd left him, in bed. I thought at first he was asleep, but I was wrong. He was awake and remarkably coherent.

'I'm sorry,' he whispered. 'Fucking silly thing to do.' I put the carrier bags on the floor.

'It's OK,' I said. 'Thank God you cocked it up.' I cupped his face for a moment with my hands. He was still freezing.

'Listen,' I began, 'this story of yours.'

'Yeah?'

'I was just wondering . . .'

'What?'

'Whether you wouldn't mind if I took over for a bit?'

'Took over?' He peered up at me. 'I'm not with you.'

I hesitated, knowing all too well the implications of the step I was taking. I'd never believed Stollmann's line on Wesley's little thesis, that the whole thing was pure fantasy, and now I knew I'd been right. The operation my ex-employers were running downstairs – the equipment, the manpower, the overtime – was a serious investment. Someone, somewhere, had a great deal to hide. Wesley was still looking at me.

'There might be a problem,' he began, 'with my memory.'

I smiled at him, picking up the plastic bags, opening them, showing him the cassettes inside.

'These might help,' I said, 'if we get stuck.'

25

Money, if you have it, is a wonderful thing.

By nightfall that same day, I'd swopped Stollmann's expenses cheque and a modest dollop or two of my Irish compensation for a brand new life. The key to this adventure was a 1987 Volkswagen camper van. I knew exactly what I wanted and the third call I made on Wesley's phone secured me the deal. The Volkswagen would cost me £8300. It was properly fitted out – cupboards, beds, water tank, a small stove – and carried a full service history. The mileage was low and the salesman would be delighted to take my little Peugeot in part-exchange. By five-thirty, I was back outside Wesley's flat, nudging the VW gently against the kerb, knowing we still had time to make a semi-organized exit. Of our neighbours downstairs, there was still no sign.

I kept luggage to the minimum. While Wesley watched from a cocoon of blankets in the armchair, I packed what was left of his life into three cardboard boxes. Clothes went in one. Drugs, food, washing gear and (at Wesley's insistence) six bottles of Guinness went in another. The third I filled with cassettes and the log from downstairs, plus a selection of the files Wesley had already got together on the table. The latter, I noticed, included a couple of videotapes. Curious, I paused, kneeling on the floor.

'Why these?' I said.

Wesley frowned. I'd already explained about downstairs. He'd been confused at first, then shocked, then angry. But the anger had gone now, and he was visibly nervous. What mattered, I realized, was his peace of mind. A month in hospital had left him with a dread of getting sick again. He wanted things to be calm and stable. He wanted to be taken care of.

'Let's go,' he said, ignoring my question. 'Let's get the fuck out of here.'

We locked the door behind us and I helped him to the camper. I'd made up a bed for him in the back, a nest of blankets and a big white duvet, but he shook his head, saying he preferred to be up front, with me. We drove west, away from Guildford, along the ridge of the Hog's Back, the lights of Woking twinkling in the distance. By ten past eight, Puccini on the cassette player, we were burbling down the A303, deep into Wiltshire. An hour and a half later, more or less the time I'd told them to expect us, we pulled up outside the Riviera Hotel.

The Riviera is in Exmouth. It stands on a hill called the Beacon, overlooking the sea, with fabulous views down the Devon coast towards Torbay. I used to attend the odd function there when I lived with my parents in Budleigh Salterton, and I'd always liked the place. Far more important, just down the road lived the couple for whom I'd worked years back, the summer I'd returned from Zaire. To the best of my knowledge, they were still there, still running the nursing home. They had medical skills, patience, masses of room and a sense of humour. Soon, I was quite certain, I would need all four. Hence the trip west.

We booked into the hotel. They'd given us a room on the first floor, facing due south. Tomorrow, we'd wake up to the views I'd been promising Wesley on the journey down, but for the time being I pulled the curtains, turned the radiators up and searched the wardrobe for extra blankets. Wesley watched me, slumped in the single armchair. He'd said virtually nothing for the last hour or so and now he looked close to collapse. His face was grey, his eyes listless. When I asked him about food, he shook his head. He was still looking at the bed. It was a double.

'The only one they had left,' I said.

'So where do you sleep?'

'In there. With you.'

'Yeah?'

''Fraid so.' I paused. 'Can you bear that?'

He gazed at me a moment, then shrugged. He looked utterly defeated, neither grateful nor upset, simply a pawn in someone else's game.

'Sure,' he mumbled, 'anything you say.'

The night was easy for both of us. Wesley barely moved and I nearly got up at one point to check that he hadn't been at the tablets again. He hadn't, thank God, and when the maid woke us both up with a morning tray of tea, he looked infinitely better. He lay in bed, gazing out at the view. His memory of yesterday's events seemed less than perfect.

'Where?' he said again.

'Exmouth.'

'Where's that?'

'Devon.'

'Ah.' He nodded, none the wiser. 'Nice.'

We had breakfast in the room. Wesley ate a boiled egg and two slices of toast, his first food for twenty-four hours. I cut the toast into strips for him, dipping them in the egg.

'Soldiers,' I told him. 'Get you in the mood.'

After breakfast, I tried another briefing. Staying in Guildford, I told him, had been out of the question. Once our neighbours had returned, it would be only a matter of time before someone or other came knocking. It might be the police. It might be Special Branch. It might even be my ex-chums from MI5, enraged enough to break cover. Either way, the outcome would doubtless be the same: questions, and more questions, and very probably a formal arrest. Hospital, I told Wesley, might have been awful, but just imagine a week or so in some Godforsaken police cell. He'd watched me carefully from the bed, toying with the last of his toast.

'You're serious?' he said.

'Yes.'

'They'd bang us up?'

'Yes.'

Chastened, Wesley agreed that we'd needed a new base. The hotel, he said, seemed fine and he was visibly impressed with the views. I smiled, happy for the time being to let him think our stay was semi-permanent. I'd already phoned the nursing home up the road, recognizing the voice at the other end, my ex-employer, Eileen. We were meeting for coffee at eleven. She'd sounded intrigued. I looked at Wesley.

'The cassettes?' I said. 'You remember I found the cassettes?'

'The ones downstairs?' He frowned. 'The ones those bastards taped?'

I nodded. Soon, I said, we'd have to go through them, one by one, hours of listening, pages of careful notes. Unless, that is, he wanted to spare us both the time.

'How?'

'By giving me the gist of it. The bare bones.' I smiled. 'By telling me how far you'd got.'

Wesley was staring at me. He'd evidently forgotten our conversation of yesterday, me taking over, and there was enough of the journalist left in him to regard any sharing of information with the deepest suspicion. I warmed to the reaction. It was the most positive thing he'd done since I'd got back from the States. He shifted uncomfortably in the bed. I took the tray off his knees. He'd developed a rash I hadn't seen before, across his shoulders and up his neck. I sat on the bed. Wesley was still looking dubious.

'I think it's important we pursue this thing,' I said, 'and just now that means me, not you.'

'Why?'

'Because you're ill.' I paused. 'And I'm not.'

'But why pursue it? Why bother?'

'Because . . .'

I frowned. It was a good question, one I'd asked myself on a number of occasions over the last month or so. Until very recently, the answer had been simple. It was my job. I'd been paid to do it. But now that excuse had gone. On the contrary, I had every reason to turn my back on the whole thing, to forget Wesley's little theory, to accept the war at face value, a walkover for Western planners, a triumph for high technology. So why didn't I do it? Why didn't I cash in the rest of my compensation, treat myself to a year or two in the West Indies and simply forget it? I was still looking at Wesley. Back on form for an hour or two, it was his turn to smile.

'Because it's fucking evil,' he said, 'that's why.'

I met Eileen for coffee an hour later, leaving Wesley amongst a litter of press cuttings. In the six years since I'd seen her last, she'd aged. A little weight had settled on her thin, spare frame and she'd taken to wearing glasses. They were very old-fashioned, black, hornrimmed NHS frames and they made her face even more severe than it already was. In the three months I'd worked at Beacon Hill House, I'd got to know her well. She swept through life at a thousand miles an hour and took few prisoners, but behind the blazing eyes and the abrasive manner she was kind, fearless and completely her own person. Her husband's name was Pete. He was quiet, amusing and utterly dependable. He'd trained as a ship's engineer, and when times were hard, he evidently still disappeared to sea, returning after a month or two with a bagful of money and a nice tan. Just now, he was back from the Far East, tending the engines on some rustbucket or other.

We were having coffee in a corner of the lounge. Residents sat around in various stages of decay. Some of the older ones looked alarmingly like Wesley. Eileen was staring at me.

'AIDS?' she said.

I nodded. 'Yes.'

'And you want to put him here? With us?'

'Yes.' I smiled at her. 'Just for a while. I may have to do some travelling.'

Eileen and Pete exchanged glances. To my knowledge, AIDS had never been a big problem in East Devon, certainly not amongst the kind of clientele attracted to Beacon Hill House. I hesitated a moment. Pete was smiling now, amused at the prospect, staring out of the window, his hands clasped behind his head, while Eileen was frowning at an elderly woman in the corner who was trying to unpick her skirt.

I leaned forward across the table, touching Eileen lightly on the knee. 'Listen,' I said, 'maybe it's not such a great idea.'

'What?' Eileen's eyes were still on the woman in the corner. Most of her skirt was round her ankles.

'Wesley,' I said, 'coming here. You know . . .' I shrugged. 'AIDS and everything.'

Eileen glanced round at last. She looked, if anything, surprised. 'Do you have a book on it?' she said, ever practical. 'Anything we might read?'

Back at the hotel, I found Wesley still in bed, the covers drawn up around his shoulders. One of the videotapes lay on the bedside table. Most of the cuttings had fallen on to the floor, except for half a page of newsprint in his left hand.

'We need a video machine,' he said at once.

'Why?'

He looked at me a moment and then nodded at the tape. 'I

should have shown you earlier,' he said gruffly. 'My fault.'

I went downstairs again and enquired about a video machine. The young assistant manager looked dubious. He said it might be possible, but only after he'd spoken to the boss. The boss was in Exeter for the day. He'd be back tonight. He'd have an answer by seven. I smiled and thanked him. In the town, in a corner on the main street, I found a TV and radio shop. The man sold me a brand-new machine. I took it back to the hotel in a taxi and got the assistant manager to unpack it and tune it in. Still flustered, he spent half an hour trying to get the thing to work. When he'd gone, I loaded Wesley's videotape. Wesley had loved the scene with the young assistant manager, following his every movement, enjoying his embarrassment.

'What do they think we're up to?' he said.

I was on my hands and knees on the carpet, peering at the controls on the video machine, trying to find the play button.

'Simple,' I muttered. 'I'm Mata Hari and you're dying of AIDS.' I glanced over my shoulder, grinning. 'Joke?'

Wesley looked at me a moment, uncertain, then he, too, grinned.

'Fuck off, you,' he said.

We watched the video for the next hour or so. Wesley, it turned out, had shot it himself, using a brand-new VHS camera he'd been given by Aldridge. It was 1989. The Iran–Iraq war was over and in Baghdad it was business as usual. To mark his birthday, Saddam Hussein had decided to organize a party. He called it a trade fair and he invited all his Western friends. Wesley had covered the show as a journalist working for *Defence Week*, and taking the video camera had been Aldridge's idea. The trade fair had attracted the biggest names in the arms business and Aldridge wanted a permanent record for the file.

The video opened with fuzzy shots through the window of a 747. Wesley clearly hadn't read the instructions properly and was waving the camera about all over the place. There was a lot of muttered cursing on the soundtrack, and when the view finally steadied, it turned out to be a piece of Baghad Airport. Then the shot changed and we were somewhere else, another airport, tents everywhere, pavilions of some kind, men in uniform, heads tilted upwards, pointing fingers.

In the hotel room, I was sitting on the floor, my back against the foot of the bed. Wesley was up above me on the bed itself, a blanket wrapped round him. He had the remote-control unit for the video machine and he froze the picture on the screen. He sounded, at last, excited.

'Watch this,' he told me. 'Bloody incredible.'

He waved the remote controller at the screen and the picture came to life again. For a moment nothing happened, the camera looking down the runway, scanning left and right. Then a tiny dot appeared. On the soundtrack, above the general hum of the crowd, I could hear snatches of a foreign language, Arabic maybe. The dot grew bigger and bigger and then resolved itself into a small jet fighter. The wheels were down and the nose was up, and the pilot was obviously trying for a landing.

'Alpha Jet,' Wesley grunted, 'Egyptian Air Force.'

By now, you could hear the jet, a high-pitched whine, softer than you might expect. The plane disappeared behind a row of heads and the camera wavered for a moment, not quite sure where to go. Then there was a roar from the engine and the plane appeared again, climbing for height, the undercarriage tucking up inside the fuselage, the pilot banking sharply away at the end of the runway.

'Overshoot,' Wesley muttered. 'Guy fucked up.'

I nodded, not really understanding, still watching the screen. Wesley was using the zoom now on his new camera, the plane getting bigger. Then, abruptly, there was a crackle of gunfire, a distant pop-popping, and the plane was caged in dirty black puffs of smoke. Bits started falling off. There was an explosion of some kind near the tail. Then the little jet seemed to stop dead in the air, one wing dipping, the nose going down, the canopy disintegrating, two black shapes blasting upwards. The camera went with them for a second or two, parachutes blossoming from the ejector seats, then it panned down again, trying to find the aircraft, and we had a brief glimpse of the falling wreckage before it disappeared behind the forest of pointing fingers, and there was a dull, heavy, crumping sound, followed by a series of explosions and a column of thick, black smoke.

The screen went fuzzy. Wesley stopped the tape. I was still looking at the screen, still blinking.

'What happened?' I said blankly.

'Guy turned off the flight path. He was heading for the Presidential Palace. They have anti-aircraft guns up on the roof, serious triple-A. They shot him to pieces.'

'At an *airshow*?'

'Sure.' Wesley shrugged. 'They thought he was about to bomb them.'

'But what happened? To the plane?'

'History.' Wesley paused a moment. 'Twenty people killed on the ground.' He shook his head. 'Crazy place.'

I glanced up at him, recognizing the expression on his face, the huge eyes, the wagging head, the astonishment and delight that life should have dished up so extraordinary a scene.

'Must have wrecked the party,' I murmured.

'Yeah . . . real downer.'

'Seriously.'

'Seriously?' Wesley looked at me. 'They loved it. You know what one guy said to me? One guy who saw it?'

'No.'

'He said it was all pre-planned. Swore blind.'

'Why? Who by?'

'The Swiss.'

'The *Swiss*? Why?'

Wesley paused a second, savouring the moment, and I suddenly realized he'd been through this scene before, probably dozens of times, his very own home movie, his party piece. He was still looking at me, demanding my full attention.

'Obvious,' he said at last, 'they made the fucking triple-A in the first place. Nothing like the real thing to flog a few more.'

I offered him a thin smile, chilled by the joke, then I turned away, hearing the seagulls outside the window and the sigh of the wind in the trees across the road. *Evil*, I thought again, *evil*.

We spooled on through the video, an agonizingly slow tour of the trade fair. We stopped at each display, each pavilion, Wesley's voice on the soundtrack supplying a running commentary. Wherever we went, wherever Wesley took us, there was more hardware on display. The components, quite obviously, were Western, often British, and there was rarely any attempt to disguise their origin. However loud the noises back home, all the parliamentary handwringing about 'responsibility' and 'restraint', here was the raw evidence of what we'd really been up to. Thousands of jobs. Millions of pounds' worth of export orders. All bound for Iraq. Winners and losers, I thought, watching the images drifting in and out of focus. Peter Devlin. And poor Clive Alloway.

Finally, inside yet another pavilion, we got to the point of the tour. Mounted on a long table was a model I didn't for a moment recognize. It was composed of lengths of pipe, bolted together, with what looked like an enormous open breech at one end. The whole assembly was mounted on a length of railway track, and tiny model figures dotted here and there gave an idea of scale. The camera panned down the object, pipe by pipe, and then drew back. On the soundtrack, in a state of some excitement, I heard Wesley mutter something I didn't quite catch.

'What?' I queried, looking up.

'Supergun,' Wesley said. 'More Brit engineering.'

I looked again, recognizing it now, the huge project the Iraqis had commissioned from British factories, the scandal that had made headlines around the world. After all the handwringing in Whitehall, and the arrests of the key businessmen, the episode had never got as far as the courts, and I'd often tapped into Registry files, looking for some clue to why the government had mysteriously dropped all charges. But the electronic cupboards had always been bare, just the terse note 'ED', Executive Deletion, sure confirmation that the records had been weeded at the highest level.

Now I looked up, puzzled. 'Why Supergun?' I said. 'What's that got to do with us?'

Wesley was still looking at the screen. 'Watch,' he said. 'Watch what happens next.'

I returned to the screen. The camera was off on its travels again, swinging round, pulling out, revealing a group of four or five people on the other side of the display. They were facing the camera and their faces were all clearly visible. They were deep in discussion, looking at the model, pointing at this feature or that, nodding and agreeing. Finally, one of them glanced at his watch and patted the man beside him on the back. There was the sound of laughter and the man with the watch began to turn away. As he did so, Wesley froze the picture. It hung on the television screen, juddering slightly. I peered at it again, recognizing the savage crewcut, the hooded eyes, the thick neck. No doubt about it. Harold Beckermann.

It was mid-afternoon. I'd coaxed Wesley out of the hotel, both of us suddenly back in a world where it paid to be careful about conversation. We'd taken a drive along the beach road into the docks and parked the other side of a narrow swing bridge. The area around the dock was derelict. A line of wooden chalets between the dock and the sea had recently been demolished. There was timber and rubble everywhere, lots of empty space, not a soul in sight. I bumped the camper up on to the hardstanding and switched off the engine. Yachts swung at their moorings. Across the river, miles away, I could see a train. I looked at Wesley.

'Go on,' I said.

Wesley glanced across at me. His recall was far from perfect, but there was no question about the effort he was making. The man beside Beckermann on the video had been François Ghattan, the name McGrath had given me in Washington, 'Mogul's' first owner. According to Wesley, Ghattan was a near legend in the arms business, a Lebanese trader who'd specialized in selling stuff into Iraq. He had the ear of the Al-Tikritis, Saddam Hussein's extended family. They trusted him completely and he'd made a fortune by marrying their grander plans to sources of Western credit. But by 1989, said Wesley, Ghattan was sick. He had a chronic heart complaint and sooner or later it would kill him.

'And Beckermann?'

'A good friend.' He paused. 'No question.'

'And Supergun? The arms fair? That scene you shot?'

Wesley reached for another cigarette, his second of the day. I couldn't make up my mind whether it was a good sign or not.

'Beckermann,' he said carefully, 'had lots of interests.'

'Had?'

'Has. He's based in Dallas, as you know. A lot of what he plays with is oil money, reinvested in the weapons business. The piece you saw, the piece I showed you, they were discussing a forward steel contract, no question.'

'For another gun? A second gun?'

'Yeah.'

'You *know* that?'

'Yeah.' He paused. 'The Supergun's 1000-mm calibre. Saddam wanted a slightly smaller version, 600 mm, still a monster. A gun like that could throw a shell nearly five hundred miles. The steel you use to build the thing is highly specialized. There's a firm in Texas makes it. Saddam wanted to buy the firm.'

'From Beckermann?'

'No. Beckermann was just the front man. Representing Texan interests. There's a little club of top Americans on the Iraqi circuit. Industrialists mostly. Beckermann's one of them.' He frowned. 'That's not the point, though.'

'No?'

'No. The point is Ghattan. Ghattan had the ear of the Iraqis. They trusted him. They liked him. He took them places they'd never otherwise go. Same with the Americans. You saw the pictures. He's Beckermann's favourite Arab. The classic middleman. A foot in both camps.'

I nodded, wondering now where Wesley was headed. Across the river, the other side of the tidal stream, a single cormorant was diving for fish. He disappeared for a long time. When he came up again, he'd got nothing. I looked at Wesley.

'Tell me something,' I said slowly.

'What?'

I smiled. Wesley's old expression was back. Deep mistrust. I glanced at the river, looking for the cormorant again, not finding it.

'Grant Wallace,' I began, 'those notes of his on Beckermann . . . for the book he was doing . . .'

'What about them?'

I sat back, closing my eyes, smelling the old Wesley smell, spindly roll-ups, shag tobacco. 'He ever show you,' I said softly, 'any of that stuff?'

I opened one eye. Wesley was concentrating very hard on a small black beetle making its way along the dashboard. For a moment, it occurred to me I'd lost him again. Then he nodded.

'Yes,' he said.

'The whole lot? Including the research he'd done recently?' I paused, remembering the empty drawer in Grant's filing cabinet, the way his mother had described the body, the gun dangling from his dead hand, the single black hole in his temple. 'The stuff about Beckermann's recent life? The last year or two? What he was up to? Where he'd been?'

Wesley gave up on the beetle, and looked me in the eye. To my relief, he understood exactly what I meant. Even better, he was smiling.

'Yes,' he said again, 'even that.'

26

Several days later, we were still talking about the contents of Grant's files on Beckermann.

I'd managed to borrow a wheelchair from Eileen and for the second afternoon in a row I pushed Wesley along the empty seafront, a two-mile walk that took us as far as the end of the beach. Overnight, Wesley had developed a hacking cough. I didn't know whether it was the shag tobacco or something more sinister, but the weather was lovely, if cold, and I told myself that the air must be good for him.

At the end of a line of sand dunes, we stopped and I peered down at Wesley. His nose was running, his eyes, too. I fumbled for a Kleenex, and gave it to him.

'That crash,' I said again, 'the Beirut plane.'

Wesley buried his nose in the Kleenex. When he'd finished, he motioned me to sit beside him. He hadn't the breath left to raise his voice and there was no way he could compete with the wind. There was a low wall beside the wheelchair. I sat down, glad of the shelter.

'You're sure about the date?' I said. 'June? This year?'

'Yeah.'

I looked away, doing the calculations. Desert Storm had ground to a halt at the end of February. According to Grant Wallace's notes, March and April had found Harold Beckermann commuting between Dallas and the Gulf, signing a string of massive re-supply contracts with the Saudis and the Al-Sabahs. The latter, the Kuwaiti ruling family, evidently had the contracts ready and waiting, prices pre-agreed, delivery dates pre-agreed, even the date of the contract signature pre-typed at the foot of each page. This was part of the story Grant had originally told Wesley back in Geneva, the night they'd first met, Wesley's first sight of the hare. At that point, Grant himself had been awestruck by the implications, though even then he'd been convinced that Beckermann himself was blameless, simply a willing contractor, only too pleased to play the State Department's game. If Foggy Bottom and the Pentagon had been that certain about the war's outcome, then so be it. With billions of dollars at stake, no one was asking too many questions.

Now I glanced back at Wesley. His nose was chafed and red. He was still thinking about the crash.

'June the sixth,' he confirmed, 'mid-afternoon.'

I nodded. In June, the local Extec agent in the Lebanon had chartered a small, two-engined executive plane. The aircraft was to carry the agent, plus three other passengers, from Beirut to Sana'a in the Yemen. Ten minutes out from Beirut, somewhere east of the Litani River, the plane had disappeared from ATC radar screens. A day later, wreckage had been found, scattered over a rocky escarpment, about thirty miles west of Damascus. The aircraft had burned on impact. What little remained of the bodies on board was charred beyond recognition.

Beckermann, in Dallas at the time, had returned to the Middle East at once. Grant, said Wesley, had made a great deal of what happened next because he felt it showed his hero at his very best. Back in Beirut, taking command, he'd organized immediate payouts for the victims of the crash. The family of the Extec agent, himself Lebanese, had received, to Grant's certain knowledge, a quarter of a million dollars. Relatives of the other three passengers, plus the pilot, had been given similar sums. In return, the grieving relations had preserved a discreet silence about the loss of their loved ones. No public handwringing. No drama. No demands for an inquiry.

Officially, the incident had provoked equally little curiosity. Weather in the area had been bad, visibility poor, winds gusting sixty knots. There'd been vague talk of an altimeter failure, or simple pilot error, or even some kind of interception by the neighbouring Israeli Air Force. The one word that no one appeared to have used was 'bomb'.

Wesley voiced the thought now, peering out to sea, watching the gulls clouding around a small trawler.

'Had to be,' he said, 'just had to be.'

'Why?'

He glanced across at me. 'The wreckage was everywhere. Big area. If the plane had hit the mountain, you wouldn't find that. It would be tight. One place. Not scattered.'

'So who'd plant the bomb? Who'd be the target?'

Wesley shrugged. 'Dunno,' he said.

'Did Grant have a passenger list? Names we could check?'

'No.'

'Photographs?'

'No.' He shook his head. 'Just notes he made at the time. Plus a couple of cuttings.'

I nodded, plucking a blade of grass from the dune, sucking it. Wesley had fallen silent again, brooding. Finally, he looked up.

'Tell you who'd know more about it,' he said reluctantly.

'Who?'

'Dickhead.'

'Who?'

He looked at me a moment, still reluctant. 'Aldridge,' he said at last.

Back at the hotel, a tray of tea between us on the bedspread, I pressed him further. How much did Aldridge know? What had been his interest? Did he have photos? Names? Theories? Wesley met every question with the blankest of stares, volunteering nothing. When the tea was brewed, he asked me to pour.

'Photographs,' he said at last, watching me burn my fingers on the hot metal handle. 'He has three or four photographs.'

'You've seen them?'

'Yes. But only briefly. They're in the library at *Defence Week*. They're definitely there. I was going to lift them. Before . . .' he shrugged, 'all this.'

I nodded, wrapping a napkin around the teapot handle.

'And what did they show? These photographs?'

Wesley frowned, still far from eager to part with the information, and I hesitated, the teapot in mid-air, waiting for a reply.

'There's a group shot,' he said at last. 'The five of them on the tarmac with the plane behind. I think it was the agent's birthday or something. Someone took it before they left.'

'Did you recognize anyone?'

'I can't remember. I didn't really look.'

'But you could,' I began to fill his cup, 'if I got the photo?'

He nodded. 'Yeah,' he said quietly, 'maybe I could.'

I looked at him again, realizing at last why he was being so slow, so uncooperative. Getting the photo would mean talking to Aldridge, and talking to Aldridge would mean going to Guildford. Wesley didn't want that. He wanted me here, in Exmouth, with him. He wanted to be looked after.

'You can come too,' I said at once. 'I'll drive you.'

Wesley shook his head, his hands around the cup, warming himself. An hour in a wheelchair had exhausted him. No way would he be able to cope with a four-hundred-mile round trip in the camper. We said nothing for a minute or two. The last of the daylight had turned the sea an unforgiving, gunmetal grey. I shivered, getting up to pull the curtains.

'I'll have to go,' I said softly, turning back into the room. 'You know that, don't you?'

Wesley nodded, his eyes still on the teacup. 'Yeah,' he said, 'I do.'

I left after breakfast next morning, a dull, wet, windy day. Wesley had given me three phone numbers for Aldridge, two at the office and a private one where he lived. I'd already tried an office number, confirming with Aldridge's secretary that he was free for lunch, but leaving no message. The last thing I wanted was a reception committee.

I took the A303, up through Somerset and Wiltshire, bumping along under a thick blanket of cloud. It was still raining at midday when I pulled into the car park behind the Royal County Hotel in the middle of Guildford. According to the AA book, the County rated three stars for its 'comfort, facilities, and skilful blend of tact and service'. I put the latter to the test at once, asking for a double room and pre-paying the daily rate. The woman behind the counter passed me the key with the change.

'Breakfast, madam?' she queried. 'Tomorrow morning?'

I shook my head and pulled a face. ''Fraid not,' I said. 'Dawn start.'

Upstairs, from the room, I phoned Aldridge. I could tell at once that he was busy, though when he heard my voice, he changed down a gear or two.

'Nice to hear you,' he said. 'Nice surprise.'

I apologized for interrupting whatever he was doing. I said I had a favour to ask. I quoted the Beirut crash story and gave him the date. I said I knew he had some photos on file. Maybe I might take a look?

'Of course,' he said, 'I see no problem with that.' He paused. 'You want to come in this afternoon?'

I hesitated a moment, eyeing the double bed. I'd already turned down the sheet and plumped up the pillows. The rest, I told myself, should be child's play.

'I thought maybe lunch,' I said, 'on me.'

'You?' he said blankly.

'Yes. I'm staying at the Royal County.' I paused. 'Can you spare the time?'

'Ah . . .'

'Is there a problem?'

'God, no.' He laughed, an easy chuckle. 'It's just that I've eaten already. About ten minutes ago. Ham sandwiches. From the canteen. You want me to bring the photos, too?'

I fingered the phone a moment. 'Yes,' I said at last, 'that would be kind.'

Aldridge arrived twenty minutes later. He had a Peter Dominic's carrier bag with him and two bottles of champagne. He pushed the door shut with his heel and crossed the room towards me. I was half-sitting on the vanity unit. He bent over me and kissed me on the mouth. He'd been drinking already. It tasted like Scotch. He took a couple of steps backwards and nearly tripped over the bed. The sheet was still folded down. He produced an envelope from his inside pocket.

'Your pictures,' he said, letting the envelope fall to the bed. 'Send them back when you're through.'

I smiled at him. 'Thanks,' I said.

He looked at me a moment, not quite so certain, then put the champagne beside the bed and disappeared into the bathroom. When he came back, he had two glasses. He began to open one of the bottles, loosening his tie, taking off his jacket. Plainly, time was short. I stepped across to him. I was wearing the two-piece I'd bought in Dallas. The blouse underneath was buttoned down the front, and I'd put a lot of thought into the choice of bra. It was a Gossard, my favourite, and it fitted me beautifully. When

Aldridge finally got the blouse unbuttoned, he couldn't believe it.

'Jesus,' he murmured, 'must be my birthday.'

He was sitting on the side of the bed. I reached for the bottle of champagne he'd begun to open and gave it to him. He put his thumbs under the cork, levering upwards, and I caught the first frothy fountain of champagne as the cork hit the ceiling. He filled the second glass, sipping greedily as I proposed a toast. When he reached for me again, I got up and stood in front of him, my hands resting lightly on his head. He was wearing gel. I could feel it.

He glanced up at me. His hands were under my skirt now, working slowly upwards. For a man with a reputation, he was quite hopeless.

'You want to talk?' he said.

I nodded. 'Please.'

'And?'

'Whatever you like,' I said, 'afterwards.'

'As cold-blooded as that?'

'No.' I smiled again. 'It's just the way I am.'

His hands were still between my thighs. I fondled his hair, easing his head towards me, belly height, maybe a little lower. He began to groan, nuzzling me.

'What is it?' he said. 'What do you want to know?'

'About the crash.' I paused. 'Why the interest? How come the photos?'

He looked up at me again. 'Is this an interview,' he said, 'or just lunch?'

I smiled. 'Lunch.'

'You mean that?'

'Yes.'

'About afterwards?'

'Of course.'

He nodded, thoughtful, briefly back behind the editorial desk. Then he shrugged.

'There was a lot of industry chatter,' he said at last. 'You may have heard.'

'About a bomb?'

'A possible bomb. It sounds obvious, but no one ever asked

the hard questions. Not even the plane makers. Though you'd have thought they'd had an interest.'

'Who are they?' I asked him.

'Rexall,' he said. 'They're big in defence sales, too. Made a fortune since the Gulf War.'

'Should that matter?'

Aldridge looked up, his eyes moist with the champagne, a curious little half-smile on his face, and I knew at once that the talking was over and that my time was up. He passed me my glass. I tipped it to my lips. Moët et Chandon. No expense spared. Aldridge was still watching me.

'You here tonight?' he said.

I nodded.

'Free for dinner?'

'Yes,' I said, 'if you think it's worthwhile.'

He hesitated a moment, looking up at me. Then he reached for the clasp on my bra and undid it, watching my breasts fall free, cupping them in his hands, kissing the flesh around the nipples. On his feet again, he headed for the bathroom, turning on the taps in the basin, whistling a tune from some opera or other, quite the gay rake.

I stooped to the phone. I'd memorized the number on the journey up from Devon. I dialled it now, local code, six figures. I heard the number trilling, then a woman's voice. I laid the receiver beside the phone in time to smile at Aldridge as he came back in. He was stark naked. He needed to lose a stone or two around the waist and find himself somewhere sunny to take care of the rest. Me, or the champagne, had stirred the beginnings of an erection. He was, in Rory's phrase, modestly appointed.

'Sir?' I said. 'Your pleasure?'

He grinned at me. 'No, no,' he said, 'I insist.'

'On what?'

'On whatever.' He shrugged, 'Your choice, my treat.'

He sprawled across the bed and pulled me towards him. He was beginning to sweat, a line of moisture on his upper lip.

'Do you do this kind of thing often?'

'Not with someone like you.'

'Oh?'

'No,' I felt his fingers in my hair, 'most of the time it's short rations.'

'Meaning?'

'The odd chum at the office. Passing ships . . .' he kissed me, 'the wife.'

We were very close, my face an inch from his on the pillow, the phone beside us. I could tell that the line was still open. I rolled over, my skirt off now, my pants still on, straddling him. I knew by the look on his face that he hadn't read the book on self-control. Any minute now, the show would be over. His thumbs were inside the tops of my knickers. He was trying to get them off. He wanted the insides of me. Badly.

I bent over him, my mouth beside his ear.

'There's someone on the phone for you,' I whispered. 'Little surprise.'

Aldridge opened one eye. He thought I was joking.

'Get those fucking knickers off,' he said. 'I need you.'

I said nothing, nodding at the phone. He began to pull at my pants again, still not believing me, and I rolled off his erection and squatted by the bed, picking up the phone, giving it to him. He stared at it, totally bewildered, then he picked it up and put it to his ear.

'Yes?' he said.

Nothing happened for a moment, then his face began to purple and I wriggled back into my skirt, buttoning my blouse, stuffing my bra into my bag, watching his eyes close, hearing the voice at the other end, nothing specific, nothing I could understand, just the low hiss of air leaving a marriage, the longest sentence in the world, the one that leaves you with absolutely no place to hide.

Dressed now, I watched him put the phone down. He was too shocked to be angry. He just lay there, staring at the ceiling, his face grey and sweating, his mouth half open, his erection quite gone. I pocketed the envelope with the photographs and stood by the bed. My hand strayed across his crotch, nails and fingertips. I smiled down at him, thinking of all the other women he must have met in rooms like these. I bent to him quickly, my hand still playful, my lips to his ear.

'Wesley sends his regards,' I whispered. 'Says thanks for everything.'

I was in London by mid-afternoon, in time to catch the bank before it closed. So far, since taking Wesley to the West Country, I'd managed to pay for everything in cash. Even the camper I'd bought with a large handful of fifty-pound notes. Doing it that way, the same logic I'd used in the States, I'd avoided leaving the usual trail of electronic footsteps that agencies like MI5 rely on. Once they'd discovered the break-in at Guildford, they'd have put a trace on my bank account and credit cards. Every transaction would come up on one of the computers at Curzon House, leading them directly to Exmouth and the Riviera Hotel. By using cash, I'd effectively stayed invisible, but now it was running out and I needed more. The best solution was a visit to the West London branch where I had a drawing arrangement, and while this would certainly be reported, I suspected there was no way they'd be able to withhold the cash.

In the event, thank God, I was right. The woman behind the glass window spent long enough on the phone to make several check calls, but when she returned there was no problem with the money. By half past four, I was back in my flat in Fulham, five thousand pounds the richer.

I spent no more than ten minutes in the flat. Staying longer, after my appearance at the bank, was asking for trouble, and I had time to check only the obvious things. A pile of mail I stuffed in my bag. A week-old carton of milk I poured down the sink. A handful of clothes I threw into a sports bag. En route to the front door, I paused by the phone. There were three messages on the answering machine, fewer than I expected. I checked my watch, then spooled quickly through them. One caller had left no message at all. The second wanted to sell me a security alarm. Only the third was of any importance.

I bent to the phone, recognizing my mother's voice. She obviously hadn't a clue where I was, which was perfectly reasonable since I hadn't told her. She chided me as gently as ever for the lack of contact ('... the odd postcard, dear? Just one?') and then said that she was organizing a surprise party. My father was retiring in a week's time. She was trying to get together all his closest friends. It would be lovely if I could be there. She knew it would make his day. There was a pause, then the kisses she always left on the tape and then she hung up. I hesitated a moment, wondering whether to phone her now, but then decided against it. A week, just now, was an eternity. Literally anything could happen.

I was back in Devon by nine. The traffic had been appalling, and I had a number of other serviceable excuses, but I knew the moment I opened the hotel bedroom door that all was far from well. Wesley was lying in bed, half watching television. He barely turned his head when I came in and refused to answer when I asked how his day had been. At first, silly me, I thought he was sick again. It took me several minutes to realize he was sulking.

'What's the matter?' I said at last. 'Mummy left you too long?'

Wesley gave me a look, much as a child might, a daughter perhaps, derision and scorn. I went over to the window, shrugging off my coat. I had the photographs out now. I'd had a look at them on the way down. They were ideal for our purposes, all five faces, perfect focus. I pulled the curtains, glancing round. For the first time, I saw the mark. It was high up on the wall beside the door, a big greasy splat, some kind of impact, not at all in keeping with the rose-printed wallpaper.

'What's that?' I said.

Wesley was still looking at the television. He scowled. 'Lunch,' he said.

'But what's it doing on the wall?'

'Brett came up. We had words.'

I nodded, beginning to understand. Brett was the assistant manager, the helpful young man who'd installed the video. He was neat, and well-scrubbed, and Wesley had taken quite a shine to him.

'What happened?' I said, sitting on the bed.

Wesley looked at me for the first time. He looked, if anything, shamefaced.

'It was a game,' he said, 'that's all.'

'You made a pass at him?'

'Yeah. When he brought the lunch up. Nothing serious. Just a joke.'

'And what happened?'

'He told me to fuck off. Said I should be locked up.'

'And then?'

Wesley shrugged, fingering the buttons on the remote control, changing the TV channel. 'I threw the plate at him.'

I looked at the door, trying to imagine Brett on the way out. Wesley had missed, but only just.

'Maybe you frightened him,' I said. 'This is Devon. Not 42nd Street.'

Wesley shot me another look.

'That's the whole point,' he said. 'That's why I was so angry. I still am. Little turd.'

I frowned, confused now. 'I'm not with you,' I said, 'I don't understand.'

Wesley looked at me for a long moment, then hauled the blankets up around his chin. 'He's gay,' he hissed, 'and he called me old.'

Later, when Wesley had recovered his dignity, I showed him the photos. He switched on the bedside light, and half-rolled over, peering at each of the faces. His pyjama top open, I could see again how thin he'd become, skin and bone, the flesh slack and pale. At last, he looked up, his finger anchored on the group by the plane.

'This one,' he said, showing me.

I studied the photograph. The face that had attracted Wesley's interest was second from the right, a shortish man, curly black hair, open shirt, strong chin, dark complexion, plainly an Arab. I'd thought already that I'd seen the face before. Now, I turned the photo over. There was a typed caption on the back, naming the faces, left to right.

'Rahman Khalil?' I said.

'That's him.'

'Who is he?'

Wesley gazed at me a moment, then nodded at the video we'd seen earlier in the week, his coverage of the Baghdad Trade Fair.

'Remember the Supergun?' he said. 'The blokes at the table?' I nodded. 'Khalil's the next one along. Beside Ghattan.' He paused. 'The two were always together. Bill and Ben.'

'Friends?' I frowned, looking at the photo again. 'Business partners?'

Wesley shook his head, enjoying himself now, back in control, the circus master. 'No,' he said, 'Khalil was his bodyguard. Wherever Ghattan went, he went. Khalil was a little present from the Iraqis.'

'Meaning?'

'It was his job to know everything.'

27

Four days later, we moved out of the hotel. Relations with the management had collapsed entirely when Wesley invited Brett to do something particularly unspeakable, and I was obliged to find somewhere else for us to live. In the depths of a recession, with money in my bag, that wasn't hard and I took a three-month lease on a second-floor flat further down the hill. The place was warm and furnished, and there were two bedrooms. I did the final negotiations on the phone, from the hotel, and Wesley monitored the dialogue with a certain grim amusement.

'Three months?' he said. 'As long as that?'

The following day, settled in, I finally phoned my mother. The party was to be held at the weekend. When I said I'd be delighted to come, my mother was overjoyed. She suggested she pop up to London to see me, do a little shopping together. When I said I was incredibly busy, and liable to be elsewhere, she sounded disappointed.

'Don't worry,' I said, 'we'll catch up on Saturday.'

'Of course, dear. But don't say a word to anyone. *Top* secret.'

'Cross my heart.' I smiled. 'Mum's the word.'

It was at this point, at last, that I managed to get in touch with Raoul again. I'd been phoning the Dallas number off and on for more than a week, but had never made contact. Either he was out on a job, or away on leave, or just too busy to talk. When I finally got through he didn't bother to apologize. In the background, I could hear office noises: phones, typewriters, chatter.

'This thing,' he said. 'I can't talk.'

'Why not?'

'Not here. You got a pen?'

He gave me a number. I wrote it down. He made me read the

number back. Then he told me to phone later, his time, half past eight in the evening. The number he'd given me was private. We'd be able to talk.

Our new flat had no phone. Armed with a small sheaf of BT cards, I returned to the call box at half past two in the morning. I'd set the alarm for thirty minutes earlier, but I was still half asleep, wrestling with my trusty recorder, wondering whether the batteries were still up to it. Outside the box, the night was wild, leaves swirling around in the orange light from the street lamps, a bitter wind off the sea. Walking down the hill from the flat, I'd seen no sign of life.

Raoul got to the phone after the first trill. He sounded more relaxed, but still cautious. I peered at my list of questions, the fruit of my intermittent discussions with Wesley, nothing I'd dignify with the word 'analysis', simply an attempt to join the most obvious of the dots.

'Grant Wallace,' I began. 'You getting anywhere? All those contacts of yours?'

'Sure.'

'And?'

There was a long pause here. I was watching the digits in the little window, the ones that tell you how much time you've got left. Silence comes expensive on transatlantic calls, even at two in the morning.

Then, suddenly, Raoul was back. 'Listen,' he said, 'you ought to level with me. OK?'

'Level?'

'Yeah. Like who you are, and who you're fronting for, and why the fuck I should be Mr Helpline.' He paused. 'Am I making any sense?'

'Yes,' I said drily, 'lots.'

'Well?'

It was my turn to say nothing. A car had appeared at the end of the street, a rusty old Capri, a big pudding face behind the wheel, unshaven, swivelling to watch me as the car cruised slowly past.

Raoul was into guesswork now. 'Press? Media?'

'No.'

'Police?'

'No.'

I cut him short, telling him as much of the truth as I dared. I'd been working for British Intelligence. Just now, I was off the case. The whole thing stank.

Raoul broke in again. 'Stank?'

'Stinks.'

'What does?'

'What I'm into. Please, just tell me about Wallace. And trust me.'

There was another silence. Then, reluctantly, Raoul told me what he knew about Grant. According to police insiders, he'd been killed after a struggle of some kind. There'd been blood under his fingernails, and contusions on his ribcage, though these looked a day or so older.

'I know about them,' I said quickly. 'Beckermann did them. Out on his ranch. With a riding whip.'

'You kidding?' I heard Raoul's soft laugh.

He went on. The gun he'd used appeared to be his own, same make, same model, but there was some confusion about the serial numbers matching the ones recorded on the original sales invoice. He'd been to the shop, the Sun Valley Arms Corp, but it was obvious that the owner had been told to say nothing. When Raoul had asked him whether he'd sold anything similar recently, he'd said he couldn't remember. When Raoul suggested he consult his records, the man said he was far too busy. Frustrated, Raoul had next tried contacts at the police laboratories, but it seemed that the slug in Grant's brain had proved useless for forensic purposes.

'Why?'

'It was soft nose. You know about these things? Soft nose goes squashy. It's the favourite for professionals. Leaves nothing but the mess inside your skull.'

I frowned, remembering now the box of shells I'd found in Wallace's attaché case. Fifty rounds. Full metal jacket. Definitely not snub nose. I told Raoul. The news didn't appear to surprise him.

'Homicide,' he said. 'Obvious to everyone. Except the guys in charge.'

'You mean the police?'

'Not necessarily.'

'Who then?'

Raoul didn't answer and I asked the question again. When he still refused to say anything, I changed the subject, consulting my list.

'I've got a name for you,' I said. 'You get this one for free.'

'Pardon me?'

'François Ghattan.' I spelled it. 'You get that?'

'Sure. Who is he?'

'Close friend of Beckermann's. We're pretty certain he died earlier this year. Probably some time in June. Probably in Dallas.'

'What was the problem?'

'Heart condition.' I paused. 'We think.'

'You want me to check it out?'

'Please.'

Raoul laughed again, a wholly pleasant chuckle, warmth in the chilly darkness. I could see another pair of lights in the distance. I hoped to God it wasn't the Capri again.

'Another thing,' I said, 'another name.'

'Yeah?'

'This Ghattan, the name I've given you, the man had a bodyguard. An Iraqi. Rahman Khalil.' I spelled the name, watching the headlights creeping up the road towards me. 'You got that? Only we'd be interested if you could come up with anything.'

I hesitated a moment, certain now that it was the Capri, same big face, same staring eyes, mouth slightly open, head turning as the car began to coast to a halt. I swallowed hard, feeling my pulse quicken. For weeks, I'd stayed one step ahead of the game, taking my chances, pushing my luck. Now, in Exmouth of all places, my luck seemed to have run out. I bent quickly to the phone. Raoul was back on the line.

'This "we",' he was saying, 'you and who else?'

'A friend,' I said, 'someone pretty special.'

The Capri had stopped a yard or two from the phone box. The door was opening. The man behind the wheel was getting out. I dropped the phone, grabbed the recorder and made a bolt for the darkness. Beside the phone box was a small park. There were trees in the park and shrubs beside a footpath. I clambered over a low wall and pushed through the bushes, crouching in a flower bed, hidden from the road. I heard a car door slam. Then there were footsteps and the sound of someone bulky crashing through the undergrowth. Already, I knew it couldn't be surveillance. Even MI5 couldn't be this obvious, this gross. No. The figure coming at me through the bushes was altogether simpler. Someone big, and probably drunk, and very definitely looking for company. I stayed motionless, convinced he couldn't see me, not understanding why he kept coming on, straight towards me, unerring. Then I looked down, realizing too late that the recorder was still on, the bright red glow of the battery warning light winking in the darkness, my very own homing beacon.

Too late, I abandoned it, throwing it into the bushes, but the figure was on me now, huge belly, baggy jeans, boots, lunging at me, pinning me to the ground, my face turned away, driven into the wet soil by the sheer weight of his body. I smelled the hot, sour smell of whisky, and I heard the man grunting as he tore at my jeans, the huge hands ripping open the fly zip. I tried to struggle free, knowing I could outrun him, badly frightened now, and then there was an explosion of lights inside my head as he began to hit me, the smack of knuckle on bone, again and again, the man grunting and cursing with the effort. I tasted blood for the first time, the side of my face numb, and as he rocked back on his heels, trying to get out of his own jeans, I rolled over, into the leaves.

He lunged at me again, half naked beneath the waist, unable to move properly, and I spotted my chance, remembering with absolute clarity one of the tricks they'd taught me at Hereford. I could see the black shadows of his groin, and I went for it, one hundred per cent, the way they said you had to do it, total commitment. Astonished, he hesitated for a second, a big mistake, giving me time to grab and squeeze and squeeze harder and twist with all my strength. He began to bellow, an animal roar that became a scream and then a whimper. When he was quite still, gasping for air, his knees drawn up, I let go, both hands finding his neck, up by the line of the chin, the skin rough with stubble. I put my hands round his neck and drove the thumbs in as hard as I dared, hearing him beginning to choke, the eyes popping in his face, the huge belly writhing beneath me. I hung on for a moment or two longer, then let go, stepping away, on to the grass, watching his body go limp. I'd no idea whether I'd killed him, and in truth I didn't care.

On the way past the Capri, I reached in and took the key. If he'd survived, the last thing I wanted was him coming after me again, so I threw the key as far as I could, over the wall across the road, into the grounds of a big hotel. Then I set off, up the hill, back to the flat, pausing twice to be sick in the gutter. Wesley met me at the door, minutes later. He'd been worried about me. Anything, he said, could have happened.

'It did,' I said, collapsing. 'I think I just killed someone.'

Wesley was brilliant, quite brilliant. He sat with me until dawn. He sponged the blood from my face and put together an ice pack with cubes from the fridge and an old drying-up cloth. He raided his supply of drugs for a couple of painkillers and found a quarter bottle of brandy. The combination of the two had an extraordinary effect, loosening my brain from my body, and as the drugs began to blanket the pain, I broke down completely, sobbing and sobbing, Wesley beside me on the narrow little bed, his thin arms enfolding me, his big face in mine.

'Hey,' he kept saying, 'hey, now.'

I shook my head, angry at the tears, all that raw emotion, but quite unable to do anything about it. Finally, at God knows what time, I must have gone to sleep because the next thing I remember is sunshine pouring in through the thin curtains, and Wesley back beside the bed with a huge mug of tea.

I reached for it, grateful. I noticed how ugly my hands looked, the nails broken, cuts and scratches everywhere. The sight of them brought it all flooding back, the smell of the man, the weight of his body, and I began to tremble again, spilling my tea. Wesley fetched a blanket from his own bedroom and wrapped it around my shoulders. I noticed, for the first time, that he was wearing a coat.

'Where have you been?' I said.

'Out.'

'Where?'

'Down the hill. Where you said.'

'And?'

'The car's still there. Police all over it.'

'What about the guy?'

'Nothing. No sign. Either he went of his own accord, or they picked him up.' He paused. 'Supposing he was still alive.'

I stared at him for a moment. 'Shit,' I said.

'What?'

'The recorder.'

'What about it?'

'I left it there. With the tape. Everything ... It was in the bushes. They must have found it. Must have.'

I risked a sip or two of tea, swilling it around my dry mouth, trying to remember exactly what I'd said to Raoul. I knew he'd been pushy, wanting to know who I was, who I worked for, and as near as dammit I knew I'd told him. Intelligence, I'd said, British Intelligence. With dialogue like that, the local constabulary wouldn't need too much prompting. The cassette was probably already en route to London, PO Box 500, one of those neat little HMG jiffy bags.

'Shit,' I said again, finishing the tea.

I didn't leave the flat for the next two days, a combination of vanity and caution. My face ballooned less than I'd anticipated. One eye was blackened, and there was more bruising along the line of my cheek bone and down the side of my neck, but nothing seemed broken. Even my precious teeth, which had survived the accident in Northern Ireland, had once again come through intact. All in all, given the physical odds, I'd been incredibly lucky.

Not that Wesley had much time for luck. Frail as he was, he'd taken over entirely, a real reversal of roles, and he fussed around the flat, keeping me supplied with never-ending mugs of soup and hot tea. He made occasional expeditions to the local shops, returning with titbits he thought might cheer me up, and after one of these trips, he reappeared with a copy of the local weekly paper.

My little adventure in the park had made page one. The man's name was Jason Livingstone and he was, thank God, still alive. From his hospital bed, he'd given police a detailed description of the gang that had assaulted him. They were, he'd said, young, a handful of teenagers who'd dragged him from his car, beaten him senseless and left him for dead. The report included a photo of the hapless victim. He was sitting up in his hospital bed with a loose crêpe bandage around his throat and an expression of wary innocence. Beside the report was a paragraph or two of editorial comment, heavy black type, headed 'HAS IT COME TO THIS?' Wesley read it to me, line by line, circling the living room, aiming the odd kick at the furniture. The editorial was full of phrases like 'motiveless violence' and 'teenage thuggery', and at the end of it – inevitably – there was a call for the return of national service. Wesley waved it at me, outraged.

'Can you believe they print this shit?' he said.

I smiled, an amazingly painful experience. 'Of course,' I said.

Wesley stared at me. 'What?' he said. 'After all that?'

'Yes.' I shrugged. 'What's so special about the truth?'

My mother's surprise party took place on the Saturday. My first instinct, recovering from the attack, was to cancel, and I got Wesley to phone from a box and tell her I'd been sent abroad. He did what I asked, but it was obvious that she'd been really disappointed, and the more I thought about it, the more I knew I owed them both an appearance. I didn't look my best, but an hour or two with the Max Factor would hide the worst of the damage, and in any case my father had never been the kind of man who worried unduly about appearances. What mattered to him was what mattered to me: the fact that we cared enough to make an effort.

The party was to begin at eight. My mother had gone to elaborate lengths to get my father out of the house in time for the guests to gather. When he returned, he'd find the lights out and my mother fretting in the hall about the fuse box. He'd come in, take off his coat, go in search of his precious tool box, and while he was still looking – hey presto! – the lights would come on again. Whether or not it had happened in exactly this order, I didn't know, but by the time I arrived in the camper, the street was full of cars, and there was laughter and music and the cheerful hum of people having a thoroughly good time.

I parked the camper down by the seafront, pausing a moment to listen to the long draw of the rollers on the pebble beach. It had always been one of my favourite sounds – audible from my bedroom when I lived here – and I drew my coat around me, somehow comforted. Whatever happened, wherever I went, I could always come back to this, one of life's precious constants.

I walked back up the road towards the house. I'd left Wesley watching television in the flat. He'd had mixed feelings about the party, mainly, I suspect, because he'd have liked to have come. The last few days had brought us very close. He'd been there when I needed him, a commitment entirely free of any kind of strings. There was nothing, I told myself, he needed me for. Not sex. Not money. Not advantage. The only things he had left to give were time and effort, gifts all the more precious because he had so little of either left. All this probably sounds infantile. But to me his devotion matched nothing I've ever experienced, before or since. I wrote at the start of this account that Wesley was the bravest person I ever met. Part of that courage, that generosity, was the bit of himself he spent on me.

I had the key to the house, but I judged it best to knock on the door. Inside, I could hear accordion music and the jaunty scrape of a fiddle. There were footsteps along the hall, the door opened and then my father was standing there, his arms wide, a huge smile on his lovely face. He was wearing the old cardigan he put on for trips to the pub, and a paper hat, the sort you get in crackers. Christmas was round the corner and there was a big bunch of mistletoe inside the hall.

'Sah,' he said, the pet name he'd always used.

I felt his arms close around me and smelled the warm Erinmore Flake smell of Sundays by the fire. I kissed him and then kissed him again. I'd brought a present, a framed Falklands sketch Wesley had found for me in an Exmouth gallery. I gave it to him.

'They let you go, then,' I said, 'poor fools.'

I stepped inside, into the light. My father was looking hard at my face. Not much got past him.

'What happened?' he said quietly.

I dismissed the question with what I hoped was a grin. 'Nothing much,' I said. 'Long story.'

'Are you all right?'

'Yes. No problem.'

'Look at me.'

I looked at him, my eyes beginning to moisten, a reaction so instinctive it took even me by surprise. I could see a blur of guests behind, up the hall, some of them looking my way. I fell into his arms again, his big hands cupping my head.

'My poor love,' he said, 'my poor darling.'

It took me a minute or two to compose myself. The make-up, I knew, was wrecked. I slipped into the little cloakroom beside the front door, excusing myself. I had my bag with me. Not everything was lost.

Repaired, I emerged again. The big through-lounge was a sea of faces, most of them turned my way. I waved as gaily as I could, my biggest grin, trying desperately to find my mother, someone I could bury myself away with, a chance to catch my social breath.

'Hi,' I said, 'hi, everyone.'

There was a chorus of answering hi's, then the music struck up again, a wild swirl of violin chords, an answering barp on the squeeze box. Across the room, against the wall, was a table of food, rows of glasses and I picked my way towards it. The last thing I wanted was anything to eat, but I was beginning to have serious doubts whether I'd stay upright much longer and I thought a drink might help. I was still pouring a large glass of my father's favourite Medoc, when I felt a tug at my elbow. I looked round. It was Ruth.

'You made it,' she said, 'after all.'

I nodded, trying not to gulp. 'I did,' I agreed. 'Bit of a surprise. My father. You know . . .'

Ruth was nodding. Her glass was empty. Without asking, I filled it. She watched me do it, surprised.

'I wasn't going to come,' she said at last, 'under the circumstances, your mother and I—' She broke off, not bothering to complete the sentence. I looked at her, a mix of confusion and mild shock.

'I'm sorry,' I said woodenly, 'if it makes any difference. I was a fool. We both were. These things . . .' I raised my glass, touching hers. 'Cheers. Happy Christmas.'

Ruth ignored the toast. Plainly, she wanted to talk.

'As a matter of fact,' she said, 'I think it was a blessing. And long overdue.'

'What?'

'Rory and I.' She studied her glass a moment, her thin lips pursed. 'If it hadn't been you, I'm sure there'd have been someone else. You can tell. Some men. There's a definite pattern. I realize that now.' She looked up at me. 'Do you know what I mean?'

I nodded gamely. 'Yes,' I said.

'So . . .' She shrugged. 'All things considered, maybe you did us both a favour.'

'What about the kids?' I said automatically.

'They're fine. Fine. There's lots of things they probably miss, but I'm astounded how resilient they've been.' She paused. 'School helps, of course. It's not as though they live at home any more.'

'No.' I nodded. 'I suppose not.'

We both fell silent for a moment. My mother had appeared at last across the room. She was carrying a plate of mince pies and she threw me a big smile, beginning to head my way. When she saw Ruth, she stopped and altered course, picking her way back towards the kitchen. I looked down, running my finger around the rim of my glass.

'And how about Rory,' I said quietly, 'how is he?'

'Rory?' Ruth gave me a hard, bright smile. 'He's fine. As far as I'm aware.'

'Have you . . .' I glanced up, 'parted?'

'Yes.'

'And his leg?'

'Better.'

'Good,' I said, 'I thought he'd have more sense. In the mountains. Climber with his experience.'

I looked up again, aware of Ruth staring at me.

'Mountains?' she said.

'Yes.' I nodded. 'I thought he'd been with the Kurds. Up in the mountains.' I paused, 'No?'

Ruth was smiling again.

'No,' she said, 'that was the mystery. It turns out he was never with the Kurds at all. He broke his leg in Cyprus. Some RAF base or other. He'd been out there in the summer. Went back in October.' She looked down at her drink. 'Couldn't stay away from the place.'

28

     I flew to Mexico City ten days later, a letter from Wesley in my pocket.

     I opened it an hour into the flight, the scene when we parted still fresh in my mind. Wesley was sick again, the symptoms obvious, all the more affecting because he tried so hard to disguise them. The dry cough I'd noticed earlier had developed into something worse, periodic spasms of coughing that shook his whole body, bending him double. He was permanently breathless, the slightest exertion making him pause and gasp for air, and the night sweats had come back, the sheets on his bed soaked through in the morning, the mattress wet to the touch. The day I called in Eileen, it had taken him nearly an hour to get dressed, refusing my help, moving slowly from task to task.

     Eileen, when she'd arrived, had understood at once how sick he was. Hospital had been an obvious option, but I knew Wesley would do anything to avoid that and if Eileen was the alternative, then so be it. I'd been careful to introduce her gradually, the *idea* of her, dropping her name over a period of weeks, saying she was a friend, no threat, with a big sunny room up the road, a limitless supply of drugs and a great sense of humour. The latter wasn't entirely true, but by the time Eileen took over, Wesley was beyond noticing. If he had a choice, he wanted me to take care of him. But he understood why I had to spend a week or so away and insisted I should go, and when he said he'd see me later, I could see from the glint in his eye that he meant it. Virus or no virus, he was determined still to be there, waiting, for when I got back.

     The note was brief, three short lines from Robert Frost, a favourite poet of his. The handwriting was terrible, spidery capitals, the sort old people leave out for the milkman. It went as follows:

> *No memory of having starred*
> *Atones for later disregard*
> *Or keeps the end from being hard*

I read it twice. It made me cry.

Later, a little drunk, I took out the map again. Raoul had been explicit about the arrangements. I'd phoned him twice in the last three days. The first time, he'd told me we had to meet. I was to fly to Texas. He had detailed news. It wasn't something he could mail, or talk about on the phone. Besides, I owed him one or two favours of my own. I'd said that all sounded fine but I was *persona non grata* with the FBI. My name was doubtless starred on all the airport computers and I'd never get beyond the queue for immigration. At this news, he'd grunted, telling me to call back in twenty-four hours, and when I did so he came up with another rendezvous, Plan B, a set of travel arrangements that took me as close as you can get to Texas without touching US soil.

I studied the map, wondering whether to risk another gin. In six hours or so, we'd be landing in Mexico City. From there, I was booked on to an Aeromexico internal flight to a city called Matamoros. Matamoros is up in the north of the country. It sits on the Mexican bank of the Rio Grande, within sight of the USA. For Raoul, it would mean an hour's flight south from Dallas/Fort Worth to Brownsville. From there, he could take a cab across the bridge and into Matamoros. He'd given me the name of a place to stay, the Hotel Jardín. He said it had only just opened. It was cheerful, air-conditioned and discreet. I was to book in and await his arrival. He might be a day or two late, but whatever happened, he promised to be there. Something in his voice, a tone I hadn't heard before, prompted me to ask what the matter was, but he'd dismissed the question with a grunt, repeating the name of the hotel, and sealing the conversation with a murmured '*Hasta la vista*'.

Now, sleepy, I pushed my seat back, and turned my face to the window. The sun was pleasantly warm through the perspex, and I stared out at the tumble of clouds below. In my heart, I think I knew I'd pursued the trail as far as I could. What happened over the next day or so would determine everything. Either Wesley had stumbled on the story of the century, or we'd been sidetracked into a series of blind alleys, colliding with nothing more sensational than the normal consequences of grown men falling out over big money. Either way, remembering Wesley's face when I left him, I wasn't even sure if it mattered any more. The knowledge of his coming death had aged him. What he cared about now, in his own phrase, was getting the pay-off more or less right. The pay-off was something journalists evidently did to stories they wanted to file. It often made the difference between publication and the shredder, though when I pursued the conversation with Wesley, he no longer appeared to know the difference. Still preoccupied by the thought, I drifted off to sleep. Words in print meant nothing any more. Shouldn't I be there? With him? Instead of here? En route, once again, to God knows what?

We landed at Mexico City in a warm, airless dusk. I waited three hours for the connecting flight. By midnight, I was booking into the Hotel Jardín, exchanging my pesos for a pleasant, spacious room on the first floor. I put a call through the hotel switchboard to Eileen, knowing she was up all night at the nursing home, but when the switchboard finally made the connection, I was fast asleep. Hearing the phone, I lifted it and muttered something incomprehensible about leaving me alone, and Eileen must have taken the hint because she hung up.

Next morning, I tried again. It was Pete this time.

'How's Wesley?'

'Not good.'

'Is he sleeping OK?'

'Most of the time, yeah.'

'Have you had the doctor in?'

'Yeah. We've got drugs. A nurse. Everything.' He paused. 'But I don't think it's going to be long.'

'Is that you I'm hearing? Or the doctor?'

'Neither. It's Eileen. She has a nose for these things.'

I thanked Pete and hung up. When I tried Raoul at the office in Dallas, they said he was on vacation. When I tried his home, I got number unobtainable. Puzzled, I gave up, ordering breakfast from room service and wondering quite what I'd do until he arrived.

The wait turned out to be infinitely longer than I'd anticipated.

The first two days, I sat around the hotel in almost hourly expectation of Raoul showing up. Every now and then, I'd check in the lobby, making sure Raoul hadn't arrived, but as the days went by it dawned on me that something must have gone badly wrong.

Day five, at last, I got through to his home number. A male voice answered, not Raoul. Carefully, I explained I was an English friend. Over for a flying visit. We'd fixed to meet. Where was he? There was a long pause. Then the voice came back. It sounded, if anything, Mexican.

'You're Sarah Moreton? The lady from England?'

'Yes.'

'My name is Luis. We met before.'

I nodded. Luis was Raoul's bodyguard, the short, squat, powerful little Latino who'd patrolled the motel car park the night Raoul had paid me a visit.

'I remember,' I said, 'so where's Raoul?'

'He's away just now.' He paused. 'With you.'

'Wrong.'

'He's not there?'

I paused, hearing the surprise in his voice, and another, harder edge. 'No,' I said, 'he's not.'

'OK.' He hesitated. 'You're still at the hotel? In Matamoros?'

'Yes.'

'You stay there. OK?'

I nodded, another question on my lips, but he rang off. Worried now, I put the phone down, wondering quite what had happened to Raoul. He was a man with few illusions. If there were risks, he'd doubtless try and avoid them. So where had he got to? Why wasn't he here?

That afternoon, I wandered down through the plaza and along the wide promenade that ran beside the Rio Grande. The river was wide and sluggish, a sickly grey/brown colour, and on the other side lay Texas. I found a bench under a tree and sat there for more than an hour, trying to work out what to do. Already, I'd been waiting for nearly a week. Clearly, I couldn't hang on for ever.

Neither Raoul nor Luis showed up that day. Next morning, I decided to give it another twenty-four hours. Keen now to make the most of my time, I hired a car and drove east, out of the city, towards the Gulf of Mexico. A local map showed a beach called the Playa General Lauro Villa, and when the woman at the hotel reception said it was good for swimming, a favourite with the locals, I bought a costume from the little kiosk next door. The weather was wonderful, like a pleasant English summer's day, still and warm, and I bumped along in the little Ford, trying to avoid the worst of the ruts.

The beach, when I found it, was a disappointment, dark, hard-packed, granular sand overlooked by a military base and an enormous water slide. The area was dotted with parasols and sun-bleached wooden shacks, and after I'd changed under my hotel towel and tried the water, that was a disappointment too. It felt strangely viscous, with a light sheen on the surface, and when I got some in my mouth, it tasted faintly of oil. There was the smell of oil, too, chemical, sickly, sweet.

Back on the beach, I began to dry myself, towelling hard, aware of a small, squat figure tramping over the sand towards me. Late now, the sun low, the beach was almost deserted, a couple of families playing football, a man in a shellsuit walking a huge dog. The figure got closer. I pulled on my shorts and sweatshirt. It was Luis.

He stopped where my costume and towel lay on the sand. He seemed, if anything, embarrassed.

'They told me at the hotel,' he said simply. 'They said you'd come here.'

We walked back to his car. He had a wide, flat, pock-marked face and longish hair, combed straight back. He walked like a boxer or a rugby player, the movement coming from his upper body, the steady tramp-tramp leaving deep footprints in the firm sand. When we got to the car, a newish Oldsmobile, he opened the door and took out two large envelopes. Across from the parking lot was a small café. There were tables outside. We sat down.

'Raoul?' I said.

Luis shrugged. 'I don't know.'

'You haven't seen him?'

'No.' He looked at me a moment, not bothering to elaborate, and then he picked up the thickest of the two envelopes. 'This is for you,' he said. 'Raoul had it ready for you at the house.'

I looked at the envelope. It had my Christian name on it, careless capital letters, a man in a hurry. I mimed opening it, looking at Luis.

He shrugged, producing a pack of cigarettes. 'Go ahead,' he said.

I slid a nail beneath the flap of the envelope. Inside was a sheaf of A4 paper. The typing was double spaced, the punctuation erratic, more evidence that time had been short. I waved away the offer of a cigarette, reading quickly through the first few pages, hearing Raoul's laconic voice behind the terse journalese.

What Luis had brought me was a report on the name I'd given Raoul, François Ghattan. It confirmed that Ghattan had been an arms dealer, with offices in Switzerland and Miami. In the process of making his fortune, he'd evidently acquired friends in high places. One of them was Harold Beckermann, who'd retained him over a period of years for deals with Iraq.

Ghattan, as Wesley had already told me, knew Iraq inside out. His first million dollars had come in commissions, from deals struck during the Iran–Iraq war. He knew, and liked, the Iraqi leadership, Saddam's extended family, the Baathist bandits from upriver Tikriti. I hesitated over the phrase, reading it again, recognizing Raoul's style. An old man had appeared from the café, jeans and grubby white shirt. Luis barely looked at him, ordering coffee in Spanish, still watching me. I returned to the report, reading on.

The Iraqis, over the years, had showered gifts on Ghattan. One of them was evidently a villa beside the lake at Lausanne. There was a photograph of it attached to the report, a handsome place with huge picture windows and an acre or so of grass sloping down to the water. It was an ideal nerve centre for Ghattan's European operations, discreet, monied, with ready access to the comforts of the Swiss banking system and to Iraq's many friends in nearby France. Jake McGrath, I remember, had mentioned the importance of the French connection, how close the two countries had been, the deals they'd done, the deals still to come. I studied the photo a moment or two longer, impressed now by Raoul's diligence, by his contacts, wondering just where he'd picked up all the information. Paper-clipped to the next page of text was another photograph, smaller, fuzzier, a head and shoulders shot, someone young, dark, swarthy, someone I'd seen only a week or so ago, in the photo from Aldridge's precious library. I turned it over, knowing already who it was, reading Raoul's scrawl on the back. Another of Baghdad's little gifts for François Ghattan: Rahman Khalil, his bodyguard.

The old man returned with cups of *café de olla*, thick, dark, brewed coffee, delicious. I picked mine up, sipping it, curious to know what Raoul had to say about Rahman Khalil. The man had, it seemed, served a number of purposes. By far the most important, from the Iraqi point of view, was the guarantee that Ghattan would remain under their control. Khalil would be with him day and night, an ever-present companion, charming, highly trained, multi-lingual, a social asset as well as armed protection. This arrangement had apparently worked well until very recently, when Khalil had abruptly gone missing, leaving Ghattan undefended and unchaperoned. Next thing anyone knew, Khalil had reappeared in Beirut, Ghattan's old stamping ground, joining an Extec party booked to travel by chartered plane to Sana'a in the Yemen. The rest of the story I thought I knew already – the plane disappearing from Lebanese radar screens, the wreckage falling earthwards, everyone on board killed – but Raoul had a different version. According to him, Khalil may not have been on the plane after all. There were rumours out of the Middle East that he'd been seen since. One source claimed to have spotted him in Cyprus, in a small bar in Akrotiri. *Cyprus?*

I glanced up. Luis was smoking again. 'You know about any of this?' I said.

He nodded. 'A little.'

'What happened to Ghattan?' I said. 'Isn't he supposed to be dead, too?'

Luis said nothing, indicating the pages of typescript on the table with a brief movement of his hand, and I wondered whether or not he'd read it, been part of this impressive piece of research. The temperature was falling fast now, a breeze from the Gulf stirring the dust at our feet. I pulled on a sweatshirt over my vest, reaching for the last two sheets of paper.

The headline, in capitals, read: 'FRANÇOIS GHATTAN: THE CORONARY THAT NEVER WAS?' Intrigued, I read further. This material wasn't as well-sourced as the stuff I'd read earlier and there was a handwritten note of apology at the end, promising more collateral, but the drift of the story was very obvious. Ghattan had been suffering for a number of years from a condition similar to angina. The blood vessels of his heart had narrowed to the point where any exertion or excitement could become life-threatening. Drugs had kept the problem more or less under control, but in June he'd finally submitted to a heart bypass, a perfectly routine piece of surgery which replaced the worst-affected blood vessels with lengths of healthy vein from the inside of his leg. This procedure, naturally enough, had been carried out at the Harold J. Beckermann Cardiothoracic Center, in Dallas, the hi-tech facility funded by his friend and business partner. The operation itself, according to the surgeons, had gone well. Yet within a week, under puzzling circumstances, Ghattan had died.

I read the final paragraph again. On 10 June, just four days after the Extec plane crash, Ghattan had been found dead in a private room at the Cardiothoracic Center. He was out of intensive care. His vital signs had all been excellent. His convalescence was utterly routine. Yet there he was, dead.

The hospital, at Beckermann's insistence, had opened an enquiry and the post-mortem had revealed evidence of a massive heart attack, yet Ghattan's abrupt exit was still – according to Raoul – a talking point amongst the Dallas medical set. Raoul was too good a journalist to build conclusions on speculation, but after the scribbled apology, at the very end of the piece, there was a final line. I peered at it in the fading light. It read: 'Injection? Thalium?'

I looked at Luis. Thalium was a particularly nasty poison, a favourite for political assassinations. It was lethal in minute amounts but left no trace in the body.

'Thalium?' I queried. 'Raoul's serious?'

Luis stared at me, uncomprehending. 'I don't know,' he said, 'I never heard that name.'

'You've read this?' I held it up.

'No.'

'But you knew where to find it?'

'Yeah. Raoul told me. He'd hidden it. He told me to give it to you if you called round.'

'*Called round?* He said that?'

'Yeah.' He paused, and then, for the first time, he smiled. 'I don't think he believed everything you told him. He was sure you knew.'

'Knew what?'

'Where he lived.'

'No.' I shook my head. 'Wrong.'

There was a long silence. A skinny dog padded slowly up the road from the beach, nose to the ground. I looked at the other envelope. 'What's in there?' I said.

Luis shrugged. 'It's for you,' he said. 'It came last night. To the house. There's a note from Raoul on it. Here.'

He passed me the envelope. It was a thick, heavy-duty envelope, the kind you use for sending photographs. Scrawled on the outside, in Raoul's hand, were two brief lines. I tried hard to read them. His handwriting was even more unformed than usual. 'Don't bother making sense of it all,' I think it read. 'Happy Christmas, and take care.'

Don't bother making sense of it all? I glanced up, frowning. Luis was looking at the envelope. Something appeared to be troubling him, something on the other side. I turned it over. There were fingerprints around the flap. The fingerprints were a browny, ochre colour. I blinked, looking up again.

'Blood?'

Luis nodded. '*Sí*,' he said, '*sangre*.'

I hesitated a moment, then opened the envelope. There were three photographs inside, enlargements, full colour. I shook them out on to the table. The old man from the café was standing there, two more coffees in his hand. Seeing the photos, he turned on his heel and walked away. I picked the top one up. It showed a man lying on the ground. He was naked above the waist, and where his throat had once been there was a gaping hole. His eyes were open, his mouth too, and his face, like his upper chest, was covered in blood.

I stood up, sickened, watching Luis reaching for the photographs, his face darkening as he recognized the body in the dirt. Raoul Delahunty. He picked up the second photo, same scene, close-up this time, head and shoulders, the inside of Raoul's windpipe clearly visible. I sat down again, shaking my head, feeling the hot gusts of vomit in my mouth. Luis was studying the third photo. He seemed, suddenly, quite calm, under control again. He showed me the photograph, Raoul's torso, the head missing completely, the blade of a new spade visible in the corner of the shot, fresh blood darkening the shiny metal.

I indicated the first two photos, the torn throat, the ripped flesh. 'Could a dog do that?' I said.

Luis nodded, saying nothing. Then, very slowly, he rolled up the sleeve of the shirt he was wearing. He had thick, muscled forearms, completely hairless. Deep scars wound around them, purple tracks, the suture marks still clearly visible. There must have been four separate wounds. Maybe five. Luis looked up at me.

'Beckermann's place?' I said.

'*Sí.*'

I hesitated a moment, remembering Raoul's story in the hotel room, how far he'd taken me, the rumours that Beckermann was arranging fights to the death, *mano a mano*, hand to hand. Luis, I thought. Luis must have been one of them, a Mexican, a wetback, desperate for citizenship, driven to wager his life against a stake in this rich, cruel, hideous society across the Rio Grande.

'You fought?' I said. 'You fought for Beckermann?'

'*Sí.*'

'Man to man?'

'No,' he paused, buttoning his cuff again, 'I was lucky.'

'What then? What happened?'

He said nothing for a moment. Then he collected the photos in a neat pile, giving me the answer I wanted.

'You fought the dogs? They made you fight the dogs?'

Luis nodded, examining the photos for a final time, his own fate, somehow avoided. 'Yes,' he said quietly.

'And you won?'

'Yes. I killed the dog.'

I nodded, sitting back, turning away, looking down the road, out towards the Gulf. A moment later, Luis was beside me, putting on his leather jacket. I peered up at him.

'Just tell me,' I said, 'what makes them do it?'

'Who?'

'Beckermann, these friends of his.' I nodded at the photos, now under his arm. 'Why?'

Luis said nothing. I stood up. Then he lifted his nose in the air, sniffing, an almost animal gesture.

'You smell anything?'

'Yes,' I said, recognizing that same sickly sweet smell, carried on the night wind from the Gulf.

'You know what it is?'

'Yes, of course.'

I glanced up at him, expecting more, but he was already walking away, back towards the car.

29

We met again back in the hotel. Luis came up to my room. I offered him a Sol from my private supplies but he said he didn't drink. He stood by the door, looking uncomfortable. He plainly wanted to go. I still had the photographs, and the report that Raoul had put together.

'What happens now?' I said.

Luis shrugged. 'I'm going back,' he said, 'to Dallas.'

'And?'

He looked at me for a long moment. He had very black eyes. Then he shrugged again. 'Maybe tomorrow,' he said, 'maybe the next day.'

'Maybe what?'

'Simple,' he half turned, wanting the conversation over, reaching for the door handle, 'I kill him.'

'Beckermann?'

'*Sí.*'

'How?' I said. 'How are you going to kill him?'

He thought about the question for a moment. 'I haven't figured it out,' he said at last, 'yet.'

'From a car? Will you need a car?'

Luis hesitated, the door half open now. Finally, he nodded. 'Yes,' he said. 'I'll need a car.'

'And a driver? Back-up?' I paused. 'Help?'

Slowly, it began to dawn on Luis what I was really saying. The realization stole across his face. He looked surprised. Then amused. Then extremely grave. '*You?*' he said softly. '*You* want to help?'

I crossed the Rio Grande at three o'clock next morning, forty miles west of Matamoros, a deserted stretch of riverbank that

Luis had used himself, only three years earlier. Luis dropped me half a mile from the river, showing me a path that led down through the scrub to the water. The river, he said, was wide. There was a current of sorts and I'd hit the further bank maybe a quarter of a mile downstream. There, I'd find an area of marsh grass. Beyond the marsh grass, back on dry land, I was to look for a broken-down old shack. The shack was occasionally used by hunters and fishermen. He'd meet me there in an hour, time enough for him to backtrack to the bridge at Reynosa and then drive down Route 83.

I repeated the instructions and he listened hard, nodding, before getting back in the car. I watched the tail-lights disappearing down the road, and then set off through the scrub towards the river. It was a warm, windless night, nothing moving except the odd bird I managed to disturb. I watched one flapping away into the darkness. I could see the river now, inky black, and I could smell it, too, the dank, muddy smell of rotting vegetation.

On the riverbank, I stripped off the clothes I was wearing – jeans, sweatshirt – and sealed them inside a polythene laundry bag I'd found in the hotel wardrobe. The rest of my luggage I'd left with Luis, including the photos and the report that Raoul had done on Ghattan. Wearing only the bathing costume I'd bought that day, plus a belt I'd fastened round my waist, I slipped into the water, surprised at how cold it was. The current was stronger than I'd expected and I struck out for the further bank, feeling myself drifting sideways. I'd tied the laundry bag to my belt but it turned out not to be waterproof after all. It filled quickly and hung down beneath me like a kind of anchor, slowing my progress.

I'm normally a very strong swimmer, but after five minutes or so I knew that I'd have to make a decision about the bag. It was dragging me down, reducing my progress to a very slow crawl. At this rate, I thought, I'd be back in Matamoros by daybreak, a sitting duck for my uniformed friends on the other side. Finally, knowing there was no alternative, I trod water for a minute or so, wrestling with the tightly knotted plastic, untying it from my belt, letting the bag sink beneath me. Minutes later my feet found the riverbed and I was wading out of the water, on to US soil.

By the time I found the shack, Luis was already there. I

approached it from the north, taking no chances, keeping my body low, moving very slowly across the baked earth. I saw Luis before he saw me and I was within touching distance when he spun round, dropping into a crouch, a small handgun levelled at my chest.

'*Buenas noches*,' I whispered, beginning to shiver with cold, glad of the towel he'd brought from the car.

We drove north for the rest of the night, and by the time it was light enough to see, we were pushing into the outskirts of San Antonio, the flat, brown landscape dotted with new developments, the towers of the downtown area visible up ahead. Luis, as inscrutable as ever, had said very little, but my performance on the riverbank had definitely warmed the atmosphere between us. Women weren't meant to take him by surprise the way I'd done. It simply wasn't in the script.

We stopped for breakfast north of Austin, a beaten-up café in the middle of nowhere, ringed by huge trucks. Back by the car, still wet from the river, I'd changed into a pair of tracksuit bottoms and a tight cotton singlet that didn't leave much to the imagination. Conversation stopped when we picked our way through the tables towards the counter and I could tell by the expression on his face that Luis loved it. He was a good three inches shorter than me and the physical difference between us clearly made a powerful statement about his *machismo*. We stayed longer than we needed to, a double helping of waffles with maple syrup, and by the time we left we had the makings of a plan.

It was, to my astonishment, Christmas Eve. Every Christmas Eve, Beckermann hosted a huge party at one of the big Dallas hotels. Luis had even attended one, accompanying Raoul the previous year, delivering his boss at eight in the evening and returning past midnight to pick him up. At the party's end, Beckermann always drove back to the ranch at Fairwater. There, with his family, he'd celebrate Christmas itself.

The plan, therefore, was simple. I'd check on the party arrangements by phone. We'd wait for Beckermann to leave. We'd tail him south, out along the road to Corsicana, and when the time was right we'd draw alongside and Luis would kill him. When I wondered aloud about armour plating and toughened glass, Luis said it would be no problem. We'd be making a call en route to Dallas. Amongst the hardware we'd pick up was a weapon that was, in Luis's phrase, *'fantástico'*. Beckermann, Luis promised, would be history. As would anyone else foolish enough to be sharing his car. His kids, I murmured, his friends? Luis looked at me and shrugged. I'd seen the photos, the evidence of what he was prepared to do. That, in his view, closed the argument.

Later, mid-afternoon, we discussed what would happen afterwards. Beckermann dead, we'd swop cars in Dallas, picking up Raoul's big Mazda, and head south again, back to the Rio Grande. Checks going into Mexico were no problem at all, especially on Christmas Day, and I would cross the toll bridge in the boot of the Mazda. Given a little luck and good connections at the airport, Luis said I could be back in the UK while there was still a little meat left on the turkey. The latter expression made me laugh out loud, a reaction which, for some reason, made Luis acutely embarrassed.

A hundred miles short of Dallas, we stopped in a city called Waco. Luis drove around for a while, plainly lost, then saw a gas station he evidently recognized. He pulled the Oldsmobile into a sharp U-turn, and stopped outside a modest clapboard house beside a timber yard. He grunted something at me in Spanish and left the car. He was in the house maybe five minutes. When he came out, he was carrying something wrapped in hessian sacking. It looked heavy. He signalled me to open the boot and I did so, feeling the car rock on its springs as he dropped the package in. Luis disappeared again, returning this time with a large cardboard box. This, too, went into the boot.

An hour later, at a wayside Dunkin' Do-Nuts, I phoned the Dallas hotel where, according to Luis, Beckermann traditionally celebrated Christmas Eve. The woman on the switchboard confirmed the function. Mr Beckermann would be entertaining his guests in the hotel's Galleywood Suite from six o'clock onwards. The function was scheduled to end around 1 a.m. I thanked her for the information and, as an afterthought, booked a room. We'd need somewhere to rest up while the party was in full swing. Where better than the hotel itself?

Back in the car, I gave the news to Luis. A grunt or two

signalled what I took to be approval. He had the cardboard box beside him on the front seat now. He opened it, taking out an automatic pistol, passing it across to me.

'You ever seen one of these?'

The question was voiced with a certain respect. I looked at him a moment. I think he was getting to like me.

'Yes,' I nodded, 'I have.'

'Know how to use it?'

'Yes.'

I slid back the firing mechanism a couple of times, then checked the magazine. The gun was Swiss, a Sig Sauer P226. I'd handled them a number of times in Northern Ireland. It's a beautifully made weapon, reliable, accurate, with a fifteen-round magazine. The SAS swear by them. Luis was rummaging inside the box again. I glimpsed a length of belt ammunition.

'What's that?' I said.

Luis looked at me, then glanced out of the window, checking that we weren't being watched. Opening the box properly, he let me look inside. There were layers and layers of the belt ammunition, hundreds of rounds. It must have weighed a ton. I looked at Luis. For the first time since we'd met, he was grinning. He extracted one of the bullets from the belt and gave it to me. It was full metal jacket, the nose tipped in blue dye.

'Specially adapted,' he said. 'Goes through most of everything.'

'Including whatever Beckermann drives?'

'Sure.' The grin widened. 'The kind of range we'll be at.'

'And the gun? That thing in the back? The one we picked up?'

'M60. Ex-Marine Corps. You can buy them most places round here. All you need's a driver's licence and a signature.' He shrugged. 'Easy.'

I nodded, taking in the technical details, sobered by the implications. The M60 is the standard-issue US Army heavy machine gun. The GIs call it 'the Pig', and you see them in all the classic Vietnam clips. For our purposes, to be honest, it was a little excessive. An act of simple revenge was fast becoming a major military encounter. At point-blank range, even through a layer or two of sheet metal, the M60 would tear Beckermann apart. I lay back against the seat, smiling at the thought, a helping or two of primitive American justice, with love from Grant and Raoul. I glanced across at Luis. He was repacking the ammunition.

'Won't you miss the States?' I said. 'Afterwards?'

Luis shrugged, letting the line of shiny brass bullets slither through his fingers. He must have paid for the stuff upfront, because he was counting the rounds, ten at a time. When he got to four hundred, he stopped, closing the box.

'No,' he said flatly.

We got to the Dallas hotel at seven in the evening after yet another stop for me to raid my case for something half-respectable to wear. In the end I settled for trousers and a simple top, and while Luis put the Olds in the underground car park, I booked in. They wanted ID, so I used my own name, showing my UK driving licence, but paid with traveller's cheques. If the FBI were any good, they, like MI5, would have a direct line to American Express. Using my credit card could see me behind bars well before midnight.

I sat in the lobby for a couple of minutes, discreetly shielded by an enormous yucca plant, waiting for Luis. Guests were already arriving for Beckermann's party, late middle-aged couples, the men in tuxedoes with armfuls of presents, the women exquisitely turned out, the kind of dresses I'd been ogling in the Niemann-Marcus catalogue. The atmosphere was loud and cheerful, big smiles, hugs, kisses and I told myself I'd seen one or two of the faces already, out at Beckermann's ranch, the day we saw the dogs fight. Watching the couples ambling towards the huge function room, arm in arm, I could smell the river smell again, and hear the snarl of the pit-bulls, and taste the hot, sour bite of Priddy's bourbon. I smiled at the line of retreating backs, thinking of the contents of Luis's hessian sack, our own little Christmas surprise, the line of full stops we'd stitch across the end of this hideous story.

Upstairs, we settled in for the evening. The room was enormous. I ordered shrimp and fries from room service, and a large steak for Luis. He'd already stationed one of the armchairs in front of the television, and was checking out the offerings on cable. I retreated to the other side of the room, reaching for the phone and dialling the Exmouth number. In the UK, as far as I could judge, it was Christmas Day. The least I owed Wesley was a phone call.

Pete answered the phone. I could hear music in the background, someone playing the piano. It sounded like a rag of some kind, maybe Scott Joplin, but much slower than usual.

'Happy Christmas,' I said. 'I'm sorry it's so late.'

'Hi.' Pete's voice dropped at once. 'Where are you?'

'Dallas.'

'Ah.'

'Why?'

There was a pause. I glanced across the room at Luis, signalling him to turn down the volume on the television. He did so, pulling the armchair closer to the set.

'Why?' I said again.

Pete came back to the phone. Wesley, evidently, had rallied. Against all expectations, he was back on his feet. He wasn't better, in fact he was still very ill, but he'd insisted on joining the Christmas Eve expedition to midnight mass, and now he was back again, two in the morning, still celebrating.

'*Mass?*' I said. 'You mean church?'

'Yeah.'

I blinked. Wesley had never been anything but caustic about religion. He thought of God as a chat-up opportunity for closet gays in dog collars, and regarded concepts like salvation and the after-life as a cop-out. Yet here he was, half dead, attending midnight mass. Was he hedging his bets at last? Or was it something deeper?

'How is he?' I said, returning to the phone.

'Drunk,' Pete hesitated, 'I think.'

'But happy?'

'Dunno.' He paused again. 'You wanna talk to him?'

'Yes. Please.'

Pete left the phone and I heard his voice again, very low, the other side of the room. The piano stopped and there was more conversation, and then Pete was back on the phone again. He sounded awkward, almost apologetic.

'There's a problem,' he began, 'it's not a good time. This is all a bit complicated. What's happened is—'

He broke off, and in the background I heard the piano again, a different tune this time, the theme all too familiar, picked out with the right hand, the notes descending, plaintive, haunting, a private message, impossible to ignore or misinterpret. Rachmaninov's Second Piano Concerto. The slow movement. I closed my eyes, listening to the dying chords, numbed. Wesley, at last, was saying goodbye.

A second or two later, there was another voice on the line. Eileen.

'He won't come,' she said. 'He won't talk to you. He says there's no point.'

I smiled, sadder now than I can describe.

'He's right,' I said.

'So? What do you want me to do?'

I could hear the frustration in her voice. It couldn't have been easy. I bent to the phone, the television a blur now.

'Tell him Happy Christmas,' I said quietly, 'and tell him . . .' I hesitated, '. . . safe journey.'

The Galleywood Suite function room began to empty at midnight. Luis and I sat in the Oldsmobile, across the street. We had a perfect view of the guests descending the hotel steps, the occasional gusts of laughter, the younger couples shepherding their children towards the waiting limousines. Inside the lobby, plainly visible, was Beckermann himself, head and shoulders above his guests, impeccably dressed, a towering bull of a man. Each time a guest stopped and thanked him, he stooped slightly, extending a hand, encircling a shoulder with an arm, accepting an embrace, and watching him I thought again of Raoul Delahunty's line about royalty, and deference, and money, and what really mattered in America. '*Harold J. Beckermann*,' he'd said, '*the living proof the system works.*'

At length, the queue of departing guests began to thin. One of the last to appear looked familiar: tall, slim, curly blond hair, the wide smile never leaving the square-set face. I glanced across at Luis. Luis was sitting beside me in the passenger seat. The M60 was on his knees beneath one of the hotel blankets.

'His name's Devlin,' I said, indicating the figure on top of the hotel steps, 'and he's English.'

'Yeah?'

Luis didn't look up. He was busy with the machine-gun's breech mechanism, sliding it backwards and forwards, listening hard, making sure the register was exactly right. Watching him, I began to understand why he'd been so valuable to Raoul, such a good bodyguard. He had a musician's care for his instruments, a fanatical attention to the smallest detail.

I looked across the street again, comforted. Devlin had been joined by a blonde woman his own age. She was wearing a long black dress, low cut. She looked wonderful. They talked together for a moment, laughing, then he leaned forward and kissed her on the lips. As he did so, Beckermann appeared through the door. He put his arms around them both, a gesture, it seemed to me, of genuine warmth. The woman reached up and kissed him. Devlin looked fondly on. Then a long black car pulled up, a stretch Mercedes, and someone inside leaned forward from the back seat and opened the door. Beckermann shepherded the woman and Devlin into the back, then got in beside the driver. I turned to Luis, telling him it was time to go, reaching for the ignition key, stirring the big engine into life.

We followed the Mercedes out of the city. Soon it became obvious that we were heading south, exactly the same route I'd taken with Priddy, all those long weeks ago. Townships came and went, empty streets, shadowed gardens, front windows twinkling with tiny decorated Christmas trees. Past Ennis, the Mercedes slowed and then turned left. From here, I knew, the countryside was bare, no houses, no townships, just the occasional stir of cattle in the huge fenced fields. I looked across at Luis, meaning to tell him, but he nodded, reading my mind. He's been here already, I thought, in the back of some pick-up or other, fodder for the afternoon's entertainment, a journey he'd never forget.

The blanket was off the machine-gun now and Luis had fed the first shells into the side port. The belt fell away from the gun, into the cardboard box in the well of the car beneath the dashboard, and Luis was sitting sideways on, the gun across his lap, his left hand curled around the trigger guard. When the time came and I drew up alongside the Mercedes, all he'd have to do was blast the shells through the bodywork of the door, keeping his eye on the driver. Four hundred rounds of blue-tipped full metal jacket would do the rest.

I fingered the switch that controlled my window, lowering it fully, taking deep lungfuls of air. The lights of the Mercedes were a quarter of a mile ahead of us, and I knew that there'd be some curiosity already about our presence. This was a tiny country road. To my knowledge, it led nowhere except the Fairwater Ranch. So who were we? And what were we doing on Beckermann's home turf?

The Oldsmobile hit a deep rut in the road and I had to fight for control for a second or two. I had the Sauer on my lap now, fully loaded, a round already in the chamber, and I recognized the churning in my belly, the anticipation and the waiting tying my insides in knots. I wasn't new to situations like these, Northern Ireland had seen to that, but I never got this far without a dry mouth and a racing heart, a mix of excitement and foreboding, my body awash with adrenalin, every nerve strung tight.

I glanced across at Luis. The road was straight here, plenty of room for overtaking. He nodded. I pressed hard on the accelerator, feeling the big car respond. In seconds, we'd halved the gap between us and the Mercedes. I looked at Luis again. He had the gun up now, the muzzle an inch or two from the door. His finger was curled inside the trigger guard. He didn't take his eyes off the road ahead.

'Now?'

'*Sí.*'

I indicated to overtake and hit the throttle again. The Mercedes began to move over, making room. Up ahead, there was nothing. I slowed a little, still travelling fast, 60 m.p.h. on the speedo, but letting the Olds creep up alongside the Mercedes. Inside the Mercedes, I could see faces turning towards us. There were three people in the back. I remembered two of them stooping to get in at the hotel, Devlin and the woman, the third one already there, leaning forward, opening the door. I eased the Olds forward, hearing Luis cocking the big machine-gun, getting ready, then I checked right again, lining us up, seeing the face at the rear window, looking directly at me, the spare, bony features, the wild ginger hair, the hand at the throat loosening the black bow-tie. I stared for a full second, then another, my foot easing on the throttle, my resolution going, everything suddenly wrong.

Luis was shouting now, cursing at me in Spanish, and I was trying to tell him it was impossible, we'd have to call it off, some terrible mistake, but I was still trying to get the words out when the M60 began to bark, one long explosion, the shells tearing through the thin metal, the machine-gun jumping around, Luis wrestling with it, forcing it back towards the door, spent cases everywhere, bouncing off the dashboard, the Mercedes swaying, wildly out of control. I hit the brake hard, throwing Luis against the dashboard. His head came up again, blood all over his face, and he made a lunge for the wheel, but I fought him off, stamping on the brake again, throwing him against the windscreen, bringing the car to a skidding halt.

After a moment or two, Luis motionless, I got out, the Sauer in my hand. The Mercedes was fifty yards up the road, slewed sideways, every window shattered. I ran as fast as I could. When I got to the car, I circled it carefully, breathing hard, smelling the cordite and the burnt rubber.

Inside the car was a mess. Beckermann was unrecognizable. Parts of his head were missing and blood was still pumping from a line of holes across his chest. The driver was slumped across the wheel. As far as I could tell, he too was dead. I reached for the back door, wrenching it open. Devlin sat in the corner, hunched up, quite motionless. His eyes were open and he was making strange whimpering noises. He appeared to be in deep shock. The woman beside him lay across his lap. Her hands were clasped tight over her ears, and as far as I could judge she was still alive. Of the other passenger, the face I'd seen at the window, there was no sign.

I stepped away from the car. Then, abruptly, there were a series of gunshots from back down the road. I peered into the darkness, quite certain that it wasn't the M60, wrong calibre, something much smaller. I began to run again, hugging the side of the road. Ten yards from the Oldsmobile, I stopped, adopting the low crouch they'd taught me at Bessbrook, the one they call the Armagh shuffle, moving very slowly, the gun out ahead of me, perfect balance, one step at a time. Close now to the car, I checked left and right, seeing nothing. Finally beside the driver's door, I peered in. Luis lay across the other seat, the M60 still cradled in his arms, his head back, the dead eyes staring at me. One of the bullets had hit the very middle of his forehead, up above the bridge of the nose, a small, black hole, a textbook killing.

I eased back, beginning to turn away. Then, very gently, I felt the pressure at the base of my skull, smelled the sharp, familiar smell of the aftershave he'd always favoured, heard the burr of the soft Scots vowels.

'Drop it.'

I did what I was told. The Sauer clattered to the ground. Very slowly, I turned round, the gun still to my head.

No doubt about it. The face in the back of the Mercedes. Rory.

30

Late the next afternoon, we were still at the Hyatt-Regency Hotel, downtown Dallas, seventh floor, a nice view of Reunion Park from the big picture windows. Rory had ordered a full Christmas dinner for us both from room service: turkey and stuffing, bread sauce and veggies, and even a couple of unopened crackers. We'd been looking at it now for the best part of five hours.

'Tell me again,' I said. 'It might help.'

'I love you,' he said. 'Just trust me.'

'No.' I shook my head. 'The rest of it.'

He looked at me a moment. As a debrief, the afternoon was going nowhere: endless questions, mostly mine; careful evasions, vintage Rory.

'You're here to keep an eye on Devlin,' I said. 'At least you've told me that much.'

'Have I?'

'Yes. You said you've been close. You said you've seen a lot of him. Socially. Business-wise.' I paused. 'That makes you either his friend, or his minder. I'd suggest the latter, no?'

Rory refused to comment, but got up and poured himself another Scotch. He'd been telling me since noon that this was strictly a Christmas indulgence, but looking at him I wasn't so sure. His face had reddened a little since we'd last been together, and there was an uncertainty in his manner that I'd never seen before. He didn't seem sure of himself, and under the circumstances I didn't blame him. Leaving three dead Americans on a country road in Texas was a lousy career move, even if his relationship with the authorities had enabled us, quite literally, to walk away.

'So let's say I'm right about Devlin,' I suggested. 'Let's say you've been looking after the man. What's he going to do now? What's he going to say about last night?'

'Nothing. If he's sensible.'

'Ah.' I smiled. 'A clue?'

'Hardly.'

'But he was there. In the car. A witness. He can't just ignore it. Pretend it never happened.'

Rory shrugged, nursing the Scotch. 'Grudge killing. Some half-crazed Mexican. Man like Beckermann. That kind of profile.' He looked up. 'This is a violent country. Happens all the time.'

'You're telling me he drove the car *and* handled the M–60? All by himself? You're telling me that?'

Rory glanced up. He looked exhausted. 'I'm telling you nothing,' he said.

'You're right,' I agreed. 'You're telling me bugger all.'

There was a long silence. Across the room, Rory stirred. For someone whose life I'd spared, he was being remarkably businesslike.

'You have a choice,' he said finally. 'You can stay here and wait for them to pick you up—'

'Them?'

'Our FBI friends.'

'What for?'

'You want the list? Arson. Illegal entry.' He paused. 'Plus probable homicide charges.'

'Or?'

'Or,' he shrugged, 'you can come back with me. To the UK.' He looked at me for a moment, then got up and went to the window. 'I gather Keogh's dying,' he said at last, 'and I gather you're close.' He glanced round at me. 'Am I right?'

'His name's Wesley.'

'Is that important?'

'Yes,' I said, 'to me, it is.'

He nodded, saying nothing, not bothering to hide his indifference, and it occurred to me yet again that I'd been lucky all those months ago, having the relationship fall apart in my hands, Rory suddenly gone, yours truly left with nothing but a rumour or two about the Gulf War and the address of a flat in Guildford.

'Where did you go,' I said idly, 'when you left me?'

'When?'

'Way back? October? After we'd been to Skye?'

'Ah.'

Rory smiled, reaching for the Scotch again. I looked at the trolley of congealed food. The custard on the plum pudding was pink. Very Dallas. I yawned, studying my hands.

'Cyprus,' I said softly, 'wasn't it?'

I looked up. Rory had reddened a little more. At length, uncomfortable, he cleared his throat. 'Does it matter?' he said.

'Yes,' I said, 'it does.'

'Then,' he shrugged, 'let's say you're right. Let's say it was Cyprus.'

'So why? Tell me why. Why would you have been there?'

'Business.'

'Whose business?'

'The usual business.' He paused. 'HMG business.'

'On Cyprus?'

'Yes.'

'Whereabouts on Cyprus?'

Rory cleared his throat, refusing to answer. His whole manner had changed. He might have been sitting in a court of law. I studied him, drawing on my years at Curzon House, the bits of useless information that stick in your brain regardless. 'Akrotiri?' I suggested. 'The RAF base?'

'There and other places,' he nodded. 'Yes.'

'But including Akrotiri?'

'From time to time,' he nodded again, '. . . yes.'

I shifted down the bed, lying full-length, gazing up at the ceiling. A year ago, Rory would have been with me in seconds. Now, he reached for the last of the Scotch.

'Akrotiri's a debrief centre,' I mused, 'MI6, your lot, DIS.' I frowned. 'Assets from the Middle East, off-cuts from the terrorist groups, the odd disaffected Israeli, they all end up there, don't they? Before you pass them down the line? To London?'

I looked sideways. Rory wasn't saying a word. I closed my eyes again. My game. My rules. My shout.

'This man Khalil,' I said slowly, 'Rahman Khalil. The one who was supposed to have gone down with the Extec plane. The one they never found.' I got up on one elbow and looked at Rory. 'Ever know him at all? Heard of him? Friend of Ghattan's? Ghattan's bodyguard?'

Rory was shaking his head now, a firm denial, transparently false, too much Scotch, too many questions.

'Never heard of him.'

'Ah.' I smiled. 'I was just wondering, the way you do. Supposing . . .' I frowned, 'he *didn't* die. Supposing he *wasn't* on the plane. Supposing he came over, defected, ended up at Akrotiri? Supposing—'

'Defected?' Rory sounded derisive now. 'Defected from who?'

'The Americans. And the Iraqis. The ones who knew about the partnership behind the war. The ones who planted the bomb on the Extec plane. The ones who wanted to kill him.' I paused. 'That would be a good reason to defect, wouldn't it? Providing he knew? Providing someone told him?'

'But defected to who? To where?'

'Us.' I smiled. 'You.'

'Why? Why should he do that?'

'Because we could offer him . . .' I smiled again, 'a new life, some kind of future.' I paused. 'A safe haven.'

Rory was frowning now, eyeing the complimentary bottle of Napa Valley Chardonnay the hotel had sent up with the food.

'To make all that work,' he said slowly, 'you have to have a motive. So why on earth would we do it? Why on earth would we get involved?'

'Because the Americans are screwing us on the arms deals. We think our noses should be in the trough, too,' I shrugged, 'and they don't.'

I paused here, wondering if this was too stark a summary of Aldridge's thesis. He'd put it to me twice and on both occasions I'd somehow missed the main point. Only now, moving the other bits around the board, did I see how obvious it all was. If we didn't export, we'd die. If we didn't export arms, we'd die even faster.

I got up off the bed and fetched a Kleenex from the box on the windowsill. Half an hour in the Rio Grande had given me a cold. Rory watched my every movement, nervous, uncomfortable, half the man I'd known in London. I sat on the bed again, my back against the deep-buttoned velvet of the headboard.

'If Wesley was right,' I said, 'then the Americans and the Iraqis would have needed channels, middlemen, people they trusted to negotiate a deal. That's the way business works. Wars aren't any different. Just bigger.' I smiled. 'No?'

Rory shook his head. 'No.'

'OK.' I shrugged. 'So let's just pretend. Let's just *say* that's the way it was. They'd need a couple of guys, one each side, people they trusted.'

'What for?'

'I just told you. The deal.'

'Deal? What deal?'

I looked at Rory a moment. His questions were beginning to irritate me, bends in my road.

I leaned forward, ever patient. 'It's December,' I said, 'and Bush knows that the war he's about to fight could be incredibly expensive. Not money. He's stitched all that up already. No,' I shook my head, 'blood, casualties, lives. That's what he needs to control. And it's dawned on him that he can't. So the man needs a deal.'

'With the enemy?'

'With Saddam.'

'Same thing,' Rory gazed at me, 'isn't it?'

'Not necessarily. Not when you've just spent most of the last ten years arming the guy.'

'You're saying Bush and Saddam were on the same side?'

'No. I'm saying Saddam got it wrong by going into Kuwait. That upset Bush. Quite genuinely. But in the end, before the fighting started . . . they both had a common interest.'

'And what might that have been?'

I looked at Rory a moment, recognizing exactly the shape of the argument, hearing Wesley's voice in the background, derisive, contemptuous and very probably right.

'Survival,' I said. 'They both wanted to survive. Bush, politically. Saddam,' I shrugged, 'for real. That's why there had to be a deal, a limit to the war. That's why the Americans stopped when they did. That's why they didn't go after Saddam.'

'And Saddam?'

'Agreed to pull his punches.'

'Are you serious?'

'Yes, listen.' I leaned forward again. 'The deal's agreed through the middlemen. Thanks to the deal, there's a timetable. First the air war. Then the land war. Everyone knew that's the way it would go. Stood to reason. You said so yourself. I remember you saying it. Air war, you said, five days. Real blitz. Bang bang. Then the big push, the land war, six weeks or so of solid fighting, up through all those berms and trenches and minefields.' I was enjoying myself now, power without responsibility, total conjecture, ten parts cynicism to one part fact, the Wesley Keogh view of history. Rory was following me closely again and I wondered for a moment how much of all this was new to him, too. The way intelligence works, no one gets the big picture, or at least no one at Rory's level. Or, indeed, at mine. I leaned across, patting him on the knee, a friendly, festive gesture. Maybe, after all, we should have opened the crackers. Maybe it would have helped. 'The air war,' I said again, 'and then the land war. Five days, and six weeks. Problem was, it didn't happen that way at all. No, we had a long air war, then a brief land war. Helped no end with the allied casualties. Got Bush out of the hole.'

Rory was eyeing me with a strange expression, a mixture of impatience and disbelief. 'The way it happened was perfectly logical,' he said, 'if you know anything about war.'

'Sure.' I nodded. 'But *seventy-nine* dead? Do you believe that bit, too? Against an army a million strong?'

Rory shrugged. 'Luck,' he said tersely, 'and bloody good planning.'

We fell silent for a while. Outside, it was getting dark. I wondered about going through the whole thing: Grant, Raoul, Eric Stollmann, but decided against it. Better to concentrate on the essentials. The hinges on the door. The guys that made it happen.

'Ghattan and his bodyguard,' I began, 'are both off the plot. One's dead. And Khalil seems to have disappeared. Mr Invisible.'

'So?'

'You know as well as I do the way it works.'

'What works?'

'Deniability. If you run an operation like that, the one thing you have to remove afterwards is the evidence.' I paused. 'In

Curzon House, we called it weeding.' I smiled. 'What's your word?'

Rory ignored the question. He was staring into his empty glass, brooding.

'You think Ghattan and the other bloke were fronting for the Iraqis?' he said at last. 'Is that it?'

'Yes,' I said, 'that's it.'

'And us? The Brits?'

'We weren't in the loop. Not until afterwards. Until Khalil came over. Joined us in Cyprus.' I smiled. 'Then we had leverage.'

'On who?'

'The Americans.'

'And who was dealing for them?'

I hesitated a moment. I could hear carols from the television in the next room. 'Silent Night', followed by a commercial for some Baptist sect or other.

'Beckermann?' I suggested.

Rory frowned. 'But why? Why would he do it?'

'Money? Big fat share of all those contracts? Plus a chance to make a little history? Mr America? The president's man?'

Rory stared at me, still holding the empty glass. 'But Beckermann's dead,' he said, 'so who'd know?'

I nodded, smiling again. 'Exactly,' I said softly.

An hour later, still wet from the shower, I towelled my hair dry, sitting at the vanity unit. Rory was slumped in an armchair across the room, his head back, eyes closed. He'd been on the phone while I was in the bathroom. I hadn't a clue who he'd been talking to or what he'd said, but I'd checked in my case for Raoul's report and the photos, and they'd both gone. Later, when the time was right, I'd do my best to get them back, but for now, reaching for a glass and the bottle of Chardonnay, I tried to revive the conversation.

'Say I come back,' I said, 'to the UK.' Rory opened one eye. 'What happens then?'

He shrugged. 'That's up to you,' he said. 'Your life. Your decision. Not mine.'

'But say I go to the press? The media?'

'With what?'

'The story.'

'What story?'

I paused, sipping the wine, taking the point.

'Then say I write about it?' I said. 'Say I get it all down? All the stuff we've talked about? Plus the stuff I've not told you? The whole lot? The right facts in the right order? Find a publisher? Get it into print? What then?'

Rory said nothing for a while. Then he got up, rubbing his eyes. He sounded, if anything, bored.

'Then I imagine people will read it,' he said, yawning, 'and draw their own conclusions.'

Wesley died the day before I got back to England. Eileen told me the news when I phoned from Heathrow Airport and I was still numb by the time I got off the train at Exeter. She and Pete met me at the station and drove me down to the nursing home at Exmouth. It was a beautiful afternoon, still and blue and cold, and we walked along the beach, all three of us, while they told me the way it had been.

On Christmas Day he'd gone into a coma. Hopelessly out of their depth, they'd called for an ambulance. Within an hour, Wesley was in hospital in Exeter, a room of his own on the fourth floor. Not getting him into hospital earlier had been a mistake. Without the right cocktail of drugs, his defences virtually destroyed, infection had run riot. His mouth was thick with fungus. Pus had swamped his lungs. A violent rash covered the whole of his upper body. He was three quarters blind. His brain had started to go.

Eileen, a kind woman, told me it was better that I'd never seen him like this, and listening, I believed her. At the end of the beach, where the sand laps up to the cliffs, we paused a moment. I knew what I wanted. I wanted a last sign, some signal, a message he'd left me, something to hang on to. I looked at her, trying to put the question into words, but it was Pete who stepped across and slipped his arm round my shoulders, knowing exactly what I was trying to say, breaking the news as gently as he could.

'At the end,' he said, 'there was nothing.'

Wesley was cremated at Exeter on 2 January 1992. In the flat I found a note he'd written me about the arrangements. He wanted nobody there except his mother, Mark and myself. All his money was to go to his mother. The rest of what he owned was to come to me. This bequest included his books, notes, tapes, diaries, everything he'd been collecting since he'd met Grant Wallace in Geneva. It also included his ashes, plus a detailed set of instructions about their disposal.

Wesley's last few weeks at Exmouth had evidently made a real impression on him. He'd loved the view from where we'd lived, the sound of the waves on the beach below the flat. Accordingly, he'd asked me to scatter his ashes at sea, in the deep-water channel, within sight of land. The weather had to be awful. The sea had to be rough and if possible, he wrote, it ought to be pissing down with rain.

The crematorium gave me his ashes in a small metal box. I put them on the mantelpiece in the flat, consulting the television forecasts every night, waiting for the weather to worsen. When a particularly deep depression appeared in the western Atlantic, I made friends with a fishing skipper in the docks. For £50 he'd take me to sea in any weather. For another £50, he'd bring me back.

I waited two days. On the third morning, I got up to the howl of gale-force winds. The trees on the Beacon were bent double and sand was blowing knee-high across the beach. Even my fisherman was having second thoughts.

I'd brought the money in cash. We set sail around noon. The little boat, sturdy enough, bucked and rolled in the heavy sea. The clouds were like smoke, torn and ragged in the wind, and there was a thin yellow light, eerie, almost livid. If Wesley had been there, he'd have found a word for it. Operatic would have done nicely.

We made it as far as the dog-leg that takes the deep-water channel into the open sea. The weather, if anything, had worsened, the wind stronger, the seas longer, the clouds occasionally parting, fingers of light lancing through. The skipper put the wheel over, bringing us bow-first into the weather, steadying the boat as best he could. In the tiny wheelhouse, we exchanged glances.

'Now?'

He nodded, and I inched open the door and squeezed through, trying not to lose my footing on the slippery deck. At the back of the boat, I steadied myself against the low rail, freeing my hands, trying to prise the lid off the box. The boat was pitching up and down, taking me with it, the sea boiling an angry brown beneath the stern.

Finally, I got the lid off. Inside, to my surprise, was a thick grey sludge, more solid and more sticky than I'd imagined. I looked at it a moment, nonplussed. There was a layer or two of ash on top, quite granular, and it was already blowing every-where. I closed my eyes a moment and muttered a simple prayer, good luck, God bless. Then I threw the lot overboard. In the wind and the rain, I didn't even see the splash, which is probably the way Wesley would have wanted it. The music, he always told me, not the fucking players.

Epilogue

Finishing this book has taken me deep into autumn. The garden outside my bedroom window is glorious, the best possible evidence that my father's time is now his own, and he potters around it for most of the day, returning to the house for meals and the odd cup of tea. Things between us have eased a lot over the summer, give and take on both sides, and once or twice, nearing the end of this account, I've wondered about telling him what it contains, letting him into our little secret, Wesley's story, but every time the opportunity comes up, something holds me back. My father's life, after all, has been based on a certain view of the way things are. He believes in the integrity of Westminster and Whitehall. In uniform, he's risked his life to defend the system. Who am I to tell him that much of it has been a sham? That money and power count for more than mere principle?

This little quandary has preoccupied me a great deal in recent weeks. Then, yesterday, came the perfect opening. The morning paper arrived late. I took it into the living room. My father was eating a boiled egg at the table in the window. I gave him the paper, turning away, hearing him chuckle.

'What is it?' I said.

'Here.'

He showed me the paper. Across the top, for once, was good news. A multi-billion-pound arms deal, preserved in the teeth of American competition. 'SAUDIS CONFIRM TERMS' went the headline, 'HUGE BOOST FOR UK JOBS'. My eye ran on down the page, pausing at the photo in the middle, the DTI junior minister who'd helped clinch the deal. It was a head and shoulders shot, less than flattering. I gave the paper back to my father. He was beaming.

'Thank God *someone's* still up to the mark,' he said, peering at the caption beneath the photo. 'What's his name?'

'Priddy,' I said, 'Lawrence Priddy.'

'Quite.' My father glanced up. 'Where would we be without people like him?'